CHOICES

CHOICES

PAMELA NOWAK

FIVE STAR
A part of Gale, Cengage Learning

Detroit • New York • San Francisco • New Haven, Conn • Waterville, Maine • London

GALE
CENGAGE Learning

LIBRARY OF CONGRESS CATALOGING-IN-PUBLICATION DATA

Nowak, Pamela.
    Choices / Pamela Nowak. — 1st ed.
      p. cm.
    ISBN-13: 978-1-59414-810-1 (alk. paper)
    ISBN-10: 1-59414-810-4 (alk. paper)
      1. Frontier and pioneer life—Fiction. 2. Dakota Territory—History—Fiction. 3. United States. Army—Military life—Fiction.
    I. Title.
    PS3614.O964C53 2008
    813'.6—dc22   2009016137

Published in 2009 in conjunction with Tekno Books.

Printed in Mexico
2 3 4 5 6 7 13 12 11 10 09

For Judy and Dave, who share my love for Fort Randall
and believed in me from the start.
And for Terry, who knows authenticity and remains my
dearest friend.

ACKNOWLEDGMENTS

This story began over twenty years ago when my husband Tim and I traveled to the National Archives to research the history of Fort Randall. Tim was preparing for his role as Project Director of the Fort Randall Archeological Project while I was along for company, assistance, and the fun of doing research. I discovered a wealth of information about the social history of the fort that refused to leave my mind. It rolled around and around, forming into story lines. In 1993, I began to put one of the stories into manuscript form and launched my writing journey. Since then, many people have taught me the ropes and shaped my craft into publishable quality. I owe them all thanks.

Tim and my daughter Katrina supported me throughout, allowing me to spend time writing and encouraging my efforts. My parents, Dick and Vauna, my brother Mike, my sister Judy and her husband Dave, and my friend Terry offered their constant confidence.

I am indebted to my critiquers (Judy, Dawna, Tim, Terry, Sharon, Janet, Sue, Robin, Liz, Teresa, Jennie, Tina, Heidi, Anita, Deb, and Leslee), who cheered me on and forced me to learn, as well as to the Rocky Mountain Fiction Writers organization. My gratitude also extends to my Five Star editors—Tiffany, John, and Alice—who had faith in me (most especially to Alice, who weeded out all those dratted pronouns).

Finally, I owe my appreciation to the U.S. Army Corps of Engineers for seeing the potential in the Fort Randall Archeo-

Acknowledgments

logical Project, to the staff at the National Archives for their unwavering research support, and to all the authors and editors of books about the nineteenth-century military, its social structure, military dependents, and personal narratives.

CHAPTER ONE

Dakota Territory, August 1876

Suffocating in the close heat, Miriam Longstreet slammed the sideboard drawer with unladylike emphasis. The sound reverberated through the cramped commanding officer's quarters like a gunshot and she winced at her lack of control. "Dash it all," she muttered.

"Uh-oh," Franny whispered. "Mother won't like that." Miriam's six-year-old sister cast a furtive glance toward the kitchen and bit her bottom lip.

Miriam stroked Franny's shoulder and rued the rapid chain of events that had forced her to this isolated outpost. Just days ago, she'd been preparing to move to Denver with her friend Sarah. Instead, she found herself stuck in this oppressive swelter with a scared little girl and a mother who had somehow become a volatile shrew.

"It's all right, pet. She's outside. She didn't hear me."

Franny's eyes welled. "She'll yell at us and call us names. It won't matter if you didn't mean it."

"I know, pet. I won't cross her." It might take every ounce of self-restraint she had, given her tendency to blurt responses out before she took the time to think them through, but she'd do it. "I promise."

"I don't like her anymore." Franny's chin quivered.

Miriam swallowed, unable to disagree with Franny's assessment. Five years ago, when Miriam had left for boarding school

9

in St. Louis, her mother had simply been demanding and distant. Now, she was an explosive tyrant whose curt orders erupted into harsh tirades without warning. Tirades that left Franny in tears.

Mother's summons to come West had been terse and direct, brooking no argument. Papa's letter had been pleading, citing his wife's rapid change in demeanor and his worry about Franny. Miriam responded out of a sense of duty, intending to buffer her sister and bide her time until the family could secure a more capable governess. At nineteen, she'd been looking forward to exploring her interests, making her own decisions about her life. Now, her mother's behavior had forced her to Fort Randall instead. She hadn't been prepared for what she'd found.

It hadn't taken long to realize Franny's governesses hadn't been lured away by marriage proposals. They'd been driven away, and everybody knew it, just as they knew Harriet had called Miriam home because no one else would take the job. Without a governess, there was no one to protect Franny during the long hours her father was on duty, away from the house.

Miriam no longer had a choice. Her mother had stolen her options away and Miriam resented it.

Glancing at Franny's worried face, Miriam offered an encouraging smile and slid the silver spoon from Franny's hand. "I'll finish things here. Go on outside for a while."

"You'll polish it good, so she won't get mad?"

"I promise."

Franny slipped out the front door. Anger stabbed at Miriam. Little girls shouldn't have to stand polishing silver for hours on end, let alone worry about being yelled at for a speck of tarnish. Miriam shook her head and an errant auburn ringlet fell in front of her face. She blew at it, and the curl swayed before drooping back onto her cheek. Using the back of her hand, she pushed the curl away, then swiped at the beads of perspiration on her brow.

Her mother swept into the room, a plump peacock with the keen, piercing eyes of a hawk. She eyed Miriam's hand still brushing its uncouth way across her sweaty forehead.

"For shame, Miriam. If I told your father once, I told him a thousand times that it was a waste to send you to finishing school. You'll never amount to anything, will you?"

Miriam bristled, then controlled herself. She'd promised Franny. "I'm sorry, Mother." She picked up a spoon and concentrated on dabbing polish onto the silver.

"Please heed what you are doing. You've managed to miss some of the tarnish." Her voice grated on Miriam's patience.

"I'll try to be more careful."

"You'll do more than try. This dinner demands perfection. I will not have the colonel thinking I'm incompetent." Her voice rose and a slight twitch pulled at her face. "He seldom visits outposts like Fort Randall. Surely even you remember the importance of impressing one's superior officer?"

Miriam smothered her annoyance. Of course she remembered. Military etiquette had been drilled into her, even if the years away had excused her from practicing the ingrained habits. Everything an officer's family did was a reflection on the officer. Everyone had a role.

"Pay attention when I'm speaking to you, young lady."

Miriam stiffened and ground the polish into the spoon.

"Colonel and Mrs. Daniels are due to arrive within hours. We have one and only one opportunity to entertain them before they continue on to Fort Pierre. I do hope they understand about the lack of servants. Mind what you're doing. I don't have time to fix your mistakes."

Miriam suppressed a groan. "I'll see that it's done correctly, Mother."

Harriet went on as though she hadn't heard. "I need to go to the post bakery. See if you can do things right while I'm gone. I want that table laid exactly as you've been taught. No deviations. And make sure that sideboard is cleared. We're serving a buffet a la Russe. No wonder my head aches, having to pay such attention to these simple little chores. . . ."

Her mother exited, still fretting, into the kitchen. Moments later, the kitchen screen door screeched, and Miriam heard her mother's clipped footsteps descend the back stoop.

Miriam sighed. Her free-spirited St. Louis friends had talked about changing the world. She'd cheered them on, pledged to help make a difference, but had only begun to find her own role. She'd waited too long to broach her ideas, to tell her parents about her interest in millinery, her desire to apprentice in a hat shop. And look where it had gotten her.

Here she was, back under the thumb of rigid military social structure where the only issues of significance were the seating arrangement and what to serve for dinner. By the time she figured out a solution to the situation, the Denver apprenticeship would be offered to someone else.

Still, Franny needed her. Independence would have to wait. She'd use the time to prove herself capable. She'd keep her tongue still and handle things like an adult. That way, when she did present her plans to strike out on her own, no one would be able to argue she wasn't ready.

She set the serving utensils on the sideboard, slipped the linen napkins through the silver rings, and put one next to each place setting. She glanced at the finished effect. The room was small but meticulously arranged. Not a speck of dust lingered on the cherry-wood breakfront, and the linens on the table were white and crisp. The organ in the corner near the archway shone with a glossy polish, and the fireplace had been scrubbed of all its ashes.

Through the arch, the parlor with its settee and side chairs was just as tidy. A bowl of potpourri sat on the corner whatnot, lending the scent of cloves and cinnamon to the humid summer air. For the first time, Miriam felt that perhaps she had done well enough to appease her mother's wrath.

A commotion on the porch drew her attention. Franny bounded through the front door. An oversized black dog trailed after her, its paws clicking as it raced down the hall.

The dog skidded across the polished wooden floor and hit the table leg with a dull thud. The impact rocked the table. Miriam rushed to rescue the tipping china. A small bowl of mint jelly tottered onto its side, its contents oozing across the snowy linen before spilling down the side of the tablecloth and onto her dress.

Gasping, Miriam turned to her sister. "Frances Longstreet, you know better than to leave that door open. Now look what's happened."

Miriam shooed the dog away from the table, then grabbed a napkin and blotted at the jelly on her dress.

Franny stood rooted to the spot, her eyes pooling.

Miriam's own eyes stung as she realized she'd yelled at Franny. She reached for her sister, regret softening her touch. The girl was a mess. Her chestnut-brown hair spewed out of her once-tight braids and her dress sported a large splat of mud.

Franny looked up and began to blubber. "I'm s-sorry, Miriam. Pl-please don't be m-mad at me."

"You oughtta be harpin' on the dog, not the kid," a deep voice chastised.

Miriam glanced to the doorway. A tall, scruffy-looking enlisted man stood there, leaning against the jamb of the still-open door. The non-military scrap of faded red cloth knotted around his neck drew attention to his tawny beard and the bronzed skin beneath his open collar. His broad shoulders filled the entryway and, for a moment, Miriam felt dwarfed.

Lessons on military social structure flooded her mind. The casual St. Louis demeanor she was so accustomed to had no bearing here. There were rules that must be followed, however uncomfortable she was with them. She was the commanding officer's daughter, and this was a private who had crossed the line. His impropriety must be tactfully addressed before she could even think about fixing the mess he'd created. Miriam straightened her back and tried to ignore the globs of green jelly that now decorated the front of her skirt.

"I assume this is your dog, Private? If you cannot control the beast, you should not be allowed to own him. You've also addressed me with disrespect. You deserve to be put on report."

The intensity of her tone caught Miriam off guard. Goodness, she sounded like . . . like her mother. She cringed at the thought, regretting the haughtiness. Returning to this rigid, class-conscious life left a sour taste in her mouth.

Franny stood, bug-eyed.

The private's shoulders shook and Miriam felt the suppressed ridicule as clearly as if he had laughed out loud. She swallowed and held her chin high, refusing to let him see her discomfort.

"Still ain't no reason to take it out on Franny," he said, ambling across the room toward the dog.

She should find out his name and speak to her father about his carelessness, but a tiny spark of admiration for his independence kept her still. She brushed it away, knowing the aura of superiority was expected. The last thing she needed was to raise Mother's hackles with a breach of protocol.

Setting her lips into the necessary expression of reproach, she stared at him.

He stared back with intense blue eyes, and she shivered.

"Miriam, please don't look at Deakins like that," begged

Franny, pulling at her arm. "She doesn't mean it, Deakins. It's just that we're gonna be in lots of trouble now."

Deakins smiled at the youngster. "It's all right, little lady. It was my fault, lettin' Blackie get away from me like that." Bending down to her level, he whispered, "Got a new one while I was gone, huh? I'll give her a month."

The private rose again and faced Miriam in a heavy silence that left her very much aware of his scrutiny.

"Beg your pardon, ma'am." He offered a slight bow but did not lower his gaze.

Small prickles jumped across Miriam's back. Perspiration glistened on Deakins' skin. She drew a breath, surprised by the pleasing muskiness. Her face grew hot and she fought to lower her gaze.

Her blush deepened while she searched for the proper tone of voice. "Not only is your uniform dirty, but its cuffs and elbows are worn well beyond what is acceptable," she babbled.

And stretched far too tightly across your chest.

Miriam forced the unbidden thought to remain silent and took another breath before continuing. "Take your dog and go. Count yourself lucky I don't report you to Major Longstreet."

The soldier's expression narrowed. She could tell he was itching to put her in her place. The impulse blazed in his eyes, and she almost wished he'd let it out. He held his remark in check, leaving a vast empty stillness.

Miriam shifted under his scrutiny. This, then, was what it felt like, the power that her mother so loved. She wasn't sure she liked it.

"C'mon, Blackie." Deakins grabbed the dog by its collar and hauled the animal out the door. Miriam watched him go, trying to shake off the odd sensation of loss she felt at his departure.

Franny pulled at Miriam's skirt. "Deakins is my friend. He keeps me an' Albert from getting in too much trouble. We missed him a bunch 'cause he's been gone on 'tached service and he hasn't been here for a month. Are you gonna whup me about the jelly?"

"No, pet, I'm not going to whip you." She hugged Franny close, then sized up the situation. They hadn't much time. Franny's appearance would have to wait, as would her own. If the table wasn't perfect by the time her mother returned from the bakery, Harriet would have a fit.

Miriam needed to keep Franny out of such situations. Besides, if she didn't prove herself capable, she wouldn't stand a chance of convincing her parents that she wanted to plan her own future. She clawed through the drawers of the breakfront for a clean tablecloth.

"Does the post trader sell table linens?"

Franny sniffled and shook her head. "Mother always complains about the sutler having nothing decent. We got another one, but it's at the laundress."

"Let's hope it's been washed." The camp laundresses lived near Randall Creek, away from the main parade ground.

"Do you know which laundress does our laundry?"

Franny nodded, and Miriam felt her patience thin. She struggled to stay calm and rephrased the question. "Can you tell me her name and take me to her, before mother gets back from the bakery?"

Franny wiped the back of her hand across her runny nose and nodded again. She offered the hand with ceremonial seriousness, and Miriam choked back a grin.

Accepting her sister's dirty hand, Miriam followed her out of the house. They crossed the parade ground toward the flat prairie beyond, Franny chattering all the while.

"The laundress who does our clothes, her name's Mrs. Jeffreys. I play over there lots. Not at Mrs. Jeffreys' on account of me not liking her kids. But I play at Suds Row—"

16

"Mother lets you play at Suds Row?"

Franny's head bobbed up and down. "Sometimes her head hurts lots and I don't want her to get crabby like she does when she doesn't have any medicine, so I just go play. She never comes after me. And when she does have medicine, she just gets sleepy so I go play, then, too."

"And what does Father say?" Somehow, despite the breech in military etiquette involved, Miriam suspected her father was more comfortable knowing Franny was safe. She tucked a curl out of the way and wondered about her mother's headaches. Both Franny and her mother had mentioned them.

"I mostly play with Albert. Papa likes him. Papa says I should have my fun while I have the chance." She grinned. "I don't think Mother likes that very much."

Miriam laughed. "I imagine she doesn't."

They followed a well-worn path, bereft of the colorful wildflowers that covered the rest of the prairie. Franny glanced up with solemn eyes. "Papa's awful busy, anyhow."

"Papa's always been awful busy." Miriam squeezed Franny's tiny hand. "He has lots to do."

"Me and Albert, we go fishing. And sometimes, we go wading in the creek and even sometimes in the big river. Once, we were gonna make a boat but Deakins said we couldn't. So we made mud pies. Did you ever feel mud squishing in your toes, Miriam?"

Miriam shook her head. "Is it wonderful?" she asked with a mixture of revulsion and curiosity.

"It just sorta hugs your feet, 'specially if it's warm. I just love mud." Franny grinned again, skipping out ahead of Miriam. "Feels good on your hands, too," she called back, "when you're makin' mud pies, but not nearly like your toes."

Miriam couldn't remember ever being allowed to do any of those things. Deep down, she knew Franny was not supposed to be doing them either. She shook her head, feeling a stab of envy for the child's freedom. And regret, because she knew her mother would expect her to curtail it.

Miriam would have the job of forcing discipline on a free-spirited sprite who cared nothing about proper grammar or ladylike pursuits. She sensed she wouldn't be any more success-ful than the governesses before her.

Franny circled back. "So, if you didn't make mud pies, what'd you do?"

"I suppose not much that you would find fun, pet. I went to endless teas, and the theater and to dances, all properly chaperoned." She smiled at her sister. Perhaps boarding school had been her playground, after all, her chance to do the forbid-den. Their forward-thinking headmistress had believed in self-direction. After classes, the older girls had been granted the freedom to roam the town together. Mother would have had a conniption fit had she known Miss Blinlee had been so lax.

"That's all you done?" Franny sounded incredulous.

Miriam shook her head. "Well, my friend Sarah took us to suffrage meetings." In fact, she'd led them from one meeting to another, forever crusading, challenging them to test their limits. Lise championed the rights of others, speaking out against Grant's Indian policy, always cautioning against intolerance. Miriam wished now that she'd done more than just cheer them on.

"Well, they don't got suffrage here, whatever that is. There's theater in Yankton but that's miles away. Mother goes to sewing bees, and the minister comes once a month for church."

Miriam sighed. Life in Dakota Territory would be neither comfortable nor interesting. Her mother was overbearing, both the breeze and cultural events were nonexistent, rules were too complicated, and she was lonely. The more she thought about her situation, the more her resentment grew. By the time she and Franny arrived at the laundresses' quarters, perspiration soaked her dress, and her corset chafed against her skin.

"Come on," Franny urged, leading Miriam past the first building.

A young woman emerged from the next doorway, a washboard in her hand. Short and gaunt, she regarded Miriam with deep blue eyes that seemed to open to her soul.

Startled, Miriam reverted to the social structure she knew was important. Fighting to ignore the still-bright jelly stains on her dress, she put on her best upper-class demeanor.

"We are looking for Mrs. Jeffreys, please."

The young laundress pointed to a crook-backed woman struggling with a basket of wet clothing.

Miriam approached slowly, her heart tightening at the woman's toil. She yearned to offer assistance and swallowed against the restrictions that forced her to keep her distance. "I am Miss Miriam Longstreet," she said, pausing as she had been taught to let the impact of her name set in. "We've had an accident and must replace this linen." Hoping the name association with the commanding officer would ensure an immediate response, she thrust the tablecloth forward. "Is our spare cloth ready?"

The woman shook her graying head. "Sorry, miss."

Miriam drew a breath. Her mother would skin both of them when she discovered the mess. Her self-assurance shriveled, blending with frustration. She murmured a thank-you to the woman and strode away, not caring that Franny had to run to keep up with her.

"Miss Longstreet. Wait, please." The voice came from behind her and Miriam turned to find the tiny sapphire-eyed young woman she had first seen at the cabin. "You come back with me and I can help you."

"How?"

"Jes' come." As they walked back to the cabin, the laundress explained. "There ain't a woman back here that don't know how your ma gets when she's angry. I reckon I don't want nobody to go through that if it ain't necessary. I got a cloth I jes' done up that'll pass for your ma's. You jes' take it with you and then bring it back later when you get done."

Miriam waited outside the ramshackle building with Franny, surveying the quarters with interest. Her mother would say it was squalor. Yet there was no dirt or filth, just a tumble-down building. Was there some sort of rule that made poverty disrespectful?

The frail laundress returned to the doorway and handed her a starched cloth. "This one ought to work out jes' fine. Nobody'll ever be the wiser. Jes' don't tell nobody I offered up somebody else's cloth."

Miriam murmured her thanks and gave her promise to keep the secret. She refused to question the solution that had been offered to her. She'd managed to solve the problem without involving her mother, invoking her anger, or making any mistakes that would threaten herself or Franny.

CHAPTER TWO

Miriam whispered a good night to Franny and stepped out of the bedroom. The warm glow of lamplight filled the common rooms and she breathed a sigh of relief at the orderliness, certain she'd achieved the standard her mother was expecting. It shouldn't be too difficult to keep her satisfied and mellow for the rest of the evening. Guests milled about, offering admiring nods, and her mother reigned supreme as hostess.

A sharp intake of breath interrupted the small talk and Miriam glanced across the room. A tight knot of apprehension formed in her gut as Mrs. Stanton waddled over to the table, staring at the tablecloth. "This is quite fine lace," Mrs. Stanton said. "Is it imported?"

Her mother's face registered momentary surprise before she masked the emotion and moved to investigate.

Miriam bit her lip and mentally kicked herself for not having asked about the ownership of the cloth before she left Suds Row. From the ladies' expressions, she had a hunch they were using Mrs. Stanton's cloth, and she suspected her mother was none too pleased. Heaven only knew what she'd do next.

Silence filled the room as the dinner guests waited out Harriet's delayed response. In the parlor, her father, Tom, glanced up from his conversation with Miss Samuels, clearly aware of the sudden quiet in the dining room. His dark-brown eyes searched the room and settled on Miriam.

She swallowed under his scrutiny and tried to look confident.

Drat it all. She waited with everyone else, watching her mother's face, praying she wouldn't lose control.

"Well," her mother coughed out, "I'm not exactly sure. You see, Mrs. Stanton. . . ." She paused and raised her hand to her forehead with a grimace.

Miriam's breath stalled at the telltale action. She forced herself to remain calm. In another moment, she would have to step forward and take responsibility, publicly admitting herself incapable in order to save her mother's reputation and prevent her mood from disintegrating into madness.

Across the room, Harriet regained herself and fingered the tablecloth. "I didn't realize Miriam used this cloth. It's been packed away. It was a gift from Major Longstreet's cousin. I imagine it could be imported lace. It never occurred to me to ask about the origin of the trim."

Miriam released the breath she'd been holding and surveyed the room. Her father's attention shifted back to Miss Samuels, who rewarded him with a quiet smile while a few of the other guests murmured in soft voices.

At the table, Mrs. Stanton continued to finger the edging, her pudgy face red. "Why, I have seldom seen such an intricate pattern repeated. I have a cloth of my own—"

Captain Stanton thrust his head forward in his wife's direction, pursed his lips, and arched his eyebrows. Mrs. Stanton's mouth closed with a snap.

Next to the captain, Tom Longstreet and Colonel Daniels stood, their mustaches both twitching.

Miriam choked her own laughter back and slipped out of the room. She was followed by Miss Samuels, who covered her amusement by coughing into her lace handkerchief.

"Oh, my," Miss Samuels whispered. "Thank heaven for hallways to hide in. Did you see the captain's face?"

Miriam nodded, feeling an instant level of comfort with the

woman. "Thank heaven my father outranks Captain Stanton. That could have been a disaster."

"Goodness, yes. Harriet's become so unpredictable. I take it you're Miriam? Your father told me you had arrived. I'm Eulalie Samuels. I didn't get a chance to meet you when I came in."

Miriam shook her delicate hand. She'd been so busy tucking Franny in that she'd met very few of the guests. "Mother mentioned you. You live with your brother?"

Eulalie's face darkened, dispelling the quiet mirth her gray eyes had shown seconds before. The transformation corresponded with her mother's description of the woman as the "pinch-faced spinster sister" of Captain Samuels.

"I've served as George's hostess for many years. When he was transferred here, I chose to come along. I've known your parents for a long time." A wistful expression crossed her face, then disappeared.

Miriam smiled, wondering at the quick changes in Eulalie's mood. "I'm pleased to meet you."

"And I you. Now we should be getting back to the others, before they miss us. Your mother is apt to be a bit touchy for the rest of the evening." Eulalie turned and left the hallway.

Miriam followed, entering the parlor. She could feel the lingering tension as guests attempted to recoup earlier conversations. Her mother touched her head again and threw a look of stern reproach toward the parlor, sending another bolt of apprehension through Miriam's stomach. A merciful knock sounded at the front door, and Harriet turned her attention to her hostess duties, parading to admit the late arriving guest.

A young lieutenant stepped in, regal in his pressed dress uniform. Tall and slim, his dark hair and mustache lent a teasing air of mystery that reminded Miriam of the actors in the plays she had attended in St. Louis. She shivered and watched him greet her mother with a box of chocolates, melting all remaining traces of strain from her face.

"Mr. Wood, do come in," Harriet gushed, greeting him according to army custom, as "mister" rather than by his rank.

Drawn, Miriam approached.

Her mother batted her eyes. "We were wondering if you were going to join us."

"Thank you, Mrs. Longstreet, I wouldn't have missed it." He smiled, revealing shining teeth, and looked past Harriet to Miriam. His stare was intense, yet full of curious warmth. Unlike the untamed passion she had noted in the snapping eyes of the private that afternoon, his gaze held respect. A smile lifted the corners of her mouth.

"Miriam, may I present Lieutenant Robert Wood. Mr. Wood, my daughter, Miriam."

He took Miriam's hand, raised it, and stopped just short of touching the back of it with his lips, proper but distant. "I'm very pleased to make your acquaintance, Miss Miriam," he said. "I'd heard a rumor that there was a lovely addition to the Longstreet household. Most of the men are convinced it's another governess. I'm delighted it's not."

"Mr. Wood," Miriam acknowledged, and stepped back into the swarm of her mother's friends. It didn't take her long to realize Robert Wood was a charmer, treating the ladies with a subtle blend of deference and flirtation.

"I would venture every one of those women is infatuated with that young man." Eulalie Samuels stood beside Miriam, shaking her head.

"He has a way with them."

"He's refined, well-groomed and congenial, with the finest manners at the fort. The men even like him. George says he's an exceptional officer."

Miriam glanced at the cluster, convinced there had to be something less than perfect about the man. Amid the group,

Robert lifted his glance, caught her gaze and winked. "He's a flirt," she blurted out.

Eulalie laughed. "And I'd wager that is the true reason he's so popular."

He was still surrounded by middle-aged women when Miriam noticed the punch bowl was empty. She worked her way through the crowd to retrieve it. Leaving Robert with his entourage, she pushed open the kitchen door.

Her mother stood at the dry-sink, swallowing from a thin glass bottle. Her gaze raked Miriam, critical and exploring. "Well, well," she muttered, "is that my punch bowl you're carrying or someone else's?"

Miriam blanched at the hostility in the slurred words.

"My head is pounding so hard I can hardly think straight. What in heaven's name are you trying to do to me?" She corked the bottle, slid it into the cupboard, and turned to Miriam. The skin around her eyes sagged and her face was red.

Miriam set the bowl down, took a deep breath and offered the only excuse she could, given her promise to the laundress. "I picked up the wrong tablecloth by mistake. It looked like something you would own. I assumed it was yours."

Her pulse pounding visibly in her temples, Harriet struggled to digest the simple explanation. Her expression flickered before her eyes flew wide open. "You impudent, lying little snake."

Miriam pulled back, shocked at the reaction.

Her mother advanced. "You did this to ruin me, didn't you? I ought to pack you up and send you—"

A sharp knock on the screen door silenced her.

Miriam closed her eyes against the onslaught. Her mother's accusation was ludicrous. Had she gone stark, raving mad?

Harriet shoved a chair out of the way, careened to the door, and opened it.

Miriam recognized the husky private who had set the whole

mess in motion and her hands stilled.

"My apologies for interruptin' your party, ma'am," he told her mother.

Miriam's glance drifted over the man's unruly blond hair and broad chest. She stared at the taut blue wool, unable to define her fascination with him. He was rough, nothing at all like the refined Lieutenant Wood. She forced her gaze to move, and it settled on his strong calloused hands and the neatly folded cloth they held.

"Carrie sent me over, as soon as she caught on that Miss Miriam picked up the wrong tablecloth. She says she hopes there wasn't too much damage done."

Timing definitely was not one of Deakins' skills. Miriam sighed and sent the soldier a scathing look. His blue eyes widened in surprise.

Her mother snatched the cloth, tossed it on the kitchen table and stormed toward the dining room. "I'll deal with your incompetence later," she hissed to Miriam as she exited.

"Ain't much of a thanks, is it?" the private ventured as the screen door swung shut in his face.

"You idiot," Miriam said under her breath. She moved around the kitchen, dumping half-empty glasses of punch into the slop pail.

"Idiot?" Deakins said from the door.

Miriam flinched. Had she really spoken out loud? Drat her tongue.

Deakins opened the door and stepped into the room, confusion etching its way across his brow. "The woman was just standin' there fit to fire you and you call me an idiot for tryin' to save you?"

Miriam ignored the implication and exhaled an exasperated breath as pent-up frustration washed over her and her self-control slipped away. She strode past the private and opened

26

the screen door, extending it for him. "Go away. I don't need saving, and I'm tired of having to tiptoe around her unpredictable moods. If it hadn't been for you and that mangy mutt, this mess wouldn't have happened in the first place."

He moved in front of her, brushing her arms with his solid body as he exited the narrow doorway. Heat coursed through her.

She retreated into the kitchen like a skittish colt and turned away from him. Moments later, she heard him slap the screen door with his hand and move off the stoop.

Proving herself capable enough to satisfy her mother and keep her calm was going to be a whole lot tougher than she'd anticipated, especially with the interference of others. The last thing she needed was any further trouble with Private Deakins.

She set the last of the glasses in the dry-sink and picked up the slop pail, then opened the screen door with her hip. Turning, she slung the pail's contents into the yard.

"Jesus, Mary, and Joseph," Deakins yelled and stepped into the dim light, punch dripping from his beard.

Mortified, Miriam stepped back. The slop pail fell to the floor as her hand flew to cover her open mouth. "I'm sorry," she whispered.

"Just go back to your damn party," Jake growled. He watched her retreat into the safety of the house's inner rooms and wondered what the hell had possessed the Longstreets to hire a twit like her. She wouldn't last any longer than the other governesses had. Except that he doubted it would be a marriage proposal that took her away. Nobody'd be crazy enough to court a demon like that.

A drop of red punch slid down his nose. Jesus, he was soaked. The stuff was starting to get sticky already. Carrie'd be up half the night washing out his only decent uniform, and he'd have to take a bath.

If it weren't Major Longstreet's house, he'd march right back in there and throttle her. Skinny, snippety, little twerp. But he couldn't afford time in the guardhouse, or the fine that came with it, not if he was going keep up with his youngest sister's tuition payments. Besides, throttling a woman was dishonorable.

He stomped out of the yard and headed to his barracks. He'd barely have time to change into his moth-eaten spare duds and get his clothes over to Suds Row before taps sounded.

He'd been back at the fort for less than six measly hours and they'd all turned out bad. He'd no sooner turned in his report on the Indian village than Lieutenant Wood had spied him and ordered him to take that damned dog for a walk. Wood's dog was a pain in the butt—mean, stupid, and troublesome. Leave it to Blackie to go barging into the commanding officer's house and wreak havoc.

He swatted at a mosquito and cursed. The bugs had smelled the sweet punch nectar. He'd be itching like crazy within the hour. They ought to go bite that new governess. Hell, he hadn't even known the old one had left.

It had been almost funny, this afternoon, her standing there with green globs oozing down the front of her skirt, all the while trying to act like she was above it. She hadn't fooled him for a minute. Sure, she stood real straight and knew how to put her nose in the air, but she sounded fake, at comfort only when she was harping like a commoner.

Still, he'd felt a little guilty by the time he stopped to visit Carrie and Ed after tattoo for his hour and a half of free time. He'd been hoping Carrie would take pity on him and feed him some leftovers of her good cooking. She sure could cook like their ma. He'd even passed on mess, looking forward to his sister's food.

He'd eaten nothing but crow. There were no leftovers, and

Carrie was fit to be tied because she'd given Miss Miriam a one-of-a-kind tablecloth instead of a plain one, and Mrs. Longstreet would have her head. He'd opened up his stupid trap about Blackie getting away from him, and she'd started in on him until he said he'd fix things.

Well, he'd fixed things, all right.

Jake rounded the corner of his barracks and headed inside to his bunk.

Miss Miriam and her snooty, good-for-nothin' attitude. If she wanted to draw a line in the sand, fine. He wasn't about to step across it again.

Two agonizing hours later, the last of the Longstreets' guests departed. Harriet had retired early, complaining her head was about to burst, leaving Miriam and her father to finish the evening without her.

"You did a nice job," he told Miriam as they turned down the lamps.

"Thank you. I'm sorry about Mrs. Stanton's cloth. Will it cause problems?"

"Only in your mother's mind, I'm afraid." He patted her arm and carried the last tray of dirty dishes into the kitchen.

Miriam pulled the cloth from the table and folded it, leaving it on the breakfront. She wondered how often her mother lost control and whether her father knew it was happening as often as it appeared. Unsure how to broach the question, she left it unasked as he reentered the dining room and bade her good night.

She slipped into the bedroom she shared with Franny, her thoughts on Private Deakins. A stubby candle provided a small, wavering circle of light. In their common bed, the child was soundly asleep. Franny seemed to think the world of Deakins, but Miriam found him quick-tempered and annoying.

29

She felt a stab of regret at having tossed the punch at him and tried to ignore it. She hadn't even known he was there, for heaven's sake, and he shouldn't have been standing in the shadows, anyway. Still, he had been, and the image of that dripping tawny beard and those hardened muscles wouldn't leave her mind.

Weary, she began the tedious process of disrobing, one of the many regrettable elements of being a lady. The many rows of buttons, sets of eyehooks, and layers of heavy, constricting undergarments seemed to occupy an endless amount of time. She yawned, placed the garments on a chair, and breathed freely for the first time since morning.

Naked in the close, late-night air, she ached to open the window, break from society's strict code of propriety, and lie down as she was to wait for the odd stray breeze to whisper across her body and wash away her haunting thoughts of the evening. What she wouldn't give to have that freedom.

Instead, she sighed and donned her modest white nightgown. It was a silly thought anyway. All she really needed was to appease her mother for a few weeks, until Franny had a new governess and Miriam could convince her parents she could run her own life.

Harriet Longstreet lay in the front bedroom next to her sleeping husband. Her head throbbed, one of those wretched poundings that haunted her with increasing frequency. Thinking about anything intensified the pain. Thinking about Miriam made it nearly unbearable.

The girl was a menace. Upon her arrival at Fort Randall a few days earlier, Miriam had certainly seemed to possess all the traits considered proper and desirable for a young woman of her status. Her behavior since had fallen far short of acceptable.

Harriet groaned and reached for the bottle of laudanum she

had stashed under her pillow. She uncorked it, took an unlady-like swig, and waited for it to wash over her and chase the headache away.

She had no doubt that Miriam had done something to her tablecloth. Otherwise, there would have been no need to replace it. It was no surprise that her daughter was incapable of laying a proper table, but to secure Mrs. Stanton's family heirloom? It suggested sabotage.

Harriet groaned at the thought and tried to shake it loose from the laudanum. Miriam couldn't mean to ruin her. Still, even if Miriam hadn't switched the tablecloths on purpose, such careless behavior would lead to social disgrace and was unfit for the daughter of a commanding officer. If Miriam could behave no better than this, how could she teach proper man-ners to Frances? And how, dear heavens, could she represent the family?

Harriet sighed and concentrated on the light she had noted in Lieutenant Wood's eyes that evening. Despite Miriam's flaws, she had drawn the attention of the most desirable young officer at the fort. Robert Wood was a man with ambition, enough ambition to rise higher than Tom Longstreet ever would. Enough ambition to carry his in-laws along with him.

Perhaps she needed to change her strategy with Miriam. As-suming her daughter was not intentionally misbehaving, she would work on molding her. Nothing could inspire a girl to model behavior like a young man. Harriet had read somewhere that girls these days responded well to older women who could guide them through all the complications of romantic relation-ships. By fostering the relationship and making herself more ap-proachable, she could kill two birds with one stone. She could reform Miriam as well as arrange an ideal husband for her.

Harriet smiled to herself, took a final gulp of laudanum, and passed out.

CHAPTER THREE

Reveille sounded and Miriam groaned. She hated army mornings. Five-thirty was too early to get up.

Franny awoke with ease, plunging into her usual chatter.

"You aren't gonna start teaching me today, are you? Can't we wait until next week? Me an' Albert were gonna go fishing today. You could come along. 'Course, sometimes, the worms are kinda squirmy."

Miriam burrowed under the feather pillow in a desperate attempt to drown out the prattle.

"Miriam?" Franny tugged on the pillow. A full five seconds of uncharacteristic silence filled the room. "Let's get up now, 'cause when the bugle sounds like that it means to get up, and if the soldiers don't do it right away, they can get in trouble a bunch. Did you know they all go eat together, and they call it 'mess' but we don't and Papa doesn't 'cause he's an officer and we're just civilians?"

Miriam pulled her head out from under the pillow and forced her eyes open.

"Can I get up and play now?"

Miriam rolled her eyes. "*May* I get up now."

"Yes. Can *I?*"

Miriam nodded, thinking about how little she knew her sister. She shifted from scared little girl to rapscallion with the ease only children possessed. Miriam sensed the wild streak was part rebellion, part escape. Franny's eyes sparkled with hopeful anticipation, and Miriam's heart tugged with unexpected love.

"Go on," she said. "You can go with Albert today, but we have to start lessons bright and early Monday morning."

Franny responded with an impulsive hug. "Thank you, Miriam," she chirped. "I'll catch you a nice big fish, and you can still come if you want to."

The little girl scrambled out of bed, dressed and was halfway through the door before Miriam managed to rise from the bed.

Miriam envied Franny's freedom. Fishing would no doubt be a lot more pleasant than trying to second-guess their mother. She sat up and swung her legs over the side of the bed. The warmth of Franny's hug lingered on her neck. She couldn't remember ever exchanging affectionate embraces with either of her parents. Papa was always too busy and Mother . . . well, Mother was Harriet. Someone must be hugging Franny. Otherwise, where in the world would she have ever learned such behavior?

She glanced out the window. The parade ground was already busy with wool-clad soldiers bustling about their duties. She chewed at the inside of her cheek. Tired or not, it was time to be up and about, facing the consequences of last night's actions. She owed Deakins a better apology and hoped she could offer it discreetly, without breeching the social lines and incurring more of Mother's wrath. Too late, she realized she should have asked Franny where to find the soldier.

Miriam rose and rummaged through the chiffarobe, then donned her numerous layers of clothing. Her efforts to fix her hair in a French roll instead of the childish, outdated ringlets her mother favored, proved a dismal failure. The result was a far cry from the stylish statement she wanted. Mother would undoubtedly tell her the time would have been better spent utilizing the curling iron.

She settled for a familiar neat coil, opened her bedroom door, and emerged, expecting her mother to let her fury fly.

"Well, good morning, Miriam. I expect you slept well. I want you to know I fully appreciated your assistance last night. Would you care for breakfast? That much the striker can do."

Miriam's jaw dropped. What was Mother up to? A pang of guilt drifted through her at the instant distrust but she couldn't shake it. She approached the dining-room table warily.

Harriet called for the cook to bring more biscuits and bacon, commenting about the shortages of eggs and the low supply of potatoes. Then she leveled a stern gaze on Miriam.

Miriam held her breath.

"You do realize there were certain elements of your behavior last evening which were not acceptable?" She paused for effect, a veiled warning in her eyes. "I do not know how Mrs. Stanton's cloth came to be on our table, nor am I sure I desire to know. I trust the linen will be returned to the laundress posthaste so I am not further embarrassed by the lie you forced me into. I also trust that your public behavior will henceforth be more appropriate to your station. Are we understood?"

Miriam nodded, unwilling to tempt fate with words.

"Good. Now, then, I was quite impressed by young Mr. Wood. Did you have a chance to speak with him?"

"I did," Miriam said, still unsure where her mother was going with all this.

"Your father speaks well of his military performance. Perhaps we might invite him again." She paused again and beamed at Miriam with a wide smile that didn't quite reach her eyes.

Miriam nodded again, uneasy.

"Now, dear, what do you have planned for the day? I observed your young charge out quite some time ago."

Heavens, this wasn't what she'd been expecting. Miriam swallowed. Her stomach churned with the expectation of some sort of reaction.

"I felt I should take some time to review the teaching supplies before we start."

"A fine idea. Perhaps you might take the time to amuse yourself a bit. Now, I have things to attend to with the sutler. Have a good day, dear."

Harriet left the room before Miriam could respond. The kitchen door swung shut, and Miriam offered a confused prayer of thanks. She'd take the respite her mother had offered, however suspicious, and use the time to take care of Mrs. Stanton's tablecloth, then find that private and eat her humble pie.

Rising from the table, she picked up the laundry bundle and left the house. The parade ground was aflutter with activity. She glanced around, hoping to catch sight of the private. A small corps drilled in front of the barracks. Here and there, men labored at their duties. Most doffed their caps at her, uniform in their courteousness despite her mother's insistence that common soldiers were impolite.

She started to nod back, then caught herself, warring against her instincts. Mother's still-fresh warning about minding her behavior raised its head, and she thought briefly about ignoring it before deciding not to tempt fate so early in the day. She made direct eye contact only with the officers and forced herself to disregard the respect paid her by the enlisted men. The snubbing felt uncomfortable, and the disturbing thought that she might one day turn into her mother sobered her.

She rounded the corner of the enlisted men's barracks and proceeded to Suds Row, passing several common-looking women busily engaged in various stages of laundering clothing. The air was heavy with the smell of potato starch and more humid than Officers' Row, but the women seemed not to notice. Their pleasant voices mingled together, punctuated by an occasional hearty laugh. Amid the wooden tubs and coppers, Miriam spotted the tiny woman who had lent her the tablecloth.

She cleared her throat to catch the woman's attention so that she wouldn't be conspicuous in announcing her presence.

The laundress looked up, then abandoned her task. "Come on up to the house, an' we can settle that matter we was workin' on," she said.

She led Miriam into an unlit wooden structure, leaving the door ajar. The inside of the one-room cabin was unpainted, a world away from the bright whitewashed walls in the officers' quarters. And a great deal smaller. The room's scant furnishings pointed to the excessiveness of her own home. Miriam swallowed hard.

The woman took the tablecloth from Miriam's hands. "Jake didn't get there in time, did he?" she asked.

Miriam filed the soldier's rugged given name away for future reference and shook her head, knowing she should keep the visit short. She doubted she should be inside the cabin, and she knew friendly conversation was to be limited to members of one's own class. Still, the little laundress was hard to resist, especially since Miriam missed Sarah and Lise so much. Besides, who was going to run back and tell?

"There trouble about it?" the laundress prompted.

"Almost. Mrs. Stanton recognized the lace."

The laundress unfolded the cloth, checked it for stains, then tossed it into a basket with an assortment of other white items. "Oh, Lordy," she said, "I can just about see it. When I figured out what happened, I was fit to be tied. I didn't mean to hand over Mrs. Stanton's cloth. She musta threw a conniption. I s'pose I'll lose some pay over that." A small look of worry crossed her face.

Miriam offered her a smile of reassurance. "Mother lied and I don't think Mrs. Stanton dares stand up to her. But she's sure to be back here to see what's going on."

"Oh, ain't you right about that one." The woman's bright blue eyes danced with mirth.

Miriam almost laughed aloud with her at the image her mind created. Instead, she smiled and held out her hand. "Miss Miriam Longstreet."

"Mrs. Carrie Rupert," the laundress responded, shaking Miriam's hand. "But you jes' call me Carrie. So you're Franny's sister?"

"I am." Miriam shifted, nervous. "I really should be on my way back. It's not proper, my being here."

"Life's a whole lot more enjoyable if folks forget about being proper. Living back here, you learn that."

The room darkened, and Miriam looked to the door. A man dominated the opening, intent on something outside. She recognized the broad set of his shoulders. It was Jake Deakins, the soldier from yesterday. She knew it was time to make amends and wished Carrie weren't here, a witness to her faux pas.

Deakins stayed in the doorway, looking toward Randall Creek. The tiny entrance emphasized his size, and a small chill ran down Miriam's spine.

"Carrie, you notice Franny's running all over down by the creek again? Her mother's gonna be up in arms." Deakins turned and peered into the dark cabin. "Where in tarnation is that new . . . well, look here if it isn't her, and all dolled-up, too," he said, sarcasm biting in his voice.

Carrie stared at him with wide eyes. "Jake, this here's Miss Miriam—"

"Yes, I remember her from yesterday, packs quite a punch as I recall."

Carrie's questioning eyes widened a fraction more.

Miriam felt her color drain. For some sudden, indefinable reason, she wanted Jake to notice her as a woman, not the harpy she'd been yesterday.

His gaze raked her from head to toe. "How do, Miss Miriam? You aware that youngster is traipsing around down there at the creek? It isn't high this time of year, but Franny can't swim, and you're putting her in danger letting her go like that. Just what are you thinking of, woman?"

Miriam bristled. The man still hadn't figured out her identity, but she'd be damned if she was going to explain it now. "Danger, my foot. You couldn't drown a flea in Randall Creek." She glared, knowing her tongue was wagging too loosely again. Drat how that man got her goat!

"So what happens if she works her way down to the Missouri?" he retorted.

"She's not a stupid child, Private Deakins, and you know it." Of all the arrogant boors in the world, Jake Deakins had to take the cake. Hell could freeze before she'd apologize to this rude, insufferable man.

"Children forget, Miss Miriam," he mocked.

"Albert'll keep her in line." The words tumbled out even as she realized she had no idea how responsible Albert might be. She sounded like a fool.

Deakins stared at her and laughed dryly. "Oh, that makes real sense, missy, trusting an eight-year-old to mind a six-year-old."

Miriam's face grew hot. How dare this oversized oaf accuse her of neglecting Franny? The fact that he was right made her even angrier. Lord, she hoped Franny was all right. She shot him a piercing stare.

Carrie's shocked gaze bounced between them.

"Dolt," Miriam muttered, driven by anger and embarrassment. She drew herself up to her full height and sent Deakins a quelling gaze.

He glared back.

She felt small, dwarfed by both his more-than-six-foot height and his condescension. It galled her to no end that she couldn't rush out of the Carrie's quarters without asking him to move. "Excuse me," she demanded, stepping toward him.

He didn't move.

Carrie stood looking first at one of them, then the other, her mouth agape.

"Why, excuse me, Miss Miriam," he taunted, ambling out the doorway. "You have a good day now," he said. Much to Miriam's relief, he disappeared from sight.

Carrie shuffled her feet. "I'm awful sorry, Miss Miriam. Jake shouldn't have done that. You send them kids on up here, and I'll see to it they stay out of trouble."

"I couldn't impose," Miriam said, regaining her composure. "Franny's my responsibility."

"Ain't no imposin' about it. They play up here all the time, anyways. 'Sides, I'll put 'em to work. Go on and send 'em over."

"You're sure?" She hated to take advantage of Carrie's hospitality, but she could use the time to draft an advertisement for a new governess. She doubted Mother would do so.

" 'Course I am. Them kids don't need to be cooped up inside on a day like this. Let Franny have her fun."

Miriam wavered.

"Go on, bring her up."

Surrendering to her instincts, Miriam nodded and murmured a quick thank-you before leaving the cabin to find her sister.

Deakins stood some thirty feet away, filling a water barrel. He paused to watch her, and she hastened away from Suds Row, toward the distant sounds of children playing. She could almost feel his stare boring into her, and she groaned inwardly at the sight she knew her bustled posterior must be making.

Maybe, after all, there were good reasons for her mother's warnings about overfamiliarity. If she hadn't forgotten herself and started chatting with the laundress, the soldier would never have dared to act so forward and she wouldn't have lost control. She slowed and fought to catch her breath, damning the constricting corset. It wasn't fair. Why couldn't she relax and be neighborly without having other people think they could forget the rules and act with disrespect?

Oh, that Jake Deakins had nerve. He could just forget about getting any kind of apology now.

Careful to stay within the sound of Franny's laughter, Miriam followed the edge of the ravine until the slope eased. If she hadn't had to worry about maneuvering in her crinoline, she'd be down there with the children by now.

She slipped through the leafy green trees and down the embankment that led to the water, drawn by the chatter of happy voices. Catching hold of a branch, she slid down the creek bank and spied Franny and Albert wading in the knee-deep water.

The sound of a now-familiar voice stopped her in her tracks. She ducked behind a bush, listening.

"You ought to come up to Carrie's," Jake said. "I reckon you could be a mighty big help to her. Why, I s'pose that Albert could tote some of the water, and Carrie might be willing to have you learn the finer points of scrubbing."

"Gosh, do you really think she'd let us help?" Franny asked.

" 'Course she would. I heard her say so to Miss Miriam. Let's pack up your things and get on up there, huh? I gotta get back to water detail before the sergeant catches me shirkin'."

It bothered Miriam that Deakins had gotten to the children before she had, but it didn't really surprise her. His sarcastic lecture hadn't hidden his concern for their safety.

Franny and Albert were barefoot and muddy. And happy as could be. Miriam was suddenly sure she had made the right decision, letting her sister spend the day playing. Franny would have precious little fun once they started their lessons, and she needed this time away from the house.

Watching Deakins laugh with the children eased Miriam's anger. He really had a way with them, gently talking the wayward children into playing at Suds Row.

His muscular chest and arms stretched his woolen gray military blouse, and sweat stains told her he'd been hard at work. He'd stuffed a military cap into the back pocket of his blue trousers. Glints of sun danced on his tawny hair, and his beard made him look both savage and playful at the same time.

He was an enigma. He'd been a boor to her, yet he treated the children with respect. The contempt he'd displayed earlier had vanished, replaced with gentle humor.

Miriam waited among the trees and watched Franny and Albert trample up the grassy embankment towards Suds Row. Jake watched them go, then reached for a pair of empty buckets. He sloshed the first into the creek, whistling.

She turned away and focused on reclimbing the creek bank. The shaded air was cool by the creek, belying the summer heat that perched, motionless, on the plains. She wrinkled her nose at the thought of another stifling day and reached for a low-hanging tree branch.

The branch snapped in her hand, and the whistling stopped.

"I might've known," Deakins said. "Took you long enough. Figured you weren't comin', so I hightailed it down here to keep an eye on 'em. They're long gone now."

Miriam wished she wasn't halfway up the bank with her rear side stuck out. She straightened her back and reminded herself to act like a lady, then turned to face him.

"Private Deakins," she said coolly. "While I appreciate your efforts, it was awfully presumptuous of you. Franny is under my care, not yours. You seem to have a knack for putting your helping hand in where it's not wanted."

"I put it in where it's needed, Miss Miriam. Don't matter to me if the person in trouble is too stupid to know it."

"Stupid?" she exploded. "If anyone here is stupid, I daresay it must be you."

"Like hell." Contempt and mockery filled his voice.

Miriam wanted to spit at him. Instead, she forced her quaking body to be calm. "Look, Private Deakins, I apologize for throwing the punch at you. I should have stepped outside and made sure you weren't hiding in the shadows. Now, I would appreciate if you would please avoid stepping in to rescue any portion of my life again." She turned away, finished with the conversation.

"Gladly, Miss Miriam, gladly," he retorted. "Now get your butt up that creek bank before you fall down and I gotta break my promise."

Miriam stiffened. She'd be damned if she'd give him the satisfaction of a response. She was not going to be goaded this time. She hauled herself up the bank, stopping to catch her wind as she reached level ground. One hand on her corseted stomach, she drew in a calming breath. With it came the belated confirmation of her earlier suspicions. Deakins thought she was a governess.

Heavens, no wonder he acted so vulgar and conceited to her. She shook her head, knowing her quick temper had clouded her observation. Gracious, if he knew who she was, he'd have never treated her that way.

She, on the other hand, had no excuse.

A few minutes later, calmed by her stroll back home and her decision to inform Deakins of her true identity and offer another apology, this time for her sharp tongue, Miriam approached the main post. A roan gelding stood in front of the Longstreet quarters. Curiosity prickled and she hastened to the house. Few infantrymen had horses, and she wondered who on earth owned this one.

Her mother sat on the covered veranda chatting with a dark-haired man. They stood as Miriam neared.

"Miriam, look whom I chanced to encounter at the trader's store. You remember Mr. Wood."

Miriam's hands flew to straighten her clothing. "How do you do, Mr. Wood?" she offered.

He extended his hand and took hers. "Miss Longstreet." His well-bred voice murmured, flowing over her name. She nodded to him in silent acknowledgment, caught the flirtatious gleam in his eyes, and felt a smile tug at her lips.

"We were just having a glass of lemonade, dear, and wondering where you had gotten off to. Some errand or another, I told Mr. Wood." Her mother beamed at the lieutenant. "I did note that you took care of the linens. Thank you, dear. Now, then, Mr. Wood was just telling me that he enjoys riding. Isn't it a coincidence that you also enjoy the activity?"

Miriam peered at her mother, disquieted by her congenial chatter and the magic Wood seemed to exert over her.

"Actually, we met at the store," Wood said, "and your mother told me how much you miss riding. While I fancy that I may suffer the unending ridicule of my brother officers, I would like to accompany you on a ride. Your mother has granted me permission to do so. If you would favor me with your presence, my day would be complete."

"I'd be delighted," Miriam answered, surrendering to the complete lack of tension in the air. As long as her mother was in an agreeable mood, why not? Robert Wood was magnetic, every inch a gentleman, a complete contrast to Jake Deakins. She bit her lip, knowing the ride would delay drafting the advertisement for the governess, but the invitation was too tempting to refuse.

She smiled and drew upon the social graces she knew a man

like the lieutenant would expect. "I've never met an infantry-man who rides, but I'm ever so pleased to find one." The words sounded sugary on her tongue. Only a role, she reminded herself. Feeling her mother's gaze, she glanced toward the horse, eager to be away from Harriet's scrutiny. "I don't have a horse," she announced. Heat crept across her face.

"Not to worry, Miss Longstreet," Wood soothed. "I've ar-ranged with the post trader to borrow a gentle mare as well as the gelding I rode over. I thought if you were agreeable to the ride, I would return with the mare after you have lunch."

Miriam nodded, recognizing the sense in his strategy. Robert would be spared from making small pleasantries with her mother for the remainder of the morning, throughout lunch, and while Miriam shed one set of clothing and donned another. It showed good forethought, admirable. Robert Wood was not only a gentleman, but one who thought for himself, as well.

They made arrangements to meet at one o'clock. Miriam completed her morning chores, then rushed for the kitchen. Harriet stood at the work table putting the finishing touches on a ham sandwich. Handing it to Miriam, she smiled, told her to have a good time, and left the room without a word.

It was the third time in a single morning that her mother had behaved with unexpected pleasantry.

A finger of foreboding scratched at Miriam.

Miriam slid a hat pin into her riding bonnet and watched from the veranda as Robert approached. He rode with perfect posture, testimony of his level of horsemanship. He dismounted with the ease of a person born to the saddle. She fought back a blush as warm appreciation for his well-toned body flooded through her.

"You ride well," she said. She accepted his offer to help her mount and tried to ignore the heat in her face. "How is it that you're not in the cavalry?"

Robert remounted, and they rode away from the house.

"My father was in the infantry. I believe it would have broken his heart had I chosen the cavalry. It was enough of a shock to him that I took up riding in boarding school."

Robert's manner was more relaxed than it had been in her mother's presence. Yet he maintained a proper attitude and a refreshing respect.

Miriam watched him from the corner of her eye. His grooming was meticulous, handsome, and ever so different from the unkempt Jake Deakins. His ebony mustache was trimmed in the latest style, and his hair was tidy under his campaign hat. She studied his charcoal eyes and dark complexion. He turned, caught her perusal, and offered a ready smile but refrained from commenting on her unladylike scrutiny.

She tugged at the tailored bodice of her riding habit until it was straight and smoothed her skirt over the pummel of the sidesaddle. Deakins would have said something, she had no doubt. And she would've tripped over her own tongue slinging some insult back at him. Robert's civilized behavior was preferable by far.

Emptier, but preferable.

As their horses trotted across the plains, Miriam let the odd impression slip away and focused on Robert. He chatted with ease and respect, telling her about the chain of forts along the Missouri River, before slowing his horse to a walk and guiding it through the wooded area near the river.

Dismounting, he turned to assist Miriam. His strong hands lingered only a moment as he helped her alight, enough to make her aware of them, but not so much as to be improper. His gaze caught hers and he paused, one hand just inches from hers.

She swallowed.

"Miss Longstreet—"

"Please, Mr. Wood, call me Miriam." The words were out before she could stop them. Oh, gracious, what would he think?

"Only if you call me Robert," he responded, easing her discomfort.

She frowned. "Mother will take us both to task. I mean, it really isn't very proper."

"It would be tedious if you and I were to go on being formal forever. I had hoped we might become much more intimate friends. If you would prefer, I'll appease your mother with proprieties in her presence. When the elders aren't around, though, I think we can dispense with the formalities, don't you?"

"I . . . I. . . ." It wasn't at all the response she had expected. The surprising discovery that he might actually feel the same way she did about all those artificial rules left her scrambling for words.

"Close your mouth, Miriam, before the flies get in." His eyes twinkled and he winked.

In spite of her heating face, Miriam laughed. The empty, artificial void evaporated. Finally, she could relax without getting herself into trouble.

Chapter Four

Harriet Longstreet hated hired help.

More precisely, she hated dealing with hired help. They seldom met with her satisfaction. She maintained rigid standards and expected that those standards be met in a willing and cooperative manner. In effect, she wanted people who enjoyed work, knew how to work, and were willing to work for her. They were not easy to find.

Her head pounded, and she knew the time had come to dismiss the private who had botched the dinner preparations the evening before. Firing him didn't bother her. Locating a suitable replacement did. The shortage of help at military forts was one of her foremost frustrations. Her head wouldn't ache so much if she didn't have to constantly deal with inept governesses and slothful strikers.

She longed for the days of her childhood and the servants who had met her every need. Marriage to Thomas Longstreet had certainly crimped that lifestyle. Thanks to her inheritance, they enjoyed a higher standard of living than most officers but she resented the limitations. A proper household would at least have a housekeeper to deal with the lesser staff.

Rising from the chair, Harriet drew a deep breath. Corsets were such a bother in the summer. Still, the discomfort was a part of life, to be endured, just as marital relations and the management of hired help must be. Trying not to perspire, she approached the kitchen. She smiled at the cherry-wood breakfront, a gift from her mother, then pushed open the swinging door to the rear room.

Private Hanson stood at the black cookstove. He gurgled as he cleared his throat, and Harriet winced as he spat a wad of tobacco juice into a tin can next to the stove. Time was well past for his dismissal. She closed her eyes and took another breath.

"Ahem."

"Oh, Missus Longstreet. How do? Didn't know you was there."

"Obviously."

She made him wait, hoping the lengthy pause would unnerve the man. She'd learned the technique from her mother and she held her breath, anticipating his reaction to the silence. In a moment, he'd squirm as the uncomfortable quiet stretched. It was only fitting that the commanding officer's wife should be able to practice the method to perfection, even if her husband couldn't.

She let Hanson contemplate his situation while she looked around. He'd kept the kitchen fairly clean, unlike the last striker. The stained floor near the spit-filled can turned her stomach but it wasn't the major issue. Miriam and Franny could get off their backsides and clean, if need be. It was the striker's cook-ing abilities that she could no longer abide.

Hanson turned to her with a questioning look.

Harriet arched one eyebrow.

He opened his mouth as if to ask her something, stood there a moment, then shut it again.

A surge of power leapt through her. It was always the same. None of them ever knew what to say. She added to his discomfort by pursing her lips and staring down her nose at him. A full five seconds. Then she smiled, striving for effect, so that Hanson would feel like a rat caught in a trap. Her trap.

"Private, you assured me that your experience in the culinary arts was without compare and that you were amply skilled in the preparation of a vast array of delicacies suitable for a sumptuous buffet, did you not?" She again arched a single eyebrow and waited for his response.

"What'd you just say, ma'am?" Hanson squeaked.

Harriet shook her head and felt the adrenaline drain away. Did she have to explain everything? "Did you not say that you could cook well for a large number of persons at one time?"

"Yes'm, I did."

"And did you not say that you could prepare a variety of foods?"

"Yes'm, I did."

She sighed in exasperation. She'd expected the man to wallow. Sometimes the sheer stupidity of these people took all the fun out of firing them. Her head ached and she grimaced. Where had she left that bottle of laudanum?

Hanson still waited. She frowned. "Can you explain your inadequacies yesterday?"

"Inadawhat?"

"Failures," she snapped, "the reasons I sent you out of my kitchen."

"Well, the way I see it, I didn't tell you no lies. You didn't tell me it was gonna be no fancy cookin'. I can cook lots of food for lots of people and can make do with just about anything, least ways I could in the minin' camps."

Harriet took another deep breath, then glared at the man. She didn't like it that he'd recovered his ability to face the situation. His poise spoiled the whole thing.

"Go back to your military duties, Private. You are no longer in my employ."

She left the kitchen, sat down on one of the hard-backed dining-room chairs and let her head sink into her hands. Her temples pounded. Now her misery would begin. Until she replaced the man, she would have to handle kitchen duties herself. Where the hell was the laudanum?

The door slammed and Franny entered the house. The little brat had been at the creek again. She was a complete mess. Where was Miriam? Someone was simply going to have to get through to the child that appearance was important. She hoped Miriam had it in her.

She turned and glared at her younger daughter. Franny froze like a trapped rabbit.

"Ah, Frances, look at you. You look like a ragamuffin again. Get over here."

Franny swallowed and inched forward.

Harriet tsked and waited for her to finish her infernal plodding. The girl didn't have the sense she was born with. When she was within reach, Harriet spun her around. She tugged the ribbons off and yanked her braids loose. A section of hair caught in Harriet's ring and Franny whimpered.

"Quit sniveling." Harriet jerked the strands of hair into the braid, the tighter the better, to keep them from unraveling. Silence settled around them. Harriet welcomed it as the pounding ache above her eyes subsided a bit.

Franny slid one foot around, then drew a breath. "Are you mad at me?" The question poured out in a tiny, needy voice.

Harriet sighed and tempered her tone. The girl sounded inches away from crying, and if she started bawling, Harriet's head would explode. "Children should be seen and not heard," she chided.

"Yes, ma'am." Franny paused. "Did I do something wrong?"

Harriet tied a brisk knot in the bow at the end of the completed braid and picked up the other one. It was as if the girl hadn't heard. Again. Still, Franny had nothing to do with her kitchen woes. Harriet supposed she really ought not to take her frustration out on her. Drawing a breath, she pasted a smile on her face.

"I have dismissed the striker, and now we have no one to cook or run the household. I will need to do it myself until such time as I can find a replacement."

"Oh." Franny paused, as if thinking. "I know a striker cooks, but what else does he gotta do, 'xactly?"

"Stand still, Frances, and mind your enunciation. Heavens, but you squirm." Harriet snapped the strands of hair together and ran the tasks through her head. It would take weeks to find someone. Her temples starting throbbing again.

"A striker must also be able to keep our kitchen maintained, make sure that there are adequate supplies on hand, and be able to prepare for and manage a dinner party such as we had last night. The food he prepares for such parties must be very special, not like soldiers' mess. If he can assist in any other way around the house such as laundry or helping teach you, that is all the better."

Franny turned, and the braid slipped from Harriet's hands. "I know someone like that, Mother. I do, really. I can help. You can ask him and then you won't have to be mad no more. His name is Deakins, and he'd be real good." She jumped up and down before sobering and handing her braid back to Harriet. "He already makes me stop doing what I'm not supposed to do. You could ask Papa about him, 'cause he just got back from doin' a real good job on 'tached duty, and Papa knows it. You'd like him, too. He's got real good manners and everything."

Someone who could handle Franny? Harriet relaxed her hand and finished the braid without tugging.

"Find this Deakins, and advise him to come and speak with me," Harriet told her. "Tell him I am willing to pay a salary of five dollars per month if he qualifies for all the duties."

★　★　★　★　★

Jake Deakins entered his sister's cabin and dropped an armful of firewood next to the stove. His muscles ached from the long day of water and firewood duty but he figured it was better work than some were assigned. Turning to leave, he found Franny sitting at the kitchen table. His heart softened, just like it always did. The kid melted him every time.

"Hello, little lady. What brings you all the way back down here?" he asked, joining her.

"She's been waitin' for you," Carrie said, fetching another cup and setting it on the table. "There's water in the pitcher. Get yourself a drink before you deliver any more of that wood."

Jake picked up the white enamel pitcher and poured himself a drink. Franny sat, watching him, looking ready to burst.

"Okay, sprite, what's on your mind?"

"Oh, Deakins, I ran all the way over, and then Carrie said you weren't here yet and I had to wait. I got the best news. Mother had to fire our striker, and now we don't have one. But I told her I knew somebody, 'cause she said all he has to do is cook and clean and keep supplies and make me be good."

Jake laughed. Mrs. Longstreet would be looking a long time if she was insisting on all that.

"Jake?" Carrie said.

He glanced at his sister and knew without a doubt that she and Franny had been plotting. There wasn't much Carrie could hide. Apprehension crept through his gut. Whatever they had up their sleeves, he didn't want any part of it.

"Don't you two be looking at me," he said, the truth dawning on him. No sir, he didn't want anything at all to do with it.

Harriet Longstreet had a reputation for using up strikers almost as fast as she did governesses. And then there was the matter of the governess herself. She'd make life hell for whoever took the job. Between Miriam and Harriet, it'd be a miserable position.

"Jake, it's an extra five dollars a month."

He shook his head. "It don't matter, Carrie. It isn't something I want to do."

Across the table, Franny stared at him with tears welling in the corners of her large hazel eyes. When her bottom lip started to tremble, it was too much. He pushed back his chair, stood, and headed out the door for the sanctuary of the cabin's shaded north side.

That one could get a fish to fly.

'Course, she sure could use some looking after. Seemed like he was always bailing her out of trouble anyway. He half expected Franny to come following him out and was surprised when he heard Carrie usher her out of the cabin and send her on her way back to Officers' Row. But he wasn't surprised when Carrie rounded the building and found him.

"Hiding?" she asked.

"I ain't gonna do it. B'sides, I gotta get back to work."

"You ain't thought it out none yet."

"Carrie, it'd be a hell of a job."

"You're darned right it would be. And if you're too thick-headed to see it, you ain't got the brains I thought you had."

He watched Carrie pace back and forth as she continued to lecture him on the reasons he ought to take the position. Poppycock, most of it. Except for Franny needing somebody. And the money. Five extra dollars a month sure would be of use.

Since their parents had died, he and Carrie had done all they could to make sure their younger sister, Becca, got an education. With extra money, she could finish up at that school back East and maybe even get her teaching certificate. It was a chance at a life he and Carrie had never known, a life filled with using her mind instead of breaking her back.

"It would help," he conceded, the rock in his stomach telling him he was beat.

"It wouldn't be no worse than workin' on the railroad like you done before you and Ed joined the army."

He laughed. He and Ed Rupert had spent hard days with the Union Pacific, months of them. No, it wouldn't be any worse than that. "I hope not. But, then, I was a lot younger. More energy." He smiled at Carrie. "You reckon a commanding officer's striker gets excused from regular duties?"

"I reckon Mrs. Longstreet's striker gets excused from jes' about everything."

"When they moved me up to cookin' on the U.P., I didn't make none of them fancy dishes she likes."

"No, but I still got that recipe book that lady gave Mama at the last place she worked. I s'pect that'd be all you need."

"It don't seem I got much choice, does it? Becca comes first."

Carrie nodded, and Jake thought about how she had quit her own schooling to take care of Becca when their ma died and how hard she worked as a laundress so there would be extra money to send. He guessed he could stomach being a striker for Harriet Longstreet.

A half hour later, standing at the commanding officer's quarters in a fresh uniform, he wasn't so sure. Harriet Longstreet answered the door herself.

"Private Deakins?" she asked.

"Yes, ma'am," he said, removing his cap and nodding.

"Frances gave me to understand you were not interested in the position. Do I take it you have reconsidered?"

"Yes, ma'am, I have, if the position is still open." He knew she was playing with him. She peered down her nose, saying nothing, like a cat waiting to pounce.

He waited, not saying a word.

After a few moments, Harriet invited him into the house and

bade him follow her to the kitchen. He questioned her about the pantry stock. She inquired about his culinary skills. He asked if the cookstove heated evenly. She informed him that chewing tobacco would not be permitted in the kitchen.

The interview continued until Harriet finally seemed satisfied that he could perform most of the duties required. Jake had no doubt the job would tax his self-control. But when she offered the position, he accepted. Promising to return the next morning to begin his duties, he left Officers' Row and returned to work detail.

Later, he'd try to find the time to go by Carrie and Ed's cabin and find out what he could about the Longstreets. He wondered if Carrie knew anything more about that new governess, Miriam. She must have arrived last week, before he got back from detached detail escorting the supply wagon up to the Crow Creek Agency.

Some of the fellows in the barracks were saying she might be related to Major Longstreet. He'd have to tell them about her being over at Suds Row and what a mouth she had on her. If she was a relative, it had to be a pretty distant one. That night she'd thrown the punch at him, Mrs. Longstreet sure hadn't talked to her like she was anything closer than a shirttail relative, if even that.

Whatever she was, he'd keep his distance. He'd stay out of her way and keep her out of his kitchen. He didn't really want to know her any better than he already did.

CHAPTER FIVE

The aroma of freshly baked tarts lured Miriam until she could stand the temptation no longer. Jake Deakins had spent his first morning as a striker baking things that smelled wonderful and refusing to allow her into the kitchen. He'd finally left the house just after lunch, giving her the chance she needed. Lord, but it had been ages since she'd had a raspberry tart.

She bit into the tender crust, savoring the tingling flavor. Behind her, the screen door creaked. She jumped. She didn't have to turn around to know she'd been caught red-handed.

"Well, now, just what will people say about the fancy Miss Miriam caught stealing a tart?" Jake closed the door.

He leaned nonchalantly against the kitchen wall, waiting, and Miriam's breath hitched. It was the sort of remark intended for a social equal, one he'd never make once he knew her true identity.

The reminder that she needed to clarify her identity reared its head. But she knew his words would take on a tone of artificial deference and he'd never flash those blue eyes at her again once he understood who she really was. He'd treat her like he did her mother, and there would be one more spark missing from her life.

"I wasn't stealing it," she retorted, letting the moment pass. She'd tell him later. "I was sampling."

"Is *that* what the upper classes are calling it these days?"

Miriam tossed her head, then finished the delicious tart.

"Don't be so arrogant, Private. You're new. How do we know if your tarts are edible? Entertaining on your striker's first day is risky. I was sent to make sure the pastries were good enough."

"Good enough, huh? And are they?"

"Oh, I guess they'll do. After all, one can't set one's expectations too high." She waited, surprised that Deakins didn't challenge her further.

Deakins raised his eyebrows and smiled at her, a slow, lingering smile that was impossible to dismiss.

"Mrs. Longstreet sent you, did she?" he said, his voice unusually smooth.

Miriam nodded, stepping further into the lie.

Deakins crossed the room without words, his lazy smile sapping Miriam's command of the situation. She struggled to figure out how circumstances had turned.

He stopped in front of her, mere inches away, his broad shoulders enshadowing her. The lingering scent of raspberries in the room merged with Jake's muskiness and surrounded her.

"She sent you to taste the tarts because she was busy, did she?"

"Yes," Miriam managed, whatever delicate balance of power they had started with now forgotten.

The touch of Jake's thumb on her cheek startled her. With the lightness of a feather, he traced a line from her cheekbone toward her open mouth. Stopping at the corner of her lips, he dabbed twice and pulled away.

"Raspberry," he whispered before sucking the stickiness from his thumb with an agonizing slowness that paralyzed Miriam. Her heart beat, fast and distant, and her breath grew ragged.

Jake stepped back. Miriam saw a brief, smoldering spark in the depths of his blue eyes. Then they clouded.

"You're a liar, Miss Miriam," Jake said, the bitterness in his voice shattering the moment. "She checked them herself thirty minutes ago. Go on back to the biddies in the parlor where you think you belong."

A half hour later, Miriam was still stewing. The last thing she wanted to do right now was teach Franny to sew and listen to a bunch of women gossip. She flounced around her bedroom gathering her sewing supplies and trying to figure out what in heaven's name had happened with Jake.

One minute she'd had the upper hand, properly in control of her servant. Until she baited him, part of her reaping a strange thrill at doing so. Then, suddenly, they'd been engaged in some bizarre ritual that she didn't understand and wasn't at all sure she wanted to. His abrupt dismissal was almost more comfortable. At least it was familiar behavior.

The irresistible pull was not.

Miriam shook her head. Lord, what a ninny she was being. He was likely standing in the kitchen laughing right now. She'd be hog-tied if she'd ever let him play her for a fool again.

"Miriam?"

She turned at the sound of Franny's voice. "What, pet?"

"Mother says to tell you the ladies are all here now."

It was Franny's first sewing bee and it would be Miriam's responsibility to ensure that she behaved courteously. She remembered the weekly sewing bees from her own childhood. Whether the officers' wives were busy with quilts or making dresses inspired by the latest pattern books, the bees provided them with the proper setting to combine their domestic talents. And to exchange the latest "news."

She didn't think it'd be any more fun now than it had been then. Not nearly as enjoyable as sewing had been with Sarah and Lise telling wild stories about the suffragists. Goodness, her mother's friends probably didn't even know about the struggle for equal rights. And they'd likely choke if anyone spoke of it.

Miriam crossed the room. Straightening the bows on Franny's braids, she admonished her to mind her tongue, then ushered her out of the bedroom. It wasn't Franny's fault she'd rather be somewhere else. She was here, and she needed to make the best of it.

The parlor was overflowing with both women and fabric. Miriam steered Franny through the sea of skirts toward the dining room where they'd be somewhat apart from the group.

And closer to the kitchen.

Miriam jerked out a dining-room chair and faced it away from the closed kitchen door before motioning for Franny to sit on a stool nearby. She took a small round wicker basket from the table and handed it to Franny.

"This is for you. It's the sewing basket I had when I was young, and it will be yours until you need a full-sized one."

Franny toyed with the Oriental coins and glass beads attached to the basket lid. Miriam suspected she, too, would rather be elsewhere.

"Open it," Miriam urged. Franny removed the lid, revealing a packet of needles, a paper of pins, and several skeins of thread. Miriam handed her an embroidery hoop fastened around a floral patterned dresser scarf.

"We'll start with a straight stitch. It's pretty easy so don't frown at me like that. Since we use it for both stems and the outline of the petals, you may choose where you want to start."

Franny peered into the basket and held up a skein of bright blue thread. "Flowers," she announced.

Eyes. Jake's eyes.

In that brief moment in the kitchen, before Jake's eyes had clouded over and he slipped into hostile indifference, his eyes had sparkled with the same luminous shade of blue. A window to his soul that he kept shuttered.

Miriam sighed at the intruding vision and carefully showed

Franny how to separate the threads and ease them through the eye of the needle.

"You start at the beginning of the pattern you want to embroider. From the back. Pull the thread through, leaving a tiny tail. Take a tiny stitch and stay on the line. Push it through. Then come back up, about there, with the tail underneath, and do it again."

She handed the hoop to Franny and watched, correcting stitch length, and offering encouragement. The stitches were longer than Mother would approve but remarkably tidy. Miriam squeezed Franny's shoulder in encouragement and took up her own sewing, listening absently to the women in the front room.

Today's project was the completion of Mrs. Appleby's new gown. The pattern had been copied from a design advertised in *Harper's Bazaar*. With rows and rows of gathered burgundy taffeta ruffles, the dress was hardly suited to the dusty prairie. Jake Deakins would have more than a few choice words if anyone ever wore that many ruffles into his kitchen.

Miriam tried to shake away the image of Jake scolding her clothing choices. But the image wouldn't leave.

"Miriam?" Franny interrupted. "How's this?"

"Very good. Why don't you choose another color for the next flower and try threading the needle yourself?"

Franny nodded and clumsily proceeded on her own. Miriam watched, giving her the chance to succeed without help, forcing her mind to focus on the words of the women in the parlor instead of on Jake.

"I was sure there was some sort of mismanagement occurring," said the pudgy Mrs. Stanton.

"How can one possibly mismanage laundry?" asked Eulalie Samuels. Her face was drawn again, a stark contrast to the brief smiles she'd displayed the night of the party.

Harriet looked up in irritation at Eulalie's interruption, then turned back to her sewing.

"Well, Eulalie, dear," Mrs. Stanton said in a patronizing tone, "I suspected for some time that my laundry was being used by others, perhaps even by the woman herself. One cannot trust such individuals, you know."

"They wouldn't have such audacity," contributed someone else.

Miriam focused her attention on Mrs. Stanton, wondering if Carrie had gotten into trouble.

"Well, my dear Mrs. Worthing, there has been more than one instance when I have noted my belongings in the possession of others. It finally got to such a state that I felt I must say something to the girl. I confronted her rather directly. She typically claimed to know nothing about it."

So she *had* gone to Carrie. Miriam imagined the tiny laundress listening to Mrs. Stanton's tirade and knew Carrie had quietly suffered through it.

"What did you say to her?" Miriam asked.

Mrs. Stanton lowered her sewing and glanced sharply toward the dining room.

"Heavens, Miriam, I hardly recall my conversations with servants. The little liar denied everything."

"Liar?" Miriam struggled to contain the anger in her voice.

"Don't be so shocked, dear girl. One knows the caliber of women in such positions."

"Why, I heard they all put in extra hours at night over at the hog ranch near White Swan," said Mrs. Worthing.

The gasp in the room was audible.

Miriam felt the insinuation as if she were included in it. There was no possible way Carrie could be involved with the group of women who made their camp a few miles distant of the military reservation. Though they never visited the fort, rumor had it that they shared their favors with anyone willing to pay.

She glanced around the room. A few of the women appeared curious, while the others sat with tight faces, their sewing forgotten.

Eulalie Samuels glanced in her direction, her face pinched into a stern expression of reproach.

"I really don't think—"

"Miriam," her mother interrupted, her tone a reprimand in itself. "I do believe you should refrain from commenting on this indelicate subject."

"Oh, Harriet, let the girl speak," Eulalie said. "We all know they're there. I'd like to hear her opinion."

Miriam glanced at the other woman and gathered her courage. "First of all, I've seen how busy the laundresses are. I can't imagine any of them trekking several miles after the days they put in here, let alone . . . anything else. Besides, they seem like decent women."

"Hear, hear," Eulalie chimed.

"Decent? The lot of them are ill-educated, dirty-mouthed thieves." Mrs. Stanton tossed her sewing aside and rose.

"Thieves?" Miriam countered, rising herself. She paced forward, into the parlor. "What in heaven's name could they steal? They're practically chained to their wash tubs. They barely even leave Suds Row." The thought of the friendly little laundress being accused infuriated Miriam.

"Oh, pooh, Miriam. You hardly know what you're speaking about." Mrs. Stanton waved her off with a swish of her hand.

"Mrs. Stanton is right, Miriam. Sit down and mind your tongue." The brittle tone of Harriet's voice held a veiled warning.

Miriam glanced at the other ladies and realized she'd come close to overstepping the bonds of propriety. Except for Eulalie, they all appeared more shocked at her defense of the laundresses than at the grossly unfair comments made by Mrs. Stanton.

The whole situation shamed her.

Lise had warned her of such people and their misguided judgments about others. She'd never expected to find such people in her own parlor.

Biddies, Jake had called them. And her, too. One of them. No wonder he had treated her so callously.

It suddenly mattered very much that he know she wasn't that shallow, that she wasn't intentionally treating him badly, that she hadn't eaten that tart simply because she had the right to but because she loved raspberries and because they smelled so wonderful.

And because he had made them.

Jake climbed the cellar stairs, cursing himself. He was a fool to think he could handle working for the Longstreets with that unpredictable redheaded governess in the same household.

Miriam would be the death of him yet.

He'd tried everything since he'd arrived there that morning. Staying out of her way, even ignoring her. Proximity to her made him so damned itchy, wound up tight as a watch spring, and he didn't know why.

Then he'd found her there in his kitchen eating his tart, drawing his attention to her enticing mouth with that little drop of raspberry filling that hung there on her lip waiting to be licked off.

Damn, she'd been saucy. Not insulting, not uppity, just plain, out-and-out saucy, teasing. He'd seen it in her eyes when she tossed that thick auburn hair of hers.

He'd only meant to teach her what kind of trouble she was opening up. She hadn't even known what hit her when he poured on the charm. He had walked her right into the lie and had her just where he wanted her.

He hadn't meant to touch her. Soft, so soft. Waiting. Wanting.

Tempting. Her lips parted. Her breath hot against his hand. His own heart tight and racing as he sucked the raspberry from his thumb, unable to move with normal speed.

He'd felt the tight swelling of his body as she looked into his eyes, searching for his soul.

Thank God he'd come to his senses. She was only playing with him, luring him in just to toss him back later because he wasn't good enough. Women like her were fishing for more than a never-amount-to-nothin' private like him.

Pulling the sack of potatoes onto his shoulder, Jake closed the cellar door and headed for the kitchen. There wasn't a governess yet who wasn't in it for all she could get. They all ended up marrying officers. He'd be damned if he'd ever let one eat him up and spit him out on her way to something better. Try as he might, he couldn't avoid pinning ulterior motives on all of them, and Miriam was falling right into the same category.

He opened the kitchen door and nearly bumped into Miriam.

Damn. "You're in the way, miss," he growled.

"Pardon me." She sounded sincere, penitent, and he almost believed she meant it. "I came to tell you I—"

"You're standing right in the way," he interrupted, purposely not looking at her. "Either get yourself back in there with the rest of the 'ladies' or get outta my way. Else I'll dump this whole sack of potatoes on your feet."

"You have no right to speak to me in such a manner." Quiet, unusually calm. And more than Jake could handle. He liked the hellcat better. He knew how to deal with her when she was fighting.

"When you're standin' in my kitchen takin' up space while I got work to do, I got every right."

"I didn't come in here to fight with you," she said, a hint of stubbornness back in her voice.

Jake looked at her, grinned, and dumped the potatoes at her feet before turning and exiting out the back door.

She stomped after him.

"Private Deakins, did you hear me?"

"I heard you, girl. Now quit gettin' in my way or I'm liable to stumble right over you again."

"How dare you speak to me in such a manner."

"You keep sayin' that. You might wanna take a step down, though, girl, 'cause you ain't no better than the rest of us."

He waited for her to yell or start some sort of lecture, relieved that they were back on familiar footing.

"Now just wait one minute, Private Deakins. You come into this household as if you are superior and treat me with contempt. The only person in this household you treat civilly is Franny. Have you no idea of the proprieties you are supposed to be observing here? I think you need to remember how things are done in the army."

She stood with her arms akimbo, daring him to respond. "Franny is the only one around here who deserves to be treated civilly," he tossed out.

"Are you trying to get dismissed?"

"Besides, what makes you think the Longstreets even care what a governess thinks?" He watched something akin to disappointment cross her face. The damned woman thought she was something special, did she? "You ain't no better'n the rest of us and you traipse around here like you're important to someone, screechin' like a hoot owl. It's a good thing those ladies inside ain't heard you yet or you might find yourself out in the cold. They ain't wantin' that behavior out of the likes of you."

"And they don't want it out of the likes of you, neither." she shouted.

Like a fishwife, Jake thought. Get her angry enough and she

loses that fancy grammar. He grinned at her again, baiting her further.

"Franny said you had a lot of sense but I sure don't know where you keep it." Her voice was calmer, but the insult still stung.

He held back his anger, realizing they were making a scene that could stir up a lot more trouble than either of them needed. But he couldn't keep the acid tone from his voice. "There ain't no one that's gonna tell Jake Deakins how he's gotta act when he ain't under their command. I don't take orders from nobody. Never took 'em from my ma, I don't take 'em from Carrie, and I ain't gonna take 'em from you."

She stood there not saying a thing, the little wheels in her head surely spinning like crazy. Jake knew it was time to end the exchange. Lord help them both if she got all wound up again. "Now get outta my way," he ordered.

Miriam stood there, looking like she was about to get soft on him until he began to wish he hadn't been so hard on her.

"I only came to apologize about the tart," she said. "I did steal it."

It was the last thing he had expected her to say. He searched her eyes for some trick and found only her steady level gaze.

"Let's go in and get back to work," he said, nodding toward the door, "before they come looking for us." He gave her a brief smile, a truce.

"Jake?"

He turned back, drawn by her voice.

Her green eyes were wide and luminous. "I'm not a governess, Jake. I'm Major Longstreet's daughter."

CHAPTER SIX

Miriam sat at the dining-room table, watching Franny practice her penmanship and ruing her own cowardice. She should have marched right after Jake and cleared the air instead of letting things fester for three days.

Jake's eyes had held utter contempt, a clear indication that he thought she'd purposely hidden her identity. Granted, she should have told him as soon as she figured out he thought she was a governess. And then she'd been too afraid to go after him. It wasn't supposed to matter what a private thought about her anyway.

Something about Jake Deakins stirred her. She both hated it and loved it. Letting go, yelling at him, verbally sparring with him, excited her. The tension of living up to Mother's expectations and her worries about Franny disappeared. At least until she realized what she was doing, and the guilt set in.

Well, telling him who she was had certainly put a stop to their verbal sparring—just as she'd suspected it would—and left an empty void.

Franny slammed her piece of chalk against her slate board. "Can I be done? I wrote the alphabet so many times the letters are swimmin' in my head."

"You're going to break the chalk if you treat it that way. Ladies do not have tantrums." *Do as I say, not as I do.* "If you're tired of writing, we can get out the flash cards."

"We already done 'em. Why do I gotta learn adding anyway?"

Franny formed her mouth into a pout and kicked at the table leg.

"Addition is necessary for a great many things." Miriam caught Franny's skeptical expression. "You'll need to add before you can learn any other type of mathematics and you'll use it for cooking, sewing and managing a household. If you don't marry, you'll need it to earn a living. We'll do the flash cards until you have your sums by rote." She heard the sharpness in her voice and realized she had taken her own frustration out on her sister.

"By what?" Franny's mouth quivered.

"By memory, pet," Miriam explained and set the slate aside.

Maybe it was time for a break, after all. Outside the window, sunlight beckoned. For once, the heat had not intensified during the early morning hours, and the blue sky held a host of puffy white clouds that called out to Miriam.

If she could get away with it, she'd drop everything, search out a solitary piece of prairie and flop onto her back to escape into the ever-changing shapes they created as they moved across the sky.

Ah, but that would tempt propriety too much. She could, on the other hand, give Franny a chance to do it.

"I think that's enough for now, pet. Let's put things away and take the rest of the day to do as you wish."

Franny's eyes widened and she smiled, a distorted grin shaped by two missing teeth. Miriam smiled back, feeling warm inside for the first time in days. She accepted Franny's quick hug, watched the youngster scamper from the room, and heard the rebound of the spring door as Franny left the house.

She picked up the small pictorial alphabet cards and took them into the parlor to search for the box. Then she'd set things right with Jake. It was well past time. She hummed softly, glad that Harriet wasn't home to chastise her for it. A solitary activity, self-absorbing and inappropriate. It felt so good to give in to the whim and let go.

Jake stood behind the kitchen door listening. Miriam's humming held a softness she rarely exhibited. Lord, the woman puzzled him. She went from an uppity snoot to a commoner and back again with a little bit of vixen thrown in until he was too confused to know what hit him. And then she slammed the truth at him after he'd crossed just about every line there was.

He'd choked down his pride and gone back to his duties with a smoldering chip on his shoulder, both insulted and worried that she might report his behavior. So far, he hadn't been thrown into the guardhouse so he figured she hadn't told anyone. Maybe she didn't intend to. It was time they talked about the situation so he could get past worrying and be done with it.

He opened the kitchen door and caught sight of her across the room. "Miss Miriam?" He kept his voice soft, hoping she wouldn't bolt.

Her humming stopped, and she turned, her face ten shades of red. God, but the woman knew how to blush. Silence. She opened her mouth but no sound came out. Only a soft breath.

"I'd like to say I'm sorry about what happened," he began, keeping his words crisp and respectful.

"I'm sorry, too." Her voice was cautious, surprising him, and he remembered the last time she'd tried to apologize. He searched her emerald eyes and saw only sincerity, a plea for understanding.

"I behaved poorly." He didn't elaborate further. She would know what he meant.

She smiled, and he saw the absolution on her lips. He'd missed her more than he wanted to admit.

"As did I. I should have realized from the beginning that you didn't know who I was, and when I did, I should have told you.

I should have behaved less like a governess and more like a lady. Not only did I forget my place, I acted abominably, and I assumed that everything you did was intentional."

When she spoke without ranting, Miriam was far from the fishwife he'd first thought. Dressed in a simple gray-and-red plaid, she seemed softer. Her hair—mahogany, not red—drew attention to her green eyes, which invited conversation.

Realizing he'd been staring, Jake drew back.

Miriam fumbled with the picture cards.

He shifted his weight. "So . . . how've the lessons been going?"

"Fairly well, I suppose. I've never done this sort of thing before." She turned away and laid the cards into the box.

Jake leaned against the doorjamb, watching her. "Seems to me someone who wanted to be a teacher would have practiced lessons a lot."

She laughed. "I never wanted to be a teacher in my whole life."

He heard the smile in her voice even before she turned around. It lit her face.

"Funny thing for a 'governess' to say."

"I wasn't planning on being Franny's governess, Jake. I guess I never really planned anything." She set the box on the table, then turned back to him, her expression wistful. "Sarah, my friend in St. Louis, has completed telegrapher's school, and Lise wants to study law. I'm not sure I'd do anything that extreme, but I always thought I'd fancy being a milliner, if you can imagine. I'm good with hats and I'd thought about going to Denver with Sarah, taking an apprenticeship."

"So why are you here, then?"

The wistful smile disappeared. "Franny needed me," she said, her voice laced with worry. "That and the fact that I frittered away my time, not planning a thing, until it was too late."

Jake watched her move about the room, straightening Franny's chalk and slate. He wanted to ask her more, about her and about Franny, but probing wouldn't be right. He was just a private, and privates didn't ask those sorts of things.

"You've been working on the alphabet?" he asked instead.

She pointed at the box of lettered cards she'd been fidgeting with. "I've been using those."

The shiny cards had detailed pictures, one for every letter, and he was sure they'd cost a pretty penny. Just the kind of thing they'd use up here on Officers' Row. "Very fancy," he said with a touch of sarcasm. Too late, he wished he could draw the comment back.

She stalked back to where he was leaning in the doorway, her gentility forgotten, and he braced himself for the tirade he knew was coming.

"They're appropriate. Are you implying they are not?"

"I'm not stupid, Miriam. Of course they're appropriate. It's just that kids don't need stuff like that to learn. Seems awful high and mighty."

"Your favorite phrase, it would seem. Just what is high and mighty about using the tools available to instruct a child? One would think that you don't believe in education." She stood with her hands on her hips, the fishwife returned.

"Now just one damned minute, Miriam. There ain't nothin' more important in all the world than bein' educated." If he didn't believe that, he wouldn't be working in her mother's kitchen, that was for damn sure.

She tossed her head ever so slightly and raised her chin a notch, drawing Jake fully into the battle.

"You ought to get your nose out of the air, miss, 'cause you ain't so grand. I don't care what your name is. What you're doin' with that little girl ain't so very special neither, even if you got them fine little cards with pictures on 'em. We manage to educate our young'uns just fine without no fancy tricks like that."

"Oh, I just bet you do," Miriam retorted, comfortable with scrapping on his level. "What do you do with them, draw pictures in the dirt?"

"We don't need no pictures. You ought to come see how we teach ours." He ignored the screaming voice of caution in his head and grabbed her by the forearm, pulling her into the kitchen, toward the back door. She struggled against his strength. When he didn't respond, she lifted her foot and brought the heel of her high-button shoe down on his toes. He flinched and let go of her.

"Damn it, Miriam," he shouted in her face. "You didn't need to do that." He poked his finger at her chest to accentuate each of his following words. "Why, I oughtta—"

She stood her ground. Face to face, she glared up the half foot that separated their eye levels and poked him back. "You wouldn't dare."

Then, just as suddenly as the spat had started, they were both laughing at the ludicrous situation. Jake felt the rich laughter rise from deep inside him, watching humor feed Miriam until her shoulders shook, and her head dropped like a puppet. She tried to stop the sound with her hand but laughter spilled out, a torrent of giggles that would not be hindered.

"Oh, Miriam," he gasped, "I'm sorry." The chuckles poured forth again. He fought them, recognizing too late how far he'd crossed the line this time. "I didn't mean to be so disrespectful, I—"

"Oh, be quiet," she choked out. "I won't tell if you don't." Her eyes were still full of laughter.

Damn, she's having fun with this.

The thought sobered him. She'd found the forbidden exchange as exhilarating as he had, he was sure of it. He was standing in the kitchen laughing with the daughter of the commanding officer, and if he wasn't careful, he'd find himself in a whole mess of trouble.

"Jake?" The sudden quiet sincerity in her voice caught him unaware. It was the tone of an equal and he wondered where she was going with all this.

"Miriam, you should go on back into the dining room. This isn't right."

She shook her head, a hint of a smile pulling at her lips. "I'd like to hear about the teaching methods on Suds Row."

"What for? So you can tell me how much better you do things on Officers' Row?" He turned away from her and started stacking pans on the counter for washing.

"So I can understand." She touched his arm, drawing his attention to her steady gaze. "A few days ago, I spent a miserable afternoon listening to the closed-up opinions of my socially correct peers and it made me uncomfortable. I don't want that to be all I know."

Jake shrugged. "It ain't so different, really."

"How's that?" Reaching for a stack of plates, she handed them to him.

Jake took them, unsure of how to handle the situation. She shouldn't be helping, and he shouldn't be allowing her to. Still, how often did someone of her station show any interest in his world? A little enlightenment couldn't hurt.

He set the plates on the dry-sink and nodded to the table, waiting until she sat, delicately perched on the straight-back chair. Reaching for the teakettle, he poured hot water into a cup, popped a tea infuser into it and set it in front of her.

"We use prompts, too, saying the words. Sometimes, we get ahold of old picture cards, but mostly our kids just learn that 'a is for apple' instead of seeing it."

"What about books?" She set the china teacup on its saucer

and tipped her head at him. "Primers and readers?"

"You mean McGuffey's?"

She nodded.

"We have a few. We're not that backward. But they're old, used hand-me-downs. Folks use what they have around, the Bible and a few stray books they've received as gifts."

"But not many?"

"Not more than a handful."

She frowned. "Is there a set time for teaching?"

Jake shook his head. "Lessons get squeezed in among the chores or at night, before bed."

She raised her gaze to his. "There's no organized school?"

"There's been talk of the army setting one up in the chapel but nothing so far." He turned back to the counter again and checked the list of ingredients he'd prepared earlier. "Why? You want to be the teacher?"

"I'm sure Mother would rather I marry into the army like she did."

The comment poked at him, reminding him that they were worlds apart, no matter how much they tried to forget.

"Listen, Miriam, we shouldn't be talkin' like this. It ain't proper and we're just borrowin' trouble here."

For a moment, she just looked back, her big green eyes pondering something or another. Then the corners of her mouth turned up the slightest bit, and she shook her head. "You're not as illiterate as you pretend to be, are you?"

He watched her eyes, looking for the barb in the question. They were sincere.

"What d'ya mean?" he asked, sliding further into the common dialect he'd grown up with, distancing himself.

"That. You don't always speak that way. Do you do it to hide?"

He shrugged his shoulders, not wanting to talk about it. "I adjust."

"You hide," she insisted.

"Like hell, Miriam," he snapped. "This is how I was raised and it's what I go back to. I don't have much call to put on airs. How do you think I'd fit in back in the barracks if I started sounding like an officer?" He moved across the kitchen to rummage through the cupboard. What'd she need to poke in all this for, anyway?

"But you can."

He slammed the cupboard door shut. "I ain't gonna talk about it." Behind him, he heard her move her chair away from the table and set the teacup on the dry-sink, the tinkling of the fragile china a sharp contrast to the slamming. As different as her fancy world was from his common one.

Any way you looked at it, she was an officer's daughter through and through, and she wasn't about to let him forget that he was a step below her.

He spun around. "You've satisfied your curiosity, now go on and get out. I don't want you in here no more. Get out."

Disappointment flitted across her face, then anger, and Jake wished the words hadn't come out so bitterly. She stomped across the room and left without another word, the door swinging behind her.

Damn it.

He'd meant to redraw the line that separated them, to somehow reach a truce. Now he wasn't quite sure if he'd erased the line altogether or built a brick wall instead.

CHAPTER SEVEN

Jake was late.

Miriam stood at the kitchen stove, stirring oatmeal while she fretted. If and when her mother ever got up, she would pitch a fit. After all the fussing Miriam had done over what a nuisance Jake would be, it shocked her that a tiny part of her was concerned for him.

She heard Franny poking around in the other room and moved the pan of mush off the heat. It didn't look very appetizing, not like Jake's.

She didn't know why she was worried about Jake, anyway.

The man was driving her insane. He could shift from fighting mad to quiet conversation in seconds. And then there were those strange moments that hung somewhere in between, the ones that made her stomach do flip-flops.

Yesterday, he'd been standoffish—no sneering comments and no overly familiar remarks. If anything, he was distant to the point of avoiding contact with her. And for the life of her, she couldn't figure out why his coldness bothered her so much.

After all, wasn't it his overfamiliarity that had so infuriated her in the first place? Heavens, here she was wishing he'd hurry and show up so she could start another fight.

He was nothing but a temptation to let loose and flaunt the restrictions that defined her life. That was all. She needed to keep her perspective, and Jake was a far cry from where she needed to be. Mother was just beginning to back off from her almost-constant hovering and had almost stopped yelling at Franny. She couldn't afford to risk that tenuous progress.

She shook Jake from her thoughts and entered the dining room to collect the bowls from the sideboard. Franny smiled at her and set down the alphabet book she'd been reviewing.

"I'm hungry. What's Deakins makin' for me today?"

"Jake's not here yet, pet." *So much for getting him out of my head.* "And Mother's still abed. I made you some oatmeal."

Franny's face wrinkled. "It ain't gonna taste like the other stuff you cooked, is it?"

Miriam frowned back at her. "Oh, hush. It wasn't that bad. Come on into the kitchen." She turned and led the way.

Franny followed, grumbling all the way. "Mother says she doesn't know how you got passing marks in cul'nary arts."

"Mother forgets how different it is, cooking on a decent stove. Besides, if she's going to stay in bed all day with her headaches, I'm the only cook you have."

"Jake cooks real good on that stove."

She ignored the comment as Franny pulled out a straight-backed chair and sat. Miriam watched her place a clean cloth napkin on her lap and straighten her posture. She was learning.

There was a certain security in the familiar rules of behavior. When it wasn't ridiculous, civility held tried-and-true comfort. On her recent outing with Robert, she'd felt a warm, reassuring camaraderie. With Jake, that same propriety felt petty, its safety stale and empty, without challenge.

She spooned lumpy oatmeal into Franny's bowl and realized she liked the invigoration of the challenge as well as she did the comfortable gentility.

The thought was sobering. Maybe Jake was right. Such invigoration would bring nothing but trouble, trouble she could ill afford. She'd keep her distance, the same as he was doing.

She carried the oatmeal to the table, set the bowl down and

tried to ignore the expression on Franny's face.

"It's got lumps."

"They won't hurt you, Franny. Eat it."

"But Jake never makes it with lumps," Franny complained.

"Eat it anyway. If you fuss about it, Mother will wake up and notice he's not here, and she'll fire him." She doubted it was true. Mother would never let a good striker go. She'd fuss about it some, though.

"All right," Franny mumbled. "But please have Jake teach you how to cook it right, 'cause the lumps are really awful."

Miriam smiled into her own bowl, letting the image of Jake attempting to teach her how to cook oatmeal fill the moments while Franny choked down the thick paste. He'd never let her live it down, and she'd end up throwing the whole batch of it on his head. Then he'd stand there with steam in his eyes and lumpy clots of oatmeal dripping into the golden hairs of his mustache and onto his upper lip, waiting for someone to lean forward and—

"Miriam?"

"Hmm?" Miriam turned her head toward Franny and swallowed against the unnerving picture in her mind. "What?"

"Are we gonna study when we get done?" She plunked down her spoon and bit her bottom lip.

Miriam eyed her mother's bedroom door and shook her head. "Not now, I don't think. I'll clean up the kitchen and run some errands since Jake's not here to do them. We'll study later."

Her mother had agreed that Franny should participate in disciplined studies for only a few hours each day. The remainder of the day would consist of subtle lessons on etiquette and life such as sewing, gardening, and social visiting. Free time would allow Franny to work off her energy as well as allowing Mother to sleep late and take naps without being disturbed, which Mother was doing with increasing frequency.

"Run and play," Miriam told her and was rewarded with an enthusiastic hug before Franny left the house.

Washing the breakfast dishes and the crusty oatmeal pan with hot water from the reservoir on the stove, Miriam made short work of the kitchen cleanup. She gathered the dirty napkins from the table and added them to the basket of clothing waiting in the corner. Hoping it wasn't too heavy, she lifted the wicker basket and began the long walk to Suds Row.

By the time she arrived at Mrs. Jeffreys' cabin, she almost wished she'd left the laundry errands for Jake, after all. She shifted the awkward basket to her hip and knocked on the door. A young boy answered, staring at her from beneath sooty black lashes.

"Mama ain't doin' laundry no more," the boy said. "She went to be a cook over to the captain's place 'cause the laundry work was hurting her back."

"I see," Miriam told him, retreating behind a charade of upper-class bearing. Her mother's instructions echoed through her mind. *In difficult situations, one accomplishes more when one takes command and a displays superior comportment.* "And just who's going to be doing our laundry now?" She cringed at her tone and wondered how such superior comportment could possibly be considered effectual. It was no surprise when the child shut the door.

"Excuse me, Miriam."

She turned to find Carrie standing in the shade of the run-down building.

"Carrie." Miriam smiled, feeling the tension lift. "What happens when a laundress quits?" she asked, nodding toward Mrs. Jeffreys' door.

"Most times, the army hires a new one and the contract jes' passes right on. But, there ain't been nobody else hired as yet. Ain't no one left to hire. If you want, I could do up your wash an' you could talk to your ma to see if she wants to have me take it on from here on out. I been doin' most of it for Mrs. Jeffreys anyways."

"That sounds like the most practical approach. Am I correct, then, to assume there's laundry to take back?"

"I was jes' foldin' the last of it. If you got a few minutes, you're welcome to stay an' wait while I finish up. Else I can jes' bring the load over when I get done."

Despite the fact that she knew she should return home and send Jake over later for the laundry, something about Carrie Rupert reached out, urging Miriam to stay. Besides, she knew Carrie wouldn't wait for Jake. She'd just take time out of what had to be a very busy day and haul it over herself.

"I'll wait, if you're sure it won't be an inconvenience."

"You want to come on in to the house or jes' set out here a spell? It's cooler outside, but you might feel there's less eyes on you if you were to come on in."

She was surprised at Carrie's acuity. Neither choice was proper. Waiting for her laundry was a servant's job, and they both knew it. Carrie's offer to wait inside was just as improper, but at least being indoors would shelter her from prying eyes and the wagging tongues that went with them. Miriam nodded and followed her into the cabin.

The inside of the building once again reminded her of the physical differences of their stations. She scanned the room while Carrie poured two cups of water. The crude furniture was constructed of local lumber, and simple homemade curtains hung by nails at the single window. Despite the log walls and bare floor, the room was spotless. Open shelves held neat stacks of mismatched dishes.

"Sit," Carrie said, pointing to an unpretentious wooden rocking chair. "It ain't much but the rocker's comfortable. It was my mama's and we brung it out from Ohio with us, like a piece of home, you might say." Her friendly chatter defied their different social positions, leading Miriam to sidestep her own restraint.

"You're from Ohio, then?" she asked.

Carrie settled down next to a basket of laundry and began folding. "We was raised outside a little town not but too far away from Springfield. My sister, Becca, she's still back in Ohio, goin' to school."

Carrie's face was full of pride, and Miriam wondered at her comment. Mother maintained that most of the poor left school to work in factories or become domestic servants. Her own experience was limited to her classmates, all from the upper stratum of society. Curious, she leaned forward.

"What type of school is she attending?"

"Springfield Academy for Women. She's been studyin' Greek an' Latin an' music an' all sorts of ladies' fancywork an' manners."

How in heaven's name could someone like Carrie's sister afford Springfield Academy? None of her former classmates had been from the working class. Miriam waited, knowing her reaction was unfair, until Carrie plunged ahead, her blue eyes bright and serious.

"Miriam, you ain't gonna like what I'm gonna say, but you're in my house, and I think it'd do you good to hear. Your face tells me you don't want to believe one word of what I said. I know we got diff'rent places an' all, but that don't mean I can't do good for my family jes' the same as those that provide for you do what's best. Becca deserves a chance to get ahead, jes' the same as anyone else, no matter where she starts from."

The words were carefully chosen, tactfully delivered. But they felt heavy. Miriam felt her cheeks burn. Like Lise, Carrie didn't shy from the truth. And the truth burned.

Lord, Carrie must think she was nothing but a snob.

And she couldn't even begin to deny it. For all her fussing

and stewing about her mother's airs, she was just as bad. Of course, Becca deserved a chance. The fact that Miriam had never encountered an educated person who wasn't wealthy didn't mean anything.

She felt Carrie's gaze and raised her own. The laundress's sapphire eyes held no anger, no resentment, and Miriam offered her a tentative smile. Carrie smiled back.

"If Becca was here, you would never even know she was my sister. You'd think she was some officer's girl or somethin'. Education can do that, make folks equal, long as no one puts a sign on their back sayin' they're diff'rent."

They sat in silence, Carrie's humbling words soaking in. Her directness was out of place, and Miriam knew she should have been offended. The fact that she wasn't pleased her, an absolution of sorts.

"I'm sorry, Carrie. I'd never looked at it from your perspective."

"It's somethin' to think about. A person can miss a whole lot of good things if they're all closed up. An open mind an' an open heart makes life a whole lot more enjoyable."

"You must think I'm conceited." It stunned Miriam that she had lived her life without a thought of how important education might be to someone who didn't have it handed to her. Guilty, she realized again how she'd wasted her studies, failing to prepare herself for anything but the life she was born into.

"Never feel you got to apologize for what you don't know, only for what you do know an' choose to ignore," Carrie added.

"Thank you."

"For what?"

"For teaching me, and for not making it an issue." Reaching into a pile of woolen stockings, Miriam began mating and folding them. They worked in companionable silence for a few moments before Miriam spoke again. "The tuition must be more than you make in several months."

"It's high, I'll grant you that. But it's important to us. Jake and me, we send all we can make extra to her. Livin' on the lower side of life ain't so easy. It ain't the life you want for those you love."

Jake? Of, course. An image of his deep blue eyes, the exact shade as Carrie's, lingered in her mind. It explained a lot about why he always seemed to be around Suds Row.

"Jake is your brother, then?"

"Him an' my Eddie worked on the U.P. railroad together an' then they up and joined the army a few years back. I got hired on as a laundress so I could come with. The extra money I make along with most of Jake's pay and the extra he gets for bein' your striker goes to Becca."

Miriam hadn't pictured Jake as a family man, nor as someone who'd spend his pay on his sister's education. No wonder he'd gotten so roiled up about her teaching methods.

"What about you, Carrie? You didn't want the education?"

Carrie's face took on a faraway look. "Oh, I wanted it, all right. But Becca was more suited to it, and we couldn't afford to send more than one of us. Becca had the best chance of makin' it. Hardest thing I ever done was leavin' school an' tellin' Jake I didn't want to go no more." She sighed and turned back to the basket. "You ready for these clothes?"

She dropped the last pair of socks into the wicker basket and pushed it toward Miriam. The action spoke louder than words, their respite from reality was over. It was time to assume their roles again.

"Thank you," Miriam said. She nodded and rose from the chair. Hefting the basket to her hip, she managed a quavering smile and left the cabin, no longer sure she liked what reality had to offer.

CHAPTER EIGHT

September sneaked in with its endless contrasts of muggy warmth and crisp chills. It tricked Miriam into choosing the wrong clothing, leaving her uncomfortable and frustrated. She almost believed nature had planned it that way so that neither her body nor her mind could remain undisturbed.

Each time she made peace with Jake, it scratched like a woolen petticoat until she couldn't stand it. Then, in a gust of heat, one of them would explode and they'd forget their places. More and more, they were crossing society's lines.

It wasn't right. He was a private, an enlisted man. She shouldn't be wasting her time on him, let alone her thoughts. Unless, of course, it was simply that time was the problem. Too much time together made for too much familiarity. And too much familiarity was leading to a very strange relationship indeed.

If she'd been spending her time with Robert Wood instead of being cooped up with Jake, she'd have other diversions. It had been almost two weeks since Robert had called on her, and it was long past time to recapture his attention.

Leaving Franny hard at work on a simple sampler project, Miriam grabbed her best straw hat, pinned it on, and struck off across the parade ground toward Post Headquarters. Adjutant's Call had been sounded, and if her timing was right, she'd run into Robert just about the time he'd be leaving morning officers' assembly.

He stood outside the office building, tall and easily recognizable amid the other officers. Their laughter quieted as she neared, and each tipped his cap in greeting before drifting off, leaving only Robert and her father. Tom Longstreet nodded at her and smiled, then turned and entered the building.

Robert lingered, waiting for her to approach before speaking. "Hello, Miriam."

"Hello, Mr. Wood," she answered, hoping her tone conveyed her discontent. "We haven't seen you for a while. You've been busy?" It wasn't what she wanted to say, but it was as close as she could come without overstepping propriety. Dissatisfaction gnawed at her. Odd that she'd never thought that much of it before. One more bad habit she could thank Jake for.

Robert appeared unbothered. "I have, but I should have found the time to stop by. Will you accept my apologies?"

"You're an officer, Robert. Please don't apologize for doing your duty." She held back the tongue-lashing that still threatened to spill out. What made duty so all-fired important that he couldn't even spare a few minutes after retreat?

"A bunch of us just got ranked out. I've got the rest of the morning to move but Peterson's got to clear out first. Want to take a walk while I'm waiting? I've got enough time to circle around the post trader's store."

"A new officer?" Miriam asked, taking Robert's extended arm as they headed north toward the chapel.

"Arrived last night and took over Simpson's quarters. Of course, Simpson bumped me. I'll be down to half the space I had, two rooms." Though his words made light of the matter, his voice was edged with frustration.

"Two rooms, Robert, is decidedly better than a hallway," she said, challenging him with a grin. He glanced down at her tone and raised an eyebrow as if trying to decide how best to respond to her lighthearted jab. The conversation felt stilted, almost hollow. Heavens, Jake would be bantering with her like crazy by this time.

"That it is, Miriam, that it is. What makes you so saucy this morning?"

"Too much time caged up in the house, I suppose."

Robert laughed, missing the barb Miriam had aimed at him, and turned into the wooded area surrounding the trader's complex. "Too much time with your mother might just do that."

The differences between Jake and Robert were sharp, and she wondered just when it was that she had come to crave Jake's pointed repartee over Robert's quiet pleasantries. She should have sought out Robert days ago, before Jake got under her skin.

"So how have the lessons been progressing?" he asked.

"It's a new experience every day. I've not done anything like teaching before, and it taxes my creativity to find new ways to present the material."

"I'm sure you do quite well at it. I always find it fascinating how skillful women are in dealing with children."

The praise failed to warm her. He hadn't even asked what she was doing. Did he simply expect her to be creative and skillful because she was supposed to be that way?

"What makes you sure I'm good with them?" she probed.

"Of course you are. How could you not be. You're well-mannered, thoughtful, and respectful. You were raised in a military family. All the necessary traits."

She bristled. "Is that how you examine all women, then?"

"Gracious, Miriam, you are saucy today. Of course that's how I examine women. The military is my career. A woman's social skills are important here."

"But what about her intelligence? Or her wit?"

"I didn't say those things weren't significant. It's just that out here, a woman's skill as a hostess and social partner can make or break an officer's advancement. That's where intelligence and wit come into play. A supportive, gracious wife can be an officer's greatest asset."

Wonderful. And here she was, barely able to keep her tongue in check. What was it Jake had called her? A screech owl? Not exactly what Robert had in mind. Not even if she was the commanding officer's daughter. And it wouldn't be what any of the other bachelor officers had in mind either. Had it really only taken her two weeks to slip into behaving this way?

"Woolgathering?" Robert asked.

"I guess I am a little distracted. I'm sorry."

"I've had an idea. How about a party? You haven't had a chance to meet many of the junior officers and their ladies. We could have a 'ranking out' party. I'm sure your mother would let us host it at your house. It'd be the perfect chance to show off your skills."

She let him ramble on about guest choices as they returned to the parade ground. Her skills? It'd be the perfect disaster. She'd almost ruined her mother's last party.

"Robert," she interrupted, "I'm not sure I'm ready to serve as hostess. I'm not very polished about menus and—"

"Nonsense. You have all the skills required, I'm sure of it. After all, you're Harriet Longstreet's daughter. She told me you laid out the table at the last party and it was perfect. And she's been boasting about how great Deakins is in the kitchen. Just put your head together with him."

No, she and Jake and parties did not mix, not at all. They'd be fighting like a couple of tom turkeys before they even got started and she'd be a nervous wreck. And then there would be Mother. She'd never be able to handle both of them at the same time.

"But Robert, he's very difficult to work with." Spending more time with Jake had not been her goal. Look what time thus far with him had wrought. Robert had completely missed the point.

"Most strikers are, Miriam."

"He almost ruined mother's party when he let that dog into the house."

"Dog?" The comment had grasped his attention.

"The big black one," she explained.

"Blackie? He let my Blackie in your mother's house?"

"Your Blackie?" Miriam sputtered. "That dog belongs to you?"

Robert frowned. "Goodness, Miriam, settle down. It's just a dog. I bought him, yes, but he's more like community property. All the single officers watch out for him."

Lord, the whole mess with Deakins had started with a dog that wasn't even his. No wonder he'd reacted badly.

"Enough about the dog. We were talking about a social. I'm sure you can manage Deakins just fine."

"I don't like him, and I don't think he'll cooperate with me." But she knew that wasn't the problem. It lay much deeper. In fact, she was beginning to suspect that she liked him a little bit more than she should. That was the problem.

"You don't need to like him, Miriam. He's your employee. Any good military woman worth her salt can control her striker." He smiled in triumph. "Let's plan for Saturday evening."

She nodded her assent and watched Robert return to duty.

He'd left her no further argument, no choice except to create a scene she wasn't prepared to deal with. She may have succeeded in recapturing Robert Wood's attention, but she'd have to survive working with Jake Deakins if she wanted to keep it.

CHAPTER NINE

The following afternoon, while Mother and Franny took needed naps, Miriam headed across the parade ground to Suds Row. This time, she wasn't about to let any unexpected accidents threaten the party. She'd already informed Jake that Blackie was banished from the interior of their quarters, borrowed an extra tablecloth from Eulalie Samuels, and checked her mother's linens for any spots or tears. A small gravy stain on the break-front scarf demanded Carrie's attention.

She needed to concentrate on Robert and making things successful. He was charming, handsome, and easily the most eligible bachelor at Fort Randall. If she remained at the fort long, she suspected their relationship would deepen. It shouldn't matter that their conversations lacked stimulation. She was approaching the relationship the wrong way, that was all. If it weren't for her irrational need for freedom, she'd find Robert perfectly acceptable and she knew it. Even with Sarah and Lise, she hadn't behaved with such abandon.

She'd given the wild, untamed element inside her far too much head. Jake hadn't helped, challenging her at every turn. It was her own fault for letting Jake get the best of her. She needed to put a stop to this nonsense before she lost every shred of breeding she had. Proper ladies controlled their whims.

Somehow, there had to be a way to pull rein on her temper, control this childishness, and act like the lady she'd always known she was to be. Behaving with propriety didn't mean she had to become an uppity old biddy, after all.

She rounded the first cabin of Suds Row and found Carrie resting in the shade of an elm tree, her blonde head bent over the back of her hand.

"Carrie? Are you all right?"

"Miriam, what a surprise. You caught me restin' a bit. Sometimes, the heat gets me a little. You brought some linens. That must mean I got work to do."

"If you could. I'll need it by Saturday afternoon."

"Not one bit of a problem." She rose, took the scarf, and motioned for Miriam to follow her into the house. "Sit," she said in that direct way of hers that would have been rude coming from anyone else. "Havin' folks over again, are you?"

Miriam nodded and sat at the tidy wooden table as Carrie put the table scarf aside. "Lieutenant Wood has asked me to help him host a small gathering."

"Wood is quite a legend 'round here."

"You know him?" Miriam asked, surprised.

"We hear a bunch. Our husbands talk about him a lot."

"And what do they say?"

"Oh, lots of things," Carrie teased. "Mostly gossip."

"Like what?" Even if it *was* pure, unabashed gossip, Miriam hungered to hear more about Robert, to understand him better.

"Well, they like to tell about what he done to Captain Tate, back when he weren't a captain yet."

"Tell me," Miriam urged. Carrie grabbed two tin cups from the shelf, filled them with hot tea and sat across the table.

"It used to be, Captain Tate and Mr. Wood was always tryin' to best each other. Tate one time sent a fake message to Wood, and Wood, on account of the note, went hightailin' it over to the colonel's, back when we had a colonel here. 'Course, the colonel didn't know nothin' about it. He didn't much like it that Wood came stormin' into his quarters just when he was climbin' into bed. The fellas had quite a laugh on that one."

Miriam inhaled sharply. "Oh, my, I'll bet Robert didn't find it very funny."

Carrie just smiled. "Well, now I don't know nothin' about how he felt right then, but it seems he figured to get even with ole Tate. Took some time plannin' it all out, too. Come down here, wantin' to know if any of us women had any sort of fancy dress he could borrow, and he done a lot of whisperin' with the sergeant. Next thing we hear is 'bout some fancy ball over to the officers' quarters and the laundresses and hospital matrons is all invited. There was a special invite to all the enlisted men, too. Last time we got invited to any of the doin's."

Robert, involved in a practical joke? Somehow, the idea didn't gel. Miriam leaned forward, interested in this unexpected side of him. "Robert had something to do with it?"

"Was his idea. 'Course we was all just delighted to go to some big fancy gatherin'. We all got prettied up and set out and just guess what we see when we get there?"

"I can't begin to imagine." Miriam waited, eager for Carrie to continue.

"There's one of the privates all dressed up in Mrs. Jeffreys' best dress. 'Course we all know him, but them officers is all fooled. Wood and the sergeant had him all fixed up with a hairpiece pinned on and color on his cheeks. He sure was pretty, in a homely sort of way. Wood introduced him as a new hospital matron and set him off a-dancin' with all the officers. 'Course it was all planned for him to spark it up with Captain Tate. Which he done. Ole Tate didn't know it was a man till he escorted him home and was about to kiss him good night."

"Oh, my."

"He was some mad at Wood for that one."

"I'll bet he was. Robert really planned that?" So he did have a childish side after all. A practical joker. It didn't seem to fit

91

with the Robert she knew, but it sure did make him more appealing.

"Earned him the hearts of the men down here. Ain't none that liked Tate too well. There's a few that grumble about Wood bein' strict, but mostly folks remember what he done to Tate. 'Course the womenfolk think mighty high of Wood, too."

"The women?" Miriam sipped her tea, curious.

"You was down a while back, lookin' at how we teach our young'uns and such?" It was more a statement than a question.

"I was, yes," Miriam said, remembering how she'd wandered over after the day Jake had challenged her to observe the education of the laundresses' and enlisted men's children. She hadn't realized Carrie had noticed.

"Tell me what you seen."

"There were many children but very little space and almost no books. Mothers were trying hard to fit in teaching whenever they had a spare minute. I got the sense that many of the women had little education themselves. Quite a bit different from Officers' Row."

"You got a good idea, then, how hard it is. 'Specially when there's so many that want to do good for their children."

"But what has Robert to do with it?"

"Seems he's taken up the cause. He's been askin' for schoolin'. The army's done already said it was good to educate the enlisted men. He's tryin' to get a real school goin' with a paid teacher and all, for the children in the day and the men at night."

"Robert is trying to start a school?" This, too, was an unexpected side of him.

"Guess he even talked to Jake about bein' the teacher. With him havin' gone to school up till he was near sixteen, he's got more schoolin' than most of the men. Army says it should be an enlisted man what gets hired as teacher, or leastwise as assistant, so might be Jake is one of those most qualified."

So that was why Jake had gotten all riled up about the alphabet cards and her high-and-mighty attitude on education. He'd taken it personally.

"He can polish up how he talks when he wants to," Carrie added, "and he reads more'n anybody I know. He just don't make no big display about it is all. Tends to blend in with folks he's with."

"Goodness, Jake a teacher and Robert a joker. That's quite a lot you've given me to think about, Carrie."

"I s'pect so." They sat, sipping the last of their tea.

"I'd best go," Miriam said at last.

"I reckon," Carrie agreed. "I hope your party goes well. Celebratin' something special?"

Miriam laughed. "Robert got ranked out. So I guess we're trying to poke some fun. I'm just glad it wasn't me. I wouldn't be able to stand it."

"Oh, you'd make do," Jake interrupted from the doorway, a bundle of soiled laundry in his arms. Meeting his eyes, Miriam held her tongue. Too many times, she'd jumped to a fast retort only to set him off.

"Only if I had to," she finally quipped, unable to resist the challenge. She hoped he'd notice the lightness in her tone.

"No, on second thought, you'd likely screech about it so much that they'd give you a whole house to yourself, just to keep you quiet." His voice was teasing this time, and a hint of a smile crept across his face. It held Miriam's attention until the silence became noticeable and she remembered Carrie.

"Jake Deakins, you mind your manners," Carrie said.

"Aw, don't be worryin' your pretty little head about it, Carrie. Miriam knows she screeches."

"Now hold on. I take great pride in that screeching. Jake's just jealous because I screech louder than he grumbles."

With that, Jake's rich, hearty laughter filled the small room.

Miriam choked back her giggles until tears sprang into her eyes. Carrie looked from one to the other, a puzzled expression on her face.

"You two about done now?" Carrie asked.

Miriam nodded, hiding a broad smile behind her hand while Jake struggled to gain control. She realized how much she'd missed him these past few days, and how easily they'd gotten past the argument this time. Perhaps there was hope for them.

"Miriam," he said, suddenly sober, "you got any idea what the enlisted men live in?"

Miriam shook her head. Where was Jake going with this?

"It don't compare to what the officers live in, even when they get ranked out."

"I . . . I never thought about it."

"Should we show her, Carrie?"

"Well, it sure beats the two of you yammerin' like a couple of fools. I ain't sure that it's a wise idea, though. 'Sides, I got work that needs doin'."

Carrie's caution wormed its way into Miriam's mind. Visiting the enlisted men's barracks was not a good idea. She didn't belong there, and she didn't belong walking across the parade ground with Jake.

Still, she didn't want to spoil what was happening. For the first time, she and Jake had initiated, and sustained, a conversation without hostility. The playful exchange bordered on friendship. Not just a friendly spark in the middle of a fight, but a whole friendly discussion, even if it was brief. Their different social classes hadn't even mattered this time—just like they didn't seem to matter with Carrie—and Miriam felt richer for it.

Besides, she was interested in the differences between them . . . and about the things that were important to him.

Before Miriam had the chance to back out, Jake was behind

her, pulling out her chair. Surprise flooded through her and she was at the door before she realized it. She nodded a good-bye to Carrie and followed Jake out into the sunshine, shooing the doubts out of her head.

The crisp autumn afternoon was quiet. Here and there, children played among themselves. Jake led the way, not waiting for her. She understood his intent at once, a courtesy, meant to shield her from the prying eyes of the soldiers and the chastisement of the officers. This was a consideration that she knew he would not have extended a few weeks ago.

She slowed her step, studying Jake as he climbed the small rise ahead of her. Across the width of his upper back, the gray wool of his military blouse was strained by the power of the muscles that lurked below the cloth. He looked back, caught her watching him, and smiled as he waited for her to catch up.

He led her northward, and they passed the deserted officers' triplex and turned west at the equally quiet post bakery. He was headed for the back side of the barracks, the side that faced away from the parade ground.

Reaching the doorway, Jake turned back to Miriam. "The men are all out on drill so the place is empty. Have a look at how the other half lives." He made a sweeping gesture.

Curiosity pulled her closer to the unfamiliar territory. Accustomed to officers' quarters and traders' stores, she'd never seen the inside of an enlisted men's barracks. She stepped beside Jake and peered into the room. Most of the space was occupied by rows of identical wooden bunks. The beds were short and looked uncomfortable. How in heaven's name did someone as tall as Jake sleep without his feet hanging over the end?

"Through there's the mess room. It's got a long table with benches, and that's about it. On the other side is another bunk room. The place gets cold in the winter and hot in the summer and almost never quiet 'cept when it's empty like now. We each got a box to put our personal gear in, what there is of it."

Miriam wandered the cramped room, spying the crude wooden box that bore Jake's name stenciled on its lid. It sat at the foot of a stark but neatly made bunk. Jake's bunk. She pictured his large shoulders on the narrow bed and realized how inadequate the bunk was, in width as well as length. It appeared hard and spare, and she had the urge to sit on it to see if the blankets covered something softer.

Instead, she noted the sparseness of the enlisted man's life. There were none of the fancy frills that filled her comfortable room. The walls were bare of personal items. Only the stenciled names on the wooden trunks gave evidence of individual identity.

"It seems so bare," she said, "but it must be dreadfully crowded." Her voice echoed in the empty void.

"You get to know each other well. Most 'specially your bunkie. When you first come into the unit, someone is assigned to show you the ropes. That's your bunkie. On campaign, bunkies team up their half-shelters to make a full tent. You get to know your bunkie real well. You get to know everyone a little better than you want to. Once the room's full of soldiers who haven't bathed for a week, it seems mighty full."

Jake's voice filled the room, and she realized how loud it must be when filled with snoring men. One lone metal wash basin sat on the floor next to the rather small stove. She glanced around the room, wondering about wintertime.

"It gets cold," he told her, answering the unspoken question.

She nodded, thinking about the bare wooden floors and thin blankets. Somehow, she suspected that life in Robert's two rooms were far superior to life here.

"Summertime's hot. Air gets real heavy inside. Once, the men could sit outside on the verandas and get cooled down but soldiers have been throwing their garbage under them for so long that it stinks like the dickens once the weather warms up."

He fell silent again and their eyes found each other across the stillness. Still, calm silence in which it seemed natural not to say a word. Miriam offered him a small, wavering smile. He smiled back, then nodded to the door and followed her out.

Later, back in her cluttered, cinnamon-scented, comfortable five-room house, the differences in their lives haunted Miriam. So, too, did the uneasy sense of closeness created by the fact that Jake had shared his knowledge with her, shared it because he wanted her to know, because he sensed she could understand and appreciate it, and not because he wanted to belittle her.

CHAPTER TEN

"That's quite a list to be asking for when you're in the middle of Dakota Territory," Jake complained. He tossed the list onto the kitchen table.

Miriam had known he'd get testy. She'd even added a couple of the more exotic items just to see his reaction. As she'd expected, his eyes began snapping the minute he saw the list.

And along with that deep blue sparkle came a ready smirk that kept the anger and hostility of their former exchanges at bay. During the past few days, they'd settled into a routine of teasing give and take. As they worked together to prepare for the party, they alternated between the quiet conversation of friends and the spirited repartee of playmates.

Miriam's worries had dissipated into enjoyment. The advertisements for a new governess had been sent off, Mother had quit hovering, and Miriam found herself looking more and more forward to her time with Jake. The new relationship was still improper, forbidden even, but she could control things, now.

"Just wanted to see if you're up to the challenge, Private," she taunted. She stood and crossed her arms. "Of course, if you don't think you can. . . ."

"Now wait just a minute, Miss High and Mighty. I just said it was quite a list. Didn't say nothin' about not being able to do what's on it." Jake slammed a handful of tin cups into the dry-sink and turned back toward her, a smile on his face.

"I wasn't altogether sure you were familiar with everything. We could make it simpler."

"What's going to be difficult is getting some of it. One can see you have no experience at all in marketing." He quieted as his gaze traveled down the list and the pause lengthened. "It's too late in the season for fresh asparagus and the sutler doesn't even carry some of the spices I'd need for the soup," he said. The teasing lightheartedness was gone, replaced with something suppressed, unidentifiable.

"So improvise." She threw one last challenging smile at him in an attempt to pull him back to the Jake she'd become familiar with. He stood in silence, watching. Puzzled and disappointed, Miriam turned to leave.

She heard his footsteps behind her and sensed his hand on her arm, a brush of his fingers on her sleeve. "I'll have to. The raspberries are gone."

The suggestive image filled her mind. She turned to face him and saw the memory reflected in his eyes. Raspberry tarts. Filled with clinging red jelly. Waiting to be licked. The experience flowed through her body and she shivered.

Jake watched the shiver, his gaze drifting across her. "If I make 'em with currant jelly, will you swipe one of them, too?"

Miriam felt her lips part and the catch of her breath. Jake's fingers stroked out a circle on the fabric of her sleeve, making a slight rustling sound in the unsettling silence. Her breath came slowly, at cross-purposes with her racing heart.

In Jake's eyes, the fire had reignited, this time as a smoldering ember. Intense. Magnetic. He swallowed once, his gaze locked with hers, then dropped his hand and turned away, the spell broken. "I'd best get to the sutler, then, and see what we can do about this improvising."

She watched him leave the kitchen and stood there alone. Looking down, she realized she was holding on to the back of the wooden chair as if her life depended on it. Lord God, the game had changed. And she no longer had control.

Early Saturday evening, Miriam stood before her bedroom mirror. She could almost taste the expectation in the air. It had built in odd bursts throughout the day. At times, anticipation was an almost-imperceptible undercurrent. But there were moments, like now, when it swelled until the eagerness hung like a heavy wave, threatening to inundate her.

Apprehension about the party, she told herself, nervousness about meeting Robert's friends and meeting with his approval.

But she knew it was neither.

It was the strange trepidation that lingered in the bottom of her stomach every time she thought about Jake.

Miriam turned from the mirror and opened her bedroom door. The sound of tinkling glassware startled her and she peered into the dining room. Jake squatted before the open door of the polished cherry-wood breakfront, unaware of her presence. Taut cream-colored suspenders crisscrossed the broad expanse of his back, straining against the rear buttons of his trousers. Below, the tight blue wool molded his firm thighs.

She watched him, unable to tear her gaze away. She waited for him to turn and notice her, half hoping he wouldn't. Since the day he brought up the raspberry tarts, she'd felt a strange pull to him that seemed to stop everything but their awareness of each other. Neither frequent nor steady, it recurred without warning, shocking in its sudden intensity.

Until today. Today, the magnetism had built like a slow, wet, summer storm, and no amount of reason could stop it.

"Jake?" she ventured, stepping into the dining room.

He turned, back muscles playing under gray wool, long blond hair brushing the collar of his military blouse. She saw appreciation register in his eyes. It stalled there, caught in the blueness, then spread into a slow smile that broadened as he stood, the vase he held in his hand all but forgotten.

Miriam felt her own mouth curve in response.

Jake's breathing was labored, like her own. She felt a need to suck in great volumes of air to feed her pounding heart. The pull of his stare engulfed her in the vivid depth of his eyes until, in the space of a second, they clouded and became hard.

Like they had in those first weeks they had known each other.

"Got yourself all dolled up for the lieutenant, I see." The bitterness in his voice stung, and her mind scrambled to figure out what she had done.

"Who else would it be for?" The answer sounded catty and she wished she could take her words back. Who else would it be for? Five seconds ago, they'd both known the answer to that one.

"Do take care you don't stick your elbow in the jelly or anything. It'd make a hell of a mess of both your dress and the buffet." He edged his way past her, clutching the crystal vase like it was some toy he refused to share.

"Well, now, we wouldn't want to spoil your buffet, would we?" Miriam quipped, wishing he'd stay and fight. Wishing for anything but this cold shoulder.

"No, Miriam, we wouldn't. Because if we did, the lieutenant wouldn't like it. And that, my dear, would put you in a hell of a pickle."

He ducked into the kitchen. In her mind, his words lingered, troubled and uneasy. Ha. She was in a pickle already. They both were, and he knew it.

Trying to be Jake's friend was stupid and futile and pointless. Over and over again it came back to the two of them fighting like alley cats. Alley cats that had more on their minds than just fighting. What in the world was she doing?

Playing at a game she ought not to have gotten herself into.

She was a major's daughter. He was a striker. A private for heaven's sake. Within minutes, Robert would be knocking at the front door, a handsome, intelligent, courteous officer who would be any woman's dream.

Miriam turned away from the still-swinging kitchen door and smoothed her dress. Tonight, she would turn all her attention to Robert.

By the time the evening ended, Miriam could feel the tension building in tight knots behind her eyes. On the surface, the party had been a success. She could see the satisfaction written across Robert's face. He joined her as they bade good night to their guests, like a couple wrapping up an evening in their own home. It should have been a heady thought.

But deep inside, a trapped feeling clawed at her.

Her parents retired with the last of the guests, giving Miriam and Robert a few minutes alone. He stood, surveying the room, and she straightened the parlor chairs they'd disturbed during their game of charades.

"You were wonderful, Miriam," Robert said, capturing her hand in his. He beamed at her. "Witty, charming, a true hostess. And the food was magnificent, even the canned asparagus salad." Pulling her hand up between them, he moved closer.

"Thank you, Robert," she answered, aware that, despite her inner turmoil, the party had gone well, with no slips of propriety, no social faux pas to mark her as a failure. Indeed, because of Jake's talent in the kitchen, Miriam's success was magnified. And her relationship with Robert was solidified.

"You fit in beautifully. I'm sure the ladies would welcome you if you wanted to visit them in Yankton. It would be good for you to get to know them more. They join us for all our socials. You could all go shopping for those fancy hats and pins."

She smiled at him and nodded. The two guests of Captains

Barnes and Wilcox had chatted all evening about nothing. They'd tittered when she'd asked them whether the suffrage movement had made it to the territorial capital, then returned to discussing dress styles. They hadn't even known the names of the candidates for the upcoming presidential election.

She didn't need another dress, and her opinion on things that mattered was not needed. This, then, was the other side of the life she would live if she stayed at the fort. She frowned and tried to concentrate on what Robert was saying.

"Everyone was impressed. The party was perfect."

She knew he meant the compliment. There was no mistaking the pride in his voice. Still, his approval failed to satisfy her. There was more to perfection than impressing everyone, wasn't there?

She searched for the words he wanted to hear and found only emptiness. "Yes, it was, wasn't it?"

"It's been such a short time, Miriam, but I feel we are so suited to each other." His arm encircled her and he pulled her close. Flush against his torso, she felt his muscles tighten. Between them, her hand still in his, she could feel the beat of his heart, strong and insistent. Moving his hand away, he caressed her softly under her chin, then raised her face.

His kiss was soft, gentle and undemanding, filled with warmth but not with fire. She opened to him, waiting for the tightness to catch in her chest. For her heart to race the way it did when Jake looked at her.

Robert's body hardened against her before he pulled away. "I'm sorry, Miriam. I didn't mean to spoil the evening. I think I should go now." He slipped out the door and into the darkness of the night.

"Good night, Robert," she whispered behind him. Caring for Robert would have been easier if her heart had raced when he kissed her, if her body had shivered at his brief touch. So much easier. She closed the door and propped her forehead against it.

"Miriam? You still up?"

Jake's voice, friendlier than she'd heard it for days, startled her. Dear heaven, how long had he been standing there?

"Y-yes. Could you use a hand cleaning up?"

"Wouldn't refuse it, I guess. Most of it's already done. How do you feel about drying dishes?"

"Better than washing." She smiled at him, turned down the lamp in the parlor, and followed him into the kitchen. For a while, they worked without words, each involved in personal thoughts, comfortable in the silence.

"Fancier, maybe, but otherwise not so different," Jake said into the stillness. He handed her the last of the china plates.

"What?"

"Entertaining. Down in the barracks, it's less formal. There's a few of the men that play the harmonica and a couple fiddles. Carrie's husband brings his banjo over sometimes. More music, less talkin', I guess."

"Well, I guess the officers can get a little rowdy, too. If they put their minds to it." Miriam glanced at him, unsure if he was baiting her. But the challenge was missing from his eyes, and she was glad she had kept her voice light.

Jake lifted the dishwater, headed for the kitchen door and tossed it into the yard. Turning back, he pulled the wooden door shut and latched it against the night.

"You don't see many footraces or baseball games outside of Suds Row," he said.

"True enough. But do you see variety shows and plays there?"

He smiled and nodded. A memory seemed to drift through his thoughts, bringing a soft chuckle. "You do. But they ain't very sophisticated. Neither is the dancin', for that matter." He smiled again, took the last plate and moved to stack it with the others on the shelf next to the dining-room door.

Lord, the light that shone from those bright blue eyes of his when he wasn't on his guard. The thought slammed into her and she was acutely aware that she wasn't going to be able to have it both ways. She couldn't be Jake's friend. Because being his friend meant drowning in those eyes.

The sound of the plates clanking onto the shelf echoed through the evening air. He turned and gazed at her.

"I'm sorry for bein' hurtful," he said. "The other day hit me like I was gut-shot." He raised one hand in a signal of silence. Reaching behind his back, he clicked the slide bolt on the door shut. "I need you to just listen. Until I say this." His voice was almost a whisper. "It took me all night to figure this out, the better part of the week, even."

She saw the change in his eyes, the merging of the bright with the dark smoldering fire. The change inside her kept pace, closing in, forcing her to concentrate on each breath.

"Jake. . . ." She recognized it now, the suppressed tension that threatened to engulf them both.

"Not now, Miriam." His gruff, struggling voice battled against reason as much as she did. "It keeps comin' down to this. We just can't stand on middle ground without it shifting on us."

They stood staring at each other while time scurried past.

"I'm not even sure who I am anymore," she told him, knowing that he would read the rest of her meaning in her eyes. Dear Lord, her heart was going to explode.

In two steps, he was there, close enough for her to feel his breath hot against her face. He took her head in his hands and tipped it back until their gazes met yet again. He closed his eyes, exhaling into the stillness, and leaned his forehead against hers. "God, Miriam."

"Jake. . . ."

"Shhh."

His lips met hers, hot and demanding, choking off further

words. Their hearts pounded against one another, waiting to explode. Her breasts ached, nipples hard, needing his touch. Aching. Farther down, where Jake's hardness touched her, but deeper inside, the ache became a dull throb.

He pulled his mouth from hers and swallowed, his breathing as ragged as her own.

"God, Miriam. I didn't want to go and do that."

"Me either, Jake. Me either."

"See, the thing is, we both know who you are. And who I am. We can't do this anymore. And I'm not sure I can stop it, what with bein' in this house with you. And I sure as hell can't take shuttin' you out." He took a folded scrap of paper from the shelf and laid it in her hand, closing her fingers around it. "My resignation. Give it to your mother and tell her I'll be over to talk with her in person and help her find someone else so I don't leave her in a pinch."

They stood still, unmoving, neither saying anything more. They didn't have to. He wouldn't be back, and anything she said would only worsen the situation.

She felt pain deep inside as the realization crept through her. Inches away, Jake closed his eyes briefly, extinguishing the spark, then crossed to the back door, slid open the lock and left the house.

CHAPTER ELEVEN

Twenty minutes later, Jake lay in his bed, cursing himself.

He was in over his head and there was no getting around it. He didn't want to desire Miriam. A few weeks back, when he'd still thought of her as a high-and-mighty governess, it was easy to dislike her. It wasn't as though she was oozing with charm. But she did have guts, and determination, and fire. It was her fire that had torn down the wall. He punched his pillow. It was a fire that would burn him if he wasn't careful.

He should have pulled back when he found out who she was. He should have respected the social lines that separated them. She was out of his class. No matter how much either of them wanted to erase those lines, the choice wasn't theirs to make.

A private in the U.S. Army didn't play around with the commanding officer's daughter unless he was up to facing a court-martial. And the major's daughter didn't dawdle with an enlisted man unless she was willing to risk disgrace.

Oh, the sparks had hit both of them, all right. And taken them both by surprise. He could read it in her face, in those huge green eyes that flashed anger one minute and hunger the next. She was in as deep as he was. Trouble was, he didn't think either one of them wanted it to stop.

Hell, he liked her. He liked her a lot. He liked her sass and her refusal to back down and the sincerity she'd let slip through that pompous facade she tried so hard to maintain. He liked the way her breath caught and struggled to stay even when she became aroused, and how it escaped her open lips like the slow, sensual drip of honey. And what she did to him deep in his gut.

Jake threw back the heavy gray military blanket and rolled uncomfortably on his narrow bunk. Damn, he was hot. His body ached, and he knew it'd be a long time before the throbbing went away.

In the morning, he'd face Harriet Longstreet and follow up on the letter of resignation he'd left with Miriam. Then he'd see the major about getting back on detached duty, somewhere safely away from her. It was the only way he could think of to put a damper on the fire.

Miriam awoke in the predawn gray of her room, unable to escape the heavy guilt that had plagued her throughout the night. She'd slept in scattered snatches, wishing she and Jake had never ignored the social barriers they were supposed to observe, that she'd never justified crossing those barriers in her head.

At first, her interactions with Jake had been a release, a way to escape Mother's anger and rules. But it had grown into something more. She wasn't sure when their relationship had turned into the mesmerizing attraction that had pulled them into the fire that had erupted last night. Or how the peculiar friendship had budded between them in the first place. She couldn't explain any of it, let alone understand it. But she knew she'd opened the door the day she'd decided they could continue to treat each other as equals.

Her stupid little escape from reality had cost Jake his extra pay and, very likely, her mother's wrath. No one quit her mother's service without retribution—retribution that could very well damage Jake's career.

Miriam swung her legs out of bed and donned her clothes. It was time to lay a fire in the kitchen stove and begin breakfast.

She estimated she had about an hour before her mother discovered Jake had resigned.

An hour left her precious little time to come up with a plausible excuse that would neither incriminate him nor set her mother off.

"Good heavens, Miriam, I hardly expected to find you up and about at this time of day." Harriet pursed her lips, her sharp gaze darting about the kitchen. "Private Deakins seems to be absent."

"He is," Miriam said. Leave it to her mother to get straight to the matter at hand. The silence stretched as she cracked the eggs into the cast-iron fry pan and discarded the shells.

"And?"

Miriam closed her eyes for a moment, fingered Jake's opened letter of resignation inside her apron pocket, and knew she could never give it to her mother. It left far too much unexplained. She took a deep breath and opened her eyes, then lifted the eggs from the pan, placed them on a plate and set them on the table.

"I fired him," she said.

Mother froze, her forkful of eggs in midair. "You did what?"

"I fired him," Miriam repeated, keeping her voice flat.

Her mother slammed her silverware down and rose from the table, her body quivering. "What in heaven's name were you thinking of? That man is the best striker I've had in the past three years. I have been the envy of every woman at the post." Her jaw clenched. "You will rectify the situation immediately. Do I make myself clear?"

Miriam glanced toward Franny's bedroom door and prayed her sister would sleep late. She drew a breath. "You make yourself perfectly clear, Mother. But I cannot and I will not do anything to change the situation."

She waited for the assault, gathering courage for her second act of defiance.

Her mother sent the wooden kitchen chair behind her crashing to the floor, crossed the room and slapped Miriam's cheek. "You impudent fool."

Miriam stared down at her mother, becoming aware of her height as an advantage. Her face stung, but she refused to give her mother the satisfaction her tears would bring. Instead, she returned Harriet's hot stare, knowing that anger blazed in her own eyes, giving it rein.

She could feel the shock as it settled about them, thick and caustic as acid. So close to burning that she could see the scars in her mind.

Dear Lord, make this work.

"There wasn't any other choice, Mother. For Robert's sake."

She left the comment hang, watching it gnaw through Mother's bitter temper. It was the only plausible excuse she could think of that would explain letting Jake go without dishonoring him.

"Robert? Miriam, what are you talking about?"

"I didn't want to have to tell you the whole thing. I had to fire him or Robert would have gotten in trouble."

"Spit it out, Miriam, what happened? What did he do to Robert?"

"Nothing. But . . . oh, Mother." Miriam let a tear slide down her face, gauging her mother's reaction. She had to pull this off. "Robert kissed me."

"Is that all? Miriam, for heaven's sake, what does that have to do with Private Deakins?" Mother's ire subsided into exasperation.

"It . . . it wasn't a very chaste kiss. Deakins walked in and he accused Robert of ungentlemanly conduct. Robert nearly hit him. I was afraid there'd be an altercation if they had any further words. So I fired Deakins."

She could see her mother's mind working through the situation, digesting it, savoring the image of Robert's interest and balancing it against the loss of a good striker. The explanation would work, she knew it, if only Jake let her lie stand.

"A pretty pickle, Miriam, a pretty pickle." She glared at Miriam and picked up the chair. "You've put Robert in a situation that could lead to public embarrassment for him and your father. While I'm delighted to know that a man like Robert is attracted to you, it is your responsibility to keep him from expressing that interest with abandon." She sat and shoved a forkful of eggs into her mouth, shaking her head as she chewed.

"Lust is a base response, but it's to be expected of men. Ladies, on the other hand, bear the burden of restraining such behavior. Are you quite sure this will be the end of the matter? Private Deakins will hold his tongue?"

"I'm sure he won't say anything. It was not his place to take notice of it in the first place."

"True enough. But if you'd held your reaction, we would have been able to use that to buy his silence and still retain him in his position."

"But what if Robert becomes provoked again?"

"True, true. Better not to risk it."

"I'm sorry, Mother."

"As you should be. Next time, you will tell me posthaste when there is a problem, and you will do so without the defiance you displayed this morning. Now, clean up this mess and let me alone. My head hurts and I have to find a new striker."

Miriam stacked the china dishes in the cupboard and frowned at the dirty dishwater. A week of kitchen duty had worn on her, but her responsibilities had kept her out of Mother's way. Franny had done lessons at the kitchen table, her whining questions about Jake more punishment than the extra chores.

Some example she was, telling a lie to cover other transgressions. Still, to have done anything else would have left Jake open to Mother's castigation. It would have been like leaving him to the wolves. She'd thought about him often, wondering what he was doing whenever she picked up a pot holder or filled the hot-water reservoir on the stove. And each time, she missed him a little more.

She felt no less guilty about the lie she'd crafted around Robert. Though there'd been a kiss, it had been a far cry from the passionate experience she'd described to Mother. As a companion, Robert was . . . agreeable. But try as she might, Miriam couldn't think of him as anything beyond a congenial associate.

A faint knock sounded at the front door, followed by the echo of her mother's footsteps. Moments later, Mother's voice chimed in the silence, blending with a masculine voice.

Miriam's stomach clenched. Robert.

Her mother's second punishment had been that Miriam have no contact with Robert for a full week. Today would be the third time he'd called on her since the party, the day Mother had promised he could see her.

Her palms sweaty, Miriam entered the dining room to find Robert in conversation with her mother. He smiled benevolently as she moved into the room.

"Miriam, I'm so glad you're feeling better. I was beginning to get worried."

She felt color creep up her cheeks at yet another lie. "I think I just overtired myself, caught some sort of vapor."

"Well, you certainly have your color back. And just in time. I've come to take you on a picnic." He held up a small straw basket covered in red-checked gingham. "My treat."

Next to him, her mother beamed. "Oh, yes, by all means, Mr. Wood. Isn't this just the most beautiful autumn day, almost an

Indian summer, one might say. Just the kind of day meant for picnics. I'm sure Miriam would be delighted to go."

Picnicking with Robert was no longer on her list of desired activities. She'd rather be visiting with Carrie on Suds Row or, better yet, walking barefoot with Franny. Or maybe even making mud pies with Jake. She felt her face lift into a smile at the impossible thought.

Miriam caught her mother's pointed stare. What could she say? That she didn't want to go with Robert because she couldn't get her mind off Jake? She doubted that would go over well; not in light of the tale she'd spun about Robert's ardor.

"I'll get a wrap," she muttered. Gathering a knitted shawl, she nodded good-bye to Harriet and followed Robert outside.

"It's not fancy and it's not as comfortable as a well-sprung buggy, but it's all I could find." Extending his hand, Robert assisted her into the high wooden seat of the wagon. "I borrowed it from the quartermaster."

"Then I guess we'll just have to make do."

They rode in silence, taking in the trees with their red and golden leaves.

"You're very quiet, Miriam."

"Just enjoying the day, I guess." Gracious, her thoughts were a thousand miles away, elusive and just beyond her control. Playing, somewhere in the mud, with Jake.

"It is perfect, isn't it?"

She didn't respond.

"Miriam?"

"Hmm?"

"Are you all right?"

"Yes. I'm sorry, Robert, I guess I'm just a little preoccupied." She knew she needed to focus on Robert. Jake was not a part of her destiny. She searched her mind for a topic that would encourage Robert to the same playfulness she'd found in Jake, a

113

last-ditch effort to find what she was missing.

"I've been told, Robert, that you are quite the matchmaker." At his puzzled look, she continued. "I'm referring, of course, to Captain Tate and the hospital matron."

Robert burst out laughing. His laughter was infectious and she gave in to it, joining in, hoping to find an elusive spark.

"I guess I was a bit of a practical joker in the past," he said. "It's one of those boyish things best left buried. Joking doesn't work well with an advancing career."

In Miriam's mind, the spark flickered, then died.

He stopped the wagon near a grove of trees, a few miles downstream from the fort. The river gurgled as it flowed past. It was an inviting setting for a picnic. Robert removed a gray army-issue blanket from the back of the wagon and gallantly spread it on the ground. He placed the basket of food in the center of the blanket and extended his hand to Miriam.

"Shall we, little one?"

The pet name sounded condescending. Deep down, Miriam knew he hadn't intended it that way, but still, it felt contrived. She was no more anyone's "little one" than Jake was a "stuffed shirt." It just didn't fit and it took something away from the moment.

She settled herself on the blanket and spread out the food. Robert spoke on, an oration on his career goals, as they ate.

"Miriam?"

"Hmmm?"

"Do you think it would be well received?"

"I'm sorry, Robert, I was miles away."

"A school? I came across some regulations that have been lying around for almost ten years about provision of post schools. If we had one, you wouldn't need to worry about teaching Frances or finding another governess."

Miriam brightened. Carrie had said something about Robert

wanting to start a school.

"But, where—"

"I thought about the chapel. It's got a full library, maybe five hundred books. But the chaplain is on a one-month rotation, leaving no one to teach."

"Could there be approval for one of the enlisted men to conduct the classes?" A spot for Jake, as Carrie had hoped?

Robert stood and proffered a hand to Miriam.

"Possibly, but a professional teacher would be so much better. It will be a feather in my cap if I can pull it off. It'd save all the officers from having to locate and pay for governesses."

"But you would also include education for the children of the enlisted men?"

"If it came down to that, I suppose." Having reached the river, Robert bent down for a handful of flattened stones and began to skim them over the surface of the water while Miriam struggled to control her reaction to his words.

"If it came down to that?"

"I hadn't thought about including children of enlisted men, Miriam." His voice was patronizing, as if it was something he didn't think she understood. She bit back a retort. "It was an angle on the regulation, a way to use it to benefit the officers. But, yes, we'd probably have to provide classes for the men and their families. There are around a hundred-fifty, maybe two hundred enlisted men. Most wouldn't even want to come to school. The only ones allowed to bring their families are those with special permission and the ones whose wives have the laundry contracts. It wouldn't amount to too many more. I guess as long as they're here, we might as well include them."

Of all the pompous, arrogant poppycock. Might as well include them? Miriam pulled away, urging her tongue to stay silent. Arguing with Robert would get her nowhere.

"Now, Miriam, I know it's difficult to understand—"

"I understand it fine, Robert. I just don't like it." The words gushed out, refusing to be controlled.

"There's nothing to like or dislike about it. It's how things are done. I stand a good chance of promotion to captain soon, and backing the school is an excellent way to make a mark that gets me noticed. It comes down to politics, Miriam, not how much an officer cares about the kids of laundresses."

"But it's not right."

"No, it's not. That's why the officers have their wives and families here. We men worry about the politics, and you women worry about family welfare." He smiled at her and reached for her hand, patting it as he began to guide her along the river. "Let's not argue. Not today."

She was tempted to pull her hand away. But doing so wouldn't solve anything. Let him think what he wanted. He was so damned haughty that he wouldn't notice anyway. Lord, he almost rivaled her mother. And what made it all the worse was knowing that a few weeks ago, she might have been swallowed up by his plan, never even caring that it wasn't just.

Robert climbed the gentle slope of the bank and pointed at something in the distance.

"Look at them. They've a miserable existence, haven't they?"

She came alongside him, spotting the small Indian village he indicated. Here and there, children ran laughing in tattered "white man's" clothing. Women bent over open pots in front of buffalo-hide tepees. They looked happy.

"It's the village of White Swan's band." Robert's voice held an edge of contempt. "We usually have a couple of men stationed over there. Gives us a chance to get a leg up on anything they're plotting. Well, little one, I'll retrieve our things and we can be on our way."

She waited, watching the camp, while he doubled back to the river and gathered up the blanket and picnic items. She doubted the inhabitants of White Swan even cared what was happening at the fort. The small village was a world unto itself, far away from plotting against the U.S. Army.

Robert reappeared. She let him ramble on, drowning out his words with thoughts about the village, until they reached the wagon. There, he stopped and turned toward her. He reached out, his well-manicured hand cupping her chin and she suddenly realized she had missed something very important.

"Have I taken you by surprise?" he asked softly.

"I . . . yes . . . you have." Her mind raced, trying to recall what he'd said.

"I hesitated to broach it so soon. I wouldn't have if your mother hadn't suggested it was time. We have her blessing. You're impulsive, but you'll make a wonderful wife, a true asset to me." He leaned forward, lifted her chin and kissed her.

Wife?

Dear God, he thought she was going to marry him.

CHAPTER TWELVE

Miriam stomped into the house, leaving Robert on the wagon seat in stunned silence. Her behavior wasn't tactful and it wasn't ladylike, and she didn't give a damn.

Robert was the most arrogant, self-centered man she'd ever met. He'd dismissed her refusal of his proposal as easily as he'd shooed the flies from their picnic basket. He'd told her she was nervous, frightened, and said he understood, that it was too soon.

She'd sat in stony stillness the rest of the way home, squelching the outburst that screamed inside of her. If Robert wasn't prepared to have her say no to him, having a conniption fit would get her nowhere. If he thought she was hysterical, he'd never listen to her. Something told her Robert would not be as easily manipulated as her mother had been. She'd have to carefully map out her further response. But that didn't mean she had to be congenial.

She slammed the door shut behind her and, out of the corner of her eye, saw her mother rise from the parlor settee.

"Miriam?"

"Leave me alone. Haven't you done enough?" The disrespectful words poured out, leaving her to wonder when she had ceased to be afraid of Mother's judgment. She slipped into her bedroom and closed the door against her mother's prying eyes. Let her go ask Robert if she wanted to know anything.

Miriam plopped onto the bed, grateful Franny was playing

with Albert and not there to ask questions. She needed time to figure out how to get out of the damned corner she'd backed herself into.

A knock sounded on her door, followed by her mother's sugary voice.

"Miriam, dear, are you all right?"

"No, Mother, I'm not." She tried to keep calm. Losing her temper any further would not get her out of this situation.

"Robert said you were upset." Harriet opened the door and spilled into the bedroom, her concern patronizing. "I thought you'd be pleased he was interested in more than friendship."

"Oh, Mother, how could you encourage him in this?" She heard the bitterness in her voice, anger merging with stung pride, and regretted that she couldn't hold it back.

Mother settled her body onto the bed and took Miriam's hand, patting it awkwardly. "Dear, dear girl, you are so headstrong. I know it's soon, but you must realize what a catch our Robert is. Why, you were made for each other, perfectly suited to each other's stations."

Miriam sighed. Suited to each other's stations, but not to each other. She pulled her hand away from Harriet and shifted to face her.

"But I don't want to marry him."

"Miriam, I don't wish to argue about this. I can hear it in your voice and I think it's time you realize you cannot have everything your way. We take the brass ring when it presents itself, not when you make up your mind that taking it is *your* idea. Robert cares for you. He, shall we say, wants you. You told me as much yourself. Why, it's plain as day that you're fond of him. A woman does not take charge as you did to protect a man unless she's enamored. Quit being so stubborn."

Stubborn? Miriam rose from the bed, trying to sort out her mother's comments. It didn't feel like she was being stubborn.

Marriage to Robert felt like a glove that didn't fit, and no matter how she tried to tug at it, it chafed. She looked out her window at the prairie that swept away into silence, feeling the pull of its freedom.

"I'm going out," she said. "I need to think."

The sound of rustling grass interrupted Miriam's thoughts and she jumped back. A small ground squirrel scampered across her path. Squinting in the sun, she scanned the area, becoming aware of how far she had wandered from the fort. A tiny knot of apprehension began to form itself in the pit of her stomach.

She searched for a landmark to pinpoint her location. A long, meandering line of burnt autumn color was just visible beyond the next rise. She topped the hill and looked down on the Missouri River. In the distance, she saw the small Indian encampment Robert had shown her earlier.

Curiosity pulled at her until she found herself working her way toward the village, her disorientation replaced by interest. She'd never find herself this close to the village again and marveled at her lack of fear. Perhaps her attitude was due to Lise's gentle admonitions. Lise was part Sioux and she'd never hesitated to object when someone spoke negatively of Indians. She'd told Sarah and Miriam stories of her aunt, stories full of mystery and life. St. Louis itself was populated with so many mixed-bloods that Miriam had long ago rejected stories of ferocious natives. Instead, she felt only a strong desire to take a closer look at life in the camp.

A small boy, naked but for a thin cloth around his loins, stepped into her path as she neared the village.

"You are from fort?" he asked with as much authority as he could muster.

"I am," Miriam responded, aware that he served in the role of lookout. "My name is Miriam Longstreet. My father is Major

Longstreet."

The boy looked at her, then peered around her, seeming surprised. "You come alone?"

"Yes, I wandered a little too far and here I am." She smiled at the boy, hoping he would understand she meant no harm.

With a tip of his head, he indicated that she should follow, then headed into the village. All the childhood warnings about hostile Indians flashed through her mind. She knew she shouldn't let her interest in the village lead her into danger, even if Lise had told her the warnings were irrational.

An image of her mother expounding on savages crept into her thoughts, followed by one of Robert blithely dismissing the villagers as pitiful. That little Indian boy ahead of her was neither savage nor pitiful, and she'd be doggoned if she was going to let their puny prejudices ruin the one and only chance she might ever have of seeing the village firsthand. With a resolute nod of her head, she followed the boy's path.

Entering the camp, she smelled the odors of the village: the stale smoke of past campfires trapped in the hides of the tepees, raw meats, grease, and the lingering smell of skunk.

The boy stopped without warning. "You stay," he ordered before disappearing into a nearby tepee.

Apprehension churned her stomach like sour milk, and she fought against the fear that she knew was building despite her best intentions. Being inside the village was wholly different than listening to tales about Lise's relatives or meeting a half-breed on the streets of St. Louis. She looked around, wondering if it might not be better to simply leave.

A short, stocky Indian woman emerged from the tepee. She was dressed in a beaded buckskin dress and examined Miriam, then grunted and reentered the tepee.

Miriam waited, unsure what to do. Instinct told her it would be impolite to depart now, after the woman had noticed her, but she didn't know whether to follow or stay where she was.

She could feel the stares of other women watching her from in front of their cooking fires. Their strange guttural comments reached her ears, and she knew they spoke about her. Aware she was alone in a village of people whose language and customs were alien to her, she felt fear creep farther into her mind. The late afternoon sun poured down, hot, and the absence of wind seemed stifling.

She felt a sudden push at the back of her dress. Against the heat of the day, goose bumps dotted her flesh and she turned, afraid, wishing she'd never come into the village. Behind her, a small naked child stood pressing dirty hands against the back of her dress, grinning at the sway of her crinoline. She felt relief sweep over her and smiled at the little girl. One by one, other children came forward, followed by mothers and grandmothers, until she was surrounded by chattering Sioux, all watching the swing of her skirts as the little girls pushed faster and harder against the crinoline.

From among the crowd, a toothless old woman stepped forward. As she neared, she spoke in a low, aged voice and pointed to the ebony buttons on Miriam's bodice. Miriam smiled tentatively and nodded, hoping to convey she was pleased the woman liked her dress. Without warning, the woman's bony fingers reached out and grabbed at a button, pulling until it came off. She held the black button high in the air and grinned.

Miriam stood in shock while the old woman's shapeless mouth stretched wide. The old hag had stolen her button, had reached out and pulled it off her dress without a second thought. What kind of people were these Indians? She was tempted to snatch the button back, just to show the old women whose it was.

Around her the crowd chattered, and other women came forward to admire the trophy button. They closed around Miriam until her indignation faded, replaced by an uncertain apprehension. They reached out to touch the cloth of her dress and its shiny celluloid buttons. Miriam held her breath, unsure how to react. The women spoke among themselves, sounding like a gaggle of geese, until the first old grandmother clucked twice and nodded to them with authority. After stripping her bodice of its remaining buttons, they retreated, those with the buttons each attracting their own following.

Miriam remained where she was, nervous and afraid, clutching her bodice shut. No one seemed to notice her state of undress or her embarrassment, and it slowly dawned on her that her open bodice was of little import to them. To them, she wasn't half-dressed. She breathed easier.

In the wake of the departing women, the young boy who had led her into camp emerged to motion at her. He nodded to the tepee from which he had emerged. "Come," he told her and reentered.

Miriam stepped to the tepee and bent under its door of buffalo skins. Inside, she stood upright, her eyes adjusting to the dimmer light. Next to the door hung bows, spears, and quivers of arrows. Piled to her left was an assortment of baskets, pots, and finely crafted beadwork. Across the circular interior, two men reclined against willow backrests. The squat woman she had seen earlier sat with two others on the ground, their legs tucked up beside them.

The young boy gestured to the group. "Go. Sit," he told her and disappeared out the door.

Left alone with the group, Miriam struggled with a renewed desire to turn tail and head for the fort. She remembered Lise saying the white man insulted her people without even knowing it. Would leaving be such an insult? Miriam fought against irrational fear and decided to follow the boy's instructions.

Moving to her right, she passed in front of the seated Indians to join the women. As she moved, the men grunted and the women whispered among themselves. Then one of the women spoke to her, and Miriam realized she was being chastised for something. The woman pointed to a spot in the center of the group, next to the oldest man, and Miriam sat.

They remained in silence, watching her. Uncomfortable in the stillness, she looked around the tepee, taking note of rolled buffalo robes, the swept floor and the small fire near its center. The women wore loose, tanned garments, decorated with bead-work. Their hair fell across their shoulders. At her other side, the men reclined, the dark skin of their bare chests shiny above their scant loincloths. Seeing their near nakedness, Miriam felt the heat rise in her cheeks and fought to pull her gaze away. The women again whispered among themselves, then laughed.

Across the circle, a bent form stepped through the door, catching Miriam's attention. Jake Deakins straightened, scowled at her and shook his head.

Of all the places she might have expected to find Jake, this was not one of them. He was dressed in a gray wool flannel shirt, without his formal blue military blouse over it, white suspenders straining over his shoulders. His gaze settled on her open bodice until she felt the urge the squirm under it.

"Time to go, Miriam," he said, then spoke to the Indians in their language. They nodded and the older man spoke back. Miriam stood, wondering what gave Jake the right to order her around like some lapdog.

"I will not. And furthermore—"

"Miriam," his voice was sharp, with an air of authority she hadn't heard before, subtly different from the argumentative Jake she knew. "Trust me on this. We need to go. You've insulted them."

His admonishment hurt, dug at her, but she realized she needed to heed his instructions. She shouldn't have come into the village without someone to explain native etiquette. She began to move to the door only to be interrupted by Jake's firm voice.

"The other direction. Stay on the women's side, and pass behind them." She turned, realizing now the mistakes she had made upon her entry, and followed Jake's instruction. Upon leaving the tepee, he continued through the village, leaving her to follow.

Her pride stung. She was ready to own up to having made mistakes, and she'd take orders when it came to a dangerous situation, but she was not about to follow him through the village like some obedient little lamb. She'd leave when she was good and ready, not just because Jake wanted to punish her for innocent errors. This was going to be her only time here, and she was going to make sure she saw her fill before she left.

She slowed her pace and savored the sights of the camp, knowing Jake was waiting but caught by scattered curiosities. An attractive young girl picked up a rawhide bag and lifted it high, drinking as she tipped one side. Two women sat in the shade, stitching beads onto moccasins. A brightly decorated shield hung behind one of the tepees, beckoning in the lowering sun. Entranced by the bright red, blue, and white design, she reached out to touch its smoothness.

Jake grabbed her arm and jerked her away from the shield. "What are you trying to do?" he muttered and scooped her up like a sack of flour, slinging her over his shoulder. She squirmed against him, shouting, as he strode through the Indian camp. Behind them, the villagers tittered in laughter.

Jake rode with Miriam in front of him, penning her with his arms. She was stiff and fuming mad with her bodice hanging open and that damned crinoline of hers scrunched up around her waist and in his way. He didn't know whether to send her home like an errant child, strangle her, or kiss her until her sassy little mouth was as hot and swollen as his body.

A week away from her hadn't made a dent in the attraction that engulfed him at the mere thought of her, but at least she'd been out of his reach. Or had been until young Stands Tall had come running to tell him there was a white woman in camp.

They rounded a bend, and Jake pulled the horse up near the cottonwood trees that lined the river. Dismounting, he cursed the tightness in his loins, and reached to help Miriam down.

"I'll do it myself, thank you very much," she snapped.

"Be my guest."

He shook his head as she struggled to locate a stirrup, then slid, lopsided, to put her foot into it. As she moved her other leg over the saddle, the crinoline swung loose, belling her skirts as she completed the awkward maneuver. Under the bell, slender curving legs extended from laced pantaloons. Jake groaned.

Once on the ground, she turned to face him, fire in her emerald eyes and hands perched on her hips. Her blouse stretched open, forgotten in her anger, breasts pushing against her chemise.

"What in heaven's name did you think you were doing?" she demanded.

"Keeping you out of trouble and preventing a diplomatic nightmare for your father."

"By slinging me over your shoulder?"

"If that's what it took, yes. You'd already insulted White Swan and his family. Then the shield."

"But I didn't mean to. I didn't understand."

"You insulted them anyway. I've been stationed over there enough to learn some about how things are done. You told them who you were. Longstreet is an important name. That made you an unannounced important visitor. From their whispers, it sounded like you walked on the men's side of the tepee and crossed between people and the fire. Those are insults. When I came in, you were staring at White Swan. Women keep their eyes averted. And women never, ever, touch a man's shield."

"But I didn't know." She turned away, and he felt a sudden need to reach out and assure her that he knew it wasn't deliberate. Instead, he watched her stand, tall and proud, and he knew the sacrifice it was for her to admit she'd erred.

"I know," he told her, the one small consolation he could offer without touching her. He glanced at the sky. The afternoon sunlight had waned, dulled by rapidly gathering clouds. Miriam shivered and pulled her blouse shut. "Time to get you back to the fort," he said.

"In a little while. I . . . are you all right? I didn't see you after the night you quit."

"I'm out of your mother's kitchen." He shrugged, feeling his mouth tip into a wry smile. "What did you tell her anyway? When I came to explain the letter, she shooed me out like I had the plague. Said you'd already told her and she didn't want to hear any more about it. I thought she'd have my head."

"I never gave her the letter."

"You what?"

"Nobody *resigns* from her employ without problems, Jake. I told her I fired you."

"And that would avoid creatin' a problem?"

"Yes, it would. Resignation is an insult in her culture. It takes her power away. Firing someone keeps her in control. I told her Robert didn't like you." She turned away, tossing her auburn hair. "How'd you end up at White Swan's village?"

"Requested it. I'm workin' with one of the Sioux scouts. We try to visit all the villages, spend some time at Greenwood Agency. It keeps up the military presence and helps us stay aware of any problems that might be brewing. Keeps me busy." He touched her arm, a reminder to turn back to him. "It's gettin' late, Miriam, and we're in for a cloudburst. I gotta get you back."

"I'm sorry about you losing out on the extra pay. I know what it meant to you."

"Me, too, but it's not like there was much choice about it. We both know I couldn't stay there."

A huge drop of rain fell, hard and cold, against his cheek. Miriam jumped as the first drops fell against her face then merged into a torrent.

"Try to find some cover," Jake shouted. "I'll grab my shelter half." Reaching the horse, he grabbed the rolled oilcloth from the back of the saddle then sprinted to Miriam. He draped the material over a cluster of small tree branches and motioned her under the makeshift tent.

In the semi-darkness of the small shelter, he could smell her, some unidentifiable flower-scent filling the closed space. She was soaked. Little rivulets of water dripped from the mahogany tendrils of her hair and ran down her neck, slipping under the cloth of her blouse. She stood shivering, arms across her chest, clutching her sopping bodice shut. Outside, the rain pounded the ground below the edges of their too-short tent, drenching them from the waist down.

He wished he'd worn his formal blouse so he could drape it around her. God, she was trembling so much. Her arm shifted, revealing the taut hardness of her nipples under the wet fabric of her open dress.

"Miriam . . . ," he said, his voice low and husky, as if mingled with the primal heaviness that hung in the air.

"Jake." There was no surprise in the word. Only his name as she exhaled a breath and gazed at him with half-shut eyes. She dropped her arms, opening herself to him. The damp white cotton of her exposed chemise clung to her breasts. He felt the corners of his mouth turn up and was rewarded with a wavering suggestion of a smile from Miriam.

Then she was in his arms and his mouth was seeking hers. She met his lips, eager, and all his plans to resist her erupted in an explosion of desire that sprang away from any self-control. She gave her mouth to him, welcoming his tongue. His breath came hot and slow. She matched each gasp for air with one of her own. Their tongues danced.

He plunged his hands into her dripping hair, pulling it up until he felt her skin, wet, but no longer cold. Driven, he pulled his mouth away from hers and dribbled kisses across her jaw until he reached her neck. She whimpered against his ear.

He nibbled at her neck, her ear, her throat. She caught his hand and showered it with tiny kisses until he pulled it away and moved it to her heaving breast. God, he'd missed her.

Her green eyes smoldered, and he knew she wanted him as much as he wanted her. He waited, giving her time to tell him she didn't. He stared back at her until he felt the charge between them come alive. Then she was straining against him, arms entwined around his neck, her mouth seeking his response, urging him on.

He could feel her racing heartbeat under his hand and the ridge of her raised nipple against his stroking finger. He felt himself harden, aching and pulsing against his wool uniform pants, and wondered if she could feel him, too, under that damned crinoline she wore.

Deep down, reason screamed out at him, shouting for him to pull back. Reluctantly, he dropped his hand from her breast, holding her in his arms as he shifted his weight away from her.

"I'm sorry, Miriam. I shouldn't have—"

"Shh . . . just hold me," she whispered against his chest. He felt her ragged breaths soften as his own thundering heart slowed. She lowered her head onto his shoulder and stood, warm and natural within his embrace as the rain slowed, then stopped.

The soft neigh of a horse came out of nowhere and she pulled away.

"Miriam? Is that you?"

"Robert!" she gasped, suddenly rigid, fear written across her face.

Jake searched her eyes, silently apologizing, wondering how long Wood had been there. What *had* he done to them now?

CHAPTER THIRTEEN

Miriam's mind whirled. Scrambling to pull the edges of her bodice together, she struggled to control her rising panic.

How much had Robert seen and how were they going to explain it? She caught Jake's assuring nod as he turned to exit the tent and realized he would stoically accept whatever blame Robert heaped upon him. She had to keep her wits about her and think fast if she were going to be of any help to him.

"Lieutenant Wood, sir." She heard the sharp salute in Jake's voice and waited for Robert to reveal the depth of their predicament.

"Just what the hell is going on here, Private?"

"One of the natives reported that Miss Longstreet had wandered into the village, sir. I was escorting her back to the fort when we were caught by the rain. I tried to shelter her as best as possible, sir."

"Private Deakins, what I noted when I rode over that hill appeared to be far more than two people seeking shelter. You appeared to be embracing Miss Longstreet. I want to know exactly what was going on. If you've done anything to soil Miriam's reputation, I swear I'll have you court-martialed."

"Oh, for heaven's sake, Robert!" Miriam pulled aside the shelter half and stepped out, hugging her arms together to hide the front of her buttonless bodice and shivering in the cool evening air. "I was dripping wet and cold and scared. Would you have had me take a chill and risk pneumonia?"

"I would have had you remain respectable."

Stepping forward, she raised her head and stared pointedly at him. "Respectable? Are you implying that I'm not respectable?"

"With all due respect, sir," Jake interrupted, "the air's still cold and Miss Longstreet is trembling. She needs a warm wrap. I could return to the village for one, sir, if you don't have anything to offer her."

Bristling at Jake's veiled insinuation of neglect and unable to refute it without losing face, Robert belatedly shrugged off his military blouse and draped it over her shoulders. She grasped its edges, pulling it around her chest, well aware of Jake's subtle table-turning. A tiny flicker of amusement in his eyes confirmed it.

Robert squeezed her arms before spinning back to face Jake. As he turned, she slid her arms into the sleeves of his blouse, buttoning it up the front to cover her still-unnoticed open bodice. Robert would never accept that the buttons had been innocently plucked away by a group of curious old Indian women.

"If Private Deakins had been properly dressed, he would have had a blouse to offer you instead of the impropriety of his physical warmth." Robert threw a hostile look at Jake's broad chest and his damp gray woolen undershirt, then turned a benevolent gaze on Miriam and brushed a damp tendril from her face.

As the touch grew into a caress, she saw Jake's arm muscles tighten. "At least I offered something, sir," he said.

Robert stiffened, then grasped her shoulders and steered her to his horse, ignoring Jake. He lifted her onto the horse, waiting while she bunched up her crinoline and smoothed her skirts. She nodded, indicating she was settled. Leading the horse, he moved off toward the fort.

They continued in silence until Jake was well out of sight and

Robert slowed the horse. He dropped the reins and turned to lift Miriam to the ground.

"Warmer now?" he asked. She nodded, wondering what he had up his sleeve. "Then it's time for you to pay the piper. Just what was really going on with Deakins?"

Miriam swallowed. His voice held more anger than she'd expected. She fought to keep the same hostility from infecting her own words.

"Honestly, Robert, how can you stand there and lecture me on the rules of propriety? Any man with an ounce of self-respect would have put chivalry first and offered his warmth. How dare you imply that there was anything more to it or that I'm less than a lady for accepting his help?"

She felt her cheeks grow hot, knowing there had been nothing ladylike in her response to Jake's passion, and prayed that Robert would attribute her flaming face to insulted indignation. His eyes flashed, their charcoal color deepening to near-obsidian.

"It sure as hell looked like there was more to it. Just why were you over at the village in the first place? A secret rendez-vous?"

"Good heavens, Robert, you're jealous," she chastised.

"As if I've no right to be. How can I not be jealous when I discover the woman I'm betrothed to in the arms of another?"

Knowing he'd given her the opportunity she needed to refute their relationship, she chose her tone with care.

"We are not betrothed."

"So you *were* meeting him? Is that why you won't say yes? Why, so help me, Miriam, I'll see him locked up, dishonorably discharged, and beaten to a bloody pulp."

She turned away from him, her mind racing for a reply that would appease his anger and move them away from further talk about Jake. Argument would only fuel his assumptions and get

Jake into trouble. If she framed her response with care, she could move the conversation back to the engagement and somehow justify her refusal. She had to make him think he was the only one who mattered.

"I only meant to come back to where we picnicked, to think about your proposal. I wanted to bring back the day, before I got all hot-tempered." Looking back at him, she saw his face soften. She let the tiniest of smiles flicker across her own face. "I must have been so caught up in my thoughts that I didn't pay attention, and then there I was at the village and the women were all laughing at me and I didn't know what to do. Deakins came and got me, and then it started to rain and it rained so hard and I was cold."

"Truly, Miriam? Truly you were thinking about it?" He reached for her hands, taking them into his, and beamed at her. Pleased that the conversation had taken the turn she desired, Miriam reminded herself to stay focused.

"I didn't want to think this was all to please Mother, as if we were her puppets. She's so strong willed, and I wanted our engagement to be because we wanted it. I was afraid that it was too soon for us to know."

"But it's not too soon. I know it."

It was the perfect opening, a chance to decline the proposal on a level he would understand, one that centered on him. She weighed her words, then plunged ahead.

"Oh, Robert, don't you see? Your reaction today proves that it's too soon. You doubted me. How can we even consider marriage when you don't trust me?"

His face registered comprehension, dismay. He grasped her hands tighter and pulled her close.

"You must know that it's only because I care so much. Perhaps I overreacted a bit."

"And will you always try to impose your will, your opinions, on me? I know a wife vows to be obedient, but shouldn't a husband respect a wife enough to allow her to express herself? You don't even know what my opinions are, Robert. How can we pledge ourselves to each other?"

She broke away from him and focused on the brilliant orange of the setting sun. She hadn't expected the silence. Behind her, she could hear Robert readying the horse. Without words, he touched her arm, led her to the horse, and lifted her up. Mounting behind her, he set the horse into motion and took her home.

They reined in at her house as evening settled fully about them. Robert slid from the horse, then lifted her down. Meeting her parents at the porch, he explained the situation to them, then returned to where she waited.

"All right, Miriam, I've thought about it." He spoke for her ears only. "You do have some very valid points, and I'm willing to wait until you are as comfortable with a formal engagement as I am, until we have worked these things through. Would that be agreeable?"

Agreeable? Her heart wanted to sing. Yes, it was agreeable and so much more than she'd ever expected as she had stood there in Jake's arms listening to Robert's shocked voice questioning if it was really her.

"That would be fine, Robert," she said as calmly as she could.

"A few months should do, I would think. That would give us both time to get to know each other better and see us through the holidays. You've shown me today that we don't have a clear understanding of each other. I think some time would benefit us both. Shall we say February?"

Four months before they had to talk about this again, time to make him realize they were not made for each other, time to find a way out of this mess without Robert blaming Jake. She felt the smile on her face as she nodded to him.

"February would be fine."

"St. Valentine's Day," he said, then kissed her forehead, nodded to her parents, and mounted the horse. "I shall consider it your pledge," he whispered in a barely audible voice. "But you just remember, darling, that if you hadn't been so obviously chilled to the bone, Deakins would have run the gauntlet. You'd better thank your chattering teeth, because that's the only reason I'm letting this go. Rest assured I'll be watching you, and Deakins. You're both one step away from a hell of a lot of trouble."

He stared at her, the threat clearly evident on his face, and urged the horse into the darkness.

Jake stood in silence, watching Robert lead Miriam away, the satisfaction of having gotten away with insulting the lieutenant somehow failing to gratify him.

Seeing Robert touch Miriam's cheek that way had almost driven him stark, raving mad.

Who was he trying to fool? A reaction that strong didn't spring out of just wanting somebody. Hell, you could talk all night about the sparks and the fire between them, but he felt something burn in his heart when Wood touched her that way.

He was feeling something here, something he didn't want any part of. Good God, when had this moved from desire to whatever it was that it had turned into?

Jake turned to the tent and jerked it off the tree branch. Rolling it into a compact bundle, he cursed again. They'd been lucky. If Wood had ridden up any sooner, there would've been no doubt that there was more involved in their embrace than the simple provision of body heat.

He stowed the shelter half on the horse and mounted up, turning toward the village. They might have gotten out of this one with a couple of half-truths, but their good fortune lay only in timing and the fact that Robert was so self-centered. It wasn't likely to turn out that way more than once.

She'd better stay the hell away from the village from now on because distance was about the only way out of this one. He'd have to keep requesting detached duty as long as he could get away with it and hope that time would squelch whatever was brewing between Miriam and him.

If he was alone with her again, he'd be a goner. If his body didn't betray him, his heart would.

The next morning, Miriam sat across the breakfast table from Franny and assessed her situation. She'd decided, during a long night of tossing and turning, that anger was unproductive and that her own attempts to mastermind her situation were doomed to failure in the face of Robert's skilled manipulation.

She closed her eyes, thinking of Jake. She shivered as she recalled their moment in the rain, the hot pressure of his hard body against hers, the fire of their stolen kisses. In those few brief minutes in Jake's arms, she'd discovered a deep, hidden passion that no one had ever told her about, a passion so great that it would consume both of them if they gave it rein, a passion so strong that Robert's inane attempts at romance paled in comparison.

And she knew without a doubt that Robert would destroy them both if he ever discovered the depth of the attraction between them.

She was thankful for the reprieve Robert had provided. She sensed the four-month period had more to do with Robert's desire to observe how she managed the hectic social demands of the Christmas season than any real desire to understand her. Either that or she'd committed enough faux pas to make him doubt her suitability as his mate.

Whatever the reason, it was enough time to plan, enough time for Jake to be farther removed, enough time to find a governess and to extricate herself from Robert's future. She just had to figure out how.

Finishing breakfast, she left Franny with an embroidery assignment and set off to Suds Row, determined to be away from the house and any chance visit Robert might make and anxious for Carrie's reassuring presence.

With November just around the corner, she was not surprised to find the air had turned brisk. As she headed southward toward Suds Row, she could almost taste the chill as she inhaled the frozen air. Her breath lingered in front of her when she exhaled. The atmosphere seemed to punctuate her feelings. She pulled her cloak around her body and hastened her step.

She neared the third cottage and spotted Carrie outside, bent over a tub of steaming, sudsy water. Miriam arrived just in time to see her clutch her stomach and run around the side of the building. The unmistakable sound of retching echoed in the pre-winter bleakness, and the acrid smell of fresh vomit filled in the air. She swallowed, then went to Carrie's side.

Carrie rested on her knees, head hung low and one hand on the frozen ground to support her weight. Her other hand was clutched against her abdomen. Her breathing was fast and shallow and a small drop of spittle lingered at the edge of her mouth.

"Carrie, what's wrong?" Miriam withdrew her handkerchief from a hidden pocket and wiped Carrie's mouth. She felt a stab of worry prickle at her.

"I'll be all right in a minute or so. It don't last too long, most times. It just gets worse when I'm bent over like that." She took the hand offered by Miriam and stood.

"Worse? Carrie, you *are* ill. Has the doctor been here?"

"No, ain't no reason to get the doctor, Miriam."

A thousand questions flashed through Miriam's mind. Surely the laundresses were allowed access to medical care? Carrie's casual answer hung between them, then her face broke into cheerfulness.

"It's the baby, Miriam. I'm gonna have a baby."

"A baby? Carrie, how wonderful. Are you sure you're all right? You shouldn't be sick like this. Let me get the doctor."

"Ain't nothin', just mornin' sickness."

Miriam searched her mind, trying to remember details from boarding school, if Sarah and Lise had ever spoken of the trials of pregnancy. All Mother had ever told her was that it wasn't comfortable. She felt the embarrassment of her ignorance creep across her face.

Carrie's eyes were tired but shone with kind awareness. "Your ma ain't told you much 'bout such as this, has she?"

Miriam shook her head, amazed anew at Carrie's keen perception. "It isn't considered proper discourse." She shrugged, sure that Carrie already knew the subject was taboo in the upper classes.

"Let's go on inside. It's cold and I could use a rest about now, anyways." Carrie led the way into the cabin and added a log to the fire crackling in the corner fireplace. The aroma of fresh coffee filled the room. "Sit," she ordered and poured Miriam a tin cup of steaming coffee.

Miriam took the cup, warming her hands on the metal. "Are you sick much?" she asked as Carrie settled into a chair.

"Mostly when I do a lot of bendin' or when I eat somethin' sharp flavored. Seems my body's changin' so fast that it can't keep up with itself. Food just seems to stick in my throat and I get mighty dizzy-headed and tired near all the time. Doin' laundry don't make it no easier. But it ain't nothin' to worry about, just happens."

"But the laundry, Carrie, you must be sick most of the day." Miriam reached a hand across the table, catching Carrie's and giving it a concerned squeeze.

"Ain't no way around it, though. Not unless I give up my

contract. The other women'll help out some, I guess, and Eddie totes up the water for me."

"So, how long?"

"Guess I'll be mostly through bein' sick before too long. Missed my monthlies startin' back in August. The baby oughtta come 'round April or May."

"Is Eddie pleased?"

"Lands, yes. He's already plannin' fishin' trips and ball games and such." She paused, and the shared intimacy of the conversation settled about them, drawing them closer. Miriam basked in the feeling, knowing that her emerging friendship with Carrie had sealed itself in what they'd exchanged. Proper or not, she was certain that they'd broken through the barriers that were supposed to keep them apart. And it felt good.

Her thoughts strayed to the barriers she and Jake had broken, and she pushed the thoughts away. Being friends with Carrie was different.

As if she, too, sensed the new level of their relationship, Carrie squeezed Miriam's hand, then rose, poured them each another cup of coffee and returned to her seat. Once settled, she raised her eyebrows at Miriam.

"But that ain't what you come all the way over here for, is it? You got somethin' weighin' on your mind?"

Miriam nodded. "I need so badly to talk about it, Carrie. I didn't want to presume that you'd even want my confidence with all the differences between us. But there isn't anyone else I want to talk to." She hoped she was right about the companionship she sensed between them.

"Shoot, I guess we crossed over that fence already. I reckon your ma wouldn't be too pleased 'bout it, but somehow or another we ended up gettin' to be friends even if we wasn't supposed to."

"You know, I would have laughed at anyone who predicted

that a couple of months ago."

"Me, too, Miriam, me, too. Now, what's itchin' at you?" Carrie's tone was light, but her voice held both an invitation to talk and a promise to understand, a *rightness* that urged Miriam to continue.

"Robert has decided that we're perfect for each other."

"And you don't think so?"

"Two months ago, maybe. But I'm not the same person I was in August, and it confuses me to no end. Everything points to Robert and me being together."

"But?" Carrie prompted.

"It just doesn't feel right." Miriam struggled to find the right words to describe her lack of feeling for Robert. Was everything wrapped up in the absence of passion, that he didn't stir a physical response in her? She thought about the emptiness, the smallness she felt when they were together, and knew that the problem ran deeper. She turned to Carrie's expectant eyes. "My heart isn't in it, I guess," she finished, unable to put her thoughts into words.

"Well, I reckon that'd make it mighty difficult. Sometimes, gettin' to know a person better brings that special somethin'. Do you suppose that could be it, that you just don't know him enough?"

"It just seems that the more I get to know him, the more confused I get."

"This ain't got nothin' to do with Jake, has it?" Carrie spoke the words with candor, and her voice held no accusations. Still, Miriam was unsure how to respond. She could hardly tell Jake's sister what had happened between them.

Carrie had hit upon the heart of the matter. Time and time again, Miriam had tried to put what she was feeling for Jake from her mind. He made her feel vital and alive and all watery inside, yet still strong, still herself. Sarah's words came to her from across the distance of time, whispered conversations they'd held in their room, deep in the middle of the night, dreams of the love they would find someday. *A woman should be consumed by love. She should never settle for something that's only half there. A woman has the right to choose.* Until this moment, Miriam had never truly understood what Sarah had meant.

And if she chose Jake?

He'd offered her no words of love, no hint of future. Only the fire of a deep, raging desire that could ruin them both. Words escaped her, and they sat in silence until Carrie's gentle voice took up the slack.

"I ain't gonna beat around the bush none, Miriam. It's plain as day there's more between Jake and you than either one of you will let on. Shows up like a hunger in his eyes when he sees you, and I see the need in yours, too. Now I ain't judgin'. Why, there's times when a body's just got needs that are bigger'n a person knows what to do with. But there's a mighty big difference in bein' friendly with a laundress and bein' more than friends with a soldier when you're the major's daughter."

"It should be Robert I feel that way about."

"*Should* is a mighty big word sometimes. Could it be that you just ain't given Robert a fair chance?"

"I don't know." Miriam wanted to believe Carrie was right, that there could be something more with Robert. It would make her life so much easier, her decisions less painful.

Carrie reached across the table, covering Miriam's hand with her own. "I ain't pushin' aside the spark you been feelin' with Jake. Spice like that is what makes bein' with a man worthwhile. If you're thinkin' about someone else like that, a life with Robert ain't gonna be worth salt. Could it be you ain't found it yet with Robert 'cause you're lettin' Jake in the middle?"

"Do you truly think that might be it, Carrie?"

"Don't reckon you're gonna find out till you put some space

between you and Jake. Could be that what stirs things up between you two is knowin' how dangerous it is. You'd best know you're settin' yourselves up for a mighty big fall if you don't get past what's goin' on and you might be lettin' somethin' good with Robert slip right past because of it."

Miriam recognized the advice as both practical and wise. She'd have expected nothing less from Carrie. Maybe it was just the forbidden element that made Jake so alluring. Staying away from him was the best strategy.

Still, a part of her raged against Carrie's commonsense advice. What she felt for Jake was misplaced, improper, and dangerous. But it felt so good. Could Robert ever stir her to those depths?

Surely love was possible without it. It had to be. Look at her parents. She'd be fooling herself if she thought there was passion in their relationship. They were distant, yet they must love each other. Surely she could find a good life with Robert if she forced herself to stay away from Jake and to forget about the burning ache her body felt at the thought of him.

Reaching for her near-empty coffee cup, Miriam lifted it in mock salute, her face resolute, a contrast to the mourning in her soul.

"Here's to Jake Deakins," she toasted, "and our time apart."

CHAPTER FOURTEEN

Robert sat in the Longstreet parlor, waiting for Miriam. He perched on Harriet's fancy red horsehair settee and tried not to make crinkling noises with each shift of his weight.

He still wasn't sure he'd made the correct decision regarding the delay in his engagement to Miriam. That little episode last evening with Private Deakins left him wondering how he was going to handle her. Delaying the engagement meant delaying his control over her damnable headstrong independence. He didn't like it, any of it, and he almost wished he hadn't let her get away with it. And he wouldn't, not when all was said and done. But until he was Major Longstreet's son-in-law, he'd need to placate her.

Still, he felt hemmed in, like he'd somehow been backed into a corner without being aware of it. She'd managed to twist things until he was making all sorts of concessions. He'd wanted to postpone seeing her until he could get comfortable with this new strategy but knew he needed to keep his eye on her. And so, here he was, on the first of what would likely be nightly courting visits.

Accepting a dainty sandwich from Harriet, he smiled and pretended to listen to her prattle. That woman could jam more words into a minute of time than she could knickknacks and frillies into the parlor. But she, too, was valuable to him, so he nodded in agreement with whatever it was that she was saying.

As soon as he was securely married into this family, he'd get

144

the major to promote him to a leadership position, transfer to some other post and leave the waddling old bird behind. Meanwhile, he'd be patient, understanding, and a good listener, just like Miriam wanted. Anything to keep the wedding on track.

Turning his attention back to Harriet, he accepted a paper-thin china teacup and tried to look impressed by it. "What a lovely cup, Mrs. Longstreet."

"Oh, pooh, this old thing." But her face beamed, and he was glad he'd remembered the pride women took in such things. Harriet might be an old bat but she was easily manipulated and handy to have on his side. Between the two of them, maybe they could keep Miriam from doing anything embarrassing.

"Be it old or new, it reflects your exquisite taste." He winked at her, then turned toward the sound of squeaking hinges, awaiting Miriam.

She entered the room without words, her form and manner in stark contrast to her mother. Robert doubted her height and slender build would be considered fashionable, but at least she didn't look like an overgrown red hen. Her willowy appearance mirrored his. Together, they formed a handsome couple.

He rose, raised the corners of his mouth in welcome, and whispered her name. She rewarded him with a tentative smile.

"I thought you might want to go for a stroll," he allowed his voice to waver, hinting of uncertainty, offering Miriam control of the situation.

"I didn't expect you."

"Why, who else would you expect, dear?" Harriet interrupted. "You two young people go on. The weather won't allow many more strolls. Then it will be evenings in the parlor with your sister and the old folks."

Miriam seemed to weigh her choices, then nodded and began to gather her wraps.

Robert waited in silence until the front door had closed

behind them and they were surrounded by the dusk of the early November evening.

"Thank you for agreeing to come."

Miriam accepted his hand as they descended the wooden stairs of the porch and returned his gaze. "I truly didn't expect you. Not after last night."

"Miriam, listen. Last night caught me by surprise. There were words said that shouldn't have been. But you need to understand how things looked." He waited, gauging her response. Once he made it clear that she had responsibilities, he could focus on winning her over. She'd stopped walking, her eyes focused on him. He had to hand it to her; she didn't flinch.

"All right, Robert, I'll accept that. But you, too, must accept that your accusations appeared as a lack of trust."

He nodded, an illusion of agreement. If there was something going on with Deakins, she was managing to pull it off with more finesse than he'd thought she had in her. One more reminder and he'd let it lie. For now.

"Others might not be so accepting. The women of this fort put great stock in appearances. Be careful."

"Your point is well taken." They walked again, the darkness of the evening falling around them as they circled the parade ground. The subtle scent of wood smoke wafted from the chimneys along Officers' Row. Robert stalled, waiting for the precise moment, then took her hand and linked it through his arm.

"You made a few other points last night, little one. About mutual respect, I believe, and your need for independence?"

Their footsteps crunched on the fallen leaves the wind had carried from the trees lining the river and he waited for her to digest his words, hoping this was the right tactic.

"I did, yes. Please understand I'm not trying to be contrary. For the past five years, my opinions have mattered to those around me. To be abruptly unimportant is like a slap in the face. I don't need agreement, just the opportunity to express myself."

"So you simply want for me to listen to your thoughts?" Any fool could do that, if that was what she needed. He pulled her closer as the colder temperatures of darkness settled in, stopping when he felt the resistance of her body. She'd need a little more stroking.

"And consider them important enough to bear weight, not simply be dismissed because they're spoken by a woman. Discuss things with me."

She sounded half off her rocker. "It sounds as though you took up with a few suffragettes back in St. Louis."

"We explored their ideas, yes. My friend, Sarah, was quite taken with Miss Anthony's views. She heard her speak at the World's Fair in Philadelphia."

Drivel and poppycock, from what he'd heard. "Ah, yes, the Women's Bill of Rights, wasn't it?" A bunch of old maids with nothing but time on their hands. Good Lord, this was just what he needed.

"Oh, Robert, for heaven's sake, don't look so worried. I'm not proposing to organize such a movement here."

He hadn't realized his shock had been written so plainly across his face. He'd have to be more careful.

"That, my dear, is a little more than I would be able to handle. I thought we did discuss things."

"Our 'discussions' have consisted of you expressing your opinion and waiting for me to agree with you. When I insert a different thought or ask a question, I'm told I shouldn't worry about such matters."

"But you do?"

"Very often, yes."

"All right, I'll do my best to listen." Within limits.

"And you'll respect that I may have my own interests, apart from yours?"

"You may have your own interests."

"Then I think we are off to a much better start this time."

They'd reached her front porch. It was a good point at which to stop. One more rotation and God only knew what she'd come up with. He turned her to the stairs, extending his hand to assist her up. At the door, she paused.

"Well, then. . . ."

"I think we've made some progress, Miriam. Good night." He kissed her on the cheek and watched her slip into the house. Perhaps this strategy might work after all.

Miriam hadn't expected Robert's acquiescence any more than she had expected his visit. But now that she had his word that he would respect her interests, she was not going to let the opportunity slip by.

She arose the next morning with fierce determination. Today, proper or not, she was going to follow the dictates of her heart and go to Carrie's. She was not going to take laundry or fetch laundry or look for Franny. She was going just for the sake of a visit, pure and simple, no excuses.

Carrie's quick dismissal of the complications of her pregnancy nagged at Miriam. She had seen the exhaustion in Carrie's eyes. She wanted to see how her friend looked today. And if Carrie got stubborn and bristled at her concern, she'd make it a gossip visit, to talk about her progress with Robert.

Mother was abed with another of her headaches, curtains drawn against the brilliant pre-winter sun, demanding the house be kept in perfect silence. Happy to comply, Miriam bundled Franny against the cold and the two set off for Suds Row.

Franny skipped alongside her, chirping away about her plans for the day. "If the sun stays out so bright, maybe me and Albert can bring a pile of leaves up from the river and flop in 'em. Otherwise, we're gonna play marbles."

"Albert and I," Miriam corrected.

"You wanna flop in the leaves, too, Miriam?"

"No, Franny, the correct way to say it is 'Albert and I,' not 'me and Albert.' "

"But what difference does it make? You knew what I was sayin' when I said it the other way, didn't you?"

"Yes, I did, but you need to learn to speak correctly."

"That doesn't make sense. Don't grownups have anything else to do besides makin' up funny rules and waitin' around till somebody breaks 'em?"

Miriam laughed. Franny's logic held more sense than the girl realized.

Ahead, under the now-bare trees, Carrie hoisted a pail of water from the ground and moved toward a large wooden tub. She emptied the bucket and sat wearily on a nearby stump, her face in her hands. A brief spasm rocked her body.

Miriam shooed Franny off to find Albert and approached. "You shouldn't be lifting so much."

Carrie lifted her gaze. Her eyes were shadowed, exhausted. "Laundry don't get done without water."

"Then let someone else get the water."

"It ain't hurtin' me any. Takes longer is all." Carrie rose and reached for another pail of water.

"For heaven's sake, Carrie. Why don't you get another laundress to help you?"

"They got enough to do." Carrie's voice was firm and her eyes flashed, deep and intense, reminding Miriam of Jake. "I'll handle my own, same as them."

"I'm sorry, Carrie. It's just that I can't help but see how sick you are and I thought—"

"You thought you could just come prancin' over and shove

my work off on somebody else?"

Lord, the woman was stubborn, a miniature version of Jake. "Just to lighten your load," Miriam explained.

"They're already helpin' what they can, but there's only so much a body can handle. 'Sides, you parcel out my work and the army will figure there ain't no need for me."

"Then let me help." The offer slipped out, surprising Miriam. It hadn't been her original plan, but why not? How difficult could it be to wash a few clothes?

"You ain't done laundry in your life. I can jus' see your ma gettin' wind of that. It'd be twice the work teachin' you anyways."

Miriam smiled at the thought of her mother's response. And Robert? It wasn't something he'd approve of either, not by a mile. But his response would reveal whether or not he was serious in his declarations of respect. Besides, if her heart changed, if she married Robert, there might come a day when the army transferred them to a small post, one without laundresses. She really should learn to wash clothes, just in case.

She smiled at her own excuses, her mind made up. "What do I do first?"

Carrie rolled her eyes and sighed. "Go home, before you get us all in trouble."

"I'm not going home, Carrie. If there's any trouble, I'll shoulder it. It wouldn't hurt me to be exposed to laundry. Who knows when I may end up without a laundress? Besides, it'll be an adventure for me. What's in the tub?" She inclined her head toward a large wooden tub full of water and clothes.

"It's full of lye soap and it'll ruin your hands." She waved her dry, chapped hands at Miriam's face. "Go home."

"I'm not going anywhere, so hush. Do you use lye for everything?"

Carrie sighed again and shook her head. The look in her eyes told Miriam she wasn't pleased with the situation.

"Jus' the heavier things and what's most dirty. You leave 'em soak for a good while and there's not so much scrubbin' later when you boil 'em in the copper."

"Can't Eddie fill the tubs?" Miriam paused. "Or Jake?"

"Eddie totes the water to the house but I gotta heat it on the stove, and he ain't got time to wait around for that." She too paused, as if weighing her answer. "Jake's volunteered for more detached duty. He'll be gone at least a couple weeks. If I let you help fillin' the tub, will you let it be?"

"I might." She wished Carrie would tell her more about Jake.

"Then I reckon you can pour them there buckets of water into that tub." A large, empty half-barrel sat on a low table. Carrie pointed to a pair of wooden buckets, and Miriam reached for the first of them.

Hoisting it up, Miriam was taken aback at its weight.

"Heavy, ain't it?" Carrie grinned.

Miriam poured both pailfuls into the tub and realized it was far from full. If she was guessing right, each of the buckets held about two and a half gallons. In front of Carrie's house stood even more tubs, all of them empty. "How much water is required to do laundry?" she asked.

"Oh, I s'pect about forty gallons or so, each set."

"Forty gallons? Dear Lord, however do you get forty gallons of water up here?" She knew, even before she finished the question, that Carrie would have to acquire the water either from the post pump house or from Randall Creek. Either way, it was a long haul.

"Creek's closest. Eddie helps some before he leaves for duty and the other women lend a hand. Usin' the yoke and all, it's eight trips down and back." She smiled while Miriam blanched at the thought of eight long trips from the creek with those heavy pails.

Carrie pointed to several more pails of water. While Miriam finished filling the round tub, Carrie filled the rectangular one next to it.

"That big one there that you filled up, that's for the rinsin'. I use this one here for the washin' since it's a whole lot easier to stand the washboard up in it. Some days, though, I use the round one and the peg dolly there, if there's gonna be too much scrubbin' for just the board."

Miriam glanced at the oddly shaped tool Carrie had indicated. Its long handle was T-shaped at the top. At the bottom, there was a circular disk. Angling out from the bottom of the disk were six wooden legs, similar to those on kitchen chairs but not as long.

"It's for stirrin' the clothes around," Carrie explained. "You had enough yet?"

"I said I was helping. It would seem we've barely started. What's next?"

"You already been help. Fillin' them buckets and tubs is what takes a lot outta me. The bendin' gets to me after a while. Ain't been a mornin' this week that breakfast stayed put. I reckon you'd be of help jus' visitin'. Else I'm jus' gonna have to do it all again to get what you miss. You think anymore on what we was talkin' on yesterday?"

Miriam wiped her hands on a towel scrap and surrendered to Carrie. Making more work for her had not been part of the plan. Before she went back home, though, she'd help hang things out to dry and dump the used water. That much she could handle without getting in the way.

"Robert came calling last night. We discussed my need for independence and he's willing to give it a go. I think if he learns to bend a little, things will be less stiff between us." The answer rang hollow, even as she said the words. Somehow, she doubted that would ever happen. Robert would always be stiff and formal and completely without the abandon Jake possessed.

"That's a step in the right direction, I reckon." Miriam's avoidance of Carrie's question stretched between them, punctuated by the sounds of wet wool being raked across the zinc washboard. Thoughts of Jake and the responses he drew from deep inside her nagged at her until she wanted to scream. She'd turned it every which way trying to puzzle out if it was just the lure of the forbidden.

Much as she was drawn to the thrill of abandon, and much as her body seemed to crave him, they had also shared simple, quiet conversations, the kind experienced by two friends. Still, how often had those conversations slipped into something hot and dangerous? Maybe, without the element of excitement, they didn't have a relationship.

"I've turned it over and over, Carrie. And every time I do, things come up the same. What you said about the forbidden making it exciting seems to be all there is."

Letting the thought settle, Carrie reached for a shirt, plunged the clothing into the water, and picked up a bar of lye soap. She stroked it across the fabric and briskly rubbed the shirt against the washboard, then repeated the action several times. When sure the garment was clean, she placed the item aside and reached for another.

"When you find that excitin' feelin' springin' up in the middle of good solid friendship, honest talkin' and acceptin' each other for all you are from deep down, then you got what it takes to base a life on."

"First things first, huh?"

"I reckon. And I reckon now that you know what you're lookin' for, you can set out to find it."

"Friendship, honesty, and acceptance. Perhaps Robert and I are finally headed in the right direction." Miriam smiled at her friend then tipped her head toward the tub of wash water. "So is that all there is to it?"

"That's it, mostly. Goes on the whole day long. Scrub 'em, rinse 'em, wring 'em out, hang 'em up, change the water when it needs it. 'Course you got to add bluing for the whites and such. But it's not hard to master. Jus' a whole lot of haulin' and bendin' and scrubbin'."

"You look worn to pieces. Will you let me spell you?"

Carrie frowned, then nodded. "For a bit, I s'pose. I am gettin' mighty tuckered, and them butterflies in my stomach are all stirred up again." She wrung out the last of the shirts, wiped her hands on her skirt and sat on the stump.

Miriam picked up a white cotton petticoat and dipped it into the tub. The water was lukewarm and she realized that somewhere along the line, Carrie had heated the water. Hours of work had already been put into the venture. The water lapped at her cuffs and she realized she should have unbuttoned them and rolled them up. She turned to find Carrie choking back a grin.

"You ain't never gonna get that thing clean just dippin' it. Like it or not, if you want clean laundry, you gotta get your hands wet and your knuckles sore."

Miriam smiled back at her friend, unbuttoned her sleeves with soapy hands, rolled them up and plunged her hands back into the wash water. "Ha," she challenged, and raked the petticoat across the corrugated zinc washboard leaning against the side of the tub. Water splattered out of the tub, leaving large wet spots on her dress. She laughed. "You might be surprised."

"That I might," Carrie agreed.

"And so, Miriam, might I," Robert's dissatisfied voice drifted across the clearing. "Would you care to explain *this* one?"

Chapter Fifteen

Robert stood in silence, watching Miriam dry her hands and roll down her sleeves to cover her bare arms.

Good God, the woman could not stay out of trouble. Every time he thought she was making progress in their relationship, every time he left her alone, she pulled something like this. The incident with Deakins had been one thing, isolated and unwitnessed, but this was entirely something else.

Lieutenant Robert Wood's fiancée did not lower herself by doing laundry with common laborers. He would not have it.

She approached him with confidence. "Gracious, Robert, you look ready to explode. We've been through this discussion before." She turned to the laundress, offered a quick wave, and draped a shawl over her shoulders. Focusing her attention on him, she offered her arm. "Let's go and I'll explain it again."

He accepted her arm stiffly and propelled her away from Suds Row. He recognized her strategy of forcing him to discuss the issue on fort grounds, within hearing range of officers and enlisted men alike. He'd be damned if he was going to take her across the parade ground until this thing was settled. He steered her toward the river, instead.

The bare trees were stark sentinels guarding the floodplain, protecting its privacy. He wound through them, down the slope, until the activity of the fort was no longer visible.

"Well, Miriam," he said when they were out of earshot of the camp, "you didn't appear to be a damsel in distress this time.

What in the hell were you doing?" He could hardly wait to hear her try to wriggle out of this one.

"Don't curse, Robert. It's low."

"You're damned right it's low," he yelled. "But it sure as hell isn't as low as laughing your head off in public, associating with a laundress, and washing clothes. Good Lord, Miriam. What were you thinking?"

"Will you stop pulling me along like we're on our way to put out a fire?" She jerked her arm away from his. Facing him, she stood with her hands on her hips, eyes blazing. "Is that all there is to your pledge, Robert? One day? One lousy day?"

"What in the blazes are you talking about?"

"Just last night, you promised me you would respect my interests. Some promise."

"Since when does a refined woman have an interest in laundry? That's the most ludicrous thing I've ever heard. If your mother gets wind of this—"

"You leave my mother out of this. You broke your promise, and I'm not about to bend to your will when you've so little respect for me that you're not even able to keep your word from one day to the next." She stomped through the trees, crunching fallen branches. Reaching out, Robert spun her around.

"This hardly qualifies as an interest. Interests are sewing and gardening and reading. Laundry is not an interest. It's labor. Women of your station do not perform manual labor."

"You're right, laundry is not an interest."

"You're damned right it's not."

"But reform is. This is what Sarah and Lise felt." Her face was vibrant and full of energy. She shook away from his grasp, talking with her hands. "Reform means something."

"Now what are you talking about?" He almost didn't want to know. Another of those odd ideas she'd picked up at that awful boarding school. His skin prickled with a chilly sweat.

"For years, New Yorkers have been working for reform to better the lives of the worthy poor. And there are new movements out there. Advocates preach of the duty of the upper classes to assist those in need." She stopped pacing and stood before him with calm assurance, no longer yelling, forcing him to discuss the issue on her terms. He felt suddenly cold, trapped.

"Not by doing laundry."

"And why not, Robert? What if you get transferred to some godforsaken place in the middle of nowhere and there *are* no laundresses? Who will wash your uniforms then? Why not take the opportunity to learn a skill that may one day prove invaluable, while, at the same time, assisting someone in need?"

"She gets paid to do the laundry."

"A pittance, and she's so sick right now that she can barely function."

"That's her problem, not yours."

"It's everyone's problem. The army doesn't ease up on her simply because she's expecting. If she doesn't do her job, she loses her job. If she loses her job, she leaves."

"And why is that supposed to matter to us?"

"It matters to me because she is a kind, generous person who faithfully performs her duties. It should matter to you because if she leaves, several officers will be short a laundress."

"Then they can hire another one."

"Robert, the only women here who aren't already employed by the army are officers' wives. Whom do you propose they hire?"

He shook his head with frustration. He hated that her reasons made sense. Still, her notions were misguided. There had to be other solutions. He felt drained. The sun slipped behind a gray cloud, and bleak half-light settled around them.

"It's not appropriate for you to do laundry. The other laundresses will pitch in," he said.

"Not if they want to get their own laundry done."

"So, what are you proposing here? Are you going to form a social reform club among the officers' wives? That way, everyone can take their turn in the wash water?"

"If that's what it takes to make it 'appropriate.' "

Good God. He sighed. "I was being sarcastic, Miriam."

"Yes, Robert, I know you were, but why not?"

"It just isn't done."

"Who better to get the ball rolling but the commanding officer's family? The other women will line up to be involved." She had again become animated, eager to pursue the insane idea. Line up indeed. She'd make a fool of herself. Of him.

"Stop it. You will not do laundry." He would not have her spending hours with that laundress, with the enlisted men, with Jake Deakins.

Miriam's chin set in that stubborn way he was beginning to hate. "Give me two weeks. Let me talk to the other women. If they go along with doing a little charity work, you will let it be. If they refuse, you may insist that I stop."

They'd never go along with the idea, at least not many of them. If he spoke to Harriet, she'd quell almost all of them. He'd put conditions on the idea. That would pacify Miriam and put an end to her tomfoolery. How many did she think would do the washing? Three? Four? She'd never get four of them to participate.

"Two weeks, Miriam, that's all. And you won't go there alone. You'll need to go in groups. Let's say four others besides yourself."

"Thank you," she said, grasping his hands. "I knew you were open-minded."

He squeezed her hands and forced himself to smile. She'd done it again, twisted the situation against him. God, he hated it. She'd damned well better not make a fool out of him.

That night, Jake stood outside his shelter half in the cold night air. He'd volunteered for another rotation of duty to the surrounding Indian encampments, affecting an attitude of nonchalance while his gut did somersaults.

The Miriam Problem, as he'd come to think of it, was not going to go away.

Even before she'd appeared at the village, he'd spent hours each night thinking about her. Visions of thick auburn ringlets, lifted high, the taste of her neck, and smoldering green eyes filled his dreams. Now his body ached at the thought of her lithe body and its yielding flesh. His imaginings drove him out into the darkness where he stood shivering, trying to remind himself of all the reasons they couldn't be together.

Moving through the darkness, he checked on his horse and cast his gaze over the village. Silence. He returned to the tent and grabbed his blanket. He figured it'd be a while before he found sleep again. Maybe another sleepless night. Might as well heat some coffee.

He stuck another log on the embers of his campfire, located his pot, and sifted through everything again. A woman like Miriam didn't just give up everything for a man like him. His problem boiled down to a whole lot more than simple attraction. Hell, if he was just horny, then release ought to cure it. But, he didn't want a quick poke. And he sure as hell didn't want anybody else. Sure, desire flooded his body at the thought of her. Yet, it ran a whole lot deeper and he reckoned they both knew it.

And they both knew there was no future in it.

Miriam wasn't the kind of woman a man played around with without promises of a life together. He pulled his blanket closer and hunkered near the unsteady fire, stirring the coals.

Materially, he had nothing to offer her. The Longstreets had some mighty fine things, finer than most other officers. A woman from a background like that just wouldn't fit into the small life he could provide.

Not that marriage was an option for him. Army regulations forbade marriage of enlisted men. If they weren't hitched up when they entered the U.S. Army, they had to wait until they were out unless given special clearance by their commanding officer. Somehow, he didn't see Major Longstreet giving the go-ahead for this one. In fact, he couldn't see Harriet Longstreet allowing her husband to give approval to Miriam's marriage to a man below their station even if it were a civilian matter.

He threw the stick into the fire and stood, frustrated. How the hell had he gotten into thoughts about marriage? All this suppressed desire was addling his brain. Maybe his attraction to Miriam did run deeper than lust, but it sure as hell didn't mean he wanted to marry her.

But she wasn't the sort who would, or should, settle for being a kept woman.

Jake shook his head and tried to erase her from his mind, then turned back to his tent to look for a cup. He'd be stationed at the Indian encampments for two more weeks. If he had to, he'd request detached duty for the rest of his stint. Staying away from her was the only escape he could think of. If she managed to get herself in trouble again, she'd just have to figure her own way out.

"Absolutely not," Harriet slammed her teacup onto the kitchen table and glared at Miriam.

Miriam bit her lip. She'd started out all wrong. She should have mentioned Robert first. Or maybe something about someone famous who supported social reform. *Think*, she told herself. If the assistance league was going to work, she had to have her mother's support. One negative word from her mother and the idea would be finished.

She glanced at her father. He sat across from his wife, observing without words. It seemed she was on her own.

"Now, Mother—"

"Don't you 'now mother' me, young lady. I've never heard such a ridiculous idea in all my life. Laundry, of all things."

"Perhaps I should explain it differently."

"It doesn't matter how you explain it, it still amounts to common labor." Mother picked up her fork and stabbed at the gravy and biscuits on her plate, glowering.

"Robert felt that I should pursue it." There, maybe that would do the trick.

"I thought Robert had more sense." Her mother popped a forkful of biscuit into her mouth and dabbed at the gravy that slid down her chin. "Whatever made him agree to such a harebrained idea?"

"Two things, Mother. First, helping one's fellow human beings is a decent thing to do and—"

"Bah! I could hardly think of anything more indecent that this melding of the classes you persist in supporting. I will not have you advancing such ideas." She pushed back her chair and rose awkwardly. At the cookstove, she added hot water to her teacup.

"Ladies, a word if I may?" Tom Longstreet interrupted, surprising them both. "I think the idea has some merit, Harriet. The fine ladies of Fort Randall do seem to be a tad self-absorbed of late. Besides, Miriam is not a little girl anymore. Perhaps we should grant her a little license here, allow her to present her idea to the ladies."

Mother dropped her teaspoon on the floor and stared at her husband. "Why, I hardly think you need to bother about—"

"This time, Harriet, I think I do. Miriam has a point. It's

about time the women around here did more than sit around all day gossiping. You've been treating her like a child since she got here, and maybe it's time to let her learn on her own, for God's sake." He glanced at Miriam and smiled through his mustache while Harriet's face grew red. "Miriam, you have my approval to approach the ladies with the understanding that this laundry business will hinge on their decision."

With that, he winked at Miriam and rose from the table. At the door, he turned. "And, Harriet, it is also with the understanding that you will not interfere. I don't want to hear another word about this matter from you."

Miriam sat in shocked silence as her father left the house. His unbidden support had taken her unaware. That she would find an ally in her usually reticent father was more than she could have asked for. Harriet returned to the table and sat, her eyes beady and intense. She glared at Miriam.

"You'll regret this," she announced in a low, steely voice. "I'll take your father at his word. The laundry business will hinge on the ladies' decision. As will the ridiculous friendship you've managed to develop with that laundress."

Harriet picked up Miriam's teaspoon and stirred her tea, a smug and self-assured smile plastered across her face.

Ten days later, Miriam paced in the small side room of the post chapel, waiting for the officers' wives to take their seats. Except for her mother, their expressions were unreadable. Harriet sat tight-lipped, obviously choking back her comments. All the other women needed to do was look at her to know that she didn't approve of the situation.

"Attention, please, ladies," Miriam announced as the last of them settled into folding camp chairs. "I'm here today with a proposal." She glanced out at the eight women and forced what she hoped was a confident smile. They stared back with a mixture of irritated expressions and curiosity.

She'd delayed this meeting for almost the entire two weeks, using the time to help Carrie through the worst of her morning sickness and to plan her presentation. She didn't intend to sacrifice Carrie's friendship without a fight. Besides, if they rejected her plan, at least she'd provided Carrie some help.

"Thank you, ladies, for offering me your attention this evening. We're gathered tonight to discuss how we can all make a significant contribution to society, both for others and for ourselves. I'm here this evening with my father's sanction to ask you to consider forming a Women's Assistance League."

A low murmur filled the room.

"Excuse me," Eulalie Samuels interrupted, raising her thin hand. "I'm not sure we understand what this would entail. Perhaps it would be best if we allowed Miriam to explain."

"Charity work. She means a charity society. Isn't that right, Harriet?" Mrs. Stanton smiled self-righteously, her plump arms crossed as daintily as possible across her lap. She seemed pleased at having put Harriet in the position of being forced to respond.

Harriet glared at Miriam, her lips pursed. "Miriam will explain it," she said. Miriam knew her father's injunction that Harriet not voice her opinion was chafing at her mother.

"That is one way to think of it, Mrs. Stanton," Miriam continued. "Let me try to explain further. There are times when class differences get in the way of common human decency, of doing what is right. Some people support assistance leagues for those reasons. Others look at the fact that there are times when the misfortunes of some impact the fortunes of others."

"Which means, dear?" Eulalie's usually pinched face was animated with curiosity.

"Sometimes it's just right to help someone out. Sometimes, if we don't help, our refusal may come back to impact us."

"What is it such a group would do?" Mrs. Appleby asked.

"One of the laundresses is in the family way. I would propose that, as our first group project, we assist her with her laundry assignments for a short time."

Mrs. Stanton gasped, Mother sat stone-faced, and most of the women looked from one to another as if gauging an appropriate response.

"Wash clothes?" the quiet Mrs. Lewis questioned, her mousy features hiding all evidence of her opinion.

"It would be a Christian service to help her through this time," Miriam prompted, "as well as assuring that the officers' families continue to have an adequate supply of clean clothes and linens. Besides, the task would be fun, done in the spirit of charity, an adventure."

"Good heavens, I've never done laundry in my entire life," Mrs. Stanton protested. "This is out of the question. I can't believe your father would approve of such an idea. Besides, the Lord helps those who help themselves."

"Mrs. Stanton, please, I—"

"I will not be insulted like this. Harriet, are you just going to sit there and let her go on?"

Her mother took a deep breath. "I choose not to offer an opinion on this, Mrs. Stanton."

"But you don't approve, do you? Look at her, ladies, you can see she'd just itching to say something."

"Mrs. Stanton, please," Miriam interjected.

"Oh, you can't tell me she's going to go over to that lice-infested Suds Row and put her hands in a laundry tub, not Harriet Longstreet. We'd all be over there, risking our health, with our hands raw and she'd be standing around supervising. Well, I, for one, am not going to participate in this conversation." With that, she rose and waddled to the back of the room.

"Ladies, please," Miriam said, "this was not an attempt to

insult any of you."

"Would we actually have to wash clothes?"

"We help those creatures just by hiring them. I'm not about to associate with them just to call myself a do-gooder."

"Couldn't we do something else to assist?" Mrs. Lewis offered.

Miriam interrupted, hoping Mrs. Stanton would grow weary of making insults. "The proposal to wash clothes was simply that, a proposal. If you have other ideas, please share them." She surrendered the floor and settled into a vacant chair next to her mother. She'd known there would be resistance but she hadn't expected the comments to be so ugly. If she could turn the flow of conversation to other proposals, the league might still gain approval. After all, in the end, Robert had only said the ladies must agree to charity work. The assistance league, in any form, would guarantee her continued friendship with Carrie. She crossed her fingers and hoped her mother would keep her mouth shut.

"Perhaps we could try to limit our laundry needs for a time," Mrs. Appleby suggested.

"A fine idea, but may I suggest we take things a bit further." Eulalie stood, fully enthused. "We all have gowns that are no longer fashionable. I believe it would be more than appropriate if we were to share them with those less fortunate. And furthermore, it wouldn't hurt us to plan something special for the holidays."

"I feel obliged to remind all of you that Major Longstreet and I presently do visit the enlisted men on Christmas Day," Harriet stated, rising from her chair.

"Bosh, Harriet. You may reap great satisfaction from your little visits, but I hardly think the enlisted men enjoy what amounts to an inspection while they stand at attention for the commanding officer. That was not what I meant at all."

"And what exactly did you mean, Miss Samuels? Are you implying that—"

"Mother, please, let's sit down and allow Miss Samuels to present her idea." Eulalie was turning out to be an unexpected ally, and Miriam didn't need Harriet's overbearing presence to nip her comments in the bud. Harriet settled into her chair with a quiet thud, glowering.

"Thank you, Miriam. It was my thought that perhaps the ladies of the assistance league might take it upon themselves to provide a small party for the enlisted men and the laundresses."

"We do have plenty of refreshments prepared for our own parties, anyway," Mrs. Lewis conceded. "A little extra would provide for them, too."

"A most gracious idea, Eulalie," Mrs. Appleby added, nodding.

Miriam glanced at the other ladies. A few nodded their heads in agreement. It was the root of a wonderful idea. Even better would be a single gathering, bringing together both enlisted men and officers. That way, it would be more than simply one class sharing their scraps with the other.

"What if we were to have one big, all-post party?" Miriam blurted out loud.

From the back of the room, Mrs. Stanton groaned audibly. Scraping her chair across the wooden floor, Harriet rose and huffed to join her. The other women were silent, glancing at one another with uncertainty.

"Why, Miriam, what a gracious thought. I propose we do it." Eulalie clapped her hands together. "Here's to the Fort Randall Women's Assistance League and the first annual All-Post Christmas Party."

"Mrs. Longstreet and I call for a vote," Mrs. Stanton announced.

Miriam turned. Her mother and Mrs. Stanton stood behind

the last row of chairs, their rigid faces twins in hostile disapproval. True to her promise, Harriet remained silent. A gnawing knot formed in the pit of Miriam's stomach.

"All right, ladies, all those in favor of the assistance league please signify by a show of hands," Eulalie instructed, raising hers first. Miriam followed. The others sat watching one another, looking to Mrs. Stanton and Harriet. After a moment, Mrs. Appleby joined those in favor, nudging Mrs. Lewis with her other elbow until she tentatively raised her arm. No one else responded.

"Hah. The motion fails," announced Mrs. Stanton, arching her eyebrows in victory. She gathered her wraps and left the room. The others followed in silence, leaving Miriam alone with her mother.

"No more laundry, no more laundress," she reminded Miriam with grim pleasure and strode out of the room.

Chapter Sixteen

A week after Thanksgiving, Miriam's mother rushed into the house. She slammed the door behind her, shutting out the dreary morning shadows. The bleak day mirrored the mood Miriam had been stuck in since being banished from Suds Row. Mother's face was harried. "Miriam?" she snapped.

Miriam set her needlepoint in her lap and sighed. Beside her, Franny stiffened. Mother had been a shrew all week, gloating at Miriam's failure to organize the Women's Assistance League. Miriam searched her memory. She didn't recall having done anything "inappropriate" since the meeting. What in heaven's name had set her mother off this time?

Mother marched into the room. "Yankton. Your father wants me to go to Yankton. He just received a telegram informing us there's an unexpected officers' delegation due in tomorrow." She paced back and forth, stewing.

"Why, Mother, how wonderful. Just think, dress shops, a milliner, fine dinners, perhaps even the theater. All the things you enjoy." Miriam smiled with false enthusiasm. To Miriam, the trip sounded petty. She'd rather be elbow deep in laundry, raw hands and all, with Carrie's friendly chatter. Still, she could think of nothing better than having her mother gone for a few days.

"Oh, pooh, Miriam," Mother waved her hand in melodramatic emphasis. "How can I leave you two here without worrying every moment I'm there. My head will ache and I won't be able to enjoy a bit of it."

Miriam reined in her exasperation. "Then don't go." She was tired of everything being her fault. For three months, she'd tried unsuccessfully to please her mother. Even her forced sacrifice of Carrie's friendship didn't seem to be enough. Her mother's mercurial moods grated on her. Nothing seemed to satisfy the woman.

Mother stopped pacing and stood with her hands on her hips. "I can hardly allow your father to make social arrangements. They're passing through en route to Fort Pierre, spending two nights in Yankton. If I leave it up to him, their stay, not to mention their impression of us, will be a complete disaster. After all, the only reason these groups stop in Yankton is because of my reputation as a hostess."

"Then go."

Harriet stared at Miriam with accusation in her eyes. "And just how, pray tell, am I to trust you to stay away from that laundress and those enlisted people?"

"Oh, for heaven's sake, we've been through this before. I already agreed to bow to the wishes of the other women. No more assistance league, no more laundry, no more laundress. Franny and I will work on lessons." She offered Franny a reassuring pat. "Besides, Robert will keep me in line."

Mother took a deep breath then exhaled, her shoulders relaxing and her eyes wavering. "I'd arrange for one of the other ladies to chaperone you, but all of them are going along."

Miriam leaned forward and tried not to sound argumentative. "I'll behave. I don't need a chaperone. If I promise to stay put, indoors, would that satisfy you? I won't wash any clothes, I won't go visiting, I won't invite anyone for tea."

"I just know I'm going to fret the whole time. Oh, dear, this better not incite my head." Her mother tossed up her hands in surrender. "I do need to purchase some more laudanum. It's the only thing that seems to ease my headaches." Her eyes narrowed. "You make sure you go to Robert if there are any problems. Any. He'll let the senior officer know. I'll have your father leave instructions for him to monitor your situation.

"Your father wants to leave immediately. He thinks there's a storm brewing, so keep an eye on the weather." Continuing to cluck about the weather and her lack of time, she hustled into the back bedroom.

Within the hour, Harriet was scurrying toward the military ambulance where the other wives already sat, chattering. Miriam watched her climb into the conveyance, settle her bulk amid them, and launch into her own gossipy narrative, forcing the others to turn their full attention to her. The women tugged at their buffalo robes as the rocking vehicle pulled away.

The day was still gray and overcast. Clouds hung low in the sky. A piercing wind promised to make the trip uncomfortable and Miriam was glad she had not been included. She stood with Robert and Franny and waved to her parents as their wagon lumbered over the hill and out of sight. She breathed a small sigh of relief, glad to be free from Harriet's constant faultfinding, if only for a few days. Then she turned to Robert, took his arm and smiled as he accompanied them home.

Her relationship with Robert had subtly changed. Their laundry argument had revealed a side of him that he had kept hidden. He did have spunk. The fact that he'd let down his rigid self-control and quarreled with her somehow made him more approachable. There was something about a man who protested, a man who believed strongly. She stopped in midstep as Jake's taunting blue eyes came before her.

"Miriam? Are you all right?" Robert asked.

She shook the image from her mind. "Yes, I'm fine," she said, and resumed walking. Robert flashed a smile and offered his arm.

Taking it, Miriam told herself she shouldn't hold her mother's ban on seeing Carrie against him. After all, he'd only intended the women's decision to apply to washing clothes. If all went well, she planned to talk him into using his influence to change her mother's mind. Robert didn't set her body on fire like Jake did, but, as Carrie had said, true relationships were built on the basis of friendship, not lust.

She'd heard that Jake had returned to the fort, his request for a third tour of detached duty denied. Their paths hadn't crossed, and she didn't have any reason to see him. She told herself it wouldn't be a problem. She was building her relationship with Robert.

She grasped Robert's arm as they walked through the brisk wind. Franny skipped ahead of them, laughing at the scattered flakes of snow that whirled around her face. Reaching their door, Robert solicited Miriam's reassurance that she would notify him if she had any problems and left them.

Miriam added another log to the cozy fire. Outside, a steady blanket of snow wrapped itself around the fort. She was glad the messenger had brought word of her parents' safe arrival in Yankton.

She turned back to Franny and smiled at her. "Supper will be ready, soon, pet."

"Do you s'pose we can make some taffy tonight?" Franny asked, looking up from her paper dolls.

Miriam saw the sparkle of hope in her sister's hazel eyes. Goodness, she hadn't made taffy since last winter with Sarah and Lise. It sounded like a wonderful idea.

"I think we could do that, but I don't know how you're going to eat any with those two front teeth missing," she teased. "We'll need to borrow more molasses, though. Mother used most of it last week."

Franny flashed a lopsided grin. "I could run and ask Mrs. Appleby." At Miriam's nod, she bounded to the hallway and grabbed her wraps, then flew out the front door.

What an imp, Miriam thought, as the door banged shut. A taffy pull was just what they needed. She might even invite Robert, see if she could get him to relax a little more.

She headed for the kitchen to check on supper. The smell of corned beef greeted her as she pushed open the heavy wooden door. Lifting the lid of the pan on the stove, she tested the boiled potatoes with a fork. Supper was simple, but it was a step up from her lumpy oatmeal. Franny shouldn't have anything to complain about tonight. And Franny would love her taffy.

Miriam put the lid back on the pot and peered out the kitchen window into the darkness. She wished Franny would get home soon. She should have returned by now. Knowing Franny, she would be sitting at the neighbor's kitchen table eating cookies. Miriam removed dinner from the cookstove, donned her winter wraps and headed for the Appleby residence.

The house was dark. Miriam's heart pounded. Lord, the Applebys had probably gone along to Yankton.

Miriam pivoted toward the deserted parade ground. The cold had become intense, and wet snowflakes fell against her cheeks, driven by the biting wind. The night was quiet, all the usual sounds of soldiers and their busy routine absent. It was not a night to be out. A shiver of fear went down her spine. She should never have allowed Franny to leave the house.

She choked back her rising concern and tried to think calmly. Lantern in hand, she peered through the darkness, searching, until she spied a child's footprint in the snow. The tiny tracks headed southward, toward Suds Row, then vanished beneath a developing snowdrift.

Miriam hesitated and glanced toward Robert's quarters. His windows were lit by the soft glow of lamplight. He'd said to come if there were any problems. She started forward, then stopped again, uncertain. Robert's assistance would come at the price of harsh interrogation and thinly veiled accusations. With a sureness she had not been aware of, she knew that Robert wouldn't, couldn't, come simply because she needed him.

Jake. I need Jake.

She turned and strode to the enlisted men's barracks. Breathless, she pounded on the door. It was answered by a thin private with thinning hair.

"Get Jake Deakins. Tell him Franny's missing."

Within minutes, Jake was at the door, shoving his brawny arms into a blue overcoat. He slipped out the door and took the lantern from her hand, no questions asked.

"I found tracks," she shouted, struggling to be heard over the increasing wind, "but they disappear."

Jake nodded. "Show me."

Already, the tracks were filling in, erasing all trace of Franny. Miriam tugged on Jake's sleeve. "Do you think—"

"Carrie's," he finished for her. "Come on."

They moved past the post hospital. Snow stung their faces and the fierce wind pushed them back, slowing them down. They approached the rear of the building and Jake pointed toward the ground. He swung the lantern into the darkness. Small footprints dotted the snow. Jake swung the lantern wider and Miriam saw the tracks veered toward the Missouri River.

Jake grabbed her hand and pulled her through the trees and down the embankment. They shouted into the black void.

"Franny?"

"Franny? Are you there?"

The sound of the wind, whistling now as it wove its way through the empty tree branches, was all they heard.

Miriam threw an anxious glance at the footprints. They continued onto the ice. "Oh God," Miriam gasped and stepped forward. The ragged sound of cracking ice mingled with the wind.

Jake grabbed at her and pulled her into his arms, back to the relative safety of the shoreline. "Stay put," he commanded. "Keep your wits. Check to see if her tracks end or turn back."

She wiped at her tears as they froze in the cold air, and she struggled to gain control of herself. Jake was right. She needed to stay alert and calm. She peered across the ice and felt the wild beating of her heart as she struggled to see where Franny had gone.

"I can't see."

Jake held the lantern low. Along the shoreline, their own footprints had mingled with Franny's, but Franny's led straight onto the ice. He guided the light over the edge of the river until the ice was lit. No return tracks, only small boot prints going forward. A set of rabbit tracks ran between Franny's prints.

Miriam clutched Jake's arm. "She must have been chasing the rabbit."

Jake nodded. "She chased it out but not back."

He swung the lantern in a wide arc. Some seven or eight feet from the shoreline, Franny dangled on the ice, half in, half out of the water. She clung tenaciously to a small bush frozen into the ice.

"Oh my God. Jake?" Miriam's grip tightened and she heard the panic in her voice. *Dear God, let her hold on.*

"Franny, hold on, little lady. We're gonna get you out," Jake called. Franny whimpered in response as he pulled his arm from Miriam's hand and clutched her shoulders, forcing her to face him. "Miriam, we're gonna need to work together on this. I'm too heavy to go out there. I'm gonna get a branch but there's no way we're gonna be able to reach her with just the branch."

She nodded, trusting his judgment without question. "Tell

me what to do."

Jake scrambled to a nearby tree and broke off a strong limb. He returned to her side and cupped her face in his hands. "That ice is weak as hell. You need to lie down flat so your weight's not all in one spot and work your way out. Take the branch so she can catch hold of it." He held her gaze and his strength and calm seemed to find their way into Miriam's soul. "You can do this. I'll be right here behind you, sweetheart."

She kissed his hand and nodded then dropped to her knees and stretched out onto the ice. The cold crept through her skirt as she inched her body away from the shore.

Behind her, Jake called encouragement. "Franny? Can you take hold of the branch? Go on, honey, you can do it. Reach." His confident tone settled Miriam's frazzled nerves.

Farther out on the ice, Franny didn't seem to hear. She lay motionless except for the visible shivers that racked her body. Her whimpers had stopped and Miriam realized Franny would never be able to grasp hold of the branch.

Oh God, Franny, hold on.

Miriam abandoned the now-useless tree limb and inched closer. She felt the ice shift beneath her. She swallowed hard and kept going. The moment she could, she clasped the shivering Franny by the arms and untangled her frigid fingers from the bush. "Hold on, Franny. I've got you, pet, hold on." She pulled her sister to her and began sliding her way back toward Jake. After what seemed an eternity, she felt him grab her ankles and pull.

As soon as she was off the ice, he helped her to her feet, then pulled her close. Between them, Franny trembled, her wet clothes already stiffening in the cold air. Her small face was ashen, her lips tinged with blue. Her shivering had turned violent.

Jake touched Miriam's cheek. "Sweetheart, we need to get

her home and get these clothes off. Her fingers don't look frozen but it's hard to tell until we have more light. Her feet may be a whole 'nother story." He gently gathered Franny into his own arms. "Send the doc, then get Carrie and Ed. We're gonna need their help. I'll take Franny home."

Miriam, with Carrie and her husband Ed, raced through the dark swirling snow and neared the Longstreet house. Eddie pulled open the front door and they rushed into the hallway.

Through the parlor arch, Miriam saw the perennially disheveled post surgeon had already arrived. He sat on a footstool in the parlor, between Harriet's red horsehair settee and the fireplace. A pail of water sat at his feet.

Jake sat on the settee with Franny on his lap, surrounding her with a woolen blanket and his powerful arms. Her discarded shoes and clothing lay in a wet puddle on the floor. The doctor held her small bare feet. She whimpered against Jake's chest, her teeth chattering.

Miriam entered the room. "How is she?"

"She's gonna be fine," Jake answered. "Doc's just now checking her toes."

"I could use a hand here," the physician stated, his buck teeth dominating his round face. "Her feet need warming, and I got a bad case back over at the hospital I need to tend to. Somebody get over here and get her feet into this water."

Eddie pulled a hard-backed chair next to the footstool, and Miriam moved to sit at the doctor's side. She eased Franny's icy waxen feet into the bucket. Droplets of melting snow ran down her cheek and she shivered. Eddie picked up a log from the wood box and added it to the fire, then lifted Miriam's winter shawl from her shoulders and moved out of the way to Carrie's side.

"It doesn't appear as though she's frozen any of the digits," the doctor continued. "However, I'm not yet certain about frostbite. She's responsive, so we'll just give her time to get warm again. I think we're safe using the warm water on her feet. Her tissue seems soft underneath, but there could still be some blistering. It'll take a few hours before we'll know. At this point, all you can do is warm her up. No closer to the fire than this and no rubbing. If she has frostbite, rubbing will do more harm than good. Warm water only, not hot. Any questions?"

Miriam shook her head and wrapped the edges of the blanket around Franny's swollen legs. She felt her composure start to slip and moved her gaze to Jake's reassuring face.

"Good. I'll file my report with the officer in charge after I get my other patient stabilized. You don't need him here asking questions right now, anyway. Send for me if she seems worse. Private Deakins here knows what to watch for and how to wrap her feet." With that, he scurried to the door.

Carrie closed the door behind him and stepped back into the room. Her eyes turned toward the kitchen. "Smells like corned beef," she noted. "I'll see about fixin' her up some broth. Eddie can get a fire goin' in the bedroom and fill up the wood box." With smooth efficiency, she disappeared into the kitchen. Eddie gathered a load of logs in his wiry arms, and headed for the bedroom.

Franny began to squirm and whimpered louder. "It hurts," she fretted. She began to thrash, and Miriam struggled to keep her from tipping the bucket over.

"Shh, pet," she coaxed.

"We know it hurts, honey," Jake told her. "But you have to keep those feet in the water. That's the only way they're gonna get all better." He tightened his hold on Franny, his strong arms surrounding her. He glanced at Miriam, a tender warmth in his sapphire eyes. "Doc said it would be a good sign, her complainin' about it hurtin'. Means the blood's flowin' again."

Miriam smiled at him and felt his comfort wrap about her as if she, too, were in his arms. Their protector. As she had known he would be. He smiled back, rocking Franny until sleep overtook her tired body.

They sat in silence, listening to the crackle of the fire and the whistle of the wind. Eddie emerged from the bedroom and nodded at them. "I'm gonna see if Carrie needs a hand," he said quietly. In the kitchen, Carrie clanged cookstove lids as she prepared Franny's broth. Eddie disappeared into the kitchen and the clanging stopped, replaced by soft giggles.

Miriam listened to the sound drift through the house and recognized the happiness her two friends shared in each other, a sound she had never heard between her parents.

"You did the right thing, Miriam," Jake whispered, catching her off guard.

"I should have never let her go out in the first place."

He touched her knee and Franny shifted in his arms. "You didn't know she'd take off chasing a rabbit onto the ice. Nobody knows what kids are gonna do. You had your wits about you, coming for help, and you kept your head." He reached toward her, caught one of her hands and squeezed it.

Franny awoke. She wriggled one foot free, splashing water, and kicked out. "Leave me alone," she complained. "It hurts and I don't like it."

Jake smiled, letting Franny turn and twist. "Seems like maybe now might be the time for you to get your wet things off, too, Miriam. You look like a drowned rat."

"How gallant of you to notice."

"My pleasure. I specialize in drowned rats, you know."

"I know," she said, and smiled at him as he pulled Franny's feet up next to him. He checked them, then tucked them under the blanket. The pail of water had cooled. Miriam rose from her chair and moved the bucket away. "It's a good thing you do, too, or there'd be two less of us around."

Her voice broke and Jake shifted, catching her gaze over the back of the settee. Franny moved out of his lap and snuggled onto the seat, her eyes drooping closed. Leaning forward, over the settee's scalloped back, Miriam caught Jake's hand again. She felt the tears well in her eyes. "Thank you," she whispered, close to his ear. His hair was still damp, holding his scent, stirring her.

"I don't know what I would have done if that ice had given way." His voice, too, was strained, barely audible. "Sweet Miri."

Stray water droplets from melted ice particles glistened in his tawny beard. He reached for her cheek with his other hand and pulled her closer. She felt the wetness of his mustache as their lips touched. His kiss was soft, oddly tentative, a kiss of endearment.

The kiss reached into her very soul, melting through her, drawing her in. She felt her heart catch and she gasped.

He pulled back, releasing her. "Go, now, and get out of those wet things. I'm gonna have Carrie come see if she thinks Franny's feet are warm enough to leave them out of the water."

Miriam's gaze followed him as he rose and crossed through the dining room and into the kitchen. Only then did she turn away. In her room, the fire Eddie had laid was burning brightly, its orange flames dancing. Warmth settled about her as she stripped off her damp clothing and reached for a green flannel wrapper.

She thought again about how effortlessly Jake had taken control of the situation. If it hadn't been for his presence, she doubted she would have been able to control her panic. He'd known exactly what to do and he'd done it all with such ease, with a natural talent of command that most officers spent years learning in military school.

She had known, instinctively, that he would rescue Franny. In that small brief moment when she realized she needed help, her heart had told her to get Jake. And she'd responded without thought, without question.

Oh, Jake, good God, it's not just lust, is it?

The thought jumped at her, screaming its implications and she sat down, hard, on the bed. You didn't put your sister's life into just any man's hands. You didn't turn without hesitation to a man simply because he made your body ache. You didn't seek out someone other than your intended if it was just lust. And you didn't feel your soul sing at the simple tenderness of a kiss unless. . . .

I'm in love with Jake Deakins.

The realization swirled around her like a cloud. She lifted her hand to her mouth, holding back the sounds of astonishment that threatened to spill out, and her eyes pooled with tears.

I'm in love with Jake, and no amount of time with Robert is going to change the way I feel.

So what do I do now?

A knock sounded on the door, followed by Carrie's voice. "Miriam, you all right in there?"

Miriam struggled to appear normal and rose from the bed. Tightening her sash into a knot, she opened the door. Carrie's bright face greeted her.

"Franny's asleep again. I thought maybe Eddie should move her into bed."

"Is she all right?"

"She ate a couple spoonfuls of broth, then fought us all when we wrapped up her feet. She's gonna be jus' fine. Her feet're a mite swollen and she's got a couple blisters on her toes, but they ain't much. Just enough to keep her off her feet and de-mandin' your attention. I get the feelin' she's gonna be a difficult patient."

"I suspect she will be."

"There's supper sittin' in the kitchen. Go help yourself. Me an' Eddie'll get her tucked in and more wood on the fire."

"Thank you," Miriam told her friend and headed to the kitchen. Tin plates sat on the table along with a pile of silverware. Corned beef and boiled potatoes sat on the stove's warming area, their smells filling the room.

Miriam filled one of the plates and sank into a chair. She wasn't hungry, but she knew Carrie would squawk if she didn't eat something. Pushing the food around on the plate, she sighed.

Jake poked his head into the room. "You all right?"

"I'm fine." *Oh, Jake, what am I going to do?*

"You don't look fine. You look worried to death." He circled the table and pulled an empty chair close to her then sat, his brawny frame filling the empty space, intimately close.

He grinned and shifted his weight. Pulling his long legs back around the legs of the chair, he leaned forward, resting one powerful arm on the tabletop. "She's gonna pull through this."

Miriam tried to summon a weak smile and Jake reached out and touched her face, a feather touch. Then he cupped her head until his hand lingered just behind her neck, stroking her hair. It spoke of comfort, not physical need.

She leaned back and felt the touch of his fingers on her neck. Strong and soothing, they slowly began to stroke her skin, massaging the day away. It was enough and yet would never be enough.

"Miriam . . . ," he began, his voice uncertain.

She raised her head and sought his eyes.

". . . did you feel it?" he continued. "The way we worked together? Like we were thinking from one mind?"

She nodded, fearing to use her voice. She had felt it. From the moment he'd slipped out of the barracks, they'd worked as one. One heart, one mind, one soul.

"You came to me first, didn't you?" His voice was full and husky.

"Only you."

"Ah, Miri," he said, sighing, and pulled her closer, onto his lap, until she rested against him in the cocoon of his arms. "I don't think we can push it away anymore, can we?"

"Jake—"

"Shh, Miri, please. I'm falling in love with you and I think you're feeling it, too. And it isn't going to go away."

The words melted into her soul, answering the prayer she hadn't dared to utter. "No, Jake, it's not going to go away."

He cupped her chin and tipped her head back, lowering his own until their lips touched. No longer tentative, his mouth sought hers, his tongue reaching. She responded in kind, exploring the depths of his mouth, seeking all of him. He moaned, deep and throaty, and she knew he felt the kiss touch his heart as it did hers.

"I love you, Jake," she told him, and he swallowed her words in another kiss before pulling away.

"And I you," he said, brushing her ear with his whisper. He moved her out of his embrace and back into her own chair, then grasped her hands in his. "And, that, Miriam, means we both have some choices to make. This ain't gonna be easy. We're asking for nothin' but trouble, any way you look at it."

Carrie's straightforward voice broke in from the dining room. She pushed open the kitchen door. Her face was strained with worry.

"Just thought you'd want to know," she said. "Eddie was just out gettin' more wood. He says Lieutenant Wood is comin' 'cross the parade ground an' he looks savage as a meat ax."

CHAPTER SEVENTEEN

"Why didn't you come for me?" Robert demanded, pacing the Longstreet parlor. "Your parents placed you under my care."

Miriam frowned at him. It hadn't taken him long to start in on her. Jake and the Ruperts had barely disappeared into the whirling snow, banished like unwelcome guests by Robert. If only they'd had more time to talk, to figure out what to do.

"There wasn't time," she told him, hearing the hard edge in her voice.

"Wasn't time? There was time to run for Jake Deakins and the damned laundress. It's been hours, Miriam, don't give me a bunch of hogwash." His eyes narrowed.

She glared back at him, angry but sure of herself and her decision. Robert's opinion no longer mattered, and she refused to let his harsh words spoil what she had shared with Jake. She looked him in the eye. "All right, then. I didn't come for you because I didn't need you here, crowing like a puffed-up rooster about how important you are and how wrong I am."

He reacted as if slapped. His face contorted and he moved toward her. She could see his rage, one step away from crossing the line between gentleman and boorish clod.

"You forget your place, Miriam. No one speaks to me like that. No one. I'm sick and tired of you always pushing, pushing. You've had your way long enough."

A small jab of fear prickled at her, and she fought to keep herself from taking a step back. She wondered if he would become violent when she told him their relationship was over. She couldn't let him intimidate her. Gathering herself, she set her expression. "I haven't begun to get my way," she uttered.

The creaking of the front door intruded. Robert choked back his response and struggled to appear dignified.

Eulalie Samuels poked her pinched-up face into the house and entered with a gust of cold wind. "Goodness, whatever is the matter in here?"

"Nothing," Robert barked, reaching for the door. "Nothing at all. I'm not done with you," he whispered to Miriam under his breath. He flashed a seething glare at both women, then slammed the door behind him. On the wall, Harriet's favorite stitched sampler swung from the force.

"Well, something has him in a snit." Genuine concern shown in Eulalie's pale blue eyes. "You don't need him stirring things up when you've so much on your mind. The officer in charge sent for me as soon as Doctor Perkins filed his report. It would seem I'm a more proper set of hands than enlisted personnel." She shed her wraps. "How is Franny?"

"She's asleep, finally. Her toes are frostbitten and she's in a lot of pain, but the frostbite didn't go too deep." She felt her eyes fill with tears. "I don't know what I would have done without Private Deakins and the Ruperts. I would have plunged right out on the ice and gone in myself. Then she cried and struggled so hard that it took all of us to wrap her feet up." She sniffled, watching Eulalie. "I really need to go check on her."

"Now stop fretting and go sit down. I'll tend to her." Eulalie's face softened, once more revealing how attractive she was under all the frowns and worry lines.

Miriam watched Eulalie bustle down the hallway and into Franny's bedroom, no stranger to the house. Funny, Mother hadn't mentioned being friends with Eulalie. Miriam sighed and perched on the parlor settee, hoping Franny was still asleep.

She longed to retire for the night, to be alone with her thoughts. She had to decide how to break things off with Robert. Thinking of how he had teetered on the edge of his anger, she wondered if a letter might be safer. And, she needed to figure out a way to talk further with Jake so that they could make plans.

Eulalie emerged from the bedroom. "She's sleeping like a baby," she announced, then joined Miriam on the settee, sitting where Jake's scent still lingered. Miriam wished again that she had the privacy to wrap herself in her thoughts.

"You didn't go along to Yankton?" she asked Eulalie.

"I've just got over a sore throat and the sniffles and bowed out at the last moment. No sense taking a chance on a relapse. It wasn't much of a hardship to give up several hours in an ambulance with Mrs. Stanton and your mother while they argued about trivialities." She smiled and the dour set of her lips vanished.

Eulalie placed her hand on Miriam's and her eyes filled with warmth. "Miriam, dear, I don't know Private Deakins but I do know Mrs. Rupert's a good woman. And a good friend, I suspect. I don't suppose your mother will like it that you went to them, but I think you did the right thing."

Miriam nodded, surprised at Eulalie's perception and her candor. She remembered Eulalie's unexpected mirth at the party and her support of the assistance league and wondered if she would judge her harshly for what she felt for Jake.

"I just reacted," she said, remaining vague. "I went to those I trust."

"Well, now, that says a thing or two, doesn't it?" Eulalie patted her hand and stood, not waiting for Miriam's response. "And now you're stuck with me for the night. I'm game for a cup of tea. How about you?"

Miriam leaned forward to rise and felt Eulalie's touch on her arm. "Just sit, dear. I can get a cup of tea by myself. You might as well know I don't stand overmuch on ceremony." She disappeared into the kitchen and Miriam heard her rummaging through cupboards for cups and the tea tin. She was an odd woman, almost always sour-looking, but never afraid to voice her opinion. Moments later, she swept back into the room and handed Miriam a cup of steaming tea.

"I just love the crisp smell of a good cup of tea," Eulalie stated and reclaimed her seat. Closing her eyes, she breathed deeply, then reopened them and offered another brief smile. "Now then, we haven't had much of a chance to become acquainted. I think it's time we do."

"Miss Samuels—"

"Eulalie. Just hush for a moment, dear. I see that quick mind of yours working, trying to figure out if you can trust me. Put your fears to rest. I see so much in you that is familiar."

"Familiar?"

"Child, look at me. I'm a middle-aged spinster who lives with her brother in a very dull, very narrow life. A long time ago, I had choices in my life and I made them poorly. Through the years, the options narrowed, and now . . . well, here I am spending my time gossiping with a flock of old birds. Why, your assistance league idea would have been the sole adventure in my life since—well, since a long time ago. And life is miserable without adventure. I wanted you to know how sorry I was that the idea didn't make it past those small-minded tarts." Eulalie's pale eyes held an unusual twinkle.

Her straightforwardness surprised Miriam in its intensity. *Goodness, she's no more content with the restrictions of society than I am.* "Me, too," Miriam admitted, at once secure about the older woman's sincerity. "There was a lot more riding on the proposal than just the assistance league."

"I thought so. It wasn't too difficult to see where the

dominoes landed. All of a sudden, you just stopped going across the parade ground every day and I knew there was more involved than washing clothes. Pity what the army does to us, isn't it?"

Miriam nodded, wondering if Eulalie's almost-constant frown had its source in something the army had caused.

"Well, I doubt it will reinvigorate the assistance league, but I intend to put in my two cents' worth with your father about what the Ruperts and Private Deakins did for you. I daresay your father is a far fairer man than you might realize."

"You know my father well, then?"

"I've known Thomas and your mother for years and, yes, I suppose I do know him well. He and my brother George enlisted together way back when. But, that's neither here nor there. Another cup of tea?"

Miriam shook her head, wishing her new friend would say more. She knew her father so vaguely. Noting the firm set of Eulalie's lips, she decided not to pursue the topic tonight. Besides, she still needed to write the letter to Robert. "No, thank you, Eulalie. I really should retire."

"By all means, dear." She rose and headed to the kitchen again. "I'll just refill my cup and drown in the aroma for a while. I've brought a Dickens novel and will be here if Franny stirs. You go sleep in your mother's bed, and I'll handle everything."

Eulalie disappeared through the swinging door, leaving Miriam alone. The woman puzzled her. Before this evening, she'd seldom seen her smile, yet she'd done so several times throughout her visit tonight. And her unexpected support not only of the assistance league but of her friendship with Carrie and Jake was extraordinary. Could it be that she'd found an ally in this small, smothering world?

Somehow, Miriam knew Eulalie would have no problem

understanding or accepting that she was in love with an enlisted man. She knew it without a doubt. Eulalie was waiting for the adventure of a lifetime, and Miriam knew she had one for her.

The letter to Robert could wait. Miriam grabbed her empty teacup and followed Eulalie into the kitchen. They had plans to make.

Miriam sat in her father's office, waiting for his reaction to her part of the two-pronged attack she had planned with Eulalie. He had returned from Yankton yesterday on the heels of the three-day blizzard. Eulalie had visited him immediately as an objective observer and told him about Franny's rescue. By now, he should be quite sympathetic to enlisted personnel.

The rest was up to Miriam. Eulalie had estimated there was but one way they could hope to convince Tom Longstreet to consider disregarding the social code that separated Jake and Miriam. He had to come to know Jake as a man, not as a private. Eulalie's story of Jake's heroism was the first step. The second was getting Jake and the major in the same room socially.

He sat behind his large wooden desk, his eyebrows raised. Behind him, the afternoon sun glinted on several feet of drifted snow, urging Miriam on.

"An all-post Christmas party?" he questioned.

"One of Miss Samuels' friends at Fort Lincoln wrote that the ladies there are planning an all-post Christmas celebration, a tradition they started a few years ago. We thought that such a gathering would be a nice addition here at Fort Randall."

Her father's mustache twitched as he digested her idea. "It's an intriguing idea, Miriam, and I can see Miss Samuels' hand in this. It seems more appealing to me than those formal little visits your mother and I pay to the enlisted men and their families every year. But we are still living on a military post. Customs and rules pervade everything here."

"Would this be a custom or a rule?" she queried, well aware of the answer.

He laughed, and Miriam saw a twinkle in his eyes. "Ah, Miss Samuels again if I'm not mistaken. A good point."

"Are you saying, then, that there is nothing in the regulations governing Christmas parties?"

"You'd be opening Pandora's Box."

"But there are no regulations?" she persisted.

"No, Miriam, no regulations. But defying the convention of her special little ritual would be throwing it in your mother's face. She does not deal well with that sort of action."

"Would it require her approval?"

"Her approval would make life easier."

"We wouldn't want to lag behind Fort Lincoln, would we?" she said, knowing that this point would be the convincing element if her mother protested.

"And let those ladies best your mother?" He smiled, a momentary fellow conspirator, then sobered. "Would this be the end of your reforms? There wouldn't be a hidden agenda here, would there? No Women's Assistance League lurking in the background? No washing clothes?"

Miriam shook her head. "No, that idea is dead. I wouldn't mind being able to converse with Carrie Rupert again, though."

"I wondered if that was coming. Eulalie filled me in on what really happened when Frances fell through the ice. It seems Robert and the officer in charge left quite a bit out of the official record. I guess there's not much I can do in the way of rewarding either of you, except to relax the ban. Just be discreet. You may chat with her when you take laundry over. No lengthy visits, though, and no more washing clothes."

"Yes, sir."

"I'll issue a directive about the party this afternoon," he stated, shuffling papers on his desk.

"Thank you." She struggled to hold her smile, then stood and turned toward the office door.

"Miriam?" He paused, waiting until she turned and he caught her eye. "I'm also authorizing a promotion for Private Deakins for his role in Frances's rescue. But I want it understood that you disobeyed orders in going to him instead of to Lieutenant Wood. Something tells me there's more to this than meets the eye. Even with the promotion, he's still just an enlisted man. There are regulations in this matter. Stay away from him."

She didn't answer, avoiding a lie, and walked out the door. She had no intention of staying away from Jake. She just hoped she wouldn't get caught until after her father had the chance to know him as more than just a soldier.

CHAPTER EIGHTEEN

Miriam emerged from her bedroom with the light of dawn, ready to explain the benefits of the all-post party to her mother. Having Mother's support wasn't necessary, but it would make things easier.

She found her mother pacing back and forth on the Brussels carpet of the parlor, her eyes hostile. She'd worked herself into a tizzy. Her plump face was red as a tomato and her fists were balled. The she-bear looked ready for a fight.

"Good morning, Mother."

"No, Miriam, it is not a good morning. My head is ready to explode. Your father informed me he lifted the ban on your interaction with that laundress."

Miriam held her voice steady. "Mother, she helped save Franny's life."

"She's still nothing but a laundress, and I highly resent you involving your father in this matter."

"He is the commanding officer, Mother."

Harriet's nostrils flared. "Don't be impertinent with me, Miriam. And that fool party idea of Eulalie Samuels, you had a hand in that, too, didn't you?"

Miriam wanted to groan. She wondered if her father had approached the subject from the right angle. "It's in vogue," she said, hoping the argument would catch her mother's attention. "They're doing it at Fort Lincoln."

"I don't care where they're doing it. It's abominable," Mother shouted.

Miriam raised her eyebrows. "Abominable? Don't you think that's a little melodramatic?"

"Miriam, you have overstepped your bounds." Her mother stopped pacing and glared. "You disobeyed both your father and me while we were gone, nearly got your sister killed because of your inability to supervise her, insulted Robert, then finagled this sordid mixed party."

The words stung. She hadn't expected Franny to do anything more than make a quick trip next door. She'd been fighting her guilt over Franny's accident for days, trying to take stock in Jake's assurances that it wasn't her fault.

Miriam drew a deep breath and reminded herself that her mother's words were only a weapon, meant to hurt. For over three months, her mother had used the same ploy, flinging one sharp insult after another. Miriam was weary of the game, weary of surrender, and weary of Mother's blustering and self-righteous indignation. What a pity, to be so self-centered that the mere thought of attending a party with the so-called lower classes was the source of such an intense, such a ludicrous, re-action. Was her mother so insecure with her own position that she felt threatened by those who weren't intimidated by her?

She glared straight back at Harriet. "Oh, for heaven's sake, stop trying to impose your narrow opinions on me. I'm sick of being told what I can and can't do. I don't intend to settle for that nonsense anymore."

Mother gasped. "No, Miriam, quite the contrary. It is I who won't be settling for this anymore." With catlike suddenness, she reached out and grasped the front of Miriam's dress. She pulled at the fabric, twisting, until it tightened. "You'll be sorry you did this. You have no idea what's about to happen to you," she screamed, her temples pulsing.

A flash of fear traveled through Miriam and settled into resentment. *I am not going to let her intimidate me.* She grabbed her mother's bodice and jerked her forward. "You let go of me now, or we'll see who's going to be sorry."

Harriet paled. Miriam watched emotions play across her face: shock and confusion. She let go of Miriam's dress, turned on her heels and strode through the dining room and out the kitchen door, slamming it behind her.

Miriam plopped onto a side chair.

She doesn't scare me anymore.

The realization startled her in its intensity. Her mother did not control her life. It no longer mattered what Mother thought or what she threatened.

Miriam felt relief wash over her. Three months of tiptoeing around her mother ceased to be important. Lord, why had it taken her so long to see the light?

Her mother was nothing but a stone in her path, to be stepped over or around or kicked out of the way. Let her throw a fuss if she wanted, as long as she didn't take it out on Franny.

Eulalie's counsel that efforts be concentrated on her father had proven wise thus far. It really didn't matter how sorry Mother said she'd be if she had her father's approval. Or at least his refusal to interfere. Miriam needed to quit worrying about her mother's empty threats and forge a closer relationship with her father.

And it was also time Robert knew she was in control of their situation. She didn't want to trigger another explosion from him but she knew she couldn't let him go on believing there was any future for them. It would be best to quietly and discreetly let him know she would never marry him.

Miriam pulled a page of stationary from the desk drawer and gathered a pen and bottle of ink. It was time to write the letter to Robert, she told herself, and pushed at the nibbling sense of unease that wouldn't quite go away.

Robert crumpled Miriam's note into a crisp wad and threw it against the wall. "Goddammit," he cursed into the silent evening air of his quarters.

First she pulled that stunt that night of the blizzard, seeking out that damn private instead of him. Then she had the gall to defy him. And now, the letter. After five days of this shit, he'd had enough.

If she thought she could break off their betrothal this easily, she had another thought coming. No one ruined his career. No one.

Stomping across the room, he scooped up the note and stuffed it into his pocket.

He did not intend to let this happen and it was about time Miriam understood who was in control.

Harriet crunched across the snow toward Robert's quarters. She didn't like being summoned by anyone. Still, if Miriam had committed another act of defiance, she'd rather hear about it directly than through the grapevine. She didn't need any more bad news. Lord, her head ached.

Arriving at his house, she pulled her laudanum bottle from her pocket and swallowed another swig of the painkiller, smoothed her skirts, and rapped on the door. He opened it immediately. She glanced in and noticed the spark missing from his dark eyes.

Harriet's heart plummeted. By the look on his face, Miriam had been up to something here, too. The little rebel was about to ruin everything. Harriet needed Robert and his ambition as much as she needed to avoid a public scandal. If Miriam had insulted Robert, she'd have to send her back East before word leaked out.

Robert held the door as she stepped in, closing it behind her. Harriet collected herself and turned to him. She'd take charge and tell him straight up that their problems were solved.

"I've decided that Miriam has embarrassed us all enough," she announced. "I'll be sending her to live with my sister in Albany as soon as arrangements can be made."

Robert's jaw dropped and he looked at a loss for words.

Harriet's mind scrambled. She could have sworn Miriam had been giving Robert problems. Had she misread the situation?

Recovering, he motioned for Harriet to sit. His furniture was meager. She chose one of a mismatched pair of kitchen chairs and perched on it. What in heaven's name was going on?

"I do hope that decision isn't set in stone, ma'am."

Harriet peered at him. "Gracious, Mr. Wood, with the problems she's been causing, I shouldn't have thought that you would want her to remain and harm our reputations."

Robert sat in the other chair and reached for her hands. "May I be frank with you, Harriet? May I call you Harriet?"

Harriet's heart pattered. "Why, of course, Robert," she stated and raised her eyebrows in what she hoped was delicate question.

Robert smiled. "I won't argue that Miriam is headstrong and requires a firm hand. I had hoped that, given a little room for her spirited nature to stretch, she might settle down on her own. You must know that I've grown quite fond of Miriam." He paused and offered another wry smile. "I am even more convinced it is time to ask for her hand in marriage."

Harriet wished she had a fan to flutter. Instead, she pulled her hands from Robert's grasp and brought them to her face. "Oh, my goodness. With all she's done? Spending time with those enlisted people and treating you with such disrespect when Frances got away from her? I naturally thought the marriage wasn't to be."

He nodded. "I've tried not to be too harsh on her, Harriet. She's young. We've really known each other for such a short time, and I wanted to wait until a more proper time to approach the major." He turned back, his face filled with desperation. "I no longer feel we can afford to wait. Do you think your husband would give his consent?"

Harriet's heart jumped. He still wanted the little troublemaker. "Why, Robert, I don't see any reason why he wouldn't. With a little nudge from me, I've no doubt he'd approve." He'd approve if she had to beg.

"I'm sure once the engagement is official, Miriam will have so much to do with wedding plans that she won't have time to get into trouble." His words were filled with the hint of threat.

"Of course, she won't," Harriet assured him. "Busy hands, you know. If she can't manage to control herself, she can always be sent East until the wedding."

At Robert's dour expression, she realized it wasn't the solution he favored. Goodness, he wanted Miriam more than she had thought. It didn't matter much to her. Let him deal with her. She smiled at him and went on. "I'm certain that, given the circumstances, we could fill her time by shortening the engagement period somewhat and moving the wedding date forward. We don't *always* have to stand on convention, you know."

Robert grinned and bent to clasp her hands again. "That would be wonderful, just wonderful. You're such a gracious and supportive woman. I think, as her fiancé, I might have a little more control over her than I'm able to exert right now. As a matter of fact, I'm sure of it." His grin softened to a benevolent smile, and he patted her hand before straightening. "Oh, and Harriet, I'd like for this to be our little secret, if possible. I'd like to surprise Miriam with the betrothal pin."

"How romantic of you. I'm sure she'll be stunned."

"I'm sure she will be." He paused. "I'm planning to give the pin to her at that little all-post Christmas party she has planned."

Jake tossed the worthless spade onto the frozen ground and reached for a pick.

Damn you, Wood.

He'd been assigned to nothing but hard-labor details every day for a solid week. Clearing trees around the post trader's complex, stocking the icehouse, chopping firewood for the guardhouse, and now, digging latrines. It hadn't stopped since Wood took over the duty roster a few days after the blizzard.

It didn't take a fancy education to figure out what was going on. Wood meant to keep him away from the parade ground, away from Suds Row, and away from Miriam.

He swung the pick in a wide arc, striking at the hard ground. The force of the contact jolted through his body. Once. Twice. Again.

He hadn't talked to Miriam since the night of the accident, when Robert had ushered him and Carrie out of the major's house like a couple of bad pennies. Since they'd given voice to what they were feeling and admitted they were in love with each other.

He swung the pick again and absorbed the shock of its strike, letting the memory ripple through him. Miriam, coming to him first. Only him. And him, standing in the bitter, blowing snow, knowing her words even before she said them. The tears in her eyes, just before he told her he loved her, telling him without words that she felt love for him, too. He'd never known anything with more certainty in his entire life.

And he hadn't a doubt that Robert had figured it out by now, too.

Why else would he have him out here in the miserable cold chopping away at the frozen ground in the middle of December?

It sure as shootin' didn't have anything to do with needing new latrines.

Damn it, he needed to talk to Miriam. He had more than two full years left before his hitch was up. There wasn't a snowball's chance in hell they'd keep things from getting out of hand before then. He wanted to hold her, to whisper sweet nothings in her ear, to tell her again and again that he loved her. He wanted to see that love shining in those big green eyes as he made love to her.

He slammed the pick into the ground and cursed the hardness straining against the buttons of his trousers. No way was he gonna keep swinging that pickax now.

He didn't see Major Longstreet granting a special dispensation for his daughter to marry a private. That left them over two years to wait. Two years of barely restrained passion calling out from Miriam's hooded eyes. Just how long would it take for someone to see those hungry eyes? How long before someone overheard their whispered pledges of love? How long before one of them slipped up and announced their feelings to the world?

A week of backbreaking labor had given him all the time in the world to digest his feelings. Much as he'd tried to avoid admitting it, he was in love. Deeply. And he intended to spend the rest of his life showing Miriam as much.

He wanted her in his arms, naked and wild, like he knew she'd be. It would happen sooner, much sooner, than later. And if they got caught, Harriet Longstreet would see to it that he was court-martialed. He'd rot in the guardhouse, waiting to be shot, while that jackass Wood claimed her.

He pulled a folded note from his pocket and opened it. Miriam's careful script filled the paper.

Dearest Jake:

We've an ally in Eulalie Samuels. She will cover for us during the all-post party so that we may steal some time to discuss our situation. I ache to be with you again.

Love, Miriam

She ached, just like he had ached, every day since they were last together, like he ached now.

No, they definitely wouldn't last a couple of years.

Carrie had tried to keep him filled in on the party plans, sending word through Eddie. He supposed it was the best they could do. He'd thought long and hard about leaving the barracks in the middle of the night and meeting Miriam somewhere. But it was December, cold as hell, and he doubted they'd survive any such meeting without being caught.

He didn't relish the thought of trying to discuss their future in a crowd, but it was better than nothing. At least they'd be able to talk. He'd have to trust that Miss Samuels truly was on their side. Maybe they could snatch a few moments to themselves. Proposing marriage in the middle of a party wasn't what he'd envisioned, but he'd be damned if he was going to wait any longer.

The way he saw it, there were two things they needed to get around. One of them hinged on Miriam. Did she love him enough to endure the disgrace that marrying below her class would bring, enough to accept the physical changes that would come with it? Somehow, he sensed she did, and he hoped like hell she was ready to take that step. It was a choice she'd have to make herself.

The other obstacle was finding a way around the damned regulations. Given the probable lack of special dispensation, it was either wait or seek a discharge. Waiting was not an option they could afford to risk. An honorable discharge would not be forthcoming. The only option left went against every fiber of his being. He'd spent his life building his honor, enduring abuse from superiors to protect it.

If he played his cards right, committed the right act, he'd net a quick trial, a couple of months in the guardhouse, a beating and a dishonorable discharge. Two or three months and he'd be a civilian. Dirt poor, unemployed, and beat up good.

All he had to do was assault an officer. He'd just have to make sure it was in self-defense and in front of plenty of witnesses.

He figured Robert Wood was about one step from taking a swing at him, anyway.

Chapter Nineteen

"You do realize the other women think we're both a little tetched, don't you?" Eulalie asked, interrupting Miriam's thoughts. She tipped her head in the direction of the several richly clad officers' wives who had just entered the festive mess hall. "They look like carefully arranged gifts, just daring someone to disturb their fancy wrappings."

"I imagine they've thought us odd for a while now," Miriam replied. "I hope the party goes well enough to prove we're not. I'm a nervous Nellie."

Eulalie patted her arm and offered one of her rare smiles. "You just leave all the hostess worries to me. Spend your time tonight letting Jake and your father get acquainted, like we planned, and some time with Jake, discussing your future."

"Have you seen him come in yet? He's been assigned to about every work detail imaginable, according to Carrie, and I haven't even caught a glimpse of him let alone had a chance to talk." She glanced around the room, spying a group of stiff, uncomfortable soldiers standing under a string of old Christmas cards hung on twine. Jake was not among them.

"Robert's doing, I suspect," Eulalie noted. "The sooner he's done being in charge of the duty roster, the better. And stop worrying about everybody else. They'll forget all about their differences just as soon as the music gets going and the cider gets spiked."

Eulalie was right. She needed to clear her mind of distractions and focus on her time with Jake. They had a lot to discuss.

Across the room, officers mingled at the refreshment table, drawn by the aroma of baked turkey and fresh pumpkin pie. They eyed the canned oysters contributed by their families and laughed with one another.

A chill gust swept through the room as a trio of laundresses and a crowd of children entered, dressed in their finest worn dresses. A few of the women sported used gowns handed down by the more progressive women of the post. Miriam located Carrie and waved. Carrie removed her wraps and turned over a pail of popcorn to the youngsters. From her bag, she pulled needles and thread, gave it to the children and watched them scamper off to make popcorn strings. Nearing Miriam and Eulalie, she grinned.

"That ought to keep them young'uns busy for a spell. Gracious sakes, but it smells good in here. Fruitcakes and pine boughs sure do make it Christmas, don't they?"

Miriam hugged her friend, then pulled back. "Carrie, I want you to meet Eulalie Samuels. Eulalie, my good friend Carrie Rupert."

Eulalie extended her hand, ignoring the differences in their stations. "I feel as if I know you already, Miriam's told me so much about you."

"I reckon I heard a great deal 'bout you, too." Carrie responded. "Thanks for offerin' to help when I was feelin' poorly."

"It was something every one of us should have done. Let's go check on the musicians, shall we? I think Miriam was going to make sure everyone feels welcome." Eulalie winked at Miriam and linked her arm with Carrie's. "Seems to me I just spotted a gentleman who looks a little lost."

The two women headed off, chatting, as Miriam glanced at the door. Jake stood just inside the room, scanning the crowd.

His blue dress uniform was molded across his broad chest, testimony of the strength and security that was a part of him. Miriam shivered as she recalled his powerful arms and the gentleness she'd found within them. She lifted her gaze to his face. He'd trimmed his tawny beard and sported a fresh haircut. His eyes met hers and he smiled.

She felt the corners of her lips lift in response and savored her anticipation as he moved toward her. Gone was the scruffy soldier. In his place was a calm, professional gentleman who couldn't help but impress anyone. She was anxious for him to meet her father.

He stopped as he reached her and she sensed his desire to grasp her hands, to pull her tight. His blue eyes were hot and intense, hungry.

"You look beautiful, Miri," he said, his voice quiet and husky.

Miriam smoothed her hands across her simple emerald damask skirt. Lord, she'd missed him. Her chest rose with a slow intake of breath and her mouth parted.

"I've been waitin' two weeks for the chance to be with you, to talk to you, and I stand here like a blubbering idiot who can't figure out what to say next."

She smiled. "Me, too."

He nodded toward an empty corner behind the Christmas tree, and they moved away from the crowd. "I've missed you. Old Robert couldn't have picked a worse time to come knockin' on your door. Franny's all right?"

"Her toes hurt for a few days and she had a limp that first week but, yes, she's fine. I, on the other hand, have been utterly miserable." She resisted the urge to take his hand. "We've got a lot to talk about."

"That we do."

"I've slipped the mitten to Robert."

"Ah, a rejected proposal would explain the work details I've been getting. If he's put two and two together, and it appears he has, it's only a matter of time before he ups the ante."

"Jake, it doesn't matter to me that you're an enlisted man. I told you how I felt the night we rescued Franny. I haven't changed my mind."

He glanced around the room then dropped his voice. "It doesn't leave us many choices, Miri. I love you. I want to be a part of your future. Somehow, I don't see your parents giving their consent to you marrying me, though."

The words slid through her like warm honey. She wanted nothing more. "Why, Jake Deakins, are you proposing?"

"Miriam, I'd marry you tomorrow if it were possible. But there are regulations against enlisted men marrying unless given special permission by their commanding officer. Your father might do that if it was a woman of my own class, but he isn't going to let me marry you."

Miriam remembered her discussion with her father on the day he had given his approval to the party. *Stay away from Deakins.* Jake was right. Her father would not be giving his sanction to the marriage; not for a while, at least.

"Then we wait."

"I've got two years left in my hitch. There ain't no way I'm gonna last two years without getting myself court-martialed for inappropriate advances. Look across the room. They're watching us already." Miriam's gaze followed his. He was right. Several puffed-up officers' wives stood in a clump, their attention drawn to what might be happening behind the Christmas tree.

"Between Wood and your mother, I'd be facing stockade time in addition to the two years, and maybe even some 'accident' or other. I figure if I'm gonna get court-martialed, I'd rather work it so I can come out on top."

"Court-martialed?" Miriam felt her voice rise. "What in

heaven's name are you talking about?" she whispered.

"I'd wager Robert gets mad enough tonight that he loses his temper. They don't punish a soldier too much for self-defense. The Board of Officers might even issue a discharge just to keep a fellow officer from doing it again."

"A discharge? Oh, Jake, not a bobtail." She felt her face drain and touched his sleeve.

"It won't matter," he answered.

"Yes, it will. It'll matter when you have to write to Becca to tell her you don't have the money for the rest of her education. It'll matter when you think about giving up the chance at teaching duties at the post school. It'll matter when you talk to our children about being a soldier and every time you look in the mirror. And when you look at me."

"Not so much as you think it will."

"It will if you provoke him, Jake, because you'll always know it wasn't self-defense and that it was the wrong way out of this. *I'll* know. And you'll know I know."

"We can't hide this, Miriam, and you know it. I love you and I want to hold you and tell you that every second of the day. But we can't even spend an innocent five minutes in the corner of the room without catching everyone's attention." He nodded toward the refreshment table where Mrs. Stanton stood, peering at them.

Miriam knew he was right. Except for Jake's plan, their only hope lay in her father. "Let's not fold our hand until we see what Father's holding. I don't think you and he spoke once while you were our striker. Give him a chance to get to know you. Eulalie seems to think he might come around."

"And this Eulalie knows what she's talking about?"

"She's known Father for years, since before he married Mother. I trust her opinion."

"All right, Miri. I'll meet your father and we'll try things that way. But if Robert does swing, I'm not going to let it pass."

"Just don't provoke it. Come, the band's warming up and we need to get out from behind this tree."

"All right, I won't start anything."

They wandered back to a cluster of couples. The group of men in the corner began to play a lively tune on their instruments. Miriam picked out the sounds of harmonica, banjo, accordion, and fiddle. The tune was unfamiliar to her but she found her foot tapping nonetheless.

"You polka?" Jake asked, glancing down at her tapping foot.

"A few times, yes, but the music wasn't nearly so lively. I'm more used to waltzes and quadrilles." She watched as couples began to circle around the floor, their heels flying. "Good heavens, I've never seen the polka done like that."

"Sounds to me like you're used to the slow polka. This'll get your heart thumpin' fast. Watch close."

Miriam stood in awe of the frenzied dancing. When a private by the name of Jenkins arrived at her elbow requesting a dance, she gulped.

"Come on, Miss Longstreet, I'll learn ya how." He smiled and she noted he was missing two teeth. But he was standing there, hat in hand, clearly not prepared to take no for an answer.

Jake nodded, smiling. "Go ahead, Miss Longstreet, give it a try."

"Are you a good teacher, Private Jenkins? I shall require a great deal of instruction."

"Then let's git to it, miss." He flashed that toothless grin again and swept her into the circle. They stood for a brief moment while dancers kicked their way around the couple. "It's a count o' three. Slow, quick-quick, an' you gotta pick up yer feet high on those quick-quicks. Ready, now? Let's git goin' afore we git runned over."

They moved into the whirling circle and Miriam wondered

just when the slow step was. Jenkins tolerated being stepped on and the repeat starts with no adverse comment. At the edge of the circle, Jake stood, a smirk on his face, watching them.

"Yer on yer way, Miss Longstreet," Private Jenkins said as the dance came to an end and he handed her off to a captain. Before the set had ended, Miriam had danced with three different partners and was beginning to get the hang of it. Breathless, she excused herself and headed to the refreshment table.

Across the room, Eulalie had Jake in tow, guiding him to Miriam's father. Miriam smiled. It was better that Eulalie introduced him, anyway. She watched Jake move with grace, his muscles bulging beneath the blue wool of his jacket.

A warmth spread through her that had nothing to do with the spent energy of dancing. She had no doubt that her father would like Jake. Jake possessed every quality she'd ever heard her father praise. She frowned, wishing she knew her father better. During her childhood, his rising military career had kept him busy. Since her arrival at Fort Randall, he'd seldom spent an evening at home. Still, she'd seen his fairness in the way he dealt with his men and sensed an open-mindedness about him that he tried to hide. Eulalie had said as much herself.

Taking a sip of lemonade, she made a sour face at the tart concoction of water and citric acid crystals and reached for a piece of homemade candy to cover the taste. She'd stick with apple cider for the rest of the evening, even if it was spiked. She dipped out a cup of the steaming liquid and listened to the children's undeveloped voices singing carols in competition with the band. Franny skipped over to her, still limping, and reached a sticky hand into her palm. Miriam hugged her and tweaked the end of the peppermint candy cane she was sucking on.

"Merry Christmas, Franny."

"Merry Christmas to you, too, Miriam. Isn't this fun? This is lots better'n what we usually do. Christmas is just the bestest time of the year." Franny grinned and headed back to the group of children. Their singing continued, until Miriam hummed along, one carol blending into another.

"Excuse me, Miss Longstreet, may I have this dance?" she turned at the sound of Jake's voice and smiled.

"You met Father?"

"And Eulalie." He held out his hand as the band shifted into a waltz.

"Well?" she asked, moving into his arms.

"You were right. There's something about her that makes you feel confident about everything. Your father was pleasant, not the usual patronizing most officers dish out."

He glided her among the other dancers, keeping a proper distance between them. His arms, strong as they were, held her delicately, even as she ached for him to crush her against him. She could feel the beat of her heart, racing, as she fought to maintain a polite facade. Jake's chest rose and fell with ragged breaths.

The music stopped, forcing them to pull apart. They stood, their eyes hungrily seeking each other until Jake shifted his attention to the edge of the room.

"Miri," he said, and nodded to the group at the refreshment table. Miriam watched her mother slam a tin cup of cider down and waver slightly as she moved away from the table.

" 'Scuse me, men, I am looking for Private Deakins," she announced with a slur. *Good God, she's drunk.* Miriam reached for Jake's hand, intent on pulling him away from the dance floor and out of Mother's line of sight. From the corner of her eye, she noticed Robert, sizing up the action, a sneer on his face.

Jake dropped her hand and veered away. He headed for a group of enlisted men and slipped among them. Understanding his strategy, Miriam moved toward Eulalie, putting distance between her and Jake.

Eulalie set her cup of cider on the table and offered a quick hug. "Your father's on his way."

Mother tottered across the room. "Where'd he go? He's not going to hoodwink me. No siree. Oughtta keep his paws where they belong, on the whores over to the hog ranch. He's not gonna ruin me. She's goin' East so fast that—"

"That's quite enough, Harriet," Tom intercepted his wife and steered her toward the door. "Too much cider seems to cause you delusions. A simple dance never hurt anyone. It's time you were at home."

Miriam's glance shifted to Jake as her father guided her mother out of the building and into the darkness. Jake's face was etched with worry and displeasure, his attention focused on Robert Wood.

She eyed Robert. He looked pleased as punch, leaning against the wall with a grin plastered across his face.

CHAPTER TWENTY

"It doesn't take much to figure out what prompted that little outburst from your mother, does it?" Eulalie asked.

"Not with Robert standing there like a Cheshire cat. How much damage do you think she did?"

"Some, but I think your father countered most of it."

"There's no way Jake and I can spend any more time together tonight, though. Not without lending credence to her comments. Do you really think she'll send me East? Oh, Eulalie, she can't."

Eulalie was unusually quiet. As Miriam stood in the room's deepening silence, Mother's threat settled about her. She was suddenly very afraid that she had underestimated her mother by dismissing her threats as idle. What if Mother sent her away and she and Jake never even got a chance to follow their love?

Jake still stood across the room. His body had relaxed, but his eyes were smoldering, revealing his anger. When Miriam glanced back at Eulalie, she saw her friend also studying Jake. She turned to face Miriam, gulped down the last of her cider, and clasped both of her hands.

"Miriam," she said, "I believe you and I are having the same disturbing thoughts. A life of regrets is a sorry life indeed. I've lived one for many years. Seize what joy you can before it escapes you." Eulalie's eyes misted and her voice wavered.

Miriam stared at her friend. Eulalie was tipsy, but clearly not drunk. "But—"

"Your parents won't be back. Between Carrie and myself, Franny will be well tended. Take the time to go with Jake so you may avoid the same regrets. I'll explain things to Carrie, if she hasn't figured them out herself. If anyone else inquires, I'll say you went to help with your mother. I'll keep my brother dancing until midnight." She pressed a tarnished silver key into Miriam's palm and winked at her. "Back door. I'll tell Jake where to find you."

Miriam closed the kitchen door of Eulalie's quarters and debated whether or not she dared light a lantern. As her eyes adjusted to the darkness, she made out the sturdy wooden furnishings and the large iron cookstove. The stove was still warm from the evening meal.

She opened the heavy door and added a log to the coals. It caught, lending a small soft glow to the room. If she left the door open, it would be light enough. She dropped her winter shawl over the back of a wooden chair and stood near the growing heat of the flames.

A quick knock echoed through the silence of the night air and she jumped.

Her heart pounded as the door opened. Jake slipped into the room, coatless and shivering. He closed the door and slid its iron bolt into the lock, then smiled at her wryly.

"Guess who?" he whispered.

She melted into his open arms and he enfolded her. Within Jake's powerful embrace, she basked in the security she felt, letting the sureness of it fill her. This, then, was where she belonged. The thought came at her, strong and sure and overwhelming. It was no longer a sense of Robert being wrong for her but a sureness of Jake being right.

Eulalie's counsel, with all its implications, echoed through her mind. *Seize what joy you can before it escapes you.* This time was a gift, made for far more than words. If all she and Jake had for the next two years were stolen moments, those moments should be fully theirs. She'd play by whatever rules she had to when they were in public to keep Jake from a court-martial but she'd be damned if she'd sacrifice their limited time alone. *Seize what joy you can.*

He pulled her flush against him and brought his head down. His lips brushed hers. Once. Twice. Then he pulled back, peering into her eyes, into her soul. It was enough for her to know, as if they were one, that his thoughts had taken the same path.

"Miri. God, girl, we shouldn't be here. We shouldn't—"

"Shh. This is too much a part of us to try to deny it with 'shouldn'ts.' We already did that. Please, Jake, if this is all we get a chance to have, we've got to make it ours. I can't not be a part of you."

"This isn't how I wanted it to be for you. You should be my wife, and I should be making love to you in some fancy hotel or in our own bed. Hell, we're in someone else's house. I'm not sure Eulalie was offering her bed when she sent us over here."

"Jake, hush. We don't need her bed. After all, we've experienced some wonderful things in kitchens so far. I don't care where we find ourselves, only that we're together."

"I love you, Miri."

"Then show me. Love me." She lifted her mouth to meet his with slow deliberation, pulling his head forward, opening her lips to his. Their tongues met and greeted each other as if for the first time. He tasted of apple cider and peppermint sticks. She sensed a gentleness about him, almost tentative, and knew he was giving her the choice, the chance to change her mind.

He stroked her cheek with calloused fingers before grasping her face in the palms of his hands and pulling her to him. His thumbs rubbed against her cheekbones even as his fingers worked their way into her hair. The tentativeness gave way and he kissed her, delving into her mouth.

She opened herself to him and encircled his head with her hands. The scent of bay rum and evergreen lingered in his blond hair and drifted about him as she wove her fingers through its soft length. She pulled him closer and felt the groan that began in the back of his throat. It echoed through her mouth, resounding inside her head, and she mewed in response.

He raised his mouth from hers and strewed tender kisses across her cheek and down her neck. She tipped her head back, arching her throat to him, and his mouth became hot against her, hungry and demanding. His hands slid from her hair, fingers brushing against the silk of her dress. They drifted across her shoulders, over her bodice. Her heart pounded under his searching fingers, and her nipples hardened against his thumbs.

Lifting his head, he pulled from her grasp and stood, watching her. Even in the dim light, she could see the intensity of his smoldering eyes. His chest rose and fell, rose and fell, a mirror of her own.

"Will you marry me?" he asked. "No matter where this takes us, will you marry me?"

"From this day forward."

"Till death do us part?"

"Till death do us part."

He moved his large hands to the tiny pearl buttons that ran down her dress and pushed them open, one by one, stopping to caress her breasts. He dropped single hot kisses against her eager mouth, then returned to the buttons.

Her hands moved to his chest and played across its wide expanse. She slid the five shiny brass buttons open and pushed the front of his blue military blouse back to his shoulders. He pulled away and slipped it off, then shed the gray army-issue undershirt.

The soft glow of the fire highlighted his golden-blond chest hairs. Miriam traced the edge of a single fingernail against his skin, outlining the muscles of his chest, winding her way through the soft hair at its center. Beneath her finger, his hot skin was like brushed velvet. She moved inch by inch, savoring his ripples of reaction at her touch. She heard his intake of breath as her fingers brushed against his nipples and sensed it surprised him as much as it did her.

He pushed her bodice open and cupped her breasts in his hands, stroking them through the thin fabric of her chemise. He bent, his fiery mouth sucking first at one, then the other. She felt her head tip back, a small sound of pleasure forming in the back of her throat.

His hand reached down and slid over the silk of her skirt until she felt it rest against her, inflaming her. She needed to feel his touch against her bare skin.

Stepping back, she deftly unfastened her cuffs, reached to slip open the back of her skirt and wriggled out of her bodice. With Jake watching, the bodice slid down, pulling the skirt along, until both landed in a puddle of green silk around her feet. One by one, she opened the eyehooks that held her corset closed, then dropped it to the floor. She stood facing him, watching him, then untied the satin ribbon at the top of her chemise and pulled the garment open.

"Miri," he groaned. Cupping a bare breast in each hand, he stroked her skin with small whorls. He eased the chemise from her shoulders until it, too, dropped to the floor. He lowered his head to her skin, and his mouth trailed kisses where his hands had lingered only moments before. Across her breast, around her nipple, she felt his sizzling breath and shivered as his tongue marked her.

The ache was intense, deep and throbbing and maddening all at once. His tongue flicked against her until she felt she would explode. Small whimpers came unbidden from her throat. She felt herself pushing, writhing, wanting more of him.

She traced his chest hairs downward until they merged in the mass that disappeared beneath his trousers. She drew her hands under his rib cage, still feeling the heavy beat of his heart. His strong hand captured hers, pulling it downward, until it was against him.

"Feel what you do to me."

Under her hand, his body throbbed, hard and erect. He groaned, a low, deep, tortured surrender. She molded her hand to his shape and felt him fill her grasp. She moved against him, stroking him through the fabric, long and hard. His mouth left her breasts, his throat arched, his head tipped back. And she knew the ache was his, too.

He pulled back, away from her hand, and cupped her chin with his hand. She looked up, into his eyes, and read the question he hadn't yet spoken.

"Yes, Jake. Now. Now and forever."

"You're sure? Miri, I wanted it to be perfect."

"It doesn't matter where, Jake. We're perfect together."

He stepped back, kneeling to spread their garments, then placed her heavy winter shawl atop the pile. As he turned back to her, his eyes were filled with apology.

He pushed her into a chair and knelt before her. Taking her foot onto his thigh, he pulled at the laces of her shoe and slid it from her foot. Inch by inch, he rolled her stocking downward, trailing sultry kisses along her inner thigh, behind her knee, down the back of her leg. He reached for her other foot and she rested her bare toes on his lap, feeling his hardness. Following her instincts, she pushed against him and watched the expressions float across his face before he bent his head to trail kisses down her other leg.

Jake stood and kicked off his own shoes, then unhooked the buttons at his waist. Still sitting before him, she watched him slide the trousers away from his body and down his hips. Hard and turgid, he stood, waiting for her. Her gaze lingered on his naked body and she smiled. Rising to meet him, she lifted her hands to his neck.

He bent to kiss her, his mouth searching and hungry. She pressed against his bare skin, feeling him against her stomach. She reached her hand between them and grasped him, discovering the unexpected velvety softness of his taut skin. Softness over hard. Pulsating stiffness. Hot and sensitive to her touch.

He groaned and touched her between her legs. The touch flashed through her and she shuddered in pleasure. He stroked her. Again. And again. Until she let go of him and braced her hands against his chest, unable to keep her balance. Again. And again. Until she heard herself cry out and collapse.

Lifting her in his powerful arms, he carried her to their makeshift pallet and laid her amid its softness. She let herself sink back, her breath hot and labored, and smiled at him.

"Like that?" he asked between the kisses he trailed across her face, her neck, her breasts.

"Mmmm," she murmured. "Mother never told me about that."

He laughed, deep and low. "I don't think your mother *knows* about that."

His fingers moved, unfolding her, until he touched her inside. She began to move with him, matching his rhythm, trusting him to teach her what to do. His mouth was upon her, impassioned kisses. Deep, intense. His tongue wound its way to her breasts, teasing. And his hand, stroking until she felt she couldn't endure it any longer.

"Jake, please . . . ," she begged, knowing.

"I love you, Miri," he told her as he moved his hand away. He entered her slowly, steadily, watching her face, urging the demand that sprang up inside of her. She moved with him, feeling a brief dull pain eclipsed by the ecstasy of his dancing strokes. He moved until pleasure swallowed her. She felt her body contract, then erupt. Her own voice, distantly crying out, mingled with Jake's ragged gasp as he exploded into her.

They lay together, tangled and breathless, and she let the wonder of it settle about her. She felt full, satisfied, content just to bask in their completeness. A smile tugged at her mouth.

Jake smiled back.

He shifted, cradling her in his arms. She rested her head on his chest, secure.

"Soon as Wood gets done as duty officer, I'll request a clerk assignment in your father's office."

Miriam raised her head and caught his gaze. "Trying to put yourself in someone's good graces, are you?"

He grinned. "I'll give it a go. Less painful than getting beat up."

"Eulalie and I will work on softening him up." She snuggled against him. Silence surrounded them as they lay, sated, until the warmth in the air began to dim and she shivered.

"Cold?" he asked. "Fire's almost out. It's getting late. C'mon, let's get you home."

They dressed in silence, feeling the loss of private time already. The room had grown darker, the once-glowing log now in ashes. Jake closed the door of the stove and placed her warm woolen shawl about her shoulders.

He pulled her into his arms and kissed her. She recognized it was meant to sustain them, to hold them together until they could steal further time, and she responded to him, answering in kind. They stood, clinging to each other, until Jake broke away.

"Time to go, Miri."

She nodded, understanding all that was not said.

He opened the kitchen door and waited while she glanced

around the room. Everything was in order. She turned and met the chill, dark winter air. Jake closed the door behind them and tucked the key into her hand. "Tell Eulalie thank you."

The crunch of footfalls on the crusty snow broke through the silence. Jake pushed her back into the shadows of the building and stepped forward, shielding her from view. A figure emerged from the darkness.

"I see you two took me quite literally when I said midnight." Eulalie stepped forward, her face heavy and concerned, "but I'm glad you're both still here. Robert Wood has just made a very public announcement. He's told the entire company that your father has given his blessing to your marriage to him. They're toasting your betrothal now."

CHAPTER TWENTY-ONE

Jake turned, framed in the moonlight, and anger flashed across his face. "That low-down snake," he muttered. "I'll see him in hell first." He moved away from the shadows of the building, his hands curled into fists.

A knot of fear formed in the pit of Miriam's stomach. This, then, was what Robert had been grinning about. She should have known he wouldn't let her get away.

In the darkness, Eulalie shook her head.

Jake's boots crunched on the snow as he strode away from her, toward the mess hall.

Forcing herself out of the inertia of the moment, Miriam moved after him. This couldn't happen. Not now. Not when they had so much to lose.

She reached for his arm and felt the tenseness of his muscles. "Jake?" She asked. "What are you going to do?"

"Aw, hell, Miriam, I don't know." He stopped and exhaled a cloud of exasperation. His jaw clenched. "I told you I wouldn't hit him but damned if he doesn't deserve it."

"I'd punch him in the mouth myself if I thought it would do any good," she told him. "But it would be playing right into his hands. Can't you just see him waiting for you to march in and take a swing?"

"Miriam's right, Jake," Eulalie said, nearing them. "In fact, it might be better if you don't even go in. Things are liable to get out of hand if Robert catches sight of you. He's suspicious enough as it is."

In the moonlight, Jake's face filled with frustration. "So I'm supposed to hide behind Miriam's skirts now, am I?"

"Sweetheart, we need to stay calm. I think Eulalie has a point. Seeing us together will only add fuel to the fire." She paused, watching him struggle with his pride. "I've tried everything I could think of to settle this privately with Robert so he could save face, but he just won't let it lie. He's going to get a fight, all right, and a very public one at that. But it's not going to be with you."

He grasped her forearms, determined. "I'm not about to let you go marching in there by yourself."

"She won't be by herself." Eulalie stood, hands on her hips, her voice sharp. "I'll be there. Consider your actions, Jake. As long as you go home instead of following Miriam to the mess hall, any accusation Robert makes in there will be seen as the rambling insecurities of a man who's just been rejected in public. But let one person catch sight of you two arriving together and there will be no end to the rumors. You'll not only get charges brought against you, but you'll ruin Miriam's reputation as well. And all to no point because there won't *be* any future for you. Not together. Now go to your barracks and show Miriam that you trust her."

Jake's shoulders slumped.

"You two say your good nights. I'll be waiting for you at the mess hall, Miriam." Eulalie headed off toward the sounds of the band, leaving Miriam and Jake alone.

Jake pulled Miriam close. He rested his chin against her head and wove his fingers into her hair. "I'd rather shove my fist down Wood's throat than have him sling insults at you in front of all those folks." He pulled back, his blue eyes deep and serious. "You know that, don't you? It wouldn't matter if they did put me in the guardhouse."

Miriam stroked his face, knowing he would make the sacrifice, whatever the cost. "Yes, it would," she told him. "It would matter to me. Eulalie's right. Nobody will pay any attention to what he says unless you and I give them reason to. Let him rant and rave all he wants. He'll look the fool, not us." She glanced ahead. Eulalie had arrived at the door. People were already drifting away from the hall. Someone was bound to see them soon. They hadn't much time. Nodding at them, she pulled Jake into the shadow of the building.

"We should've figured out he wouldn't give up that easily," he whispered.

"Yes, we should have. But we didn't and that's that." She kissed him. "I don't want what we shared tonight to be ruined by regrets of any kind. I love you, Jake. Forever. Now go on home so I can get in there and set this straight before everyone clears out. It looks like people are leaving in droves."

He stole a quick look at the mess hall, then pulled Miriam tight. "God, Miri, I love you, too. I'll be there in a heartbeat, if you need me." His lips touched hers, a kiss of desperation, then he backed around the corner of the building and into the night. She stood, savoring the new dimension of their relationship, then drew in a deep, fortifying breath and stepped into the light, toward Eulalie and the others.

"Look, here's Miriam," one of them noted. "Poor dear." Tsking and clucking, they disappeared into the cold darkness, leaving Miriam and Eulalie alone.

"There's no sense even going in," Eulalie stated. "There's just the band left in there, putting their things away. Your father just made an announcement. A group of prospectors trespassed onto the Ponca Agency and there's been trouble. The first detachment leaves at dawn."

Robert stood in Tom Longstreet's office, waiting. It was three in the morning, he was tired as hell, and he felt sicker than a dog. The night had not gone well.

Kicking open a folding wooden chair, he plopped down. It'd had been amusing at first, Harriet making a fool out herself and Deakins at the same time. He'd only needed to make one well-placed comment about the private, and she'd almost taken care of his problem for him. Too bad the major had shown up.

The whole scene had been hilarious until Miriam disappeared, ruining his presentation of the betrothal pin. Robert slapped at a wrinkle in his dress pants. The best laid plans destroyed by a daughter's proper duty to her ailing mother. So much for Harriet being funny.

Delaying the announcement until New Year's wasn't what he'd intended, but he'd accepted it as a necessary inconvenience until he realized Deakins was missing, too.

Robert leaned back in the chair, tipping its front legs off the floor. He hadn't wanted to believe there was anything to Miriam and Deakins being gone at the same time. But if Miriam had truly gone home to take care of her mother, she wouldn't have left her kid sister there at the party. Harriet had her too well trained for that.

And Deakins. First he was there, squaring for a fight and some time in the guardhouse, and then, bang, he was gone. A man like Deakins didn't just back down like that. Not without a damned good reason.

"Shit." He clenched his teeth. *They'd been together.*

The chair teetered and Robert threw his weight forward. The impact of the front legs hitting the floor ricocheted through his body, churning the whiskey in his stomach until he could taste it, stale and rancid, working its way upward.

Damn.

He leaned forward, heaving great gulps of air, and willed the whiskey to stay put. Trying to drown his suspicions hadn't worked very well. Every drink had stirred things up more, and the rotgut whiskey that was being passed around had been an insult to both his palette and his system. He felt like he was going to be puking for days.

Goddamn it. How long had they been gone? He'd lost track of time after the first of the whiskey settled in. All he could remember was his anger when he realized the kid was still there and Miriam and Deakins were both missing. Long enough, he guessed.

"Ah, Robert," Major Longstreet's voice shattered his speculations.

"Major Longstreet, sir." Robert rose unsteadily to his feet, hoping Longstreet hadn't been standing there watching him, and saluted feebly. Longstreet was uncharacteristically disheveled, his face tired and clouded.

"At ease, Robert. Thanks for waiting. I was afraid things would come to this." Longstreet crossed the room and settled himself behind the desk. "Cigar?"

Robert swallowed hard. "No, thanks."

"Those miners have been making a mess of things for two years now. They're not even supposed to be entering the Black Hills. But they just keep on coming, crossing over agency lands to get there and stirring things up way out here."

Robert fought to keep his head clear enough for Longstreet's small talk to register. "I suppose the tribes have become harder to handle since Custer?"

"The miners have become harder to handle, Robert. They blame every Indian they see for the massacre. In their view, pilfering the winter stores at the agency is what the Indians deserve, even if the Poncas had nothing to do with the Little Bighorn massacre. Now that there's been bloodshed over it, it's going to take immediate action to keep it from getting out of control."

Robert watched Longstreet settle back into his chair, wondering what the major wanted of him. He didn't give a damn about the Indians; he just wanted to get his hands around Jake Deakins' neck and choke the truth out of him.

"Sir?"

"I'm sorry, Robert. Here you sit, tired and obviously hung over, while I babble on. I'm surprised Miriam let you get away with drinking the stuff, especially after I had to haul her mother out of there. I thought she'd keep you in check."

Robert straightened, focusing on the major's words. Miriam clearly hadn't been at home with her parents. His neck felt hot as he realized the implication. Son of a bitch. If they'd—He clenched his hands to retain control and looked at the major.

"That's the trouble with cheap whiskey, sir. It only takes a little to make a non-drinking man sick. Miriam never even knew I nipped." Never even knew, all right. Damned bitch.

"You see to it you treat her right." The major's tone sharpened. "I wouldn't have agreed to give you her hand if I'd been aware there was a problem, Robert. I hope I wasn't too hasty in doing so."

Not hasty enough, maybe. He needed Miriam but, damn, if Deakins had violated her, he'd pay. Nobody—nobody—did that to Robert Wood and got away with it.

"I'm sorry, sir. It won't happen again."

"See to it that it doesn't."

"Was there anything else, sir?"

"No, son, that's all."

Robert nodded and turned toward the door. Halfway there, he stopped, and turned back. "Major Longstreet, sir, something's occurred to me. We need to delay the first detachment."

"Delay it? We can't take that kind of chance. If we hold off, we risk an all-out fight between the rest of those miners and the Poncas."

"Delay the full detachment for a few hours, sir. Just until we can do some reconnaissance. Something doesn't feel right about sending the troops in blind."

"I sent Hastings to the miners' camp. I don't have anyone else trained as a scout, Robert. We discussed this at the staff meeting earlier. If Anderson hadn't gotten sick—"

"But we do have someone familiar with tribal ways." Robert held back a grin, fighting to look serious. "I didn't even think of it until just now. Private Deakins did several rotations on detached duty at the villages. He'd be the perfect candidate to send as an advance detail." *The perfect candidate.*

CHAPTER TWENTY-TWO

Jake stood in the shadow of Major Longstreet's house waiting for the sentry to pass. It was less than an hour until reveille, two until first light and his appointed hour of departure.

The thought made his stomach tighten.

The sentry strode past the house, crunching across the snow as he made his way around the parade ground. Jake forced himself to stay put until the guard's footsteps had melted into the night. He had to be extremely cautious. It had taken him almost fifteen minutes to sneak over from the barracks.

Jesus, it was cold. Jake pulled his clenched hands from the pockets of his overcoat and blew on them. The sudden bitter winter cold had seeped through the soles of his boots, too, numbing his toes. He eyed the chimney smoke with envy, then moved cautiously to the side window that marked Miriam and Franny's bedroom and tapped against the cold glass. The sound seemed to echo through the winter air.

Lord, let her be a light sleeper.

Jake tapped again, a deliberate pattern this time. Didn't want her thinking it was just the wind.

Damn Robert Wood to hell and back again. This was his doing, no doubt about it. There he'd be, alone, heading straight into a bunch of justifiably angry Indians hours before Miriam was even aware he was gone. The plan was so obvious it was almost laughable. Or at least would have been if it wasn't his life in the sling.

A slight movement caught his eye, and he pressed closer to the house. A lone soldier crossed the edge of the parade ground, a second sentry. Jake held his breath.

The new man stopped in front of the commanding officer's quarters, bent to strike a match on the sole of his boot, then straightened and lit a cigarette. He stood, stamping the snow, clearly cold, and clearly not intent on moving any time soon.

Jake waited for him to move on, back to the small fire at the corner of the parade ground. It'd be warmer there or moving around. He blew on his fingers again. Damn.

Flattened against the side of the house, Jake could no longer see Miriam's window. If she'd risen in response to his knock, she'd have seen nothing. He eyed the soldier again and weighed his options.

As long as the sentry remained stationary, stomping around in one place, Jake could do nothing. The night was dark enough to hide him as long as he stayed against the building, but it wouldn't cover any noise. Any further tapping on the window was out of the question, and the crunch of the crusted snow would betray him before he took more than a few steps. He was stuck.

His mind drifted to everything that needed to be done before first light. Back at the barracks, his gear was only half packed. His Springfield rifle needed one last inspection, and he hoped like hell that the sergeant had taken care of arranging for the horse.

In a way, he almost hoped the horse wasn't ready. It'd at least give him a little extra time to get used to the idea of this unexpected cockamamy notion of scouting. It made no sense. He didn't know shit about tracking and hadn't been on a horse since he'd joined the infantry. It was like they drew his name out of a hat or something. He'd figured Tom Longstreet for a smarter man than that.

He shoved his freezing hands deeper into the pockets of his overcoat and thought about Miriam. Come morning, she'd be searching for him among the troops. Her green eyes, so full of love, would find him gone. He'd wanted to tell her he'd be back to do whatever it took to prove to her father that he was worthy of her. That he loved her.

The sound of the first sentry's footsteps broke the silence as the man completed his circle of the parade ground. Jake knew he didn't have much time. He waited for the guard to move closer. The rear corner of the house was some fifteen feet distant. If he timed his footfalls, he might be able to hide the sound of his own movement behind the noise of the sentry.

He strained to pick out the pattern of the soldier's steps then prepared to move in tandem. Crunch, two, crunch, four. He picked up his left foot and moved it to the side. Crunch, two. Then his right, crunch four. The guard in front of the house rubbed his hands together and coughed into the darkness.

Jake waited, watching to see if the man turned, then repeated his movements, edging closer to the rear of the building. He could hear the sound of the second sentry as he passed in front of the captains' duplex. A few more steps and he'd be in the man's line of sight.

"Cold enough for ya?" he heard the second guard call.

"Hell of a Christmas morning, isn't it?" came the answer. Jake slipped around the corner of the building and breathed a sigh of relief. If they kept talking for a few minutes, he'd have enough cover to slip back toward the barracks.

"Yeah, a campaign for Christmas. I was hopin' to wake up to a two-day hangover and instead I get an Injun fight. A hell of a Christmas, all right."

Jake moved away from Longstreet's house, slipping into the darkness as the soldiers' voices echoed behind him.

"Say, it's not time for my relief yet, is it?"

"Nah. Lieutenant Wood put me on extra. Said we oughtta keep a close eye on the major's quarters just in case the Injuns get the idea to strike first."

Jake spit in disgust. *In case of Indians, or in case Jake Deakins tries to tell the love of his life good-bye?*

The thought slammed into his head, bringing the events of the past two hours into sharp focus. They'd underestimated Wood. Grossly underestimated him. For the first time since learning about the campaign and his unexpected assignment, he considered the very real possibility that he might not return alive. It was a hell of a Christmas, indeed.

Morning dawned clear and cold. Miriam rose just after mess call, amid the first streams of light, and slipped out into the crisp morning air. A hint of pink edged the eastern horizon as she pulled her hood against the bitter wind.

Already the camp was bustling with activity. The sounds of the men as they left morning mess drifted across the parade ground. She scanned the area, hoping to catch sight of Jake. She'd half expected to find him standing at the back door this morning. A strange unease began to gnaw at her.

Behind Miriam, the screen door creaked and her mother emerged, a bottle of laudanum tucked in her pocket. The strong smell of bitter coffee floated from the dainty china cup clutched in her shaky hands, and its steam curled in front of her haggard face. "I don't want you even thinking about wandering away from this house," she announced. "Robert can come here to say his good-byes."

"Robert can go to hell."

The cup shattered on the wooden flooring of the porch.

"Dropped your cup, Mother. Better pick it up." She turned and stomped inside, tossing her cloak on the back of the settee. She'd need it when she went to find Jake, just as soon as her mother bustled away to join the other wives in their collective send-off.

Franny stood in the bedroom doorway, rumpled and sleepy from her late night. Miriam crossed the room, hugged her, and slipped into their room. Franny turned and closed the door behind them.

"What's goin' on, Miriam? Nobody'd tell me anything last night, and you look like you're gonna cry, and Mother's all shaky, and all Papa's gear is piled up."

"Oh, pet, I'm sorry. I'll try to explain." She led Franny to the bed and lifted her up before settling down next to her and pulling her close. "Papa and the soldiers have to go down into Nebraska to check on the Indians who live there."

"What's N'braska?"

"It's the name of a place that's a few days' travel from here. So the soldiers, and Papa too, have to pack up their tents and their cooking gear and their rifles and all the other things they might need for the trip. Then they'll march to Nebraska and find out why the Indians and the miners aren't getting along and straighten out the argument they're having. After that, they'll all march back." She offered Franny a smile and hoped it matched the light tone of her words. Inside, though, the knot of her worry tightened.

She'd read horror stories about the Indian wars. The fighting could be brutal, atrocities common. Jake and her father would be walking into a tense situation. Lord, if even half the accounts were true, they might never return.

"Is that all? How come everybody has such long faces?"

Miriam forced her fears into the back of her mind. "We're just going to miss them while they're gone." Squeezing Franny's shoulders, Miriam stood, then headed to the chiffarobe. "Let's get you dressed so you can help see them off."

Franny yawned before scrambling off the bed and joining the

search for a suitable dress. Happy for the distraction, Miriam guided her clothing choices, then brushed and braided her tangled auburn hair. She left the room a half hour later and found Harriet passed out in the parlor rocking chair, snoring erratically. The laudanum bottle lay empty, overturned on the floor.

Miriam frowned. She fought the desire to leave her mother in the chair and bent to waken her.

Mother peered at Miriam from her clouded eyes, incoherent. She'd never make it out of the house.

Motioning for Franny to help her, Miriam tugged her mother's pudgy form forward in the chair. "We'll get callers later," she explained. "They can't see her like this." Franny slipped under Harriet's other arm and they pulled her up, half-dragging her into the bedroom. Settling her on the bed, Miriam left Franny to cover her with an afghan while she disposed of the laudanum bottle.

She grabbed their cloaks, motioned for Franny to follow, and moved to the front door. They emerged into the morning sunshine. The broken cup lay on the floor of the porch, chips of white amid the brown-stained snow. They steered around the mess and picked their way down the icy steps.

The parade ground was full of gear, scores of identical packs, each awaiting a soldier. Finding Jake's without him would be impossible. A group of hospital matrons and laundresses was gathering near one of the barracks. Voices mingled, wives, soldiers, children as families clustered for final moments together. She spotted Carrie, clasped in Eddie's arms. Jake was nowhere to be seen.

Her father beckoned from a trio of officers. Taking Franny's hand, Miriam crossed to the small group. The officers tipped their forage caps before drifting quietly away to their own families.

Miriam suddenly regretted the distance that had dominated her relationship with her father since her return to the fort. He used to tease her and talk with her, when she was a child. Now, they seemed to hardly know each other. She made a silent vow to regain their former closeness. They stood in uncomfortable silence until Franny looked from one of them to the other.

"What's the matter with you two?" she blurted.

"Shh, I just wanted Papa to know how much I'll worry about him while he's gone." She smiled at him and shrugged her shoulders. "I just didn't know how to say it."

Tom chuckled, at once the loving father she recalled. "She just said it pretty well, didn't she, Frances?"

Franny nodded her head, then hugged him fiercely. "Me, too, Papa. I'm gonna miss you. I'm sure Mother will, too, but we couldn't wake her up."

He looked to Miriam. *Laudanum,* she mouthed, and he nodded.

"Come on, Miriam, you gotta hug Papa, too." Miriam joined the embrace, then pulled away and turned her gaze back to the parade ground, searching for Jake. She should be in his arms, saying good-bye to him. Where *was* he?

"Looking for someone?" her father prompted.

She wanted to ask. Her mind raced, seeking a way to find the answer without asking it directly, hating it that she didn't trust her father enough to confide in him.

"Are they all here?"

"All but the advance detail. Ah, here comes Robert to offer his good-byes."

"I have nothing to say to him. Father, I am not going to marry that man. He announced a betrothal that I have not consented to and to which I do not intend to consent." She sighed, relieved to have said it.

"So that's what has your feathers ruffled, is it? Robert jumped

the gun a little. Here he is. Don't let him leave on a sour note."
He turned, pulling Franny with him, as one of the other officers
neared and forced Miriam to leave his comment unchallenged.

Robert sauntered over to the group and saluted. At her
father's nod, he made his report. "Everything's ready to go, sir.
The advance detail departed at first light. Deakins volunteered
for the duty, acted anxious to go." He turned and smiled at
Miriam. "Something about having made a mistake and needing
a way out."

The stinging comment pierced through her. Behind her eyes,
tears clustered with an instant, uncontrollable pressure, and
misted her vision. The worry crescendoed into hurt as she realized Jake had left without a word. The emotion slammed into
anger as it dawned on her that Robert was far too smug for him
not to be behind this. She raised her hand and slapped him as
hard as she could.

The sharp crack of her hand hitting his cheek punctuated the
cold morning air. A deep red welt surfaced.

He stared at her, his smile fading, and an unfamiliar emotion
filled his gray eyes. Then, the sound of the bugle filled the air.
He shrugged and turned back to her father.

"She *does* get angry, doesn't she, sir?"

Miriam stood in silence, the initial shock of Robert's announcement settling and her emotions in numb paralysis.

Her father peered at Robert and shook his head. "Let it be a
lesson, son, on the evils of not consulting a woman before you
speak on her behalf. She'll settle while we're gone."

Robert nodded, then moved away to join the other officers.

Franny tugged at Miriam's arm, her eyes wide with shock.
Miriam offered her a trembling smile. Franny swallowed hard.
"Gosh, Miriam, you really whacked him a good one."

"Hush, Franny," Father interjected. "Miriam's not very happy
with Robert right this moment. He's been speaking for her a

mite more than she's ready to put up with. Now, let's have another hug."

"Bye, Papa," Franny said, though her face retained its puzzled expression. "Have lotsa fun on your trip to N'braska."

"And you be a good girl. Miriam, I can't say that I blame you for that slap one bit, under the circumstances. Think about your decision, though, before you make it final. Tell your mother I said good-bye." He hugged them each once more, then strode across the parade ground to join the troops.

Taking Franny's hand, Miriam moved toward Officers' Row. The soldiers began to move forth, past a long line of laundresses, matrons, and families. She caught sight of Carrie saying her good-byes to Eddie and fought the urge to rush to her friend for some word of Jake.

Here and there, women stepped forward, breaching public etiquette and offering quick last kisses to their husbands. Their choked voices drifted across the parade ground, making her acutely aware of the anguish that was once again threatening to overflow her soul.

CHAPTER TWENTY-THREE

Jake watched the sun drift ever closer to the western horizon. It'd been a hell of a long day.

He guessed he'd crossed into Nebraska along about noon and met Hastings on his way back to the troops to report on the miners. It hadn't been too much longer before he'd spotted the miners' camp himself. He'd been able to stake them out from a nearby hill, and he doubted they'd even suspected he'd been there. Well-armed and half-drunk, they looked to be an angry bunch. Angry, but not much of a threat. At the rate they were drinking, they'd be passed out soon.

The Poncas, however, might be a little more of a problem.

Jake reined in his horse and looked across the endless plains stretching out before him in their winter bleakness. This close to the agency, he'd need a place to hide his horse. Any closer and he'd be seen. If he'd learned one thing during his time on detached duty, it was that it was damned tough to sneak up on an Indian village.

Sighting a small ravine, he led his gelding into it and tethered him under a group of aged willows. Giving the animal a pat, he pulled his shelter half from his pack, spread the oiled tarp on the snowy slope of the ravine, and settled down to wait until nightfall.

The cold wind bit through his uniform coat and he shivered. If he couldn't start a fire, he might at least keep his butt dry. He moved his shelter half and sat in a group of rocks, hoping the hard discomfort would be enough to keep him awake.

Once situated, he fought to stay alert. Thoughts of Miriam intruded, bringing a vision of her the last time he'd seen her, her worried eyes as he disappeared into the darkness of the night, a soft good night falling from her lips, still puffy from their shared kisses. He shook the thoughts away and reminded himself to concentrate.

What was she thinking now?

He'd heard enough about women to know she might be feeling alone and unsure and maybe even betrayed. She'd been a virgin, for Christ's sake. From all he'd ever been told, more than a few had second thoughts come the next morning.

Was she doubting him?

Hell, Miriam wasn't like most women. She'd know he wouldn't just ride off and abandon her. Wouldn't she? He slammed his foot into the nearest rock and cursed.

He should have gone straight to Longstreet and told him his intentions, right then and there, instead of bowing to orders. Robert Wood had set him up, and he'd fallen right into Wood's trap, leaving Miriam without so much as a good-bye, let alone a reassurance that their lovemaking had been a pledge.

Shit.

Jake shifted his weight and wished he could light a fire. It was damned cold out and his toes were near numbed through. At this rate, by the time it got dark enough to approach the village on foot, he wouldn't be able to walk.

He stood and stomped his feet to keep the blood moving. Had Miriam waited out there in the cold early morning light, searching through the troops for him? He pictured her standing alone, anxious and on the verge of being angry, looking over the faces of enlisted men.

He didn't even know if anyone had bothered to tell her what happened. Of the few who knew of his last-minute assignment, only Wood would know that it mattered to Miriam. And Wood sure as shootin' wouldn't have told her.

Damn it. He should have knocked on the window again, the sentries be damned. So what if he'd been caught? He'd be sitting in the guardhouse right now instead of standing in a snow-packed ravine, shivering in the cold.

Jake reached into his pack and broke off a piece of hardtack. He stuffed the crumbs of hard biscuit into his mouth until they soaked up enough spit to soften, then swallowed. Darkness had fallen. Time to get moving.

Anderson, the scout who lay ill in the hospital, had told him to watch for a well-worn path leading away from the river. Jake moved downstream, above the ravine, his eyes focused on the dry winter grass. The grass seemed to go on endlessly, with no change. He noticed the smell of distant campfires and was just about set to veer away from the river when he found the trail.

He was close enough to the agency now that caution would be needed. Every footfall mattered. Thank God there was little snow left on the windblown prairie. He didn't need another situation like the one this morning, when he'd been trying to say good-bye to Miriam. Particularly with no house to hide behind.

Jake fought to keep his mind on his mission. He was to approach the Ponca camp, unnoticed if possible, to determine how many Indians were there and what mood prevailed among them. He couldn't do that if Miriam strayed into his thoughts again.

The village lay in sight. Jake glanced around. If he could see the village, anybody looking his way would be able to see him. He spotted an outcrop of boulders and slipped behind them, pressing himself to the ground. The rocks weren't much cover.

Things looked to be pretty active in the village. Women and children moved about the campfires, but it didn't look as though there were any special precautions being taken. Jake knew the Poncas had assessed the miners, too, and figured there wasn't much to fear as long as they were drunk. Still, here and there, small groups of braves stood in conference. They wore fresh paint, bright red and white in the firelight. No, the camp wasn't afraid of attack. They were ready to launch one.

He heard the drum beats before he noticed the dancers assembling. The dance wasn't much of a surprise, not after seeing the fresh war paint. They'd be heading out tomorrow. He'd need to hustle back to the troops if they wanted to have any chance of heading off the attack.

The sound of a horse startled him, a Ponca sentry. He leaned low behind the rock and held his breath. They'd be looking for miners, expecting carelessness. The brave rode past, circling the village. Jake made a quick estimate of the size of the village, then began to inch back to where he'd hidden the horse.

The small cluster of willows was just ahead when he realized, too late, that he was being followed. His mind had barely registered the presence of another person when he felt the hand encircle him and cut off his breath. A sharp sudden pain bit into his neck.

Jake surged against the force, thrusting his elbow at his attacker. The jab connected, and the man's hold slipped, the biting knife no longer at Jake's throat. He twisted, counting on his size to help him, and wrenched out of the man's grip.

He'd moved fast enough, but the threat wasn't over. His opponent crouched in the darkness, small and wiry, ready to spring. It was a white man. His features were vague in the darkness, half hidden by a ragged hat. A flash of steel caught Jake's eye as the man circled. Jake countered, knowing full well his Springfield rifle was no match for the blade. Damn, why hadn't he attached the bayonet?

Blood trickled from the cut on his neck, oozing slowly, like the tickle of a feather. Jake wiped at it, irritated at the distraction. It continued to drip, a soft whispering touch at the hollow of his throat, like the brush of Miriam's finger.

A twig snapped and he jumped. From the corner of his eye, he saw the little man rush forward. Damn. At the same time, a lone rider charged, hell-bent for him. A searing pain ripped into his thigh, blinding in its intensity, and he dropped to the ground. The rider pounded forward, looming above him. He saw the flash of the tomahawk as the Indian slipped from the horse, just before he slid into unconsciousness.

"And you truly believe he'd just leave?" Eulalie's words were sharp.

Miriam stared at her, wounded and somewhat astounded at her friend's lack of sympathy. She'd carried her troublesome thoughts with her all day, masking them behind a stoic front, while she did her duty as hostess for the officers' wives. As she'd expected, they'd arrived at her door soon after the troops departed, anxious for one another's support.

Harriet had remained abed, passed out, leaving Miriam with the burden of hospitality. Pounding out hymns on the organ, she'd allowed a tear or two to slip out only to hide them the moment she turned back to face the others.

Now, with daylight and the other women departed, only she and Eulalie remained. Franny lay asleep on the horsehair sofa.

"I don't know what to believe," Miriam told her friend. "I don't know what Robert has to do with this, and I have no idea how much of what he said is true. What I do know is that Jake didn't volunteer. The more I think about it, the more puzzled I am about him leaving with no word. He wouldn't do that unless something was wrong." She slammed her fist into an embroidered pillow and plopped into the rocking chair, the pillow clutched in her lap.

"See, you *don't* believe he'd just leave." Eulalie sat down on the ottoman and took Miriam's hands in hers. "So, something or someone had to force his hand."

"What if he had doubts about me? What if he thought I wasn't sincere? What if he started thinking about being court-martialed? What if—"

"Miriam, stop it. You're babbling on about things you know aren't true."

"And how do I know that?"

"Faith, Miriam. Faith and trust."

"Trust like you had in the man you loved?"

Eulalie stood, pulling her hands away from Miriam's. "The man I loved was a long time ago and the situation was much different." She took a deep breath and peered into Miriam's eyes. "And when I felt him being pulled away, I didn't fight to keep him. I let myself be so consumed with self-doubt that I just gave up. Don't you dare let yourself slip into that trap."

Miriam nodded, then impulsively jumped up and hugged her friend. "I didn't mean to hurt you," she said.

"Balderdash. It was a fair question." She paused, collecting herself. "Now, then, what's the next step?"

"I think I need to go talk to Carrie," she said, pacing with sudden nervous energy. "If he didn't leave word with her, I'll know for sure that his leaving was beyond his control. If he had a chance to talk to her, I'll find out what's going on."

"Well, now, that sounds like a plan you should have hit upon quite a bit earlier." Eulalie smiled.

Miriam offered her a wry grin. "I did. Except I had a house full of miserable women who were all too stubborn to have a good cry and too uppity to admit it. And Mother."

"The laudanum again?"

"How did you know?"

"She's used it for years, for the headaches, but your father

240

mentioned that she's started using it more often."

"Does anyone else know?"

"I don't think so, dearling. And so what if they do?" Eulalie moved to the hall, pulled Miriam's cloak from its peg and made a grand sweep toward the door with her arm. "Go on, go see Carrie, I'll stay and watch Harriet."

"Thank you," Miriam whispered, pulling the cloak around her and stepping into the night.

"Son of a bitch. There's blood all over the place, sir. Deakins an' two others a-layin' there, ain't none of 'em movin'." The private stumbled away from the willow copse and emptied his stomach under the bright moonlit sky.

Robert tapped his foot as the private finished puking. Damned sissy. Instinct had told him something was amiss. Otherwise, he'd have stayed with the troops instead of coming all the way out here with this idiot. He eyed the horses wandering along the bank of the ravine. He'd *known* there was a problem.

The private lifted his head and stared at Robert. He was nothing but a delicate kid. Robert shook his head and moved past the soldier.

"You wait here. I'll check out the situation myself."

He moved toward the trees, watching the ground. Hoof prints and two sets of tracks, plus the inept private. No one else hidden, waiting. The cluster of trees hid the bodies from view until he moved past them.

Congealed blood covered the area, frozen and dark brown in the moonlight. A small white man lay crumpled by a rock, an Indian tomahawk buried in his chest. One of the miners, no doubt. A pool of blood covered his plaid shirt and had saturated the surrounding ground. Robert knelt and fingered the puddle. Still sticky in the thickest areas. It hadn't been more than a few hours since the carnage occurred.

The Indian, a Ponca, was clothed in buckskins. His throat was severed almost straight across, a clean swipe. But he hadn't gone down easy. Dried blood sprays were everywhere, dark against the scattered patches of snow. He'd probably killed the miner after being sliced.

Deakins lay apart from them, a shallow knife wound along the side of his neck. Enough to be bothersome, but not lethal. Robert's gaze moved across his body, resting on his left thigh. A great gaping gash was torn across the leg. Blood had emptied out of it like water through a dam and raw muscle screamed out of its depth.

Jesus, Mary and Joseph.

He turned away, feeling his own stomach rebel, and struggled to suppress his nausea. He moved away from the bodies until he had control of himself.

"They all dead, sir?"

Robert didn't respond. Were they? Deep inside, he recognized what decency demanded of him and felt it rage against what he was about to do. Once the step was taken, his honor would be fractured forever.

Hell, he didn't even want to know. Besides, even if any of them were still breathing, they'd never get them back to the fort alive, not with that much blood spilt.

"They're dead. We'll send a burial detail later. Right now, we need to get back to the column and alert them to what happened. Grab those horses and let's head out."

CHAPTER TWENTY-FOUR

Franny burst into the parlor, yelling at the top of her lungs. "Rider's comin'! Rider's comin'!"

Miriam's breath constricted, and the knot of worry she'd tried to keep at bay for the past two weeks reared its head again. Carrie had been unable to offer any insight into Jake's sudden departure, and apprehension continued to weigh on her.

She glanced around the room, seeing anxiousness reflected in every face present. Almost with one motion, the women gathered in the Longstreet house lay down their needlework. No one spoke.

Her mother sat in the rocker, humming absently and stitching away at her embroidery, the only one of them still involved in her task.

"Mother?"

Harriet raised her head and smiled blandly.

"The ladies are waiting. Did you want to hear the report?"

"Oh, of course." Harriet smiled again and went back to her sewing.

Miriam frowned. Her mother had been in a stupor for days. Her condition was becoming harder to explain to others. She and Eulalie had tried taking the laudanum away only to have Mother become enraged beyond control. With the other women constantly calling at the house, they'd agreed it was better to allow her limited amounts of the tincture rather take it away completely and face her fury. But Miriam doubted the other women would continue to believe their explanations about Harriet's lack of focus much longer.

She glanced at Eulalie, unsure of protocol.

"Why don't you receive the news, dear? Your mother is beside herself with worry. Whatever the messenger has should be delivered to the Longstreet women first."

Miriam nodded and rose from her side chair. In the faces of the others, she read both desperation and hope. They all knew that news of any casualties would bring salvation for some and hell for others.

Franny stood at the front window, peering out from behind the lace curtain. Miriam gathered her winter shawl from its peg and waited until Franny gave the word.

"He's here," she announced.

Closing her eyes and taking a deep breath, Miriam opened the door and went out into the frigid January air.

Lieutenant Peters reined in his gelding and slid from the horse. "Miss Longstreet, ma'am."

"You have news?"

"Yes, ma'am. The troops were engaged while attempting to control two separate skirmishes between the Poncas and the miners. While the hostile parties were subdued, I regret to report that we lost three men."

She felt the statement settle in the pit of her stomach and she shivered.

"Do you have names to report?"

"An officer, ma'am, and two enlisted men. Second Lieutenant Jefferson and Privates Rupert and Deakins."

The blood seemed to drain from Miriam's body, numbing it in shock. "No." She shook her head. Jake wasn't dead. There was a mistake. A deep rage filled her. "You're a liar, a goddamned liar!" She screamed the words at him and surged past his horse toward the edge of the parade ground. She'd see for herself.

"Miss Longstreet."

The soldier's words came to her through a haze, as if he was talking to someone in a dream. His hand grasped her arm, a vague pressure holding her back, and she struggled against the restraint.

"Let me go." She tried to pull away, hearing Jake's words echo through her mind. *Till death do us part.*

Oh my God.

The realization slammed into her, and she gulped for air with a great, twisted gasp. Shudders racked her body. *Oh my God.* Knees weakening, she allowed herself to be pulled into Lieutenant Peters' supporting arms and guided into the house.

"Miriam?" Eulalie's voice broke into her cocoon of darkness, shattering the silence. Miriam uncurled her body from the tight ball she had formed on her bed and turned toward the doorway. A searing emptiness overwhelmed her.

"Are they gone?"

"They're gone, dearling," Eulalie said, sitting on the bed and reaching for Miriam's cheek. She brushed away the tears that lingered on her skin, soothing with the touch of her hand until Miriam poured herself into her embrace. Eulalie held her, rocking, saying nothing, mothering her as Harriet had never done.

Drawing from her friend's quiet strength, Miriam breathed in and pulled away. "Thank you," she whispered, hearing the distant sound of her own voice.

"I sent Franny on to Mrs. Appleby's. Your mother's abed."

"Franny? Oh, God, did anybody tell Franny?"

"Shh, dear. Franny's been told. She's pretty shook up, but she's in good hands."

Miriam nodded, relieved. She couldn't be the strong adult

Franny needed. Not now. She felt as though the world was spinning around her, out of her control. She shivered.

Had Jake been cold? Had he lain in the snow, waiting, as life slipped out of him, or had death come at once?

She swallowed. Her eyes felt heavy. Tears trickled down her face and she fought against the helplessness closing in on her.

"Did . . . did anyone tell Carrie?"

"Yes, dearling, Carrie's been told."

Carrie. The realization struck Miriam with the force of a locomotive. How did you tell a woman that both her brother and husband were dead?

"Is there anyone there with her? Dear Lord, Eulalie, we need to go."

"Are you sure, dear?" Eulalie's voice was filled with concern.

Miriam nodded. "Jake would want me there."

Carrie's cabin was just ahead, a whisper of smoke wafting from its stone chimney. The brief puff of white blended away into the late afternoon sky. It had been a long day, and Miriam dreaded the hours yet to come.

Eulalie offered her hand a squeeze. "I'll check on Mrs. Jefferson. You'll be all right?"

"I need to do this, Eulalie."

Eulalie gave her a brief hug, then disappeared over the hill.

She rapped on the door, half wishing Carrie wouldn't answer. But the door opened and Carrie's drained face peered out at her. She gestured for Miriam to enter.

Carrie's rocker sat before the fireplace. A pair of knitting needles and a half-finished baby blanket lay on its worn leather seat. Miriam swallowed and familiar pressure built behind her eyes. Sighing, she searched Carrie's sapphire eyes. As the silence deepened, so, too, did their color, until it became a deep, liquid blue. Jake's blue. She felt the first tear slip down her cheek.

Carrie backed into a wooden chair, hugging her unborn baby and staring vacantly into the far corner of the cabin. Miriam touched her own abdomen, suddenly deeply afraid, as the reality of Carrie's anguish settled about them.

She pushed the unwanted thoughts away and waited, unsure, as Carrie brought a single hand to her mouth. Slow sobs rocked her friend's body and her head sagged into her arms until her cries were absorbed by the table.

Crossing the small room, Miriam knelt next to her and grasped her arm, sharing her pain. Carrie took her hand, then raised her head, a question in her gaze. "You loved him, didn't you?"

"With all my soul, Carrie. With all my soul."

The throbbing pain registered in some deep recess of Jake's mind long before he was ready to face up to it. The first time it screamed at him, painted faces had coursed like visions through his mind, bearing down on him, until he'd escaped back into blackness. Now, however, the pain would not be ignored.

He shifted his leg. A spasm raced through him and he gritted his teeth.

Damn.

The pain settled back into a consistent ache and he tried to summon the energy to open his eyes.

The air was warm, and it dawned on him that he was no longer lying on the prairie. No wind. He was indoors. He concentrated on the air. It smelled like grease and dogs and some kind of stew. His stomach growled and he opened his eyes.

A pair of dark eyes peered down at him from a chubby face.

"He's awake, he's awake. Grandmother, come." Jake listened to the child call out in Lakota and looked around the tepee.

An elderly woman approached in the dark firelight and nodded sagely at the youngster. "So he is, my son. Go and tell your father." The woman sat on the skins next to Jake and grinned, a large gaping hole where her front teeth should have been. "It is good to have you with the living, my son."

"Where?" The question came out as a scratchy whisper.

A cool gust of air penetrated the tepee and Jake's attention was drawn to the door flap. A tall, self-assured Sioux entered and crossed around the edge of the lodge, then squatted next to Jake's pallet.

"Spotted Elk," Jake croaked. He'd visited with the Indian several times during his detached duty at White Swan's village.

"Yes, my friend."

"How—?"

"The Poncas did not wish to let you die. They also did not want the army to find you in their village. They brought you here, to our winter camp."

Jake nodded. Wading through the hazy images of his memory, he recalled the wiry white man who had tried to slit his throat. He'd taken his eyes off the man when he saw the Ponca brave riding hell-bent for them. Assuming the white man had cut him, the Poncas would want to avoid the army thinking them responsible in any way.

"Who saved my hide?"

"Grandmother watched over you. She remembered how you listened to the children when the army sent you to the village. She also remembered how you carried the white woman away."

"Miriam?" How long had he been here, and had anyone told Miriam? He pictured her sitting back at Fort Randall wondering where he was. They'd probably listed him as a deserter.

He needed to get back to her. Pushing against the pallet, he struggled to rise. A wave of pain splashed over him. He gritted his teeth and swallowed hard. *Jesus.* He waited for the intensity of the spasm to ebb, then allowed his body to sink back down into the buffalo robes. Damn. His leg hurt like hell. His eyes felt heavy, and he wished Grandmother would bring him something for the pain before he drifted off again.

"How long have I been here?"

"More than half a moon."

"Did anyone go to the fort?"

"The men have not been there because of the Poncas and the miners. If we go while the men are gone, the sentries will think we attack. The fort will be there when you are ready. The journey will be long for you. You must heal first. We will go when I return from the hunt."

Jake groaned. He needed to get word to Miriam. Somehow, he had to let her know what had happened. If Wood got back there first, he'd be telling Miriam all kinds of lies. She'd think he left her high and dry.

Thank God the troops were in Nebraska. With them still on campaign, the reports of his "desertion" wouldn't have yet reached the fort.

CHAPTER TWENTY-FIVE

The troops arrived on a sunny January afternoon. Miriam watched them from the bare wooden porch of the commanding officer's quarters. It was three weeks since the last time she had seen Jake, since the night they had given themselves to each other. Each day brought with it growing dread and uncertainty and took her one day farther from her already late monthly.

At the edge of the parade ground, a line of women had gathered, laundresses and officers' wives alike, sharing the anticipation of their husbands' return. Carrie and Mrs. Jefferson were conspicuously absent.

"Are you all right, dearling?" Eulalie asked. She grasped Miriam's hand and squeezed it.

"No, but someone needs to welcome Father home."

Eulalie nodded, saying nothing. Franny sat on the bottom step, squishing the melting snow together with her feet. Mother sat inside, muttering nonsense to herself. Miriam offered a tiny smile of appreciation to her friend for remaining with her.

The troops crossed the parade ground, and all sense of military discipline vanished. Wives and children rushed forward with hugs and words of welcome. Unmarried soldiers and officers made their ways to their quarters and Father continued on alone.

His expression was stoic, and Miriam wondered how many lonely entrances into various camps he had made. She doubted her mother had ever rushed forward with a welcome hug. She imagined Mother standing grandly on the verandah, or perhaps at the center of the parade ground, dragging out Father's homecoming. Or had the headaches always kept her away?

As her father neared their quarters, Miriam noticed the fatigue in his face. He looked drained. His heavy eyes brightened as he saw them waiting and his step quickened.

"Hello, ladies," he greeted, and he scooped Franny into his arms. "Goodness, sprite, you've gotten heavy while I was gone."

Franny giggled at the remark, then sobered. "Our friends got killed," she told him.

"Yes, Franny, I'm afraid they did." His smile melted as his gaze lifted to Miriam and Eulalie. He climbed the stairs and set Franny on the porch before opening his arms to Miriam. She slid into them, her eyes tearing.

"It's good to have you safely back at the post, Thomas." Eulalie's voice eased the moment, absolving Miriam of the need to offer a greeting. Enfolded in her father's embrace, she let Eulalie's gentle welcome settle about them, knowing that her mother would never have uttered the meaningful words.

"Thank you, Eulalie. It's good to be home. You've been seeing to my girls?" Miriam pulled out of the hug and watched the exchange with interest.

"What little they've needed me. Harriet's been under the weather."

"Worse?"

"I'm afraid so." Eulalie turned to Miriam. "I'd best be on my way. I imagine my brother is wondering where I am." She offered Franny a quick hug, then strode toward her own quarters.

Miriam turned back to her father.

His gaze followed Eulalie. "That woman has more compassion in her little finger than I'll ever have," he remarked. "I'm sorry about Rupert and Deakins. I know you considered them friends."

She nodded, not trusting herself to speak.

Franny hugged Miriam's skirts and looked up at her father. "Carrie's awful sad, Papa, and us, too. Deakins was our pal." She sniffled and Miriam hugged her before Franny broke away and ran into the house.

Tom watched her disappear, concern etched across his face. He started to follow and Miriam stopped him with a touch to his arm.

"She seems to need the time to herself," she explained, wishing she, too, could flee.

"I'll visit Mrs. Rupert later. Has she said whether she intends to finish out her contract?" Tom leaned against the porch rail, lending an air of informality to the conversation.

The action seemed to make him more approachable. Miriam warmed to it. "She plans to, if you don't cancel the contract."

"I see no reason to force her out. It's bad enough that Mrs. Jefferson is left adrift. As long as the army allows the laundress to remain, I don't plan to send her away. Her contract's good through June, I think."

"What happens to Mrs. Jefferson?"

"She's not an employee, so the army doesn't recognize her presence here. She'll have to leave as soon as she can make the necessary arrangements."

"It seems so cold." Miriam's thoughts drifted again to her own circumstances. If she were carrying Jake's baby, she, too, would be facing a grim future.

"Strange, isn't it, how the officer's widow has to leave but the enlisted man's wife has options?" her father said.

Miriam nodded, knowing such options would not apply to her.

Robert slammed the Lewis Carroll novel shut and shoved it back onto the library shelf. His concentration was shot. He strode across the empty room and plopped into one of the straight-backed chairs near a pile of outdated newspapers.

He'd given the matter quite a bit of thought. In fact, he'd thought of little else but the Miriam problem since he'd left Deakins lying on the frozen prairie.

He picked up a *Harper's Bazaar* and paged through it. So far, no one else knew Deakins was missing. Shit, he could hardly report that the body he'd left for dead had disappeared. So he'd waited. He didn't know where the hell Deakins was, and he didn't care. As long as he didn't show up at the fort again.

But the private haunted his dreams.

He awoke in cold sweats, visions of Deakins staggering into the post echoing through his mind. His report on the burial was overdue, and he was fresh out of ideas about how to cover his ass.

He tossed the paper aside and reached for another. An engraving showed bodies strewn across some desolate desert landscape. The dramatic account told of a massacre along the Santa Fe Trail. The victims had been stripped and two had been scalped so viciously that their faces were unrecognizable.

Robert devoured the rest of the article with avid interest. It was the out he'd been looking for. It was so simple he'd almost overlooked it. Unrecognizable bodies. He'd thought it was Deakins, but who could really say for sure?

He folded the tattered periodical and tucked it into his military blouse. He could finish the report tonight with a clear conscience. Half the problem was solved.

But there was still the issue of what to do about Miriam.

He pushed back his chair and grabbed his overcoat before leaving the library. Yes, there was still Miriam. Her and Deakins' mutual disappearances from the dance couldn't have been co-incidence, and, since the soldiers had returned, she'd done nothing but mope around the post like she was one of the widows. He knew he should avoid jumping to conclusions. She was friends with that laundress, after all; maybe she was grieving for Mrs. Rupert's loss. He slammed the library door behind him. Suspicion wasn't going to get him anywhere.

She was the major's daughter, and that fact alone carried a lot of weight. Advancing up the promotion ladder was not a quick process, not on the frontier. If he'd been stationed back East, things would be different. But out West, a man could stagnate as a lieutenant forever. If he wanted to advance, he'd need every edge possible.

Besides, Deakins was out of the picture. If anything had happened between them, maybe he could use it to his advantage.

The parade ground was deserted except for a few scattered soldiers finishing up their assignments. Not much time left in the day. Enough time to finish the report, but not enough to call on Miriam. He'd need to make his move soon, though. She was still shaky and a prime target if he played things right. Lots of sympathy, he figured, but he'd need to tread lightly. If he pushed too hard, she'd rebel for sure.

He opened the door of his quarters and stepped into the dark interior, already playing the scene through his mind. He'd visit her tomorrow evening. He'd be supportive, a friend there only for her, someone for her to turn to in her hour of need.

"I sure never expected to see what I seen this week," Carrie announced, settling into a chair opposite Miriam. The scent of apples and cinnamon wafted from the oven, filling the room. "There ain't been one day yet that I been alone."

Eulalie circled behind her and began kneading her shoulders. "To tell the truth, I didn't expect it either."

Miriam grasped her cup of tea with both hands and looked at her friends. "It's just a shame that it took something so desperate to force their hands. Have they been much help?"

" 'Bout as much as you were that first day." Carrie smiled, then sobered. "I got to thank you two for bein' behind this. Don't know how I'd manage all by myself. Didn't know how much Eddie done for me till I didn't have him no more." Her eyes clouded, and she looked away.

"It seems desperate circumstances make us all see things differently, dear. We've pledged to see to it that you don't lose that contract. Except for Harriet, one of us will be here daily to help." Eulalie finished the massage and poured herself a cup of tea. She settled into her own chair and breathed in the aroma of the tea. Then, she peered across the table, her eyes full of questions, and arched her eyebrows.

Carrie glanced from one woman to the other and sighed. "This ain't a regular social call, is it?" she asked.

Miriam gathered a deep breath and plunged in. "I trust you both as my closest friends, and I need your help. I thought that together, we might produce more ideas."

Miriam focused on Carrie, wondering how much she had guessed about the night she and Jake had disappeared from the party. They'd never discussed it, and she'd wondered more than once if Carrie hadn't preferred it that way.

"My monthly should have started two weeks ago," she said. The statement seemed to drift across the room, hanging above them, waiting for someone to latch onto it. Eulalie took in the words with another slow blink. Carrie, too, sat in silence, tears welling in the blue depths of her eyes.

"Christmas Eve?" Carrie asked.

Miriam nodded.

The cup of tea in her hands grew cold before anyone interrupted the silence again. Eulalie rose and poured more tea for each of them, checked on the pie, then sat back down and launched in with her usual brisk manner. "First and foremost, dearling, you mustn't jump to conclusions."

"That's true," Carrie joined in. "Bein' late don't always mean you're carryin' a child. Worry'll mess things up somethin' awful. You got any other signs?"

"I don't know." Miriam spoke the words with frustration.

"You tired? Food seem like it jus' wants to stick in your throat or come back up? Are you touchy 'bout things, cryin' at the drop of a hat?"

Miriam thought about it, trying to piece things together. Tired? Touchy? She'd been both. "Some. I cry a lot, and getting out of bed is a struggle. I hardly eat at all, though."

Eulalie leaned forward. "With all that's happened, those would be natural reactions. I don't think we can make any assumptions at this point."

Carrie nodded in agreement. "I reckon she's right on that one. So, you're just gonna have to wait it out. In the meantime, though, you got some thinkin' to do. If you are carryin' Jake's baby, how you gonna provide for it? Straight up, you ain't got no skills. You're educated, but families don't hire no governesses with families of their own, and you don't earn nothin' for being an expert in the social graces."

"I'll learn whatever it takes. I wanted to be independent."

"The plain fact is that folks are gonna hire on those who know what they're doin'. That ain't gonna be you. If you're gonna look at what's best for the baby, you can't close up on other ideas."

"Carrie's right, dear," Eulalie added. "The way I see it, your choices would be limited. I'm sure you've already been mulling this over and have reached the same conclusion. Am I to assume that you'd be determined to have the baby?"

Miriam nodded again.

"That's good," Carrie added. "Ain't many doctors that'll take care of it and it ain't safe havin' somebody what don't know what they're doin'. 'Sides, I wouldn't be wantin' you to do that anyways." She reached across the table and clasped Miriam's hand in her own.

"My guess is that brings you to either marrying quickly or visiting an 'aunt' back East?" Eulalie prompted.

She was right. Staying at the fort would be out of the question. The commanding officer's daughter couldn't have a child out of wedlock. She'd be sent away. "Not much of a choice, is there? I could stay with my friend Sarah. She wouldn't judge, and maybe she can find another millinery position."

Carrie pulled her hand back and rose from the table. She crossed the room, opened the cookstove, and pulled an apple pie from its depth. Setting the pie on the windowsill to cool, she returned to the table and sat, her expression sober.

"And if that don't work? If there ain't no place to go?"

Miriam stood and left the table. Marrying Robert was not an option she was willing to entertain. She'd declined his calls every night, and she wasn't about to start accepting them. Not now, not ever. She didn't know how, but her heart told her Robert was somehow responsible for Jake being at that Indian camp.

She heard the scrape of a chair, then felt Carrie's soft touch on her shoulder. Turning, she saw concern in her face. She melted into Carrie's arms and felt her suppressed tears begin to overflow her eyes.

"We ain't gonna tell you what to do on this, only that you gotta think beyond what you're feelin' here and now. You gotta think about that might-be baby and how it's gonna survive. If you are pregnant, you ain't got much time for makin' plans."

Robert stood in the early evening darkness and knocked on Miriam's front door. She'd refused to see him every night for a week, and it was getting humiliating. How the hell was he going to carry out his plans if she wouldn't let him in?

The door opened and Major Longstreet peered out. "Ah, Robert. She's finally consented to see you." Longstreet pulled the door open and gestured for him to enter.

It was about time. Robert briefly wondered what had caused her to change her mind then dismissed the thought. It didn't matter.

He'd analyzed the situation and determined none of it mattered anymore. If Miriam had lain with that son of a bitch, she might very well have problems of her own by now. Problems he could solve. She might need him as much as he needed her.

"Thank you, sir." He pasted a smile on his face and willed his body to relax as he stepped into the house and hung his overcoat on the coat rack. The parlor was warm and smelled of cloves. Miriam sat on the settee, involved in some needlework project. Harriet and Frances were nowhere to be seen.

"Please sit down," Miriam told him, her voice stiff. She placed her project in a sewing basket and stood. "I'll check on Franny and make sure she's tucked in and put a pot of tea on."

"Coffee would be fine."

She nodded and left the room. The major leaned against the side of the archway, watching him. "Seems as though she's making you start from scratch," he stated.

Robert sat, taking care to project confidence as he settled into the upholstered parlor chair. Longstreet looked amused, and Robert didn't like it one bit. Perhaps the major needed taking down a little.

Robert's mind scrambled for the right barb, something that would sting without appearing to be intentional. Rumors had been flying about Harriet. Perhaps it was time to toss that issue out. "And where is the lovely Mrs. Longstreet this evening?" he asked.

The major arched an eyebrow, giving away nothing. "I'm afraid she's abed with another of those wretched headaches of hers," he replied. The easy answer irritated Robert.

"Pity, isn't it, how they seem to have taken over her life?"

"Yes, Robert, it is a pity." Odd, he almost seemed to be enjoying the exchange. "I see you've finally turned in your report on the burials."

Robert frowned at the turn of the conversation. "Yes, sir, I'd quite forgotten about it until Captain Ellis reminded me."

"You hadn't mentioned the butchery before."

Shifting in the chair, Robert searched his mind for an answer. Damn, what was Longstreet trying to get at here? "No, I, uh, felt it might incite the men. We didn't need that."

"Ah, here comes Miriam with your coffee. If you'll excuse me, I'll retire to the dining room and get some paperwork done."

Robert rose as Longstreet ambled into the other room and settled himself at the table. He watched him with a sense of foreboding. He'd expected he and Miriam would be left alone, not chaperoned like a couple of youngsters. It was insulting.

And it meant he'd need to change his tactics. No frontal assault, no direct questions. Damn, he hated last-minute adjustments.

"Robert?" He turned at the sound of Miriam's voice. She stood next to him, a cup of steaming coffee in her extended hand. "Your coffee?"

Damn it. He felt like an idiot. It was carelessness like that that led to defeat. He needed to stay alert, to be aware of any flanking maneuvers Miriam and the major might make.

"Thank you," he said. "Shall we sit? You look pale." He let the comment drop, watching her face.

Miriam stared for a moment, then recovered. She moved to a small rocking chair with some type of fancy embroidery on its back. He waited until she sat, then sank into his own chair.

The silence stretched. She was forcing him to make the first move. The situation called for caution, a specific mix of charm and caring. He leaned forward, letting his eyelids close into what he hoped was a mournful expression. "I'm sorry about your laundress friend's husband and about the private. I know he saved Franny's life."

Surprise registered on Miriam's face.

Confident, he continued on. "Despite my initial reservations about it, I think you and the other ladies are doing a generous thing, helping Mrs. Rupert out in her time of need."

"Thank you, Robert. I didn't expect your endorsement."

"I think the time away gave me the opportunity to reevaluate a lot of things. The frontier calls for responses different from those appropriate for a civilized place." He paused, watching her almost-imperceptible nod. He gave her time. As he'd hoped, she seemed to be considering what he'd said, digesting it and adjusting her response to him. It was his attack on her flank.

"You're full of surprises this evening," she said. "But I'm not so sure I'm ready to just sweep everything under the carpet." She glanced toward her father, then leaned forward. "You've said and done things I'm not prepared to gloss over."

The remark stunned him, an unexpected counterattack he hadn't expected from her. He eyed her again. Her expression offered him no clue to the direction he needed to take. Experience, however, told him to counter rather than advance.

"You're right, Miriam. I have. I have allowed pride and petty jealousy to get in the way again and again."

She offered no response. He shifted in the chair again, uncomfortable in the silence. Damn her. She was deliberately leading him in deeper, forcing him into making ridiculous statements, then letting him stew. He could have kicked himself for falling into such a trap.

It was time for him to steer the conversation. He smiled at her blithely, enough so she would see his meaning. "I just want you to know I understand *perfectly* how difficult these last few weeks may have been for you."

Her face paled and she swallowed hard.

"Finished with your coffee?" she inquired, standing to receive his empty cup. Another unexpected response. He handed the cup to her, unsure of his next move. "Then I think the evening is finished," she stated.

Stunned, he stood. It was a challenge, he surmised, and forced himself to check his response. Anger would only serve to give her what she needed to throw him out for good. And he'd be damned if he'd give her that kind of satisfaction. When the relationship was no longer useful, *he* would end it.

He'd learned what he needed to know. Though she hadn't said anything, her facial expressions indicated things were less than perfect for her. She might very well be carrying Deakins' child. He'd accepted the possibility. It wasn't quite the way he wanted her, but he'd take her any way he could get her. He needed her.

She walked with him to the door, again a gracious hostess, and stood aside as he slipped on his coat. He buttoned it, watching some stray thought overtake her.

He smiled as he thought about how heroic he would be, saving her. Leaning, he brought his mouth close to her ear. "I'm worried about you, little one. You mean the world to me and I'll be here for you. No questions asked. Just let me know when you're ready to wear the betrothal pin."

He kissed her on the cheek and strode into the darkness.

Things might work out well after all.

CHAPTER TWENTY-SIX

Miriam closed the door behind Robert and leaned against it before returning to the parlor.

"Do you want to talk about it?" her father asked.

She sighed as she met his concerned gaze. "I'm not sure I know what to say," she answered, crossing the room. Robert's brief visit and his pointed comments had revealed much. She wouldn't marry that man if he was the only option she had left.

What did you say to your father when you were rejecting his chosen suitor? How did you tell a pillar of respectability you suspected you might be in trouble, very unrespectable trouble?

Father pushed his chair back from the table and offered her a smile. His gray eyes softened, reminding her of treasured childhood moments. "I'm not sure I know what to say, either, but it's not too hard to see we both have a lot on our minds."

Miriam nodded and pulled out a chair for herself. She sat heavily, propped her arms on the table, and let her head sink against them. It was time to tell him. She sighed again, thinking about Robert's artificial sweetness. She'd start there. "I feel like a trapped fly."

Father chuckled. "He *is* a bit syrupy, isn't he?" He paused then reached across the table and stroked her hair.

"I realize you and I haven't been close for a long, long time but I can't sit here and watch you struggle with this without saying something. Before Christmas, I gave my consent to Robert to ask you for your hand in marriage. At the time, I thought it was the perfect step. I'm no longer convinced."

Miriam lifted her head and caught his gaze. "It never was, Papa. I could have told you that, if you had asked."

Tom pushed back his chair and rose. He crossed the space between them and squatted next to her chair. Understanding and regret moved across his face. "I thought him an outstanding officer and a fine young man who would provide you a good life. I thought he cared for you and would do well by you."

"And now?" she asked.

Tom stood and paced the room. "It's as if he tries too hard. I'm beginning to have questions about his character."

"Papa, you know I can't marry him." The words, once spoken, cast a finality to her decision. She'd write to Sarah tonight, just in case.

"I know. I'm glad you recognize it, even if I almost missed it." He paused in front of the cherry whatnot, fingering knick-knacks, as if sorting through the memories attached to them. "You don't love him, do you?"

His quiet words startled Miriam. "You knew?"

"I truly thought I was looking out for your best interests. You both come from respectable families and seemed to have much in common. I thought you would grow to love him."

"What made you change your mind?"

He didn't answer immediately. He fingers grazed a small framed daguerreotype of a young Harriet. Miriam rose and joined him. The image he held had always fascinated her. It was as different from the mother she knew as night was from day.

"A lot of things," he said, his voice quiet. "The gossip about your mother, watching her grow hateful over the years, my own unhappiness, what might have been. . . ." His comment trailed off into the dimness of the lamplight.

Miriam thought about her parents, realizing she'd never seen a moment of tenderness between them. That her father was

Pamela Nowak

unhappy came as no surprise.

"Did you ever love her?"

He silenced the comment with a finger to his lips and reached for her hand. Squeezing it, he pulled her to the settee. She sat, waiting until he eased onto the seat beside her, knowing it was he who needed to talk and she who needed to listen. She'd tell him about Jake later.

"Tell me, Papa," she urged. For a moment, she thought he would retreat. Then his eyes softened, as if he were remembering happier times. Miriam waited, allowing him time.

"Your mother and I were perfectly suited. I was a rising young officer. She was wealthy, with political connections, and her father was a colonel. At the time, I thought my career meant everything. She was pretty then, vivacious, sought after." He clutched the daguerreotype still in his hand. "I gambled everything I had on our marriage, telling myself it was worth it, that love would grow. Through the years, I've watched her become overbearing. Every year, the headaches get worse and she drinks more laudanum. The rages are worse and the stupors last longer. I can't hide her drinking anymore. The woman I married for my career is on the verge of ruining it."

Miriam saw the pain in his eyes as he gazed across the room. The admission had been difficult for him. She touched his hand, wanting to lend reassurance. The picture she'd always had of her parents' relationship was clouded, false. The realization brought her closer to her father than she'd ever been. She puzzled at it, mulling it through her mind, as he held her hand. The image she'd always held of their relationship would be a difficult thing to lose.

"There's not much left in my life anymore but you and Franny and that career. I tossed everything else away. But realizations this late don't make much difference." He sighed, squeezed her hand, and offered a smile. "You have my support in your decision about Robert."

She squeezed his hand back. "Thank you, Papa."

His eyes filled. "Will you give me yours?"

Miriam nodded, questioning only with her eyes.

"You've taken your stand against Robert. It's time for me to take mine. You feel up to helping me do battle with your mother? Saving what little dignity I have left?"

"Battle with Mother seems to come naturally," she stated. "What do you want me to do?" It was oddly comforting that, this time, the battle would not center around her.

"I want every bottle of laudanum in the house dumped out."

Mother sat on the parlor floor clawing her way through a basket of yarn. One by one, the balls of yarn sailed across the room, accompanied by her low, frustrated mutterings.

Miriam stood near the kitchen doorway, watching. Yesterday Mother had located two bottles, drinking most of one before she'd been caught. It'd been enough to keep her passed out all night and to renew the vomiting and the tremors this morning.

Running a hand through her loosely flowing hair, Miriam sent a mental thank-you to Carrie for taking Franny again. Yesterday she'd dealt with both Mother and the discovery that she wasn't pregnant. It had been a miserable day fraught with both relief and loss. In a way, it was good she had Mother to tie up her time. She would focus on getting her through another day, one day closer to sanity. She'd promised her father.

A rolled skein of yarn flew past her head and Miriam ducked.

Harriet laughed gleefully. The sound was an eerie contrast to the ragged woman on the floor.

"You scheming, vicious girl, why are you doing this to me? I should have left you to rot in that boarding school. This is the thanks I get for bringing you here and nurturing you, finding you a suitable man."

Miriam drew a breath. Mother had been bringing Robert up all day, pushing her. She tried to shake off her words. It was the withdrawal from the laudanum talking, that's all.

"Can't I have just a little bit? For my head?" Her mother whined.

Miriam crossed the room and knelt beside her. "There's no more. How about we fix your hair?" She ran her fingers through the tangled mess of fading auburn. Never had she imagined her mother allowing herself to look this way.

Mother slapped at her hand. "Get away from me."

"Mother, please, I'm only trying to help." Something akin to pity filled Miriam's heart.

"If you were trying to help, you would have accepted Robert's proposal instead of flinging him away. Think of what people must be saying." Mother scrambled to her feet and stomped across the room like a child in a tantrum.

Miriam watched her go. Reason wasn't working. Perhaps she needed to be more direct. She joined her mother in the dining room, facing her across the table. "What people are saying is that you are an opium addict. They're not talking about me. They're talking about you, with gossip and nasty comments."

Her mother's face registered shock. "They're not. Oh, they're not." She dropped her face into her hands and sobbed.

"Do you think the post trader kept it a secret that you bought his entire supply of laudanum? Do you think the post surgeon didn't blab that you came begging for his stock?"

As suddenly as the tears had come, Harriet snapped out of them. Her face filled with anger. "It's your fault," she shrieked. Her hands rose to her head and she clutched it hysterically. "My head, my head!" she screamed. She moved around the table, stalking. "The headaches weren't this bad until you came back and started to embarrass me."

The venom of her accusations registered. For days, every effort Miriam had made to keep peace had been flung in her face. Her patience snapped and she glared at her mother. "You've been drinking the stuff for years," she shouted. "Papa told me."

"It's his fault. He pushed me into it, forcing me to come here to this godforsaken post in the middle of nowhere." She continued to move around the table, the hysterics sliding into a slow, deliberate monotone of voice and movement. "He should have been a general by now, stationed someplace civilized. Somewhere I would have been appreciated."

"Stop it, Mother. That's enough."

"Can't you get Mother one more little drink? Be a good girl and help Mother?"

Miriam shook her head. "No more."

Her watchful eyes followed Miriam. The contour of her face changed from blankness to contempt. "I saw you looking at him."

Miriam's legs trembled. Jake's memory slammed into her, forcing the thoughts she had banished to resurface. She felt the pressure behind her eyes and willed the tears to stay put. *Jake*.

"Be quiet," she whispered, not trusting her voice further.

Her mother advanced, a leer on her face. "You thought I didn't notice, but I did." Her voice rose sharply. "You looked at him like some whore. Like you'd get down on your knees for him. And he looked back at you like he'd take you then and there. Like an animal."

Miriam felt the tears slip down her face. *It wasn't that way. It wasn't.* She stood against the kitchen door, watching Mother move closer. *Oh, God, Jake.* Her knees felt weak, and she fought against the haze of emptiness that surged through her.

Harriet stopped, inches from Miriam, and smiled vindictively. "Your father used to have that look. But I taught him, taught him good. Just like Robert would have taught you. Civilized people don't behave that way."

Miriam fought against the looming wave of loss. "Stop it!" she screamed. "You are a hateful woman."

Mother's smile froze in place, a visible tremor moving through her body. She grinned. "And *you* are a whore."

Miriam stared back, stung by the insult, but refusing to surrender. The silence stretched as they stared at one another. Mother's eyes blazed with a strange intensity and Miriam felt herself gasp for breath. She watched her mother's hands clench, the image registering in her mind at the same time she felt her attack. The force of the blow sent her reeling backward, into the door. It gave way behind her and momentum carried her to the kitchen floor.

"Your father said I'd find you here." Eulalie's soft voice interrupted the quiet solitude of the post chapel as she slid into the pew next to Miriam.

"Oh, Eulalie." She fell into her friend's ready embrace. "I'm so glad you're here."

"I would imagine so, dearling. I'm so glad you're not hurt. I don't know why your father refused to let me come sooner. He took the laudanum away, didn't he?"

Miriam nodded, grateful to finally have someone to talk to. "He poured every bottle we could find into the slop pail and dumped it all into the privy." She pulled back and Eulalie stroked the tear trails on her cheek.

"He should have sent for me to help you with her."

"He couldn't, not without you seeing how bad she was." Miriam pulled her hands away and reached into her pocket for a handkerchief. She wiped her eyes. "The first day or so was easy. She was still pretty ill. Once past that, she settled into a pattern of not sleeping and accusing us of plotting against her. Then she got worse, yelling and screaming at the drop of a hat, and I sent Franny over to Carrie's. I gave in and sent for you after she attacked me."

Eulalie offered a smile. "You're all right?" She glanced around the empty chapel. "The baby?"

Miriam shook her head. "No baby to worry about. In a way, I wish there had been. It would have been a part of Jake."

Eulalie hugged her with unspoken understanding. "I'm sorry, dearling, that you had to go through all that alone." She nodded toward the door. "Let's go for a walk, hmm?"

They gathered their wraps and stepped into the warm February sun. The unseasonably high temperatures had melted the snow away, leaving a brown prairie in wait of the call of spring. Eulalie led the way up the hill, away from the post.

Miriam thought about her mother and tried to wade through her resentment and unexpected sense of abandonment. "Papa says she wasn't like that when they first met," she mused aloud.

"She wasn't," Eulalie responded, shading her eyes and peering across the prairie. "Look at that, would you? God's earth, waiting to bloom." She turned back to Miriam. "She was quite personable back then."

"Papa told me. There's so much I didn't know."

"I'm so glad he finally told you about it. I've wanted so many times to tell you, every time you and Jake tried to push away what you were feeling. Your father and I ruined our lives doing that."

Miriam stopped in her tracks. Eulalie and her father?

Eulalie's face paled. "Oh, my, he didn't tell you all of the story, did he? Oh, dear, he should be telling you, not me."

Suddenly everything made perfect sense to Miriam: Eulalie knowing both of them, her refusal to be taken in by Mother, the pinched expressions she wore when Mother was around, her unique relationship with Father, the inexplicable bond that had drawn them together. "I don't know why I didn't see it. Tell me. I need to hear it, and you know he won't tell me. He can't without betraying her."

Eulalie continued walking. Sighing, she spoke. "It was the summer of 1848. Your father had just returned from the Mexican War, a bright young lieutenant with the future in his hands. He and my brother George had both served under Harriet's father, Colonel Pierpont. Thomas received several promotions during the war and came home as an acceptable suitor for Harriet. George came home as he had left, a private."

The memories crept across Eulalie's face, a smile, shining eyes, and her smooth sure voice. Miriam held her tongue, letting the tale spin around them both.

"We met on the Fourth of July. Harriet left the festivities early because of a headache. George ran into Thomas, and he joined us for the evening, for old times' sake, I suppose." She turned and faced Miriam. "By the end of the night, I was smitten. I believe he was as well. My heart raced every time I saw him. His eyes seemed to devour me. Much like your Jake." She left the thought for a moment, as if trying to decide what to say next. "Throughout the summer, we laughed and talked and grew to know each other. I fell in love, and I believe he loved me. And all the while, Colonel Pierpont was promising him the world, priming him to become his son-in-law."

"Oh, Eulalie, no."

"Harriet was a sparkling woman, accomplished and very much the lady. She'd set her sights on Thomas and let her daddy know it. He offered Tom promises of quick career advancement, maybe even a political appointment. He was well connected. Harriet was desirable. I was the plain-Jane sister of a lowly private."

Miriam reached for her hand, catching it in her own. Though Eulalie hadn't been forbidden, she would have cost Tom both his career and the social position that Harriet offered. In a way, there were so many similarities. "What happened?"

"He was being pressured right and left, by Pierpont and his own well-intentioned friends, to propose to Harriet. Even George felt I was standing in his way. Thomas was so bright and had so much promise. Pierpont could have ruined him."

"You let him go, didn't you?"

"I never told him how I felt and I never let him tell me. I shared passionate kisses with him, knowing that anything further would bind us together forever. Then I pushed him into Harriet's arms because I thought I wasn't good enough and because I was afraid of holding him back. I've regretted it every day since."

Tears gathered in the corners of Eulalie's eyes. Eulalie wiped at them with her free hand and sighed.

"Pierpont died, and all his promises died with him. Thomas has crawled up the career ladder rung by rung through gradual field promotions. And so has George. I became acceptable, the sister of an officer. Harriet became a shrew. And here I am, living as an old maid with my bachelor brother just to lap up the crumbs from your mother's table.

"So, you see, dearling, I couldn't sit back and let you ruin your life. Even if declaring and consummating your love has changed your life forever, you will at least always have the memory of it."

"Oh, Eulalie, I never knew. Does he know how you felt?"

"I don't know, dear. We've never discussed it. Since I joined George here, your father and I have become true friends, something I believe we missed during the first go-around. I treasure that too much to dredge up the past."

Miriam nodded, sifting through all the new information her friend had provided. It made the Christmas gift she and Jake had shared seem all the more precious. It also made her realize how fickle fate could be.

"Yes, dear Eulalie," she said, seeing what her friend could

not, "but do you treasure it enough to find a way around the past? Perhaps it's not buried as deeply as you think."

CHAPTER TWENTY-SEVEN

Jake lay in the rough travois, gritting his teeth at every bump. Hell, it was halfway into February and he'd lost both a month out of his life and the use of his left leg.

He was a goddamned cripple.

The thought slammed through his mind with each jarring pain. Over and over, Old Grandmother had wagged her bony finger at him and lectured him to be still. Twice, he'd ignored her and tried to set out for the fort. He'd ripped the stitches, and Grandmother had thrown up her hands in frustration. When Spotted Elk finally returned to the village, she'd loaded him on the travois herself and ordered Spotted Elk to get him out of her sight.

The travois hit another rut and he swore under his breath. "Shit."

"Keep quiet, my friend," Spotted Elk responded. "You have no one to blame but yourself. You will be lucky now if that leg does not swell with sickness. A grandmother's wisdom should not be ignored. Not even once."

"She could have at least sent a messenger."

"No, she could not. You know this. It was my message to send, not hers. I am sorry that I was delayed on the hunt. I did not know how important it was to you. But if you had stayed put and healed, you would be riding home on a pony instead of bumping along the ground in pain."

He'd only wanted to get back to Miriam, to let her know he

was alive, that he didn't desert like that bastard Wood had probably reported. He'd planned to present his case to her father, as he should have done before he left. Now, he'd cost himself an extra couple of weeks, the pain to go along with it, and all hope of ever being able to provide for a family.

And, most likely, my leg.

He'd noticed the swelling when he rewrapped it, before they set out from camp, and his fever was growing worse. Most army surgeons weren't too good at saving limbs. He thought about the crude bone saw poised above his thigh and swallowed.

How could he expect Miriam to live the kind of life he'd be stuck with now? Hard, brittle poverty in the shadow of a half-man who couldn't pull his own weight. Hungry years and—just to survive—hour upon hour of labor like she'd never known, making her old before her time and robbing her of her spirit.

Jake tried to will the pain away. His mind brought images of Miriam, stamping her foot, her green eyes blazing with challenge then reaching for him, her lips parted and expectant. With the vision came the thought of himself, with a stump for a leg, stuck in some wheeled contraption, watching while her eyes filled with pity and disgust as she grew to hate him.

His heart filled with pain as the picture lodged itself in his brain. Everything would be poisoned, even their memories. He might just as well have died, because pushing her away now would be hell on earth.

Watching her mother parade down the hallway to answer the door, Miriam sighed. Though past the worst of her withdrawal, her disposition had softened little in the two weeks since they'd removed the laudanum. The whole household was tense.

Mother swept into the room like a reigning queen. "There is a dirty little boy at the front door who refuses to leave until he's spoken with you. Get rid of the impudent little thing before I have him removed."

Miriam lay down the spelling primer and gave Franny a re-assuring smile. "Keep working on those words. I'll be right back." She crossed the parlor while a purse-lipped Harriet settled into the rocking chair and picked up her wooden knitting needles.

Miriam neared the front door and recognized Franny's friend Albert. He stood on the porch, shifting his weight from one foot to the other. No doubt he'd heard her mother's sharp comment through the open door. Miriam opened the screen door and debated with herself. Mother wouldn't like it if she invited him in out of the chilly air, but Albert looked cold and Miriam decided to risk raising Mother's hackles. "Come in, Albert, you must be freezing."

He entered, glancing furtively at Harriet and biting his bottom lip.

"It's all right. What did you need?" Miriam prompted.

"Carrie Rupert sent me." Lowering his voice, he spoke in a whisper. "She said to tell you that that Indian what rode in a little while ago brung in her brother an' he ain't dead."

Miriam's knees buckled and she gripped the doorjamb. The pounding of her heart echoed in her ears like a train, disconnected from her body. "Jake," she murmured, collapsing against the wall.

Jake.

"She said to tell ya that they brung him to the hospital an' that his leg is messed up real bad."

Jake's alive?

She grasped the open door and pulled herself away from the wall. "Are you sure?" The shocked thumping of her heart settled into a rapid patter of anticipation.

"I heard her say it plain as day. I even seen the Indian my own self." At the sharp sound of snapping wood and rustling fabric, Albert glanced toward the parlor. "I gotta go, Miss Miriam." He scooted past her and out the door as her mother emerged into the hallway, a broken knitting needle in her hand.

"That boy ought to be ashamed, telling such stories."

Miriam moved away from the door and faced her mother. "What makes you think it's a story?" she asked, forcing an even tone into her voice while her mind raced. Jake was alive, here, at Fort Randall. She reached for her winter shawl, not caring if her mother responded.

"And just where do you think you're going? Gracious, it was Robert himself who discovered the private's remains."

"Precisely why I've no problem believing Albert. Franny, get your wrap. I'm taking you to Eulalie's."

"Miriam." Mother's mouth pinched and her eyes narrowed.

Miriam stepped closer, emboldened. "Robert has gone out of his way to lie, slander, and injure Jake again and again. Believe what you want, but you can rest assured that if it is Jake lying in the hospital, Robert will have more than a little explaining to do. Now, excuse me, I'm going to see Jake."

Mother sucked in a huge gulp of air. "You are doing no such thing. Why, of all the harebrained ideas. Visiting an enlisted man. Do you want the entire fort gossiping about you?"

Miriam's fists clenched. How could her mother be so blind? "I don't care what the entire fort says. None of it matters." She moved, pacing and gesturing with her hands. "For months, I've let you control my life by listening to you insist that I do everything according to society's expectations. I refuse to throw away any more of my choices. Besides, you should be used to gossip by now. After all, there was no end to it the whole while that you were on your little laudanum kick."

Mother's eyes widened. "If you go out that door, so help me, I'll—"

"You'll do what, Mother? Disown me? You did that a long

time ago. Let's go, pet." She waited for Franny to exit, then stepped onto the porch and closed the door on her mother, her thoughts scampering ahead to Jake. She needed to see him, touch him, tell him she loved him.

Then, she would see her father. It was time he knew what was going on, time she made her choice known.

Forty-five minutes later, she was still sitting in the post surgeon's office, waiting impatiently for the doctor's return and some word on Jake's condition. The bare white walls offered her nothing to focus on except her thoughts.

A thousand questions filled her mind. Had Jake been captured and become an easy target of Robert's lie? Or had he been left out there on the prairie somewhere? The smell of ether lingered in the building, choking in its pervasiveness. Had the cold January air seeped into Jake's body the same way? Had he lain there alone, wondering when help would come, while Robert told everyone he was dead? Had he lain there thinking about her, wondering if her inability to publicly declare their love meant she was in doubt?

At the sound of footsteps, she glanced up. The surgeon entered the room, disheveled and obviously fatigued.

"The matron said you were inquiring about Deakins. Knife wounds, some of them healing, some of them not, neck and chest area and upper thigh. Broken ribs. Missed the vital organs. Looks like he was pretty well tended. Probably by the Indian that hauled him in. Ripped out the stitches in his thigh more than once, though, and the leg's infected."

Miriam's stomach roiled at the image. "May I see him?"

"I'd just as soon not have you in the way. We're going to be fighting that infection all night if we want any chance of saving the leg. If the infection progresses, we won't have any choice but to cut the leg off. I'm already having to work around his sister."

"I just need to see him, just see him." The words tumbled out.

"In and out, or rotate with Mrs. Rupert. I don't want you both in there disrupting things and getting in my way." He bustled away like a tired chipmunk.

Miriam walked the deserted hallway to the ward, listening to the click of her heels on the bare wooden floor. She pushed open the plain swinging doors and entered. The room appeared clean, but the subtle odor of stale blood and sweat and urine mingled together as she walked past the beds of the sick and injured, smells of daily use that could not be removed by any amount of scrubbing. A hospital steward glanced up then returned to his duties.

Near a bed at the end of the ward, Carrie sat in a straight-backed wooden chair, dozing. Her usually bright face was etched with worry lines, her eyes ringed with dark circles. One hand rested on her swollen abdomen.

Miriam approached, reluctant to disrupt Carrie's sleep but unable to stay away. Jake lay on his back, his chest bare, sweat glistening among golden hairs. His breathing was fitful. She neared. His body twitched, stopping her in her tracks. *Oh, God, he's in pain.*

A threadbare cotton sheet covered him to the waist. Her gaze traveled to his left thigh. A dull red stain had dried into the sheet.

Jake.

Carrie stirred and opened her eyes. "Miriam?"

"How is he?"

"Mostly out cold. I've been trying to keep his fever down with a washcloth but I guess I fell asleep. Doc says he's in a bad way."

"The leg?" Miriam eyed the bloodstain again, wondering if Jake could feel the wound.

"They been treating it with burnt alum."

"Can he hear us?"

"It ain't likely, but I keep talkin' to him anyways, when Doc's not workin' on him."

Miriam touched his hand, drawing bask at the surprising heat. After Carrie lumbered away to the privy, Miriam pulled the chair closer to Jake's bed and reached for the washcloth on the bedside table. Dipping it into the basin of tepid water, she wiped his brow, then sponged his face.

"Jake? Sweetheart? I'm here. I thought you were gone. My heart ached. I'm not going to lose you, not after that, not ever. I love you, Jake."

She felt tears slide down her face as she moistened the washcloth again and bathed his chest. She stroked the still-fresh scars on his neck, his upper chest, and fought to keep from crying. Christmas Eve seemed so very far away.

Jake moaned and twitched again.

"Shhh," she told him. "You're here, and you're going to be all right. Shh, my love, shh."

She laid the washcloth across his forehead and leaned over him. She caressed his face, kissed him, and laid her head on his chest.

The night dragged on.

Carrie had reluctantly left, persuaded by the doctor that she was threatening the baby. Miriam sat vigil, leaving only when ordered away by Doc Perkins.

Twice, the wound had bled without restraint, soaking both bandage and sheet, and throwing Perkins and his steward into a panic. They'd staunched the bleeding with more burnt alum while acrid smells had saturated the air. Miriam had hovered nearby, hurting for Jake, as they'd flung back the sheet in their hurry to get to his leg. The wound was swollen, red and puffed, straining against the black stitches that were meant to hold it closed. Yellow pus had oozed out with the blood and she'd turned away.

Now Jake lay quietly. It had been five hours since the leg last bled.

"Miss Longstreet?" Doc Perkins approached. "You need to get some sleep."

"A little later," she told him.

"Your father's in my office again."

Miriam nodded. Perkins had interceded last night, but his tone made it clear that he expected her to speak to her father this time. She touched Jake's face, found it cooler, and turned to Perkins. "His fever's down."

"I'll tend to him. Go on now."

She rose and crossed the ward. Sun shone through the windows, striping the floor with light. Several patients sat, propped by pillows, eating their breakfasts. Last night's odors were masked by the scent of bacon and fried potatoes.

She entered Perkins' office and her father rose from his chair. "Close the door," he told her.

The click of the latch echoed through the room, and she took a deep breath. She smoothed her wrinkled skirt, her fingers brushing across a small bloodstain. It was time. She turned and faced him with determination. "Papa."

He nodded toward the empty chair and waited until she was settled before sitting back down in his own. "Your mother is ranting, and I've had my own worries about you and Deakins for some time. The fact that you've been at his side for hours seems to confirm that something is going on here. I think it's time you filled me in."

Miriam tried to read his face. His familiar brown mustache

twitched and his gray eyes were filled with expectancy. No other emotions were apparent. It was now or never. "I think I should have done that a long time ago."

"Eulalie says you love him?"

Simple and to the point. Leave it to Eulalie.

"Yes, Father, I love him. And he loves me." She stated it as evenly as she could, hoping he would understand.

"Miriam, he's an enlisted man. What are you thinking?" He stood and paced the small office.

"We tried to avoid loving each other. When we realized we couldn't, we meant to get you used to the idea slowly. But the campaign got in the way and I thought he was dead."

"Get me used to it? How I happen to feel about it is not going to change facts, here. There are lines that aren't supposed to be crossed."

She stood and faced him. "Whose lines? Lines drawn by upper-class hypocrites who fear the loss of their superiority if someone discovers good fortune is the only difference separating them from those they look down upon? Papa, I can't take the risk of losing him again while we try to make this work within society's rules. Don't you ever wish you had crossed them?"

A stunned silence hung between them.

"It just isn't done, Miriam," he stated. "You don't challenge the system like that and come out unscathed. Your social standing—"

"I couldn't care less about my social standing."

"And my career?"

"Papa, you're already stationed in the middle of nowhere. Unless you're in line for a promotion you haven't told us about, what can they do to you?"

He closed his eyes for a moment and sighed.

Miriam approached him and pressed her point. "You, of all

people, should know what happens to your life when you refuse to follow your heart's choice."

His face registered surprise, then concession tinged with pain. "God, how I wish I could do it all over again."

"Then don't make me do it."

He opened his arms and she melted into his hug. "You are wise beyond your years, girl."

She embraced him, then pulled back. "I need to let Carrie know Jake's fever's down. Then I intend to come back here and sit with him. I'd like your blessing, Papa, but I don't need it."

"No, you don't. Not anymore. But you have it anyway."

"You awake yet?"

Jake struggled to focus his eyes at the sound of Doc Perkins' voice and watched the busy little man make his way to his bedside. The doctor sank into the chair and leaned forward, his busy face illuminated by the afternoon sun.

"I'm awake, Doc," he croaked, his voice raspy from disuse.

"Good, good. You been drifting for a couple days, now."

Jake pulled his thoughts together, remembering bits and pieces—Miriam sitting vigil with soft words of encouragement. He tried to sit and experienced a wave of pain so intense that it forced him backward. *Oh, God, they took the leg.* He lay without moving, gathering his strength, then tentatively felt for his limb. The leg was intact. He heaved a sigh of relief.

"Easy, there, son. Don't move so fast." Perkins waited for his attention. "You with me? We need to talk about your prognosis. Messy wound. Serious in the first place. Made messier and more serious by your own stupidity. You should have stayed put until those stitches set. We saved the leg, but it may not be of much use. Don't think it'll bear full weight again. Tore up the muscle pretty bad. Longstreet requested a field promotion for you. We'll file for medical discharge as soon as the promotion comes through. Give you a little more in disability payments. Figure it'll take a few months, though, to get the paperwork through. Any questions?"

Doc's clipped words blazed through his mind like fire. Messy. Not much use. Disability. He'd be a cripple, just like he'd thought, unable to provide for Miriam ever again.

"Questions?"

Jake swallowed against a wave of powerless misery and struggled for his voice. "When you say it won't be of much use, what exactly do you mean?"

"No doubt on the limp. Cane'll be likely."

"But I'll walk?"

"Depends on keeping infection at bay, how hard you work and how things heal."

"How long do I gotta lie here?" The thought of Miriam, visiting every day, her pity building into resentment, plagued him. The thought tasted bitter. God, he hoped she'd stay away.

Perkins shifted in his chair and cleared his throat. "I want you off the leg until the danger of further infection is gone and the wound starts to knit. We'll take the stitches out in a couple of weeks. Stay put for a week or two. Then, if you still got the leg, you can start using that crutch that's leaning by the wall." Jake's glance drifted to the corner. A stark wooden crutch stood there, reminding him that he was a cripple. "No weight on it until the stitches set. As for how long you stay in the hospital? It depends on the paperwork. Heard about one fellow who waited eleven months. Figure at least two or three."

Jake groaned. "Months? Just to get out of here?" He covered his face with his hands, searching for strength. He'd get through the physical discomfort without a hitch. But there'd be the rest of his empty life. How the hell was he going to survive life without Miriam?

"If you're lucky," Perkins chuckled. "You ever try to hurry the army?"

"And how long before I can walk?"

"Pretty much depends on you. Won't be easy. First off, that crutch'll rub your armpit raw. Your right leg's going to ache from bearing all the weight. That thigh muscle was partially severed. It'll be inflamed when you start using it. It'll put stress on your knee every time you use it. First couple of weeks, the pain'll be intense. No way around it. Get yourself through it and we'll give you a cane. But let me warn you, if you try using that leg too soon this time, you'll destroy that muscle. You'll be looking at a crutch for the rest of your life. If you don't lose the leg altogether."

Jake looked away and closed his eyes. Already, he could feel the needlelike spasms coursing through him every time he shifted in his bed. The pain would only get worse. If only he'd stayed off the leg like Old Grandmother had advised.

"Thanks for the encouragement." He spat out the words.

"Look, son, I can sit here blathering all day about how lucky you are and how nice that disability check will be and how you'll do just fine. But when it comes right down to it, I'm not going to paint you some rosy picture or make you a bunch of promises. You know you're alive. The rest is up to you. Recovery isn't easy, but it is possible. Understand?"

"Yes, sir," he said blandly.

"I understand your sister's contract is up come June?"

Jake shifted again, gritting his teeth, remembering his visit from Carrie earlier in the day. He turned back to Perkins. "That's right. Baby's due next month."

"She figure out yet what she's going to do?"

"We know a couple of folks in Yankton from when her husband and I worked on the railroad. Fenkelstein over at the mercantile and Smith at the hotel. I think Smith has a job for her."

"You might be thinking about yourself, too," Perkins advised. "You're not going to be doing any more railroad construction, son, and I'd advise against homesteading. Leg'll be fine for the business world."

Jake nodded, his mind already picking through the narrow choices he'd have available. For an enlisted man, he reckoned he was pretty well educated. But he sure as hell wasn't prepared for the business world.

He pictured himself limping around some small godforsaken town, doing lonely odd jobs, emptying chamber pots in some fancy hotel or washing dishes. Hell, he could wash dishes and peel potatoes real good. Maybe he'd head back East and labor in some damned factory from dawn to dusk six days a week and live in some rat-infested tenement with a slew of other tired people who had no lives.

Perkins slapped the bed and stood, glancing around the ward. "Got work to do, son. I'll stop back later. Stay put."

Jake watched him move across the empty ward. Stay put. As if it really mattered.

When Jake woke next, Miriam sat in the chair next to the bed, asleep. He watched her, studying her face, remembering how the light of Eulalie's cookstove had illuminated her skin, and wondered how in the hell he was going to turn her away.

For a moment, he considered rousing Miriam, telling her he loved her, planning their future. Then he pushed the thought away.

What good was a leg if he couldn't use it? He'd be a cripple. Shit, he'd messed up that leg muscle so bad, he'd be lucky to walk on it at all. Not much a man could do for a living when he couldn't walk. Not much of a man at all. The picture of Miriam living in abject poverty, hating and pitying him, spread through his mind, taking over.

How could he do that to her? He had to let her go.

He watched her, memorizing every inch of her face, letting the memories of their night together wash over him. Her thick auburn hair, curled around his fingers, her neck, arched in ecstasy, hooded emerald eyes, her silken skin, her heart pounding beneath his hand, her breasts.

He shook the picture away and gathered his resolve.

"What are you doing here?" he finally asked. His voice echoed against the quiet walls of the ward.

Miriam's eyes flew open. Her face registered a mixture of pleasure, surprise, and puzzlement in rapid succession.

"Jake." She let his name drift from her lips, an endearment. "Oh, love, I thought you were dead."

"What are you doin' here, woman? Ain't you got nothin' better to do?" He forced contempt into his voice and spoke roughly. Pain seared through both his body and his heart.

She leaned forward, touching his arm gently. "Jake, sweetheart, rest. You've been through—"

He shook her hand away. "Damn it, I asked you what you were doin' here. Seems to me you got lots of other things to keep you busy."

Her face faltered, her lower lip trembling, and he fought to keep from crushing her into his arms and confessing his love.

"How can you ask that? I love you. We—"

He snorted. "Yeah, right. We sure did, didn't we?" He turned his lip up, attempting a sneer. "Had a real good time. And I sure as hell paid for it, too. Shoulda left you alone."

Miriam's eyes welled with tears and he looked away. *Damn. Damn it to hell.* He swallowed against his own misery. *Dear God, let her leave. Don't make me hurt her any further.*

"Jake, what's going on? I love you."

"Love? Like hell." He glanced back at her, willing it all to be over, and saw only her devastation. It was written in the disbelief that painted her face, in the anguished tears that fought their way down her cheeks. The memory would torture him forever. "You needed takin' down off your high an' mighty perch. Well, you're down now, ain't cha? We're both payin' for it. Get out of my sight."

He turned away from her, agony and unspeakable pain washing over him. He heard the chair push back and the clip of her heels as she moved away. The swoosh of the door at the end of the ward cast a finality on her exit. He listened to it swing back and forth, each lingering swish cutting to the core of his soul.

CHAPTER TWENTY-EIGHT

Miriam sat on the kitchen stoop, still numb with shock. The late afternoon sun cast a long shadow against the house, mirroring her gloomy mood.

Jake wasn't coherent. He couldn't be. He wouldn't have said those cruel things to her if he'd been in his right mind. She'd return to the hospital and find Doc Perkins. Perhaps there was a head injury he hadn't mentioned, some medical reason for Jake to be talking so crazy. In a few days, he'd be all right. He'd remember what they had shared—

The door opened behind her, and she frowned at the interruption.

"Miriam Elizabeth Longstreet, you get into this house this minute." Her mother's voice rose to a squeal.

Miriam closed her eyes, wishing she could somehow make her mother disappear. "I'd prefer to sit here a little longer."

With hawk-like suddenness, Harriet latched her hand onto Miriam's upper arm. Her fingers dug in like talons, forcing Miriam to pay attention. She tightened her grip, her nails biting into Miriam's skin through her woolen dress. "Get up," she hissed.

Miriam tried to shake loose but her mother only grasped her arm tighter.

"Get up," she commanded again. Her eyes glazed with a look of temporary madness.

Miriam recoiled. "Let go."

Harriet pulled at her, surprising Miriam with her strength. Stumbling up the wooded steps, Miriam struggled to her feet as her mother jerked her into the house. The vice-like grip on her arm neither wavered nor relented.

Once inside the kitchen, Miriam planted her feet and twisted until her mother's grip faltered and she broke free. "What are you doing?" she yelled, moving out of Harriet's reach. She rubbed her arm, soothing the muscles that had been shocked by her mother's wild grasp.

"Bringing you inside where you belong. You didn't sleep in this house last night." Mother's face was beet red and she moved toward Miriam, stalking her. Miriam backed up, alert, remembering their last incident.

"No, Mother, I did not."

"Where were you?" Mother's low voice filled with rage. Miriam eyed the door behind her mother and ruled it out as an escape. She backed toward the dining room, weighing her answer.

"At the hospital, helping Doctor Perkins."

She watched her mother's eyes narrow and knew the answer had failed to satisfy her. Harriet sprang forward, closing the space between them, and her fist landed sharply against Miriam's mouth. Miriam fell backward, stunned that she hadn't seen the movement coming. She tasted blood and wiped at her mouth, then scrambled back to her feet and slipped into the dining room.

Mother rushed after her, grasping Miriam's dress. Miriam propelled herself across the room, her skirt ripping apart as her mother stood rooted, a tattered scrap of Miriam's dress in her hand. They faced each other at opposite sides of the table. Between them, an empty bottle of laudanum lay discarded on the tabletop. Miriam eyed it, and her mother, warily.

"I watched Jake struggle for his life. The life he almost lost because I was too cowardly to stand up to you."

"You are his whore, aren't you?"

Mother leered at her but the words were empty. They were just one more pitiful drug-induced utterance. Miriam fought to keep her breathing even, her head clear, looking for a means of escape. She had only to make it through the parlor and around the settee to the hall. Then it would be a straight shot out the front door.

A slight movement caught her attention. The bedroom door opened and she saw Franny's worried face peering out. *Oh, God, Franny.* Miriam stood, waiting, until Franny's gaze locked on her. She shook her head slowly, steadily, until Franny nodded and closed the door.

"Quit playing your games. Vulgar names are useless here. I love Jake and I intend to spend my life with him."

Harriet's nostrils flared with anger and her face reddened. "Over my dead body," she hissed.

"If that's what it takes." Miriam dropped the words and rushed into the parlor. Her mother sprang for her, catching her wrist and wrenching it. Sharp spasms of pain jolted up Miriam's arm. Mother twisted it further, forcing her to be still.

Miriam gasped, slumping forward and feeling Mother's grip loosen. The pain began to ebb. Miriam forced her body to relax, a simulated surrender, and waited for her mother to seize the victory.

Harriet dropped her hold and began to gloat. "You forget who makes the rules here, who runs things. I'll see to it that you never—"

"Like you saw to it that Father gave up Eulalie? How you must have loved watching him slowly realize the mistake he'd made, making him suffer because he loved her, not you." The words tumbled out of her mouth before Miriam could stop them, and she backed away from her mother.

Mother's face crumpled and her hands flew up, as if trying to block an attack. "Shut up. Shut up."

Months of bitterness rose like bile in Miriam's throat and words continued to pour out. "It must burn, it must burn something awful to look into your husband's eyes and see what you see, all the while knowing that you have to be polite and sociable to the woman he really loves. So much so that you can't let anyone else have what you can't have."

"Shut up!" Harriet screamed.

The surge of power that had fueled Miriam's tirade calmed as she watched her mother's defeat, melted into a solid realization that Harriet no longer held any control over her life. She savored the exhilaration of her independence for a moment before turning back to declare it to her mother.

"How does it feel to realize you don't have any power anymore? Because I won't let you make my choices for me anymore. This is love's choice, not yours."

Her mother sagged against the words as Miriam moved across the parlor and into the hall. She threw open the front door, recognizing the rustle of her mother's skirts as she pursued. "You're not leaving this house," Harriet screeched.

Harriet's stampeding footfalls echoed behind Miriam. Miriam glanced backward as Harriet balled her fist and lunged. The punch slammed into Miriam's lower back. The intensity of the blow brought Miriam to her knees. Gasping, she fought to stay conscious, only dimly aware of Harriet's next forceful push. Miriam tumbled down the stairs and her shoulder hit the ground. A hot stab of pain rocked through her body and she drifted into blackness.

Tom Longstreet paced the parlor, unable to separate worry from rage. Franny sat on the red settee, her knees pulled to her chest, a panicked expression in her big hazel eyes.

"I'm scared, Papa," she whispered.

Tom turned to her, forcing his face into a disciplined picture of calm and reassurance. "I know you are, sweetie, but everything's going to be just fine. You were such a big girl to run all the way to the hospital. You knew just what to do." He smiled at her and waited for the praise to pull her self-confidence out of her.

"Mother hurt Miriam bad, didn't she?" she asked, maturity merging with innocence.

"She'll be just fine. Doc Perkins is with her now. He'll take care of her."

He settled down next to her and pulled her onto his lap. Lord, she was growing up already, almost too big for such baby-ing. Where had the years gone? He was tossing them away, like he had Miriam's childhood, on a career that had long since ceased to advance or even be important to him. Somewhere along the line, the army had become his escape from Harriet, his refuge, and he'd left the girls as his line of defense. He should have been there on the front line, not them, never them.

Offering Franny another hug, he slid her back onto the sofa and rose. It was time he stopped retreating and made a stand.

"Doc?" he queried, knocking on Miriam's bedroom door.

Seconds later, Perkins poked his head out. "Be right there," he said, then closed the door. Tom glanced back at Franny and smiled again for her benefit before leaning against the wall. On impulse, he raised his arms in a rodent-like pose and made a chattering sound. Franny giggled.

A warm feeling melted over him and his smile became genuine. God, he'd missed so much.

"Major?" Perkins emerged from the bedroom and darted past Tom into the parlor. Tom followed as the doctor launched into his report. "Left shoulder dislocated. Minor bruises, except for her kidney area. That'll be a nasty one. Slightly sprained ankle. I popped the shoulder without much problem, wrapped the ankle. Keep her immobile for a few days, maybe a week or so."

"Is she awake?"

"Passed out early on. Don't know if it was the laudanum or the pain, but she'll be out for a while. From here on out, give her whiskey if she needs something. Might be better if I didn't leave the laudanum."

"Thanks, Perkins."

"Fetch me if necessary. I'll send one of the matrons over to help out. Anybody find your missus? She injured?"

"I found her sitting out back, shaken up and pretty well out of it but otherwise fine. Don't know where she got the damned bottle this time. I took her to the Applebys' place to sleep it off. I didn't want her here."

"Very well, then." Perkins moved swiftly to the front door and disappeared outside without another word while Tom wondered what he was going to do about his wife.

Robert sat on an empty wooden crate on the verandah of his quarters and studied the frenzied evening activity at the Longstreet household.

Well, the old bat had finally gone too far. The major himself had ushered her out the door and across the parade ground to the Applebys. Frances had been bawling her head off and the doctor had come running. Whatever was going on, it was enough to have kept the major occupied. And whatever kept the major busy was good. Anything to keep him from pondering overmuch on what exactly had happened to Private Jake Deakins.

Robert stood and kicked the crate.

He sure as hell hadn't expected that stupid heathen to come riding into camp hauling Deakins' not-so-dead carcass behind him. Sooner or later, Longstreet would question him about it.

He had no doubt. He would just need to be ready.

Nor had he any illusions about Miriam. As soon as that wreck of a soldier healed up enough to think straight, she'd be cozying up to Deakins, and his own ticket up the career ladder would be gone for good. He heard she'd been sitting over by the private's bed almost round the clock. The only good news he'd had was that Deakins had sent her away in tears.

He leaned against the porch rail and scraped at the peeling white paint. He knew Miriam well enough to realize she wouldn't give up. She'd be back there hounding Deakins every day until he gave in and talked with her.

Shit.

The sound of voices caught his attention. Doc Perkins stood at the Longstreet door, apparently offering last-minute instructions, then slid into the growing darkness.

Robert straightened up, smugly satisfied that he'd made the decision to watch and wait. He willed his face to soften while Perkins strode back to the hospital.

"Evening, Doc," he said when the physician neared.

Perkins stared at him, offering nothing, forcing him to probe. His thoughts flew. The only person he hadn't seen leave the house was Miriam. It had to be Miriam.

"Is she all right?" he asked with just the proper amount of concern for a fiancé.

"She's lucky, Lieutenant, lucky. Dislocated her shoulder. She'll be in pain for a while. Best she keeps to her bed."

"I'll do my best to keep her there, sir," Robert said and watched the busy little man drift away toward the hospital.

He'd keep her there, all right, even if he had to tie her down. It would give him time to get rid of Deakins for good.

Thirty minutes later, Tom sat in Eulalie's parlor and listened to Franny's once-again-cheerful chatter. She was enjoying cookies and milk in Eulalie's kitchen with Eulalie's brother, George. Eulalie closed the kitchen door on their spirited conversation.

"Thank you for taking her," he said.

Eulalie crossed to the parlor and sat down in one of the simple straight-backed chairs that comprised their company furniture. "Miriam will sleep better this way. Besides, she's always welcome here, Tom. You know that."

"I know, but thank you anyway." They sat in companionable silence while Tom tried to sort through the hodgepodge of thoughts in his head. "I'm so damned angry at Harriet."

"Of course you are."

"What she did was inexcusable."

"What she did, Tom, was beyond the Harriet I know." As usual, Eulalie's voice was that of reason.

He frowned at her, unwilling to be swayed. "I wish I could say it was beyond the Harriet I know. But she's become a complete stranger. I haven't known her for years. Maybe I never knew her in the first place. There was a time when I thought we had common dreams. We'd spend hours planning my military career, plotting out every turn of events. Then, somewhere along the line, I realized it was her goal, not mine, and that we didn't have anything in common after all."

"I'm sorry," Eulalie said.

He rose and began pacing. "What happens the next time she finds a bottle of laudanum? Does she kill one of my girls?" He stopped and stood in front of her. "God, Eulalie, how did things get to this point? What am I going to do with her?"

Eulalie looked up at him, refusing to be drawn in. "Tom, I can't answer that for you. I'm not even sure you should be discussing this with me."

"If not you, whom? A commanding officer has no friends."

"Perhaps the chaplain?"

Tom kicked the chair, wishing he could throw it against the

wall. "So I can listen to him tell me again to forgive her and to maintain this farce of a marriage because it's a holy sacrament? I've already heard all the advice he has to offer."

Eulalie stood and crossed to him, her usually quiet eyes ablaze. "And what is it you want from me? My nod of approval to do whatever you have in mind? I can't do that. I won't."

"Why not? You gave your approval when I married her." He flung the words at her, words he should have uttered more than twenty years ago.

She let the comment pass. "I know you're angry. But this is not something that involves me. Right or wrong, you made your life with Harriet. I wasn't part of that decision, and I won't be made a part of this one."

But Tom had come too far to let the matter drop. He hadn't made the decision alone, and she knew it. "Oh, but you were. We might not have sat down and discussed my decision, but you know you were a part of it. By your very silence you were a part of it."

"Tom." Eulalie looked away from him.

He touched her face, turning her gaze back to him. "One word from you and I—"

"And you what? You would not have married her?" She threw up her hands to emphasize her point. "Tom, if you didn't know how you felt, it wasn't up to me to tell you."

"I didn't know how *you* felt."

"You didn't ask."

The comment settled into Tom's mind. She was right, he hadn't asked. He'd simply pulled away from her, pulled away without facing their feelings for each other. And he'd been doing it ever since.

He touched her face again then headed toward the door.

This time, it was his move.

★　★　★　★　★

Early the next morning, Tom stood outside his office door, wishing he'd been able to get a good night's sleep. He'd tossed fitfully, rest evading him, until he'd settled on a course of action. Having done so, he'd summoned his wife.

He opened the door and peered in.

Harriet sat in one of the office side chairs staring vacantly out the window. She looked as haggard as he felt. Her face was sallow and her hands twitched. She fidgeted.

"Harriet," he said.

"Major." Her face remained devoid of emotion as he entered the room.

"It would appear we have much to discuss." He closed the door behind him and circled his desk, realizing he was speaking to her as he would a soldier. Good Lord, when had they lost the ability to talk?

His thoughts drifted to last night's conversation with Eulalie. The words came so easily with her, more so than they ever had with Harriet. Still, this barren gulf was more than he'd realized existed.

It hadn't always been that way. Harriet had been vivacious, perfect at filling silences. They'd talked about the future, his advancement, their future social status. The divergence had been so gradual, so unremarkable, that he hadn't even realized it was happening. Not until he had suddenly found her conversation overbearing and her efforts to placate his superiors phony. Not until the headaches had become so bad that she began to drink the laudanum to escape.

But even then, she had never been so hostile. Or had that, too, been something he hadn't noticed? Hadn't wanted to notice?

"Harriet?"

"It wasn't supposed to turn out like this." She turned to him, her voice wooden and empty. A deep despair filled her eyes.

Tom stared at her, seeing the emptiness, and knew she, too, felt the loss. He pushed himself on, refusing to let things go unsaid any longer. "What happened yesterday can't—"

She rose to her feet with deliberate suddenness. "Your life wasn't the only one that was sacrificed. I could've had my pick of suitors. My pick. You could have gone so far, Thomas, so far. Papa was going to—"

"Yes, Papa," he shouted, unwilling to be drawn into her self-pity. "Your papa was going to see to it that I jumped up that career ladder. Well, your papa died." He pushed back his chair and stood, looking down on her. "He died, and we both got the hell we deserved for selling our souls to ambition."

"It didn't have to be that way. You failed." She hissed the words at him from across the desk and her eyes narrowed.

Somehow, it always came back to his failures. He'd listened to her innuendos for years, the little rubs about his lack of advancement. Tom felt his anger rise and gave it full rein for the first time. He slammed the desk with his fist.

"I didn't fail. I got stuck in the system. I didn't have the proper lineage or the connections, and I spent the damned War Between the States in a godforsaken supply depot because you had just enough pull to get me stranded there. I lost any chance I had of rapid field promotions. You held me back even while you complained. So don't you dare tell me I failed."

"Would you rather I had been a widow?"

"Just let it be, Harriet. It's over and done with, all of it. It's been over for years."

She placed her palms on the desk and leaned forward. "I tried to save you. I gave up everything to help you make an impression, to get you promoted. I've lived in squalor. It makes me sick to think of everything I could have had." Bitterness filled her words, the Harriet she had become overtaking all else.

"And while you were busy thinking of everything you didn't have, you didn't even see the treasures you had in Miriam and Frances." He moved toward the window. Harriet's heels clicked on the wooden floor as she followed him.

"Defiant children you left me alone to raise while you twiddled away your time pretending to be someone of significant rank. You couldn't even manage to get a post where I could keep a governess. Those girls ran wild and you let them. My head pounded and still you foisted all the discipline on me."

The words were hard. His mind raced through thoughts of what might have been if he'd only put his foot down earlier, if he'd tried harder, for all of them. "I shall regret not being there for them every day of my life."

"As you should. You let me suffer for years."

He turned, inches from her, and let anguish flow with his words. "I let them suffer, Harriet. Them."

"I could have gotten you transferred back East if they'd been better behaved."

Tom listened to her whine, watched the pout form on her face. A petulant child. She should have stayed home with her father in the first place.

"Be quiet, Harriet. We've all suffered enough."

Harriet wandered across the room, drifting in the sea of silence, emotions moving across her face as she let go of her train of thought.

He recognized the now-familiar behavior borne of laudanum withdrawal and waited for her to come back to reality. He felt tired, incredibly tired. God, how he wanted it all to be over. The tick of the gold clock on his desk filled several minutes before she turned back.

"How is Miriam?" she asked hesitantly.

Tom weighed the question. Did she really even care?

"How the hell do you think she is? You punched her in the

kidney and pushed her down a goddamn flight of stairs with enough force to dislocate her arm. You could have killed her."

"I didn't mean to hurt her. You know I didn't mean to hurt her." Harriet's face was remorseful, and Tom wished remorse was enough.

"But you did, Harriet, so quit whining about whether you set out to do it on purpose. You hurt her, and you'll hurt her again. Or Franny. Next time you find a bottle of laudanum, it'll be the same thing all over again." He faced her and pushed on, taking his stand. Finally. "I'm not going to let that happen. You don't belong here anymore."

Harriet's eyes widened in shock. "What are you saying?"

"I will not have you living in my house anymore."

"*Your* house?" she quavered.

"You are not army personnel. You are here at the pleasure of the commanding officer, and it is no longer my pleasure to have you here. In fact, it is no longer my pleasure to be married to you. You can start fresh, find a rich politician who will appreciate your skills. Nobody need even know about your little mistake." He heard her intake of breath as he neared and watched stunned disbelief display itself on her face.

"I'll arrange transport for you to whatever destination you desire. The divorce can be accomplished as discreetly, or as openly, as you wish. I don't care if I have to throw you in jail to do it. I'll never advance beyond major anyway, so I have nothing to lose. You can handle the public explanation in whatever manner you feel appropriate."

"How dare you."

He caught her raised hand in midair, gripping her wrist. He lowered her arm, shaking his head at her utter hopelessness.

"Be quiet, Harriet. I'll set it up for you to stay with the Applebys until arrangements for your departure can be made. I figure it will be about an hour, if you're lucky, before the women of the fort start gossiping about it. By then, you'd better decide if I'm throwing you out or if you're leaving me."

Robert waited for Longstreet to answer his knock, knowing he'd been summoned to explain Deakins' rise from the dead. He'd had two days to prepare. Two days that Longstreet was tied up with trouble at home. He was ready. He doubted Longstreet was.

Major Longstreet opened the door himself. "Come in, Mr. Wood." He nodded toward the sole empty office chair. His words were polite, but Robert immediately caught the distance in his voice and the formal address.

Sitting, Robert pasted a puzzled expression on his face and tried to erase all sign of defensiveness. He straightened his back and placed his hands on his knees. "Major?" he asked innocently.

"I assume you know why you're here." Longstreet settled himself behind his desk and peered across the room.

Robert forced himself to project a casualness he didn't feel. "I'd guess this is about Deakins, sir. I've been reeling from shock."

"I imagine you have."

Longstreet let the silence drag and Robert resisted the urge to fill it with excuses and explanations. That's what the major wanted, for him to babble on and trap himself in the process. Or maybe he should prattle a bit? He *was* supposed to be surprised about the whole situation.

Across the desk, the major's gray eyes revealed nothing but business. He shuffled a few papers on his desk, stacked them, and set them aside. Except for one. He lay that single page in front of him and stared at Robert.

"It seems there are a few details about Deakins that we need to clarify."

Sweat broke out on Robert's hands and he fought to stay relaxed. "Is there a problem with my report, sir?"

"Your report," the major repeated, picking up the paper. "Could you go over the information for me again?"

"Yes, sir." Robert drew a breath, pacing his answer. "I arrived at the scene of the attack with one of the privates. There were three bodies behind a clump of trees. I examined the bodies and determined one of them to be a Ponca. There were also two white men, both stripped and mutilated. One was small and slight. I could make no identification."

He paused, letting the impression of discomfort drift through the room, and leaned forward in his chair. "The other was large, like Deakins. The few tattered pieces of his scalp that remained indicated he'd had blond hair. His face was gone. The only remaining clothing was a faded red neckerchief, like Deakins always wore, and military boots." He stopped again, deliberately setting his next comment apart. "Knowing that Deakins failed to report, I identified the individual as him."

Longstreet nodded and reached for a cigar. He lit it and let the smoke drift across the desk. The aroma filled the air, reminding Robert of Christmas. He shifted. What was Longstreet up to? "There was no other identifying evidence?"

"No, sir."

"And the burial?"

"I led the burial detail as well, sir. I felt it was the least I could do for Deakins. If he hadn't been so mutilated and starting to decompose, I would have had him brought back." He brushed his hand through his hair and shifted his body again, transferring his gaze to the window as if the thought of poor Deakins bothered him.

Longstreet sat without words for a full twenty seconds. "Let's see, your report on the burial?" He again shuffled noisily through the papers. "Ah, yes, here it is. Yes, exactly as you've explained."

"Yes, sir."

"Oh, on the identification, you didn't say, did that private make the same determination?"

"I'm afraid he couldn't stomach it, sir. Turned back and pitched his lunch at first sight of the bodies. I doubt he even got close enough to dope out whether they were white or Indian."

"Private Simms, wasn't it?"

"I believe so, sir."

"Hmmm. Seems like he was asked to write a report, too. Now where did I put that? Maybe I didn't even bother, seeing as it was you who did the official report. Or I could have just looked it over and figured I didn't need all that extra paper, tossed it away." He smiled as if they were old friends again. "Well, I guess that about covers it. Everything seems to be in order and reflects how it happened?"

"Yes, sir."

"That seems to be all."

Robert covered his surprise. He had the old man more buffaloed than he had thought. He leaned forward to rise from his chair, choking back a grin.

"Well, son of a gun, Wood, here it is."

"Sir?"

"That other report I was looking for. You know, the one Simms wrote." He paused and the silence stretched. "I think you'd better sit back down, Lieutenant."

Robert slumped back into the chair, his mind racing. What did he have on Simms? A drinking problem would be handy, a big chip off his credibility.

"You almost got away with it. It took a while to track down the private whose name you so conveniently left out of the report. But you see, Wood, when Deakins showed up alive after all, it cast more than a little doubt on your report. From conversations with my daughter, I've learned you had quite a motive. I've already dispatched a detail to exhume the body. If there is a body."

Longstreet rang his brass desk bell and two soldiers entered the office. "You are under arrest, Mr. Wood. Because you are an officer, you will not be placed in the guardhouse. However, you will be confined to quarters. These gentlemen will escort you there. I'll schedule your court-martial to occur as soon as possible."

CHAPTER TWENTY-NINE

Two days later, Tom left his office with an armful of paperwork Fort Pierre had requested. He paused and watched Harriet climb aboard a battered military ambulance. Across the parade ground, her friends pursed their lips and glared at him.

He offered the group a lazy smile and tipped his hat to them. Word had spread quickly. The old hens had, he was sure, been shocked by Harriet's sudden announcement that she was leaving him. But they'd soaked the story up anyway, sympathetic to her outrage. Who, after all, could blame her for being fed up with him and his lack of ambition? Not to mention his refusal to take his daughter to task for her irresponsible behavior.

Tom chuckled to himself, feeling lighter in spirit than he had for months—years, maybe. Liberation was a wonderful thing.

He'd expected Harriet to resist just to make him miserable. Yet her demeanor in the past days had been unlike the Harriet she'd become. It was as if, by declaring their independence from Harriet's overbearance, he and Miriam had taken the wind from her sails. Their refusal to bow to her manipulation had removed Harriet's weapon. And, he supposed, her joy in fighting.

As she settled her girth onto the ambulance seat, he felt a brief pang of guilt for his lack of emotion at her departure. But he'd spent his disappointment, despair and his grief during the twenty-eight years of their marriage. Now, watching the wagon pull away from the fort, he felt nothing but relief.

305

An image of Harriet, prim and formal in her wedding gown surfaced in his mind. She stood behind a wicker chair, regal and attractive, before she'd let herself go to ruin. The perfect wife. But the vivaciousness that had been hers in those days was masked by a stoic expression, forced by the lengthy time it had taken to expose the glass negatives. The face in the picture was the tight, sour one that she had assumed over the years. Perhaps he should have seen her inner demons then. Thank God he had seen them now.

His thoughts turned to his daughters. Franny, who still had her childhood ahead of her, one which he could fill with happiness and love. And Miriam, who lay in her bedroom, refusing to see her mother off. Miriam, who had fought for her independence and who had announced her desires with such courage, courage he hadn't possessed at her age.

The days of forced bed rest had been torture for her, emotionally as well as physically. Through her tears, she'd told him about Jake's abrupt dismissal of her. Jake, pushing her away, deciding for both of them, changing their lives.

Tom stopped, realizing the mistakes he and Eulalie had made didn't have to be repeated. He had time for a brief stop before he left for Fort Pierre. Turning toward the hospital, he crossed the parade ground. The cool March air was heavy with the promise of new life, and it filled his heart. When was the last time he had noticed springtime? When had he last cared?

Entering the double doors of the hospital, he headed to the ward. Jake lay at the far end, away from the few other patients. Tom moved past the empty beds, wrinkling his nose at the unfamiliar smells. He ought to spend more time with the recovering soldiers.

"Private Deakins?"

Jake opened his eyes. Tom watched recognition flash through them, followed by an effort to bring his wounded body to attention. "Major Longstreet, sir."

"At ease, Private. I'm not here as your C.O."

Fresh scars crossed the top of Jake's chest, where the sheet didn't quite reach, and along his neck, hidden by his blond beard. Marks of a soldier, of courage. "Private," he began. Damn, the word felt distant. "Jake." The unfamiliar use of his given name was uncomfortable, but somehow more appropriate. "I felt some things needed to be said. By now, you've noticed that Miriam hasn't come back to visit. No doubt you've assumed that she took your dismissal to heart."

Jake swallowed but didn't respond. His silence confirmed Tom's words. Tom sat and leaned forward.

"Mrs. Longstreet . . . uh, went a bit mad a few days ago. She pushed Miriam down the stairs and she dislocated her shoulder."

"Is she hurt, sir?" Deep concern filled Jake's blue eyes.

"Doc confined her to bed and she's on the mend. I have a hunch that her heartache is worse than her bodily discomfort."

Jake inhaled and swallowed again but said nothing more. Tom recognized the barriers instilled by years in the army. It was just as well—what he needed to say was best done without interruption.

"Miriam told me about her feelings for you and announced her intention to marry you. I've given her my blessing. It didn't set well with me when she revealed you'd sent her away."

Jake's jaw tightened and he glanced away.

"Six months ago, she would have received neither my blessing nor my concern over your actions. However, I have discovered of late that the rigid rules of society are less important than I always thought, and that noble sacrifices in the name of those rules are worthless."

Jake's stoic expression wavered, then he turned his face toward the wall.

Tom leaned closer, nearing Jake's ear. "You're a fool to lie there and push love away because you presume to know what's best for the woman you love. She doesn't care a bit that you're a private, and she doesn't care if you have a torn-up leg. She's figured out those things don't matter. It took me almost thirty years to learn the same lesson, from my own daughter.

"Having done so, I'll be damned if I'm going to sit back and watch you behave like a jackass because you can't see the forest for the trees. My daughter loves you. Pushing her away won't change that, nor will it help you walk again. That struggle's going to be there either way, son. Having her by your side would make it a whole lot easier. For both of you."

Jake's face clouded and his fists clenched. His shoulder muscles tightened, and Tom knew he'd struck a nerve.

Good. It was about time Jake Deakins started feeling some emotion other than self-pity. Now let him stew in it a while. Tom pushed the chair back and stood.

"Waiting thirty years to discover what's truly important is a worse hell than letting the woman you love see that you have a few weaknesses. Worse even than letting her share a failure or two. Especially as you'll be a lot weaker and fail more often without her. I'd think it over, son. She's a lot stronger than you're giving her credit for right now, and I think you know it."

He turned and left Jake alone at the end of the nearly empty ward, knowing that the choice was now Jake's.

"Miriam?"

Miriam shifted her weight at the sound of Carrie's voice and pushed herself up against the pillows propped at the head of her bed. She winced at the spasm of pain in her shoulders and neck, hugging her left arm to her stomach in an effort to calm it. The sharpness subsided to a nagging ache.

"You all right?" Carrie asked, concern etched across her face.

Miriam forced herself to smile. "I'm fine. As long as I don't try to move so fast. How are you?"

"Waddlin' around like a duck but lots more rested. Seen your pa headin' out."

Miriam nodded. "He had to go up to Fort Pierre to make arrangements for Robert's court-marital. He'll need to bring in officers from another post to hear the case."

"Seen your ma leavin', too."

"Mm-hmm."

"You talk to her before she left?"

Miriam shook her head.

"That settin' all right with you?"

"Nothing is setting right with me. Why should that be any different?" The bitterness she'd felt over the past few days had long since evaporated, leaving only a residue of emptiness which still echoed in her voice.

"You feel a need to talk about it?" Carrie prompted, reaching to touch Miriam's arm.

"She didn't even come in to say good-bye. I should have been sad, but all I feel is hollow. That and angry."

"I don't think she would have done this to you if it weren't for the laudanum."

Carrie's smile lifted Miriam's spirit. She was right. No matter how distant and demanding Mother might have been, she had never been violent until she'd started taking laudanum.

"I know. But that doesn't make it any easier. I've done nothing but lie here and feel miserable for days. I should have been back at Jake's side long ago."

"Well, if it makes you feel any better, he ain't talkin' to nobody. Sent me away every time I come by. Guess he don't want to hear what I got to say."

"Then his mood is not related to his injuries?" Miriam leaned forward, seeking to understand.

"He's healin' up, slow but steady. He's just so darned mule-headed. I reckon he's about fit to drown in all that prideful stubbornness, and he don't even see it." Carrie shook her head.

"Because of his leg?"

"Doc don't know yet how much use the leg's gonna be. All his life, Jake's made his livin' by hard work. I'd wager the thought of havin' a gimp leg is drivin' him pure mad. That and not knowin' how he's gonna provide for you."

"I don't care how well his leg works, just so he's alive. Doesn't he know that?"

"Too pig-headed to even think about it, I reckon."

"And stewing in his misery, isn't he? Lord, Carrie, how are we going to fix this with him lying over there and me stuck here?" One of them was going to have to do something, and it clearly wasn't going to be Jake. She tossed the quilt back and swung her legs out of bed, wincing at the movement.

"Doc said you ain't to get up," Carrie pointed out.

"Doc isn't losing the person he loves. Moving might be painful but it's not going to do any lasting harm." Miriam stood, ignoring the ache brought on by the movement, and turned to Carrie. "Now, are you helping me or am I doing this alone?"

"All right, all right. Quit fussin'."

"Oh, I haven't even begun to fuss. I love him, and it's taken me far too long to realize that it doesn't matter what anybody else thinks or how hard life is going to be for us. It's time he realizes it, too, no matter what it takes."

CHAPTER THIRTY

Jake scowled and pushed his supper tray away. He was sick and tired of chicken broth and beef broth and cream of whatever soup, and if the steward brought him one more damned bowl of the garbage, he'd throw it clear across the room.

The hinges of the ward door squeaked, drawing his attention away from his half-eaten soup.

Miriam stood, framed by the doorway. Even from his corner bed, Jake could see the rigid set of her mouth. She walked slowly, holding her left arm against her waist. Her shoulder. His heart slammed against his chest, and he fought the urge to reach out and invite her into his arms.

Jesus, he needed to hold her, protect her, take her pain away. But he couldn't. Not anymore. He gulped, knowing he would love her forever and that he'd never be able to reveal that love again. He turned his face away, studying the wall. Her heels clicked against the wooden floor, coming ever closer.

Damn. He didn't want to go through all this again. Turning her away once had been hard enough. He heard her pause, felt her presence next to him, and tried to will her away even while her father's words ricocheted through his mind.

"You're a spineless coward," she announced.

A spineless coward? How on God's green earth could the woman think he was a coward? Who did she think she was? A biting retort formed on his lips. He held it back. Her tone dove into his memory, conjuring up a picture of Miriam yelling at him like a fishwife while he stood powerless to resist her. *She's baiting me.*

"Jake?"

He closed his eyes and forced himself to stay calm, to ignore the memories and the pounding of his heart. *Go away, Miriam. Go away so I don't have to do this.*

"You can't lie there and pretend you know what's best for both of us. You can't. I love you and damn it, I won't let you do this to us."

The vehemence of her words startled him, and he rolled away from the wall, needing to see her.

He pulled himself into a sitting position. Sharp pain traveled down his leg as his weight shifted. She stood next to his bed, a modest straw hat pinned atop her auburn curls and her good hand on her hip. Green fire blazed in her eyes. Her simple dress was the color of wild sage, devoid of bows and ruffles, so that her natural curves were undisguised. His memories of the night they had made love boiled within him, torturing him as he pushed himself to resist her, to force her away.

"Don't you even dare open your mouth. You come back here, drowning in self-pity, thinking you know what's best for me. There's no going back now, Jake. I've already given you my future. Is this what you think honor—"

"My, my, isn't this a sight to behold." Robert Wood's self-righteous voice cut the comment in half.

Rage boiled through Jake. Rage at everything Wood had done, the destruction he'd wreaked. Rage compounded by helplessness that he couldn't beat him to a bloody pulp.

Robert stood just inside the door of the ward, smirking. "You haven't taken a shine to cripples now, have you, Miriam?"

Cripple. The word, spoken aloud, held even more power than it had when only floating around in Jake's mind. He watched Robert amble toward them while Miriam stood stock still, not saying a word.

Miriam's breathing grew ragged. "Robert's not supposed to be here," she muttered. Her glance moved past Wood, to the door, then back to Jake. "How in God's name did he get past the sentry?" She left the words dangling and moved away from the bed toward the door, still clutching her arm to her body.

Sentry? Wood had been under guard?

Jake watched Miriam cross the ward. She eyed Wood, and Jake sensed something was very wrong. Wood touched her arm and her wince hit Jake squarely in the gut.

The son of a bitch was hurting her. He moved his legs over the side of the bed. Sharp pain swam over him, his back arching against it. He sank back against the bed, fighting to keep from passing out. Wood's voice came to him, distant.

"We'd invite you to come along, Deakins, but, then, you aren't going anywhere, are you? Must be hell to be so worthless. I could say something about the best man coming out on top, but seeing as you're less than a man now. . . ." Wood's voice trailed off.

Jake focused on Miriam. She stood, still and scared, watching Jake and shaking her head.

At the other end of the ward, a soldier stirred in his bed. "What's goin' on?" he muttered.

"Nothing," Wood barked. "Miss Longstreet and I were just ending our visit. We need to go take care of a little unfinished business before her pa gets back." Robert's dark eyes shifted, settling on Jake. "See you soon, gimpy."

Wood muttered something in Miriam's ear. She shook her head. Wood's grip on her arm tightened and he pulled her from the ward.

"Let me go, damn you, Robert. Let me go!" Miriam struggled against him, her voice full of pain and tears pooling in her wide emerald eyes. The door closed behind them.

Pamela Nowak

"What the hell?" the other soldier questioned.

"Damn it, get some help," Jake ordered. His mind spun as he tried to figure out what to do. Miriam was scared, damned scared.

The other soldier shook his head. "I ain't gonna risk openin' this up," he said, patting the bandage across his abdomen. "Doc told me to stay put."

Perkins' words echoed back through Jake's mind. He'd told Jake to stay put as well. Move and he'd lose the leg. Shit. Then Miriam's panicked eyes flooded his thoughts. Wood was going to hurt her. But he'd do it over Jake's dead body.

Jake shook his swirling head and gritted his teeth, forcing himself to sit. He reached for his pants and pulled them on, wincing as his thigh muscles stretched and the rough wool of his trousers chafed at his injury. He grabbed the crutch and hauled himself forward. Nausea engulfed him.

He stood still, letting the bile settle and the blackness fade. Then he swung his weight forward, using his good leg. His bad leg dragged. *Holy shit, it hurt.* Sharp spasms of pain raced up his leg as his foot scraped across the wooden floor. Tensing his muscles, he lifted his foot and felt the stitches rip apart.

A cry of agony poured from deep within him and his head fell back. Blood dribbled through his blue woolen pants, and a slow red stain spread down his leg. He sucked in another breath and closed his mind to the agony, then took another step.

"You're hurting me, Robert. Let go," Miriam demanded. She tried to blink away her tears. Each movement brought new needles of pain. She glanced at the open area around the hospital, wishing it weren't so isolated from the main parade ground. How in heaven's name had Robert gotten past the guards?

"Shut up, Miriam. You ruined me. You ruined everything,

314

and it's time for you to pay the piper."

His voice was ragged, as hysterical as Harriet's had been. An involuntary chill crept through her as she realized Robert was beyond reason. Screaming for help, she pulled away.

Robert jerked at her injured arm and the abrupt sting of her muscles made her gasp. He slapped his hand over her mouth and pulled her back against his chest.

"Not so fast. I have other plans." He pulled her through the wide expanse of trees that lined the Missouri River. Remnants of the winter's half-rotted leaves crunched underfoot as she struggled. Every movement set off a new spasm of pain. Under Robert's hand, she fought to breathe.

Miriam focused her mind. The farther he pulled her into the woods, the less likely anyone would be to hear her cries for help. She had to stop him. She shook against him and opened her mouth then bit down, tearing into the skin of his palm.

"You bitch," he screamed, pulling his hand away. She squirmed and thrust herself away from him. Recovering, Robert grabbed at her arm and jerked her back. She screamed.

"Bitch," he yelled again and slapped her cheek. She winced as he glared at her with open hatred. "You destroyed my life, and now I get to destroy yours. We'll see how much Deakins wants you after I take you. And we'll see just how proud you are when you're helpless and spread-legged on the ground."

She struggled against the image of Robert forcing himself on her, destroying the act Jake had made a gift of.

Pulling away, Miriam ducked out of his reach and scrambled behind a tree. Her shoulder muscles protested each movement. Robert stood on the opposite side of the tree, feinting first right, then left.

She backed away, putting distance and a second tree between them. He followed, intent on her, but not on the ground. Miriam noted his carelessness. If she could find a way to use it to her advantage, she'd have a chance. Her only chance.

Circling a fallen log, she continued to back farther into the woods. Robert stalked after her, a sickening sneer pasted on his face. In the distance, she heard a twig snap but the sound didn't seem to faze Robert. She moved deliberately through a pile of leaves, crunching them with her feet while she searched through the trees.

Behind Robert, Jake's form emerged from the trees, plodding along on a crutch, his wounded leg dragging the ground and his face ashen. *Jake.*

He topped the hill. Even with Robert's narrow focus, it would take only moments before he noticed Jake's stumbling progress. She fought to keep her expression level as she caught Robert's gaze.

"And you, Robert? You don't think you ruined anything for us?" she asked, trying to buy Jake a few extra moments.

"Ha, you think I'm to blame for your blind independence and Jake's carelessness in battle?" Robert's tone conveyed surprise. "You have some nerve. I gave you every opportunity."

"Opportunity? Good God, Robert. You were in this for you, not for me. You never gave me anything." Robert stepped forward. Behind him, Jake picked his way down the hill, agony filling his face. Miriam focused on moving away from Robert.

"And all you gave me, my dear, were a lot of problems. I'd say it's time I got something more out of this whole thing."

"I've given you everything you're going to get."

"The hell you have. You stripped me of everything. It's time I stripped you of that damned pride of yours." He lunged forward, reaching for her. Miriam scrambled back. Behind them, Jake slid down the remaining few feet of incline, his face deathly pale.

Miriam's heart rushed into her throat. *Jake.* She stepped forward, no longer conscious of Robert's presence. *Jake.*

Pain jolted through her body as Robert slammed her against a tree. Too late, she realized she had let her attention drift.

"Going somewhere?" he snarled. He shoved one hand against her sore shoulder and grabbed her breast with the other. "I think not." Robert shoved his mouth onto hers, groping her, still unaware of the sound of Jake's approach.

Miriam struggled to free herself, fighting the spasms from her shoulder. Jake moved forward. He stood on his good leg and swung the wooden crutch, catching Robert across the back.

Robert turned with surprising agility, grabbing the crutch and pulling. Jake pitched forward, uttering an agonizing yelp as he hit the ground. Miriam watched, time slowing to a crawl, as Robert stood above Jake and planted his foot on Jake's thigh.

"Thought I didn't hear you? No wonder you got jumped." On the ground, Jake groaned, then went silent.

Miriam rushed forward, mindless of anything except Jake. Robert's elbow caught her in the stomach. She staggered backward. Robert shook his head and casually reached for a large granite rock.

On the ground, Jake turned, his eyes seeking hers. "The crutch," he mouthed. Her glance darted to the crutch even as she realized she'd never be able to wield it, not with her bad shoulder. Her mind raced in search of another weapon, seizing upon her hat pin. She pulled the pin from her hat in one swift stroke and plunged it into Robert's back, targeting the sensitive kidney area, where Harriet had kicked her.

"You bitch!" he howled, sinking to his knees. "Jesus, what'd you do to me?"

Miriam raised her foot and pressed the bottom of her boot against the jeweled hilt of the hat pin, driving it deeper into Robert's kidney. He yelled, then fell forward. His face settled into the half-decayed leaves. Twisting and cursing, he tried to reach the pin.

Behind her, Jake stirred. Leaves crackled as he pulled himself closer to Miriam and Robert and reached for the abandoned crutch. His injured leg stretched out, useless, stained dark with blood. Miriam blanched. Robert struggled to reach the pin, still held tight by her boot. He grabbed her ankle, pulling at her, and tried to rise.

Jake swung the crutch. It smacked loudly as the wood make contact with Robert's head. Robert stilled and Jake sank to the ground, surrendering at last to unconsciousness. Miriam moved to Jake and knelt. Cradling his head in her lap, she caressed his face while tears streamed down her own.

The soft, lukewarm touch of a sponge drifted across Jake's chest. His eyes creaked open.

Bright afternoon sunlight streamed across the hospital bed. Beside him, Miriam sat, her thick auburn hair pulled back in a simple braid. Water dripped from her fingers as she swept her hand to her mouth, the wet sponge forgotten.

Dear God, she's safe. A flood of relief washed over him. *We're both safe.* "Hello, darlin'," he whispered into the room. The effort scratched his throat. "I forgot to tell you that I love you."

"I love you, too." Her voice was sharp with relief and tears glistened in her emerald eyes.

They stared at each other, unable to find any other words until the chill of the sponge that still lay on his chest crept through him and he shivered. "Welcome back." She lifted the sponge, her hand brushing his chest hairs. He shivered again.

Thank God she was safe. He'd wasted so much time, so much energy, letting uncertainties dictate their future. If his pride had hurt her. . . . He pulled his thoughts back and attempted another smile. Lord, he was tired. "How long was I gone?"

"Two days. Oh, Jake, I thought I was going to lose you." She kissed him on the forehead then dried his chest.

A dull throb pounded from his thigh, increasing in intensity as he became more alert. He closed his eyes briefly and steeled himself to ask. "Did I lose the leg?"

She shook her head. "It took Doc a lot of hours and some of the finest surgery he's ever done, but he saved it. And you are *not* getting out of this bed until those stitches have set."

He nodded, too sleepy to ask more. "Anything you say."

"Anything?"

He nodded again. "Anything, Miri."

"Will you marry me, Jake Deakins?"

Sweet Jesus, she still wanted him. He savored her words, knowing it was somehow right that she ask them. He reached, seeking her hand and stroked the soft skin of her palm.

"If you'll still have me."

She smiled and bent close, whispering for his ears only. "Yes, Jake, I'll have you. Over and over and over, my love."

Visions of her, wrapped in his arms, coursed through him. God, how he loved her. He wished he could give her everything. It sobered him to realize he couldn't.

"I can't give you an easy life, Miriam. You sure you want to be stuck with a cripple?"

"I thought I made it very clear to you that your leg has nothing to do with this. I love you, no matter what." She brushed her lips across his, then pulled back and touched his cheek. "You need to rest."

"I know. Wood?"

"He's in the stockade. Between my screams and Private Carpenter's yelling"—she glanced across the ward and wriggled her fingers at the private who watched them with interest from the other side of the room—"we must have alerted half the post. Help arrived just after the two of you passed out. I guess I punctured his kidney pretty bad, but Perkins wouldn't have him here. They didn't want to risk him sneaking out of his own quarters again, so he gets to recuperate in a cell. Papa was livid. The list of new charges against the lieutenant is a mile long. He'll serve a pretty long sentence in addition to getting a dishonorable discharge." She stopped and brushed Jake's hair from his forehead. "The court-martial is set for late April."

Jake felt a deep stab of bitterness and tried to brush it away. They'd take their revenge through justice and let Wood suffer with his own hate. He and Miriam had better things to do.

"Good. That's gives me enough time. God willing, I'll walk into the courtroom under my own power. And, then, Miri love, I'll walk into that chapel and make you my wife."

Miriam caught her bottom lip between her teeth and nodded. "Forever and always," she said between tears.

Jake brushed them from her cheek with his finger and she kissed his hand. A radiant smile lit her face as he pulled her close and kissed her. His mouth took hers, offering her dancing promises of love.

EPILOGUE

Warm September twilight settled across the Dakota sky as Jake and Miriam picked their way through the trees lining the creek. Jake led, maneuvering carefully with his cane.

Through her crocheted slippers, twigs jabbed at Miriam's feet, making her wish Jake hadn't volunteered them to gather firewood. Still, with baby Anna to tend and the last of their belongings to pack for the move to Yankton, Carrie could use their help. "I should have worn shoes," she said.

Jake turned and opened his arms. "Sorry, Miri. I forgot about the twigs." He drew her flush against his body and kissed her. Her mouth opened to him, their tongues met, teasing each other, and she forgot about the twigs. Then Jake pulled back, smiled at her with twinkling blue eyes, and moved away.

Miriam laughed and ducked under a branch. "We have plenty of time," she offered suggestively. "Papa and Eulalie probably won't even miss us. Did you get a gander at Mrs. Stanton's face when they announced their engagement?"

Jake nodded and piled wood onto his free arm. "I'm not sure which surprised her more, that or our announcement about Fenkelstein offering me a partnership in his store in Yankton. You'd think she'd be used to this family's surprises by now. She'd faint if she knew about your mother's letter. Come on. There's something I want to show you. *Then* maybe we'll take a little extra time before we drop off this wood at Carrie's."

Savoring his implied promise, Miriam slowed and let her

thoughts drift to Harriet's simple congratulatory message. Though it had taken her six months, she'd finally acknowledged Miriam's marriage to Jake. Not warmly, but at least she had. The note had come last week, along with her father's official divorce decree.

Ahead of her, Jake pushed on. He passed a pair of squirrels chattering among the autumn plants, then stopped and dumped both his cane and his load of firewood onto the ground. Turning, he grinned. "We're here."

Miriam recognized Franny's favorite play area, fresh with mud from recent rains. She raised her eyebrows. "Here?"

She followed Jake's glance to a gnarled ash tree. A large heart was etched into its rough bark. It was already well-weathered, indication that it had been there some time. Miriam read the carved words.

Jake loves Miriam.

Unable to trust her voice, she turned and melted into Jake's arms. He held her in comfortable silence until she was able to speak. "That's been there a while."

"Since last September. Funny how my heart made the choice way before my head did." He kissed her head. "I wanted you to see it before we left. I love you, Mrs. Deakins." His voice caught and she lifted her face toward him.

"And I love you."

He offered her a single deep kiss, steadied himself, then gathered her into his arms. "Now, surprise number two," he announced and scooped her off the ground.

Caught off guard, she gasped, amazed anew at this man she'd married.

Grinning even wider, he plucked off her slippers, limped to the puddle, and set her in Franny's mud hole.

The mud squished around her feet, smothering them in the

day's lingering warmth. She curled her toes, reveling in the sensation.

Jake slipped off his boots and waded into the mud. "Time to play," he invited in liquid tones. His strong arms encircled her. In the warm, sensual mud, his toes nudged at hers.

Miriam looked up into his sapphire eyes and found them full of merriment and love. Then she laughed out loud, secure that they had both made love's *only* choice.

AUTHOR'S NOTE

Many of the choices that confronted Miriam and Jake were real to those who lived at nineteenth-century army posts. Personal narratives and scholarly works detail the rigid social structure of the army and the lifestyles of fort inhabitants. Though my characters are imaginary, Fort Randall existed much as I have represented it, its layout inspired by maps, photos, and written records. White Swan's village and the hog ranch were actual places, Yankton was the nearest town, and miners did skirmish with the Poncas. Except for the chapel, the buildings of the fort no longer exist, but archeological evidence confirms their locations and keeps the post alive for South Dakota residents. If I have made errors in my representation of life at the fort, people, places, and events, the mistakes are unintentional and entirely my own.

ABOUT THE AUTHOR

Pamela Nowak has loved both history and romance for as long as she can remember. She graduated from South Dakota State University with a BA in history and has taught classes at both the high school and college level as well as adult basic education and GED classes at a state penitentiary. She served as a historic preservation specialist for the Quechan Indian Tribe at the Fort Yuma National Landmark and spent thirteen years as director of a homeless shelter. Her interests include reading, historic research, directing community theater, and visiting historic sites. She lives in the Denver area and invites you to visit her at www.pamelanowak.com.